The Elephant and Macaw Banner

The Elephant and Macaw Banner

a novel by

CHRISTOPHER KASTENSMIDT

GUARDBRIDGE BOOKS
ST ANDREWS, SCOTLAND

Published by Guardbridge Books,
St Andrews, Fife, United Kingdom.

http://guardbridgebooks.co.uk

Elephant and Macaw Banner, The

This is a work of fiction. All characters and events portrayed in this book are fictitious, and any resemblance to real people or events is purely coincidental.

Cover art by Ursula "Sula Moon" Dorada
Interior illustrations by HET

ISBN: Hardcover: 978-1-911486-30-5
Paperback: 978-1-911486-31-2

Contents

Dedicated to *my* heroes,
the teachers who spend their lives passing the torch of knowledge to the next generation.

Chapter 1

The Fortuitous Meeting of Gerard van Oost and Oludara

IGH ATOP THE CHURCH OF THE IMMACULATE CONCEPTION, in contrast to the subdued hues of the building's unpainted mortar and stone, a scarlet macaw perched upon a wooden cross. The macaw cocked its head from side to side, watching people pass through Salvador's principal plaza. After a few minutes, it paused to stretch out its wings, presenting its full array of colors—ruby, amber, emerald, sapphire, chalk, and coal—a combination found nowhere else in nature.

The flash of color caught Gerard's eye. From far below, in the plaza's center, he looked up and examined the macaw. The exotic bird symbolized everything which had brought him to this strange New World: beauty, mystery, and magic. All thoughts of returning to Europe faded before the bird's gorgeous display. Certainly that one sight, unknown to most European eyes, was in itself worth braving the six-week journey across the Atlantic.

When the bird took flight, disappearing beyond the city's northern wall, Gerard returned his focus to the plaza: the heart of activity in Salvador. People congregated in groups, trading the latest news, or rushed by on some unknown business. Guards with harquebuses stood in towers along the dilapidated city walls, watching for threats from without, while others, bearing halberds, stood near the Governor's Palace, watching for threats from within. Not one person in the plaza, however, paid any attention to him.

Out of habit, Gerard tugged the bottom of his linen doublet, fitting it snugly around his broad chest. He then stroked his palm-length goatee with his right hand and tapped the pommel of his Bolognese rapier with his left, as he considered the problem at hand.

He had come to Brazil under the assumption that anyone courageous enough to face the perilous trip across the ocean could earn a spot in one of the adventuring troops, but unfortunately that had not been the case. Antonio Dias Caldas, the most renowned adventurer in the province, had firmly declined his services, and no other group had stepped forward to explore the local wilds. Gerard could attempt to raise his own standard, but he would need to form a strong group, and he hadn't yet met anyone in Salvador with whom he would trust his life.

A coffle of slaves approached, interrupting Gerard's thoughts. The Portuguese merchant Pero de Belem led them on a chain, and he tipped his wide-brimmed hat at Gerard as he passed. Gerard responded in kind, then stared in gloomy silence as the slaves crossed before him one by one, heads held low, the chains joining their neck collars swaying between them. Their only clothing consisted of one-piece cotton tunics which hung to their knees, while their exposed parts—arms and faces—displayed pockmarks, relics of disease from their terrible journey. Most shuffled along with unfocused eyes, as if they could no longer think, just act.

One of the local mill owners approached Pero for a word, and the line came to an abrupt halt in front of Gerard. Gerard, who despised the practice of taking men from their homelands in chains, grimaced as the depressing sight cast a shadow over the idyllic image he had formed just moments before.

"And so, even in paradise there are slaves," he sighed.

The slave who had stopped nearest Gerard turned to look at him. Gerard, startled, noticed the man did not bend like the others; he stood proud and erect. Already inches taller than most, his upright posture made him tower above the rest. His bulging muscles stood out, even through the unfitted tunic. The man exuded power and grace, his wide nostrils and high cheekbones heightening the effect. His eyes possessed none of the stupor displayed by the others, instead, they stared at Gerard with a surety he had seen few times in a lifetime of travels. Gerard looked away, embarrassed, wondering if the man, just arrived from Africa, could have possibly understood his remark.

Trumpets sounded from the North Gate, drawing his attention away from the awkward moment. Shouts erupted around the plaza as the massive doors opened and Antonio Dias Caldas strode through, a native carrying his gold-and-red standard close by his side. Behind him followed his band. Gerard counted forty in all, many less than had left on the mission a few weeks before.

Without breaking stride, Antonio crossed the plaza to the Governor's Palace. The two halberd-wielding guards did nothing more than nod as he passed between them and slammed the door shut behind him. At that sound, his troop dispersed around the square, each member immediately surrounded by curious bystanders. Among the movement, Gerard spotted Diogo, a man he held in high esteem.

"Diogo," asked Gerard, "what happened?"

"We killed the Botat!"

"The monster that's been ravaging the countryside? Tell me more! I've heard only rumors here."

"It was truly a marvelous beast. During the day it hid in lakes and rivers, so we had to hunt it at night. It took days to corner it, but when we finally did, we discovered a serpent large beyond belief—as wide as a cart and long as a main mast, I swear. Its body blazed with a blue flame which burned beast but not bush, and which no water could douse. The flame made the beast appear blue, but when we cast light upon it, its scales shone with all the colors of the rainbow.

"Its eyes were giant balls of fire, each the size of a boulder. Two of our companions, Afonso and Paulo, made the mistake of looking the beast in the eye; both of them went mad. The Botat burned and struck without respite, killing everything it touched. But that is all I can say for now. Antonio will want to relate the victory himself, after he collects the governor's reward."

"And the recognition." Gerard's wistful tone did little to hide his envy. "It appears you lost some men?"

"Yes, we lost ten during our encounter with the beast."

"Then I suppose you'll be looking to fill your ranks?"

Gerard hoped his insinuation would receive a positive reaction, but Diogo's frown revealed the opposite. Before Diogo could voice his concerns, Gerard hurried to make his case.

"Diogo, you know I want to serve under a standard more than anything. I didn't spend six weeks cramped in a caravel just to visit this wattle-and-daub colony on the edge of nowhere. I came here for adventure! I've the strength of a bear, and I'm one of the best harquebus shots you'll ever meet. I know Antonio respects you, please help me."

"I don't know if there's anything I can do, Gerard. We still have twenty harquebusiers, more than enough for anything left roaming these parts. But your biggest problem is that Antonio isn't fond of Protestants."

"I'm not going to convert to Catholicism just to join his band."

"And it wouldn't help," came a voice to his right, "I don't like converts, either."

Gerard turned to see Antonio approaching, his chest jutting forward under his rich, blue doublet and his black beard cropped close around his long chin.

"Go back to Europe, Gerard," said Antonio, "you're not wanted here. I formally requested that Governor Almeida have you arrested for vagrancy if you're not on the next ship out. Given his delight at my defeat of the Botat, I have every expectation my request will be granted."

"I didn't know vagrancy was a crime in Brazil," Gerard replied through clenched teeth.

"It is if the governor says so."

Gerard took a deep breath before responding. "I'm willing to risk my life in your service and you treat me this way?"

"I don't need your help, Gerard." Then he paused. "Although there could be a way. A man who can think on his feet is worth a dozen harquebusiers. Brazil is filled with all types of wily creatures, and many times a sharp wit is more useful than a sharp sword. If you can guess how we defeated the Botat, I'll withdraw my request for your arrest and consider a place for you in my band."

Gerard tugged on his goatee. Quick decisions were not his specialty, and being put on the spot muddled his thoughts. He wiped the sweat from his forehead.

"Time's up," said Antonio, "any ideas?"

Gerard had no idea how much time had passed. He'd worried the entire time, unable to bring his full focus to the problem. "Hmmm," he said, "I don't know."

"A serpent is best defeated through its stomach."

All three men turned to see who had spoken. Although spoken in Portuguese, the strong African accent on the words made the speaker undeniable; the voice had come from the nearby slave whom Gerard had noticed before.

"How did you know that?" shouted Antonio. "I told the story to Governor Almeida just five minutes ago."

Pero de Belem came running.

"What's going on here?" he yelled. "Is this slave babbling something?" He held his face close to the slave's, as if examining him for some defect.

"Actually," said Gerard, "he appears to speak perfect Portuguese."

"Oh right," Pero said, scratching his beard, "that one. I can never tell them apart. He's the only one of these monkeys who speaks Portuguese, and he gave me a mouthful too much of it on the way over from Africa."

"Do not call us monkeys," said the slave. "We are not animals. You who take men from their homelands and sell them like vegetables are the animals. But I comprehend your denial, Mr. Pero de Belem, and I pity you. If you ever truly accept what it is you do, it will haunt you for the rest of your days."

"See what I mean?" Pero said, holding up his hands. He turned his attention back to the slave. "No one asked for your opinion. One more word will get you a lashing tonight."

"That won't be necessary," interrupted Gerard, not wanting to see any harm come to the man. "He just responded to a question. His insight was quite remarkable, in fact."

"Really?" said Pero, squinting his eyes. "Well, if you think he's so special, I can sell him to you."

"What? You take me for an owner of slaves?"

"I'm just saying. He's supposed to be shipped down to Fernando Alvaro's sugar mill in Porto Seguro on Thursday, but if you give me forty thousand *réis* before then, you can do whatever you want with him. I can settle something else with Fernando."

"Forty thousand? That price is absurd!"

"What was that you called him again, 'remarkable'? Well, that just means you have to pay a 'remarkable' price. Of course, you could always just leave him to Fernando. Five of his slaves were killed in Indian attacks last month, and he's eager to fill the ranks with fresh fodder." Pero turned back to the line and yelled, "Move out!"

Antonio burst out laughing.

"See, Gerard?" he said. "You're not clever enough for an expedition like ours. Even a slave just arrived from Africa knows more than you."

He walked off chuckling.

Diogo placed a hand on Gerard's shoulder. "I'm sorry, Gerard. Antonio's words are often unnecessarily brusque."

Gerard watched the line of slaves moving away.

"Not at all, Diogo," he replied. "I think he may be right."

Gerard sat patiently in Pero's office with a spoon, a pewter cup of water, and a full plate of food on the table before him. To pass the time, he studied a painting of Belem, Pero's native city. He recognized the port from its unmistakable ornamented tower, which he had passed on the start of his voyage to Brazil. The quality of the painting could not compare to those produced by the schools of Venice and Flanders, yet still provided a reasonable representation of the port.

Pero entered with the slave in tow. The slave stared at Gerard in silence, then took a long look at the plate on the table.

"Please, sit down," offered Gerard.

The slave sat down on the other side of the table.

"Could you please leave us alone?" asked Gerard, looking at Pero.

"I suppose it can't do any harm. But if anything happens to the property," Pero motioned toward the slave with a flick of his chin, "you're responsible." Just before leaving, he looked back and said, "Remember, forty thousand by Thursday or he's on his way to Porto Seguro."

After Pero slammed the door, Gerard looked at the slave and asked, "What's your name?"

The slave studied him. Their eyes made contact and Gerard held his gaze without blinking.

"Tell me yours first," the slave replied.

"All right, my name is Gerard van Oost, twenty-nine years of age. I'm Dutch, from the Duchy of Brabant, but I've lived more years in other parts of Europe than I have in my homeland."

"Well, Gerard, you are the only white man who has ever asked me my name. I am Oludara. I hail from the kingdom of Ketu, which bears the misfortune of lying within a region you Europeans call the Slave Coast. I have lived for twenty-three years."

After a pause, he continued. "Why do you seek me? From what I heard of your conversation in the plaza, I understand that you are not a sugar mill owner."

"First, I'd like to offer you a gift." Gerard pushed the plate and spoon forward. "Are you familiar with the local food?"

"Just the black beans and rice, which we receive only when we are lucky. Most days we eat cooked green bananas, which makes me think Mr. Pero de Belem really does believe we are monkeys."

Gerard didn't know whether Oludara made the comment in bitterness or jest. After a short pause, he chanced a chuckle. Then Oludara smiled and they both laughed heartily.

"Yes, Gerard," continued Oludara, "even in a situation like mine, a man must keep his humor. My people say, 'Do not lament spilled water. As long as the calabash is not broken, one can still get more.' Times are dark for me, but my body and will are strong, and for this reason I do not despair. However, it is indeed difficult to live on bananas alone."

"Well, you may find this to your liking." Gerard pointed to each item in turn. "The fish is grouper. It is dense, yet mild on the tongue. This is roasted cassava. It comes from the ground like a potato, but is richer in flavor. The yellow bread is made from corn, and mixed with a bit of coconut for sweetness. And these slices are from a fruit known as pineapple, regarded as one of the sweetest flavors in the world. It is so treasured by the Portuguese, they ship the plants to all their colonies, even to India."

Oludara stared at the plate, but made no move toward it.

"It is truly a feast, but no one offers a meal for free. Let me know what you seek before I accept your generosity."

"Tell me how you knew the answer to Antonio's question yesterday."

"Is that all? I would tell you the story if only for the courtesy you have shown. But I accept your offer, as I am so tired of bananas that my pride would not stand in the way of any handout."

Oludara ate his first spoonful of rice and beans, closing his eyes as he chewed it. After washing it down with a sip of water, he looked Gerard in the eye.

"Let me tell you a story. It happened five years ago, in my homeland of Ketu..."

Between bites, he told his tale.

Oludara stopped clearing weeds and leaned against the hoe. The wrapper around his waist weighed heavy from the sweat which trickled down his bare chest. He could afford to rest; three weeks remained before yam planting, and the field appeared to be in good shape. He scanned the expanse of rust-colored dirt and watched his two younger brothers working farther upfield.

As he removed his straw hat to wipe the sweat from his brow, he noticed movement to his left. Bale Akeju, master of the village, approached with another man—tall and confident—walking by his side. As they came closer, he saw that both wore fine, indigo robes. The bale wore such robes all the time, but Oludara knew no one else in the region with the status to wear one. Oludara couldn't imagine what would make the bale come out to the fields at midday. It would be much easier to find him in his hut that evening, after the day's work.

The two men came straight to him, without stopping, and he greeted both with a handshake. The imposing stranger studied him carefully, but the bale spoke first.

"Oludara, this man has come all the way from Ketu to speak with you."

"Are you Oludara," asked the man, "oldest son of one known as the 'Slayer of Monsters'? "

"I am Oludara, but my father passed away years ago."

"That fact is known to the oba, for it was he himself who sent me with orders to escort you to Ketu. He wishes to have words with you. I am Oyewole, one of his personal messengers."

Bale Akeju gasped at the message.

Oludara frowned. "For one such as I to be called before the oba without warning cannot be good."

"You may be right," said Oyewole. "I know not why he has sent for you, but from my experience, a surprise summons from the oba is rarely good news—I would not trade places with you right now. Nevertheless, we must leave immediately; the oba does not like to be left waiting. Take time only to say goodbye to your family and collect clothes for your audience."

"Very well, it shall be done."

Even though Ketu was only a three-day walk from his village, for Oludara, it might as well have been on the other side of the world. He had only been to Ketu once before, as a child, while his father still lived. They had gone for one of the festivals, and Oludara had seen the oba in full royal attire. He did not remember many details, just the feeling of awe he had experienced upon visiting.

The journey was well spent, as Oyewole told him much of the politics and history of Ketu. Oludara liked the man and imagined they could have been friends if Oyewole did not hold a rank in society so far above his own.

As they neared the city, they passed through a multitude of farms. They then navigated the complex system of bulwarks and moats, with the innermost courtyards surrounded by walls twice the height of a man. The locals used different colors and fashions than those in Oludara's village. Massive squares full of wooden stands sat empty, waiting to be filled by crowds and merchandise on market day.

Oyewole led him to a guest house and told him to prepare himself for his audience with the oba. A young woman helped him draw a bath and he washed off the red dust accumulated during the trip. He then dined on stewed beef, figs, and yams.

For his meeting with the oba, he vested a short-sleeved robe and tied it around the waist with a sash. A close-fitting cap completed the ensemble. The outfit was not elegant, but the best that could be expected from a poor farmer.

Oyewole escorted him to the palace. The sight of the grandiose building—a towering clay construction—awed him. Two massive gates stood open in front. The guards, upon seeing Oyewole, motioned them through.

Warriors guarded the hall inside and out. Most held swords or bows, but some were equipped with Portuguese crossbows. As Oludara walked the long hall, he glanced at the brass heads on each side: representations of all past obas of Ketu. These were interspersed among fine ivory carvings.

When he reached the end, he saw the oba's council: seven chiefs sitting on lion-skin mats. Several eunuchs, the personal servants of the oba, stood at attention. Oludara identified them by the way they wore their robes bunched upon their shoulders. Drummers and other attendants waited around the hall.

Oyewole shook Oludara's hand goodbye and motioned to a leopard skin mat, where Oludara knelt to wait. Two eunuchs carried a wooden stool to the front of the hall. Oludara could see elaborate carvings covering the stool, but could not make out the details from his vantage point.

Shortly after, one of the attendants shouted, "The Alaketu, Oba Ekoshoni enters!" A trumpet blast and drums accented his announcement.

The oba entered, flanked by two guards bearing halberds topped with thick bronze blades. In the few seconds that ceremony allowed, Oludara soaked in as much detail as possible. The oba wore a coral collar and silk sash upon his chest. A crown of red beads came to a point above his head, and lines of beads cascaded down from it, leaving little of his face exposed. Rings covered his neck all the way to his chin.

As the oba approached the wooden stool, Oludara and all others prostrated themselves upon the ground. After a few moments, they returned to the kneeling position. Oludara kept his eyes pointed down in reverence, but longed to stare at his regal lord.

"You have been summoned because my diviners consulted the Ifa Oracle." Oba Ekoshoni spoke in an even voice, just loud enough for Oludara to hear every word clearly. "They told me to seek the eldest progeny of a man who aided me long ago."

Oludara felt honored to hear the voice of the oba; it was a rare privilege. In public, the oba whispered through a cow tail whisk and a eunuch shouted his words to the people.

"Your father helped me once when I was young," continued the oba. "Through his cunning, he killed Souyuu, a terrible beast which ravaged the local villages. Now, I face a similar problem, so I assume that you are the one I seek.

"Six months ago, a dragon stopped one of my sons on the road and demanded that a sacrifice, taken from the vassals of my court, be tied and left at the sacred grove of Ofru every full moon. When my son told me the news, I refused. When the sacrifice was not sent, the dragon went to a village and killed everyone there. The next full moon, I sent fifty warriors to slay the beast. Only a few survived, and they reported that not even the bolts of the Portuguese crossbows could penetrate the beast's scales. Since then, left without options, I have sacrificed one of my vassals every month to this abominable creature. I would continue no longer."

After a pause, the oba spoke again. "I fear the beast cannot be bested by force alone; cunning is also required. I hear you have faced many trials, even at your young age. You battled our enemies from Dauma, and you tricked and slew the very beast which killed your father."

The reminder sent a pang through Oludara, but he pushed it down.

"I regret sending such a fine man," continued the oba, "so recently turned to adulthood, on such a terrible task. However, the oba does not question, he does not ask, he orders. Thus, I order you to do everything in your power to slay the beast. Do you understand?"

"Yes," responded Oludara, "it will be an honor to serve the great Oba Ekoshoni."

"Good. I am gladdened to see you here before me. You remind me of your father in both build and manner. I do not know if you realize the depth of his wisdom. When he slew Souyuu, I offered him anything in my power as a reward. He could have chosen riches or land or anything else which could have brought him temporal pleasure in this world, but he was too wise for that. Instead, he asked me to choose a name for his newborn son." At this, the oba laughed heartily. "He knew the gift would cost me not the price of a yam, but that an oba surely would choose a princely name. And thus I did. I chose the name Oludara for his son, and brought great honor to his family for all generations to come. I have no doubt he will stand by your side in the trial which awaits you."

After a pause, the oba asked, "Do you remember the dagger your father wore?"

"Yes."

"He carried that dagger because your name was not the only present I gave him. I could not leave such wisdom unrewarded, so I also gave him that dagger, one of the greatest treasures in all Ketu. Since all ivory belongs to the oba, your village elders rightfully returned it to me upon his death. However, the chiefs agree," he held a hand toward the seven counselors for emphasis, and they nodded in response, "that it would make a fine present for you now, to help with what you must face."

The oba motioned with a wave and a eunuch carrying a fine brass tray stepped forward. The eunuch knelt before Oludara, holding out the tray and presenting the dagger which lay upon it.

The dagger was exactly as Oludara remembered it: fine ivory tinted red from palm oil. The hilt contained intricate carvings; the side with a lightning bolt rested on top. The other side, he knew, showed a double-bladed axe. Those two symbols represented the god Shango, as his father had taught him long ago. The sight flooded him with memories, but he shook them off and reached down to accept the gift, not wanting to appear unappreciative. As Oludara touched the hilt, a strange sensation passed through his arm, causing him to jerk in surprise.

The oba saw his reaction and said, "The enchantment on that dagger is strong; it is rumored to come from Shango himself. Whether or not that is true not even I can say, but guard it well, because you will never again find its equal."

Oludara grasped the hilt firmly and lifted the dagger. The eunuch with the tray walked away.

"The Iya Kere controls my treasury," said the oba. "She will see to it that you have whatever equipment you need."

"Great Oba," said Oludara, "How do I find the dragon?"

"No one knows where it lives. You must go to Ofru on the next full moon, two days hence, and witness the sacrifice. Hide yourself as best you can and observe. The beast is treacherous; you must learn as much as you can before you confront it. Do not interfere with the sacrifice, no matter how much it pains you to watch. That is my command. May Olorun protect you."

The oba rose and everyone prostrated again.

Before the oba even left the hall, Oludara's mind swirled with ideas for the task before him.

Oludara, his body camouflaged by red clay dust, hid among bushes in the sacred grove of Ofru. Some eighty paces before him, at the foot of an enormous baobab tree, the sacrifice lay tied and gagged. Oludara regretted he could do nothing to save the man, but he respected the oba's order and knew it made sense; it would be foolish to face the dragon before observing it. At the moment, Oludara's main concern was concealment. If the dragon caught a whiff of his scent, it would mean a quick end to his task.

When the moon reached its zenith, the dragon appeared. It resembled a massive green snake, except for some tiny, apparently useless wings and several stubby pairs of legs which propelled it along in a half-walking, half-slithering fashion. The scales appeared impenetrable, like painted iron plates stacked upon each other.

The sacrificial victim, eyes wide, thrashed in his bonds and grunted muted screams through the gag. The dragon ignored him at first, flicking its tongue repeatedly to test the air around it. Oludara tensed, but the dragon completed its examination without incident and returned its attention to the sacrifice. The moment it made eye contact with its victim, the man stiffened and fell silent.

Without ceremony, the dragon unhooked its jaw and clasped down over the man's head. With the eye contact broken, the man resumed thrashing. It made little difference, however, and his body receded down the dragon's gullet. His movement stopped after a minute, when, Oludara presumed, either his head had been crushed or he'd run out of air.

"Olorun save us!" Oludara whispered under his breath.

Shortly after finishing its meal, the dragon looked around, flicked its tongue a few more times, and turned back in the direction from which it had come.

Oludara waited half an hour, then crawled to the middle of the grove and found the tracks made by the dragon's slithering. Using the stealth he had developed while hunting the savannah with his brothers, he trailed the beast. He crawled for at least three hours before discovering the bedded dragon. It had coiled itself up near a tree. In the moonlight, Oludara could see a glint where one of the beast's eyes remained open.

As he crawled away, Oludara formed a plan.

Two days later, Oludara found himself kneeling once again before Oba Ekoshoni.

"The Iya Kere informs me that for some reason you require an elephant in order to slay the beast," began the oba. "I have but one, and he has been with me for many years. I am loath to part with him, but I told you I would give you anything in my power, so it shall be done. However, the Iya Kere also informs me that there is something else you require which could only be discussed in my presence. I am curious to hear this request."

"It is indeed something only you can provide, great Oba," replied Oludara. "I need you and the village chiefs to impart a nobleman's status upon the elephant."

A commotion arose among the counselors.

"Outrageous!" shouted the oba, rising to his feet. "Our ancestors will laugh at such folly."

"Nevertheless," replied Oludara, "I must ask it. As it is said, 'a thief is more merciful than a fire,' and we must choose the lesser of these evils."

Oludara dared to look up at the oba, who, to his relief, seemed more interested than angered.

"Elephants and dragons are ancient enemies," he continued, "and in this case, one noble elephant can do what a thousand men cannot. I do not think our ancestors will mock us if we succeed in our task. If you will but let me explain, I will make my plan clear."

Oludara sat in silence as the dragon entered the grove and cocked its head in puzzlement at the bound elephant. It flicked its tongue and immediately turned to spot Oludara, sitting at the foot of the baobab. Oludara felt the dragon's gaze bore into him and his stomach clenched.

The dragon slithered to within a few paces of him, never breaking eye contact. Its forked tongue flicked out, almost touching him. Oludara concentrated on holding himself steady, but knew the dragon's gaze kept him from moving his muscles, even if he wanted.

The dragon spoke in a hissing voice, "What trickery is this? Why is this cursed elephant here?"

Oludara struggled to begin his speech, but surprised himself when the words came out confidently. "Did you not ask the oba to send a sacrifice each full moon? One of his choosing?"

"Yes, but I asked for a vassal, fool, not an elephant. I think I'll have you instead."

"There has been no mistake, mighty dragon, the elephant is the sacrifice. I am but a farmer, yet this elephant is a noble of the oba's court."

"What?"

"As you are such a marvelous being, the Oba Ekoshoni wished to offer a meal worthy of your stature."

"No man may look into my eyes and lie, this elephant must indeed be a noble." The dragon paused, as if thinking. "But this insult will not go unpunished. When I'm done with this wretched creature, I'll eat you and your presumptuous oba as well."

The dragon turned, allowing Oludara the opportunity to take in a deep breath.

The dragon wrapped itself around the elephant's neck. The elephant fought mightily, throwing its weight from side to side. The dragon absorbed several blows during the struggle, but eventually managed to strangle the tied animal. After a short rest, it unhinged its jaw and fit its mouth around the elephant's legs. The dragon's skin expanded as it crushed the elephant bit by bit. It required hours to ingest the entire animal, ending when the trunk receded into its bloated body.

When it finished, it slithered away heavily, without even sparing a glance at Oludara. Oludara grinned as the dragon's boast of devouring him remained unfulfilled, much as he had expected.

Oludara waited a half-hour before setting out after the dragon. He walked leisurely, unconcerned with concealment, and found the serpent at only half the distance it had crawled the previous time. It lay spread out, too bloated to coil. This time, the creature slept with both eyes closed.

All along the dragon—its skin stretched to the limit by the elephant within—the scales had separated enough to expose the flesh beneath. Oludara spotted a bulge formed by a tusk, and he chose that point to make the first incision with his ivory knife. The dragon could do nothing more than shudder as he opened it.

"So I gave the head to the oba and he allowed me to take the skin to my village, where we used it to create many wonderful things. And that is the end of my tale."

Gerard sat quietly, digesting all he had heard.

After sipping the last of the water, Oludara broke the silence. "So Antonio's group must have done something similar?"

"It appears they found a giant tapir, probably the closest thing to your elephant in these parts, and tied it to a tree as bait. But even with their ruse, it still took fifty men and over a hundred rounds of harquebus fire to bring down the beast. I'd say your kill was much more elegant."

Oludara smiled at the compliment.

Gerard leaned forward. "I have a proposition for you. Brazil is a land for the taking. Precious stones, magic, and adventure without limit are spread throughout this giant, unexplored territory. There would be hundreds arriving daily if not for the monsters which inhabit the wilds. Fame and fortune await those brave enough to face them—and quick enough to find them first."

"Yes," agreed Oludara, "both here and in Africa, two places the white man has not yet overrun with his cities, the ancient magics still live strong."

"I believe that destiny brought me here," said Gerard. "My earliest memories are of the Brazilian Festival held for King Henry. It was unbelievable, an entire forest had been erected in the middle of Rouen, can you believe it? My parents took me to see it, and we watched a show of beasts, natives, and fireworks the like of which I have never seen since. A thousand times in my childhood I imagined myself adventuring through the wilds of this strange land, and even when adolescence turned my thoughts to other pursuits, the memory lived on in the back of my mind.

"Then, a few months ago, I happened to meet a captain preparing an expedition here, and I sold what I had for passage. This is a chance to live like the ancient heroes of Greece, battling monsters and magic. Europe has forgotten those times. The nations are constantly at war, killing each other at the whims of monarchs, switching alliances like most men switch clothes. Here, one can become a true hero, not a mercenary butcher of men."

"So why do you come to me?" asked Oludara.

"Because Antonio won't allow me to serve under his standard. Worse, he's accused me of vagrancy, and I could be arrested at any moment. But I won't desist. I want to form my own band and explore the wilderness. To do that, I need your help. I need someone clever, fast on their feet. I'm not a stupid man, I'm educated, but I'm not shrewd enough. Like yesterday, Pero doubled your price on the spot. A clever man would have tricked him into getting you for half, don't you think?"

"Yes, a clever man would have pointed out my insolence as a defect, not a strength; made me look like a troublemaker, so that Pero would want to pass me off on an outlander like yourself, rather than risk problems with an important buyer."

"See, that's it," said Gerard. "Defeating monsters requires guile, and if all you say is true, I'm sure you know better than anyone. I need your cunning, and it sounds like you can hold your own in battle as well."

"It is true," replied Oludara. "I have fought both men and monsters, and still I live."

"So, if I find a way to free you, will you go with me?"

"You would go with two men where others walk in fear with fifty?"

"Yes, if those two are us!"

Oludara laughed deeply. "Sorry to laugh at you, Gerard van Oost, but how can one not laugh when presented with such madness? Yet I must also be mad, for I accept your proposal. I see you are sincere, and I am sincere in saying that nothing in this world happens by chance. Who can say if the gods themselves didn't have something to do with our fortuitous meeting? Perhaps they placed me into the slaver's hands so I could live out some purpose here on the other side of the world.

"However, I have no desire to spend the rest of my life in the Brazilian wilderness. I must return to my people and start a family, for a man without children lives a sad life in the afterworld. If you agree to release me from this service in five years' time—and see me safely back to Ketu—I will accompany you."

"Agreed," said Gerard. "Just one question, though, what about the others?"

"Which others?"

"The other slaves, are any your kin?"

"No. None are from my tribe."

"You were the only one taken?"

"Yes."

"How?"

"I alone held off thirty rival warriors for three days so my people could escape. They came raiding for slaves to sell to the Portuguese."

"How did you hold them off for so long?"

"Traps, misdirection. If we travel together, you will find I have many tricks at my disposal."

"I look forward to seeing them," said Gerard. "Although we still face an important dilemma. Thanks to my indiscretion yesterday, Pero is asking forty thousand réis for you, almost double the price of most slaves. I don't have nearly that much money."

"Sacy-Perey."

"What?"

"A voice which reminded me of my father spoke to me in a dream last night. It whispered that to be freed, one known as Sacy-Perey must be found. I can say no more."

As he descended the hundreds of steps to the docks, Gerard admired the crystal-blue expanse before him. Salvador's immense Bay of All Saints was one of finest ports in the world, capable of harboring every ship in every fleet in Europe, many times over.

When Gerard finished his long descent, his mind returned to his task. He had roamed the merchant's street and the plaza, and was running out of people to ask about Sacy-Perey. Not a single person recognized the name.

He found a group of sailors resting under a tree. A native stood nearby, staring up curiously at a ship. The native wore no clothes, just some intricate designs painted on his body in black dye. The nakedness of the natives still shocked Gerard, even though he had seen hundreds of them since arriving in Salvador.

"Excuse me," Gerard asked the sailors, "but do any of you men know a Sacy-Perey?"

The sailors grunted and shook their heads. Gerard scanned the docks for others.

"I can tell you about Sacy-Perey."

Gerard jumped in surprise at hearing the native speak in Spanish-accented Portuguese. Upon closer inspection, he saw that the man's features were not native, but European. He appeared to be around sixty years old, with skin tanned dark by the sun.

"Pardon my surprise, I thought you were a native come to trade in the city."

"Many make that mistake," the man replied with a smile. "I suppose it might have something to do with my choice of attire. Or lack of it."

"I have little doubt." Gerard held out a hand. "I am Gerard van Oost."

The unusual man shook his hand firmly. "I am called Piraju, but long ago I was known as Miguel."

"I assume I'm not the first to ask, but how did you come to take up the customs of the natives?"

"You have heard of the legendary Caramuru?"

"The shipwrecked Portuguese who became a native chief?"

"Exactly. His story and mine are intertwined. I was a sailor on the Spanish carrack Madre de Dios, which shipwrecked here some forty years past. A tribe of Tupinambá killed most of the survivors, and took the rest of us prisoner, to be devoured in one of their cannibalistic feasts. Just as they prepared to cook us, however, Caramuru arrived and convinced them to set us free. Most of my shipmates returned to Spain, but the daughters of Caramuru and his wife, the Tupinambá princess Paraguassu, were the most beautiful women I had ever laid eyes on. So I joined the tribe and, after some time, convinced one of them to marry me."

"Amazing. So you never returned to Europe?"

"No," replied Piraju, staring at the dozens of ships docked in the bay, "but it looks like Europe is coming to us. I visit Salvador from time to time, to hear the latest news, and the city never stops growing. Now, weren't you asking about Sacy-Perey?"

"Yes, I need to find him."

"*Find* Sacy-Perey? Intelligent people find a way to avoid him. And even if you do want to meet him, it doesn't matter. No one finds Sacy-Perey, he finds you."

"I don't have time to wait around. I must find him within three days."

"Be careful. Dom Sebastian of Portugal may be king of this colony, but Sacy-Perey and his cousin Curooper are the lords of the wilderness. They protect the forest and don't take kindly to strangers."

"But a friend of mine heard in a dream that I must find him."

"A dream?" Piraju studied him. "Yes, in that case, you must seek him out. Visions cannot be ignored."

"How will I know him?"

"Recognizing him is the least of your worries; he looks like none other. His appearance is that of a young black boy with a pointy red cap, and he has but one leg. Don't be fooled though: it's not a handicap. He can hop faster on that leg than most men can run."

"And how will I find him?"

"Like I said, you don't find him, he finds you. But it is said he has a penchant for tobacco. You might attract him if you can find some quality herb."

"Tobacco? I'll try it."

"But beware, he is mischievous. If little things go wrong, if you lose that which could not possibly be lost, it is because Sacy-Perey is near."

"And how might I obtain a favor?"

"Sacy-Perey does favors for no one. The best favor you could ask for is him to leave you alone. Although it is rumored his power lies in his red hat. That might be the key."

"Thank you, uh, sir," replied Gerard, forgetting Piraju's native name. "I must be off immediately. I hope our paths cross again."

"If Sacy-Perey allows it, I'm sure they will."

⤙◇⤚

Gerard, a heavy pack on his back, was crossing the plaza toward the

North Gate when a voice shouted his name. He turned to see Antonio waving at him. Gerard, in a hurry, considered ignoring the unwanted distraction altogether, but courtesy demanded he at least trade pleasantries.

A crowd of onlookers surrounded Antonio. It seemed like half of Salvador had come out, including several women, a rare sight in that remote colony where the men outnumbered them ten-to-one. In their midst, Antonio stood next to a cart. A canvas draped over the contents formed a small mountain, concealing something enormous.

"Gerard, what luck!" called Antonio. "Just the man I was looking for. I received great news today and wanted to tell you myself."

"What news?"

"The governor accepted my request to try you for vagrancy. It appears you spent the last of your coin on tobacco and don't have enough left for the passage home."

Gerard fought to control his temper. "Word travels fast in Salvador," he replied.

"Even faster when such news is propitious. I myself advised Governor Almeida of your predicament. Vices can so easily push a weak man over the edge, such a pity." Antonio shrugged his shoulders and shook his head, playing to the crowd around him. "With the evidence at hand, a conviction is assured. If you're still in Brazil by noon Thursday, you must present yourself before the governor."

"The same day Oludara will be sent to Porto Seguro," whispered Gerard under his breath.

"What was that?" asked Antonio, squinting.

"None of your concern. Is that all you have to tell me, Antonio? I have important business to conduct outside the city and your prating is causing me delay."

Antonio glared at him. "Don't try me, Gerard. If you're leaving Salvador, I suggest you don't return. None here dare to cross me, because *this* is what I do to my enemies."

With a flourish, Antonio whipped the canvas from the cart. The crowd gasped and shrieked as Antonio unveiled the macabre contents within. Gerard stood face to face with an enormous serpent's head, taller than a man. Black, empty sockets stared at him from where hot fires had once burned within. Even in death, the Botat remained a frightful sight.

Gerard turned away from the terrible trophy and resumed his march toward the North Gate, while Antonio's laughter bellowed behind him.

Gerard sat against a fallen tree and pulled out a pipe and tobacco pouch for the twentieth time that day. He had roamed deep within the forest, stopping randomly to smoke. Just looking at tobacco was starting to make him ill. The unusual plant had become the latest fashion in Europe, Gerard had seen people snuffing and smoking the stuff everywhere, but he could barely stand it. His only consolation was that traveling in the woods allowed him to leave his formal clothes back in the city and wear a cotton shirt and breeches more suited to the tropical climate.

He fumbled at the knot on the pouch for almost a minute, unable to open it.

"I don't remember tying the pouch with this knot," he said to himself. "I don't even recognize it."

He shrugged and reached into a pocket for his knife. He felt around, unable to find it. After searching for several minutes, he finally discovered it deep within his pack.

"I don't remember putting that there."

He removed the knife from the sheath and began cutting the knot. The knife passed harmlessly over the cord. Upon closer inspection, he noticed the blade was completely dull.

"I just sharpened this today!"

Then came the realization.

"Sacy-Perey!" he said.

"Correct," came a high-pitched voice from beside him, "but don't bother calling me by my full name, it's much too formal. Just call me Sacy."

Gerard spun to see an individual exactly as Piraju had described: a young black boy with one leg and a red cap. He wore short red leggings but no shirt, his chest uncovered and hairless. His musculature was undeveloped, like that of a prepubescent boy. When he smiled, it reminded Gerard of a guilty child feigning innocence.

Sacy hopped to the log and dropped down beside Gerard.

"That smells like a good smoke. You wouldn't happen to have a bit for me there, would you?"

Gerard held out the pouch. "If you can untie the knot, you can take as much as you like. I have plenty more."

Sacy grabbed the pouch and untied the knot so quickly that Gerard couldn't follow the movement of his fingers. Sacy then lifted his red hat, shook it three times, and a wooden pipe fell from it. Intricate carved symbols covered the pipe, and Gerard didn't recognize a single one. After filling the pipe, Sacy took a puff and the tobacco lit without fire.

"Now that *is* a good smoke," he said, leaning back and blowing smoke rings. "So tell me why you've entered my forest."

"I came seeking you."

"Then you must want my permission to travel the wilderness. Most don't have the courtesy to ask, and they soon regret their lack of manners."

"I do indeed plan on traveling these wild lands."

"You seem like a nice gentleman, so I'll allow you passage, on the condition you always have a pouch of tobacco ready in case we should ever meet again."

"Fair enough."

"And you must do as little damage to the forest as possible; use only what you need."

"When you say 'do little damage', does that include the monsters?"

"Monsters? I know not how you separate man from monster, to me they are all the same. If you mean the perilous creatures which crowd this wilderness from one end to the other, do with them what you will—for they would do the same to you."

Sacy's speech had caught Gerard off-guard. Sacy looked and acted like a child, and spoke with a voice so high it almost hurt the ears, but his words were those of someone much older. Gerard knew not to underestimate the strange being.

"I thank you for your permission," said Gerard, "because I plan to confront those creatures. In fact, it is the entire reason I came to this land. But, in truth, I have come here to ask something else of you."

"Sorry," said Sacy, annoyance in his voice, "but I grant no other favors. I have offered to leave you be, and that is much."

"I appreciate that, but I was told to visit you and request something which only you can give."

"Then whoever sent you is a fool."

Sacy laughed at an even higher pitch than his speaking voice. Then he disappeared, leaving only a puff of smoke from his pipe to show he had ever been there.

A rustling sound came from Gerard's left and he turned to see a wave of movement charging at him through the brush. He jumped and grabbed a nearby tree branch, scrambling up the trunk with his legs just as seven boars burst into the clearing. The boars paused at the bottom of the tree and sniffed. Gerard could hear a high-pitched laughing in the distance. He found a nook in which to sit and waited several minutes for the animals to leave.

Ever since his encounter with Sacy the day before, such torments had become commonplace. A hole had mysteriously formed in his pack, forcing him to backtrack and find everything which had fallen out. Hot peppers had been mixed into his water. A few drops of honey hidden in his breeches had led to a nasty surprise from some ants. Also, every knot tied was soon untied, and vice-versa.

After climbing down from the tree he yelled out, "Sacy-Perey, stop tormenting me! I must speak with you."

Out of thin air, Sacy appeared several paces in front of him.

"Well then, go ahead and speak."

"I need a favor which only you can provide."

"Tell you what, if you can catch me, I'll grant your wish."

"All right!"

Without thinking, Gerard ran forward. His first step, however, brought him face-first with the ground. With another high-pitched laugh, Sacy vanished from sight.

Gerard looked down to find that a rope bound his boots together with an incredibly complex knot.

"So, he likes knots, does he?" he mused as he reached down to remove the boots.

It was Thursday, the day of reckoning for both himself and Oludara, so Gerard prayed for one final appearance of Sacy. If the imp did appear, Gerard knew he would have to make the most important shot of his life.

"No harder than shooting a fly off an apple at twenty paces," he joked to himself.

To relieve the cramping, he shifted his body within the blind he had built. Even with the harquebus resting in the crook of a branch, it was painful to spend so much time in firing position.

Thirty feet before him lay a path, upon which he had left the most complex knot he could have ever imagined. He had used twenty cords of varying sizes, and spent no less than four hours tying them together as intricately as possible. In the end, the knot attained a diameter of three feet. Visions of Alexander and the Gordian knot flashed through Gerard's head and he chuckled, wondering how that ancient knot compared to his own masterpiece.

A movement caught his eye, and he froze. Sacy came hopping along the path and stopped just before the massive wad of cords. He bent down to examine it, then righted himself and looked around carefully. Gerard held his breath as Sacy's gaze passed him by.

After several visual sweeps, Sacy bent down and began untying the knot with blinding speed. Gerard knew he had only seconds to act. He held his breath and fired the harquebus. He waved his hand to clear the smoke and saw Sacy frantically patting his bald head with both hands, searching for the cap which Gerard's perfect shot had sent flying.

Gerard loosed a rope beside him, releasing a heavy net hidden in the canopy. He ran to the path and scooped up the red hat. To his surprise, the hat showed not a trace of the shot which had struck it.

Sacy lay sobbing beneath the net. "Please, free me, I will die without my hat. I did you no harm."

"I wouldn't say the prank with the ants was exactly harmless, but don't try to fool me, Sacy, I know you're a trickster. You won't get your hat back until you grant my favor."

Sacy stopped his pouting and sighed. "Very well, tell me your wish."

"My heart's greatest desire is one-hundred gold *cruzados*."

"Is that all? Most men would ask for an entire gold mine."

"I want to make my own way in this world, earn my own fortune."

"Then why are you so concerned with a hundred cruzados?"

"Because today I must pay the price of a slave."

Sacy turned away. "Then you might as well strike me down. I would never help a man acquire a slave." Sacy's voice lowered, for the first time serious. "I was once a slave, a boy on the first black ship ever to arrive from Africa, until a treacherous death and magic made me Sacy-Perey."

"You don't understand," replied Gerard, "I don't wish to buy him, I wish to buy his freedom. In return, he has agreed to aid me for five years. He will accompany me through the wilderness, braving the mysteries here."

"Is all you say true?"

"Yes."

Sacy paused. "In that case I will give you what you need, and allow both of you to travel my lands. But I'll keep an eye on you. If you don't hold your part of the bargain, I'll torment you for the rest of your life."

"I'm a man of my word."

"All right, give me the hat."

"First," said Gerard, "make an oath."

"I swear I will give you your one hundred cruzados."

"Swear it on the forest."

"I swear upon my realm, the forest."

"Very well."

Gerard hoisted a corner of the net and Sacy crawled out. Gerard tossed him the hat. Sacy shook it four times and a golden nugget fell into his palm. He placed the hat back on his head and proceeded to rub the nugget between his hands. As he did so, golden coins appeared, clinking together as they fell to the ground.

After a pile had formed, Sacy shoved the nugget back under his hat and said, "That should cover the price. I could give you a golden nugget in its place, but people might think you found it in the wilderness and come in hordes, looking for more."

"I think you're right about that, Sacy," agreed Gerard. "If gold is ever found in Brazil, the invasion will be so great that not even you could hold it back."

Sacy blinked out of sight without warning. His voice came from the woods, "Don't forget, I'll be watching you!"

Gerard stooped to gather the coins.

Gerard, panting, burst into the governor's office. Governor Almeida sat behind an exquisite mahogany desk. He wore a black, flat cap with a puffy white feather and a burgundy shoulder cape clasped at the neck by a gold chain. Antonio, also formally dressed, leaned by the governor's side, apparently in the middle of some conversation.

The governor frowned and said, "Gerard van Oost, you're late."

"Sorry, Governor," he replied, "I came running with a sack of gold weighing me down."

"Gold?" replied the governor, raising an eyebrow.

Antonio squinted menacingly at Gerard.

"Yes," said Gerard, "one hundred cruzados. Gold enough to buy the freedom of a slave. His name is Oludara."

"What is this?" shouted Antonio. "Where did you acquire such a fortune?"

Governor Almeida raised a hand to quiet him. "One hundred cruzados, did you say? That's forty thousand réis! Quite an extravagant price for a slave."

"I don't consider it right to put a price on any man," replied Gerard, "but by any measure, this one is extraordinary."

"I expect the usual tax will be paid?"

"Pero de Belem will pay what is owed."

Governor Almeida studied Gerard for a few moments before speaking. "Antonio has charged you with vagrancy and practicing the Protestant religion. Protestantism isn't a crime under the local laws, and I can't see how a man of your means could be called a vagrant. Thus, I am forced to dismiss the case."

"But, Governor," started Antonio.

"I'm sorry, Antonio, but I must uphold the law."

"Governor," said Gerard, "if I may, I would ask a boon."

The Governor raised his eyebrows and leaned forward. "What is it?"

"I wish to form a troop under my own banner, to explore the wilderness at will."

Antonio choked back a sound.

"And who will serve under your standard?" asked the governor.

"Myself and Oludara, the man I'm to free. That is, if he chooses to accompany me."

"You mean to form a banner of yourself and a slave? Just the two of you?"

"You're not the first person to ask me that question this week."

Governor Almeida held his sides and laughed. "Antonio," he said, "why are you spending so much effort to lock this man away when he's practically offering to kill himself? I can't arrest him, but I can do you this favor." He looked at Gerard and said, "Gerard, your request is granted."

Antonio glowered silently.

"Now will that be all?" asked the governor. "I'm busy preparing an expedition against the French raiders in Paraiba."

"Governor," said Gerard, "today I have gained all that my heart desires. I'll take no more of your time, as I also have an expedition to plan."

He bowed and left the office.

As Gerard passed through the main hall of the Governor's Palace, he heard quick footsteps behind him. He turned just as Antonio grabbed his sleeve.

"Play the hero as long as you can, Gerard," he said, "but the wilderness is *my* domain. Pray we don't cross paths."

"Even after all your treachery," replied Gerard, "I hold you no grudge. And there are greater dangers than you in the Brazilian wilderness."

"So you think," replied Antonio. He turned his back and stomped from the hall.

Oludara, wearing a brand new cotton outfit Gerard had purchased for him, stepped into Pero's office. Even in a rotting tunic, Oludara had impressed, but in his new clothes, he was imposing.

"So, do you like the clothes?" asked Gerard.

"They are suitable. Although it might be more advantageous to travel naked, as the natives do."

Gerard, his Protestant mind jarred by the suggestion, couldn't help but blush. "I don't think we'll be doing that, the clothes are fine. By the way, I bought something today from Martim, one of Pero's crew. He said it gave him the chills every time he touched it, but perhaps you might like it."

Gerard placed a cloth bundle on the table and unwrapped it to reveal Oludara's ivory dagger. Oludara picked it up and passed his fingers slowly across the carvings. A single tear slid down his face.

"Thank you," he said.

"I have but one sword, but I do have a spare harquebus you can use."

"I won't use the gun; their accuracy is not to be trusted. The long bows the natives carry suit me better."

"My harquebuses are nothing like those clumsy sticks the soldiers use. A master smith grooved the barrels and their accuracy is unmatched."

"However fine they may be," said Oludara, "guns are not my

weapon."

Gerard shrugged and handed Oludara a backpack. "I've obtained food and equipment, everything I could think of, including some local remedies. It appears that Sacy even added a few herbs of his own when I wasn't looking."

"Really? I thought you told me Sacy did favors for no man."

"It appears he's taken an interest in our journey."

"That could be very good, or very bad."

"Most likely both," said Gerard. "But I still have one question: do you go willingly on this dangerous journey?"

"You would offer me the chance to refuse?" asked Oludara.

"I didn't pay to buy you," said Gerard, "I paid to free you. To go or not is your choice. I would not face the dangers out there with a man who does not go of his own free will."

Oludara smiled. "You have proven yourself quite a man this week, Gerard van Oost. Catching Sacy shows that you are more resourceful than you believe. And you could have asked him for anything, but you chose to free me. I do not choose companions lightly, but I can see already that you will be a worthy one. I would serve you for five years to pay my debt, but since you would have it so, I will accompany you as a friend."

At that, they shook hands.

"Then I suppose that makes it official," said Gerard, "now we're a band. Look at what I made."

He unfurled a linen standard. Upon it, sketched roughly in black dye, appeared an elephant and a macaw.

Gerard noticed Oludara cringe at the poor drawings and added, "It's just a rough idea for now; we can improve it later."

"I speak truthfully when I say that what you have there is the ugliest, yet at the same time most inspiring standard I have ever seen."

"Then we are in full agreement," said Gerard, "and since we have our standard, I don't see any reason why we shouldn't leave immediately."

"Indeed, the dawn does not come twice to wake a man. Many adventures lie before us; let us not make them wait!"

High atop the Church of the Immaculate Conception, a scarlet macaw cocked its head and watched two men, one white and one black, as they crossed Salvador's central plaza and left the city through the North Gate.

Chapter 2

The Parlous Battle against the Kalobo

 THREE-BANDED ARMADILLO AMBLED along on her nighttime search for dinner. Every few steps, she clawed the ground and shifted her snout through the upturned dirt in a quest for ants, termites, and her favorite treat: grubs. She paused a moment when a breeze carried over an unusual scent—two of them, actually. The smells resembled those of the tall, two-legged beasts that lived in the forest, yet with a complex blend of unfamiliar, exotic odors: none of them pleasant. However, she sensed no immediate danger, and returned her attention to the nearest clump of dirt.

Gerard van Oost and Oludara lay motionless behind a patch of hibiscus. Some fifty feet before them, a squat, fidgety animal ambled through a clearing. Snorting contentedly, it paused its erratic wandering every few steps to plow the ground with its disproportionate front claws and sniff around.

Squinting in the fading twilight, Gerard studied the unusual beast. What appeared to be ochre-colored plates of armor covered it from head to tail. Coarse hair dangled from its underbelly and brushed the dry grass as it walked.

"What is it?" whispered Gerard, pushing back his wide-brimmed hat for a better look.

"It looks a bit like an animal we have back in Ketu," replied Oludara, "the pangolin."

"I've seen nothing like it in Europe," responded Gerard. "Although it does remind me of a woodcut I once saw of the famed rhinoceros of India, with its overlapping plates of armor."

"We have rhinoceroses in Africa as well," replied Oludara, "which I have seen with my own eyes. I can tell you they have no plates of armor, just thick hides. And they look nothing like *that*!"

"Do you think it is one of the magical beasts of this land?"

"It is probably harmless," said Oludara. "But the Brazilian wilderness has surprised us many times. We should be cautious."

With a nudge on the flash pan cover, Gerard confirmed that his harquebus was primed and ready to fire. He left the weapon at his side for the time being; he disliked using force until absolutely necessary. Nevertheless, the hard ground felt none too comfortable against his stout frame, and he longed for a quick resolution to the situation. At his side, Oludara shifted his body enough to slip the ivory knife from his belt.

"We should attempt to capture it," said Gerard. "Do you have any ideas?"

Oludara pulled a deep breath through his broad nose and studied the area around them.

"There are many vines nearby. I should be able to prepare a trap, and you can lure the beast."

"Wait," rasped Gerard, "it approaches."

With one smooth motion, Gerard lifted his harquebus into firing position. He pulled back the cock and placed a finger on the trigger.

A high-pitched laugh screeched behind him.

The shrill noise made Gerard tense up and fire. The accidental shot passed high above the creature, but the sound of the blast caused it to curl up in self-defense, snapping into an armored ball.

Gerard and Oludara turned in unison to face the source of laughter. Gerard dropped his harquebus and grabbed for his rapier, while Oludara extended his knife arm.

At their feet, Sacy-Perey hopped on his one leg and giggled uncontrollably. Gerard and Oludara had spent months exploring the wilderness near Salvador, and Sacy had appeared more frequently than either would have liked. He had both aided and tortured them, depending on his mood. The two men relaxed their weapons while Sacy continued hopping and laughing.

"Why do you laugh, Sacy?" asked Oludara.

Sacy spouted a final guffaw before controlling himself. He wiped a tear from his eye and responded, "Because of the way you reacted to that harmless animal."

Gerard stood up and brushed the dirt from his cotton vest and leggings. "And what exactly *is* that animal?" he asked. He turned and motioned toward it just in time to see it unroll itself and scamper off.

"It's a 'tatu'. Although I believe the Europeans call it 'armadillo'—the kind of ridiculous name your people give to everything. It is of no danger to any creature larger than a beetle, unless that creature happens to be dead, in which case the tatu will happily chew the rotting meat from its bones. So the question is, seeing how you're not a corpse, how could a strong man like you be so scared of a creature no taller than your boots?"

"I've learned never to judge a creature by its size, Sacy," responded Gerard. "Were it so, I would doubtless take *you* more lightly than I should."

Sacy smiled at the compliment. "You make a good point," he said, sitting down on a fallen trunk. "And as long as we're chatting, do you happen to have some of that wonderful leaf on you?"

Gerard sat on the log beside Sacy and removed a pouch from his backpack. Ever since his first encounter with the prepubescent demon, Gerard had learned to keep a stock of tobacco on hand. A smoke always seemed to make Sacy more amenable, and Gerard shuddered to think what the imp would do if he ever found him without. He grabbed a generous wad of leaf and handed it to him.

Sacy removed his red cap and shook it three times, causing his intricately carved wooden pipe to appear. He packed the pipe and, as always, lit it by merely taking a puff.

Gerard removed his hat and waved it back and forth, providing a momentary respite from the insects which hounded them relentlessly through the wilderness. In an effort to relax, he extracted two guavas from his pack, one of which he tossed to Oludara. Gerard retrieved a knife and peeled the bitter yellow-green skin away from the dark pink center. Oludara bit directly into the skin, eating both parts together.

After a few bites, Oludara said, "This is what I have been telling you, Gerard. We have been fortunate on our adventures so far, escaping peril by our wits alone. But the deeper we travel into the wilderness, the more vulnerable we become. We can no longer tell the difference between danger and deliverance. Our only hope is to live among the natives for a time and study their way of life. Their knowledge is invaluable to us."

Gerard frowned, as he did every time Oludara broached the subject, and tugged nervously on his palm-length red goatee. "Oludara," he said, "I'm not sure how much I can learn from naked, heathen cannibals. There is much in their culture that opposes my Protestant beliefs."

"Would you not say the same of my people, Gerard? We do not share your faith. But have I not been a most trustworthy and steadfast companion?"

"Well, of course," said Gerard, lowering his reddening face, "and I didn't mean it that way. It's just that, well, I mean to say...they eat people! Human life is sacred."

"Do not your people war in the name of religion?"

Gerard conceded with a nod. "They do even now," he responded, sighing and looking away.

"Try to understand, Gerard. To the people of this land, the consumption of the enemy is a ritual: an honor for both the eater and the eaten. It isn't like the herding of buffalo for meat; it is ceremony."

"Well," interrupted Sacy, "if you really want to speak with some natives, there's a tribe of Tupinambá not far from here. I suppose you could visit them, although I wouldn't recommend it." He took a long pull from the pipe.

"And why not?" asked Gerard.

Sacy blew a series of six perfect smoke rings before responding. "They don't take kindly to strangers."

"We should go there," said Oludara. "No matter their prejudices, we shall earn their friendship."

Gerard sat thinking for a long time before responding. "Very well then. Your council I value above that of all others, even my own. Let's make camp while there is still a hint of light in the sky, then leave first thing in the morning.

"And if you don't mind, Sacy, please tell us the way to the village before you disappear again."

⤙◇⤚

Sacy left shortly after his smoke, lingering just long enough to hang

Gerard's hat from a bees' nest in a nearby tree. Gerard and Oludara enjoyed a reasonable sleep before setting off in the morning, although the bee stings on Gerard's hand did cause him some discomfort during the night. Following Sacy's directions, they headed west.

Gerard had to admit, he did find the forest daunting. Vegetation surrounded them above, below, and on all sides. At times, the canopy closed so completely that he could not spot the sky. The odor of decomposing leaves mingled with the fragrant trees, the scents of death and life suffocating in the sweltering forest air. The seemingly endless forest, mighty and mysterious, made him feel insignificant.

They walked for six hours until arriving at what Sacy had called "the Black River". There was no mistaking the murky, fifty-foot wide watercourse. From what Sacy had told them, they would find the village downriver, one league to the south.

Gerard bent down to splash water on his face when Oludara's hand on his shoulder made him pause. Oludara pointed toward the other shore, a little ways upriver. Gerard followed the indication and spotted movement on the other side: a woman. He and Oludara watched in silence.

As with all Brazilian natives, the woman wore no clothing, just dye-painted designs to ornament her physique. She appeared to be around nineteen years old, her body young and fit. Straight black hair descended to her waist. In her left hand she carried a woven basket, but Gerard couldn't discern the contents. True to form for the devout Protestant, he kept his succinct examination above neck level as much as possible, then turned away for modesty's sake. That's when he noticed his companion thoughtfully examining the woman up and down—repeatedly.

"Magnificent," whispered Oludara. "Such beauty is rare indeed. Have you ever seen such curves, Gerard?"

"As a matter of fact, I haven't," he responded. "And I don't plan on starting now."

"Well, you should. Every part of her is perfect, from top to bottom. Her delicate feet, her firm legs, her well-formed..."

"Oludara," Gerard interrupted, blushing, "perhaps we should speak with her? Isn't that the reason we're here, to make contact with the natives?"

Oludara nodded and straightened up.

"Excuse me," he shouted in Portuguese, "we mean you no harm. We wish to parlay with your tribe." Oludara made elaborate gestures as he spoke, trying to convey calmness.

The woman jumped upon hearing his voice. When she looked over at the two of them, her body tensed, as if to run. "Go away!" she yelled in heavily-accented Portuguese. "My tribe does not want your religion or your disease, whichever it is you bring."

"Well," mumbled Gerard, "at least she speaks Portuguese."

Oludara spoke again to the woman, "May we cross the river and speak with you?"

"No. Come no closer, or I will call to my tribe."

"Our only wish is to visit your tribe."

"That would be foolish," she said, "for they want no visit from you. Who are you anyway, that you search for us?"

"My name is Oludara, and this is my companion Gerard van Oost. Our banner is the Elephant and Macaw."

"If you serve a banner, then I know why you seek my tribe—you are looking for slaves!" She spit on the ground.

"We formed a company because only those who serve one can attain the governor's permission to travel the wilderness. Our desire is to confront the legendary dangers of this land, not enslave its people." Oludara held his arms wide. "I was once a slave myself, until Gerard rescued me. I would never put another in such a condition."

The girl paused at the words. "Easy enough to say, but for the right price, a man will turn against even his own people. There are too many liars among the Pero," she said, using the name given the Portuguese in the Tupi language, the one spoken by the Tupinambá and many other coastal tribes.

"We are not Portuguese," said Oludara. "Gerard is Dutch. He is his own man, neither ally nor enemy of the Portuguese. And from the color of my skin, is it not obvious I was brought from Africa as a slave?"

"It is true you do not look or speak like the Pero I have met."

"We have told you our names," said Oludara, "what is yours?"

"Arany," she replied.

"Arany, please let us accompany you back to your tribe. Our intentions are peaceful."

"And where is the rest of your company?"

"It is just the two of us."

"Now I know you are lying," she scoffed. "I have never seen a banner with less than twenty soldiers."

"Our banner might be unusual," said Oludara, "but we face the same dangers nonetheless. May we accompany you back?"

"No," said Arany.

"And what if we make our own way to your village?" asked Gerard. "We were told it is but an hour walk from here, following the river."

"Who told you that?" asked Arany, squinting.

"Sacy-Perey," replied Gerard.

"Ha!" she said. "You take me for a fool to believe such a story?"

Gerard looked at Oludara and shrugged.

"Lies upon lies," she continued. "Walk to my village if you wish, but not by my invitation. Once you arrive there, the warriors will know what to do with you. Your presence will certainly give them cause for a *feast*."

She sneered and headed off down the river.

"I don't think that was a jest," said Gerard. "If we go, they're going to cook us."

"Gerard," replied Oludara, "I have never known you to shy from adventure. Did you not tell me one of your people said, 'the greater the difficulty, the greater the glory'?"

"Not my people, some old Roman said that. But didn't you once say 'Whoever tries to shake a tree will only shake himself'?"

"Ha, very good, Gerard, you have been listening. But we also have a saying, 'If you do not go to the market, the market will not come to you.' We require the knowledge of the natives, and we must go to them and make our case."

Oludara set off south along the river.

Gerard put his hands on his hips and said, "Don't think you can just say something like that and lead us into danger. This isn't adventure, Oludara, it's suicide! Oludara?"

When Oludara made no sign of stopping, Gerard sighed and followed.

Oludara kept pace with Arany as she walked along the far bank. She looked back from time to time and shook her head when she saw them following. While Gerard kept his eyes always on the path ahead, obviously trying to ignore the girl's splendid nakedness, Oludara found he couldn't keep his eyes off of her.

Oludara still couldn't understand his companion's Protestant ways. Gerard could speak for hours about paintings by the masters of Europe, so why would he waste the chance to study a beautiful woman with that same eye for detail?

After a while, Oludara could not help but voice his thoughts. "Do you not think she would make a fine wife?" he asked, breaking a long silence.

"Only if you'd like to be the meal at your own wedding," replied Gerard.

Oludara laughed. "Perhaps. But, to speak the truth, she would make an excellent child-bearer. Her proportions are perfect. I wonder if her smell is as pleasing as her countenance."

"Can we speak of something else?" grumbled Gerard. "Is that why we're walking to our slow-roasting deaths, because you're infatuated with the native girl?"

"Well, she is fascinating," replied Oludara, not taking his eyes off of her. "But I have no fear for us. You are a good man, Gerard van Oost, and your sincerity shines through. I am certain it will charm even the natives. And the fact that Arany speaks Portuguese is a good omen. Who would have expected to find a native speaking Portuguese this far from Salvador?"

"That's an interesting observation," said Gerard, stroking his goatee. "Arany," he shouted across the river, "how is it that you came to speak Portuguese?"

Without breaking pace, she called back, "My tribe lived with the Jesuits near Salvador when I was a child."

Gerard raised an eyebrow at Oludara. Salvador lay some thirty leagues away, no small distance.

"Do the others of your tribe speak Portuguese as well?" asked Gerard.

"Only a few of us still know the language of the Pero, and we do not speak it among ourselves. Most have forgotten it, or have sworn never to use it again."

At that moment, Oludara caught sight of a fence made from ten-foot tall stakes placed at regular intervals. He could make out a closed palisade beyond them. Some round, white objects hung on top of the outer stakes. As they closed the distance, he recognized them as human skulls.

Gerard stopped in his tracks. "I don't like the look of *that*," he said.

"Not particularly inviting," agreed Oludara.

"It's not *meant* to be inviting," came a voice beside them.

They both jerked in surprise to find that Arany had crossed a ford in the river to reach their side.

"Well, aren't you coming?" she said. "My tribe will be most disappointed if you don't join us for a *meal*." She walked toward an opening in the fence.

Gerard shrugged and said, "I suppose we've come this far; let's try our luck."

They followed Arany through the outer stakes, and Oludara noticed Gerard raise his head to study the skulls as they passed underneath. Oludara kept his focus on the path before them.

Ponderous logs formed the inner palisade, with eye-level arrow slits at regular intervals. Once through the gate, he could finally see the village itself.

Five huge cabins, each over a hundred feet long, circled a central square. These longhouses were built from stakes, leaves, and dirt, with three-foot layers of palm leaves piled on as roofs.

As Oludara and Gerard entered the ring of longhouses, hundreds of curious natives emptied out to gawk at them. None wore clothing, though most sported some type of decoration. Black-painted designs, similar to Arany's, appeared on many bodies. Piercings filled with polished stones adorned ears, cheeks, and the skin below the lips. Several natives wore necklaces made from shells or stones. Elaborate arrays of feathers decorated heads and arms. Cotton sheets, tiny infants swaddled within, draped across the backs of many women. The women all wore their hair long, but the men wore it shaved on top and cut to one length around the sides, like the tonsures of the European friars. None showed any sign of body or facial hair.

The natives shouted at Oludara and Gerard, the women loudest of all. Children ran circles around them, taunting. Men nocked arrows in six-foot long bows and held them at the ready. Arany separated herself from the two companions.

Oludara held up his hands in a show of truce, and spoke calmly, "Please, we come in peace."

Many natives pointed at Gerard's harquebus, which he carried at his side.

"Gerard," said Oludara, "put down your gun!"

Gerard placed the weapon on the ground and raised his hands.

The natives crowded closer. Some yelled at Arany in Tupi. She responded calmly to all questions, making motions to distance herself from the two of them, with the air of one who has nothing to do with the situation at hand. Neither Oludara nor Gerard understood a word of the language.

The men raised their bows and drew them, ready for an attack.

"Please, Arany," said Oludara, "persuade them to speak with us."

Arany paused and studied the two carefully. Then she turned and dashed off.

"Oh no," said Gerard, "she's abandoned us. We should flee."

"Perhaps not," said Oludara, "see where she goes."

Arany ducked into a tiny hut at the edge of the village. Oludara hadn't noticed it before: the massive longhouses dwarfed it. Within moments, Arany appeared again, pulling a bald, elderly native by the arm. He wore a feathered headdress which stretched down his back, and multiple collars rattled around his neck. As he approached, men and women parted for him.

The old man spoke; he talked with force but without raising his voice. Several of the men, those who wore more feather decorations than the others, shouted at him in what appeared to be an argument. He replied by holding up his chin and pointing to the center of the village.

At this, the natives lowered their bows, one by one, but most kept them half-drawn. The old man walked to the village center and sat on a log. Five other men, the most-decorated, followed.

"Arany," asked Gerard, "what's happening?"

"The man I brought is Yandir, our *pajé*," she answered.

"What is a pajé?" asked Oludara.

"He can communicate with the spirits. Using their wisdom, he both heals and guides us."

"So he is a type of priest?" asked Oludara.

"Priest?" scoffed Gerard. "More like a sorcerer."

"Call him what you wish," said Arany. "Yandir is not a chief, but he is old and well-respected, both of which carry much weight. The five chiefs have agreed to a council. You have gained some time, for however long it lasts."

"Thank you," said Oludara, bowing his head.

Arany frowned and walked away. Oludara admired her grace as she moved. She disappeared into one of the cabins.

The scent of tobacco smoke caught Oludara's attention, and he looked to see the chiefs smoking from a long tube formed from rolled-up palm leaves. One by one the chiefs stood and spoke, while the others passed around the tube and smoked. When the chiefs' discussion passed ten minutes, Gerard and Oludara sat down. Almost thirty natives watched over them, many with bows at the ready. After twenty minutes, one of the chiefs motioned toward them. Younger than the rest, not more than thirty years old, he wore a headdress made from yellow-and-red feathers, and a light blue stone shone under his lower lip.

"Come here, strangers," he said in Portuguese.

The two of them approached the chiefs' council.

The man who had called them over held up a hand in greeting. "You may call me Jakoo," he stammered in sluggish Portuguese: not nearly as good as Arany's, yet comprehensible. "Only Cabwassu and I speak the language of the Pero." He pointed toward one of the other chiefs.

Oludara and Gerard turned to study Cabwassu. Blue and green feathers fanned out from his armbands, and pointed stones stuck from his earlobes, cheeks, and lower lip, so many as to make him appear almost inhuman. Most striking were the numerous scars that covered his muscular body, in particular the ones which laddered down each arm like stripes. He appeared to be the toughest and meanest of the group, and he scowled when they looked at him. They both turned away their gaze.

Jakoo continued, "The others want me to ask you questions, so we may decide your fate. Some think we should eat you."

Cabwassu bared a malicious, toothy smile. Gerard removed his wide-brimmed hat and wiped the sweat from his forehead.

"However," continued Jakoo, "it has been many moons since we have tasted the flesh of our enemies, since before our days with the Jesuits. The younger chiefs, like me, no longer think it right."

"That's quite reasonable of you," replied Gerard, straightening up and nodding briskly.

"For us, it is better to kill you, with no eating."

"Oh," said Gerard, his shoulders slumping back down.

"First, though," said Jakoo, "we want to know why you come to our village."

"To learn from you," replied Oludara. "We travel the wild lands of Brazil, and your knowledge would help us greatly."

Cabwassu spat on the ground near Oludara's feet. Jakoo ignored the gesture and turned to translate for the other chiefs. Most of them shook their heads. Yandir, the pajé, said something to Jakoo.

"Yandir says," said Jakoo, "we are Tupinambá. You are not Tupinambá. Why share our knowledge with you?"

"We can offer trade," said Gerard. He pulled off his pack and rummaged through it. After a few seconds, he pulled out a knife and mirror and held them up.

Jakoo laughed, as did some of the others. Cabwassu spat again. Jakoo spoke to some nearby women, who went into the huts. A minute later they appeared again, arms full of objects. Jakoo motioned them toward Gerard and Oludara and they emptied their arms before the two. Mirrors, hoes, knives, machetes, and other items of European origin piled at their feet.

Oludara frowned. "We can work," he offered.

Cabwassu stood and yelled at them, "We don't need your help!"

"We battle monsters," interrupted Gerard. "That is why we travel this land."

Cabwassu laughed, but Jakoo turned and translated to the others.

Yandir looked them over thoughtfully, rubbing his bald head as he did. He said one word, "Kalobo."

Cabwassu shouted at the old man in Tupi, and a couple of others joined in. Whatever his idea, they obviously didn't like it.

Jakoo motioned away Oludara and Gerard. "Go sit down. We will tell you our decision soon."

Shortly after they sat down, Arany appeared, carrying round objects in both hands. She knelt beside Gerard and Oludara and offered them the objects, which turned out to be cups made from hollowed-out gourds, warm to the touch. They were filled with a fishy-smelling paste.

"What is this?" asked Gerard.

"It is *mingau*," said Arany, "much like your porridge. This type is made from cassava, with fish and peppers for flavor."

Gerard scooped some paste with his fingertips and licked it. "Delicious!" he said. "Thank you, Arany." He shoved his hand in for the next mouthful.

Oludara sat staring at his gourd.

"What's wrong?" asked Gerard, spraying bits of food from his stuffed mouth.

Oludara held up the cup. "They use the calabash, just as we do in Ketu; it reminds me of home. Funny how things can be so alike, here on the other side of the world."

"Hmm," replied Gerard, gulping down another handful of mingau. "Not just here, we use them in Europe as well." Gerard became thoughtful. "Back home, the bowl and calabash are used as symbols by the Dutch rebels in their war against Spain."

"Sorry," said Oludara, shaking his head to clear it. "I should have said before: thank you, Arany. This food was unexpected and much appreciated."

Arany turned down her eyes. "It is no less than you should expect," she said. "Even our enemies are treated with respect, until the moment they are slain." She grimaced as she said it. "I almost forgot," she said, hopping up, "there is something else."

She ran back to the hut and brought back a wooden tray filled with white bits. "This we call *pipoca*," she said. "It is made by heating bits of corn, which releases the tiny spirits inside with a bang."

"Popped corn," said Gerard, grinning. "I've heard of it, but never seen it before." He reached in the bowl and pulled out a handful.

When Arany offered the bowl to Oludara, he stared into her eyes. She held his gaze for but a moment before looking away.

After choking down several handfuls of popped corn, Gerard said, "Arany, that chief over there, Cabwassu..."

All three looked toward the chiefs, where Cabwassu shouted and made suggestively violent motions toward Gerard and Oludara.

"Yes?" she asked.

"What does he say of us?"

"He would see you killed quickly."

"Hmm," said Gerard, pulling on his goatee. "Does he hold much sway?"

"You saw those scars on his arms?" Arany asked.

"Yes."

"Each scar represents one of his names."

"So he has a lot of names?" asked Gerard. "What does that mean?"

"The men take a new name and a new scar every time they kill an enemy. He has many, many names."

"Oh, I see," said Gerard, mentally adding up the lines, but eventually losing count.

"Why do your people dislike the Portuguese?" asked Oludara.

"Why?" replied Arany. "Don't you know? The Pero are sometimes friends, sometimes enemies. Sometimes saviors, sometimes slavers. Who knows what they think? The old governor allowed the banners to sack many tribes. Our tribe was spared because we were under the protection of the Jesuits. However, the smallpox arrived and claimed the lives of other tribes under their care. We fled before it found us as well. The Jesuits could protect the Tupinambá from the governor, but not the smallpox, so we returned to our old way of life."

Arany paused before continuing. "Cabwassu hates all foreigners. He lost much of his family, as have we all. But while most of us were happy just to leave the Pero behind, he has sworn revenge."

They were interrupted when Jakoo approached them.

"Return to the circle," he said. "We have made a decision."

Oludara looked Gerard in the eye. Gerard nodded and the two stood and walked to the chiefs' council in silence. Arany followed close behind.

"Yandir suggests we give you a chance," said Jakoo. "You must defeat Kalobo, a beast which has killed and eaten many Tupinambá. A group of hunters disappeared two days past, and we believe that Kalobo is to blame.

"Our bows are useless against the beast, our arrows bounce from its hide. If you find a way to defeat Kalobo, Yandir says you can be Tupinambá."

All around Jakoo, men nodded in approval, understanding the words "Kalobo" and "Tupinambá", at least.

"Yandir is a powerful pajé," said Jakoo. "The chiefs accept his suggestion. But if you will not or cannot defeat Kalobo, you will be dinner for it or for us. Do you accept?"

Without the need to confer, both nodded their heads in unison.

"We will send a guide to show the way," said Jakoo, "one of our warriors."

"If she is willing," said Oludara, "we will take Arany as our guide."

Cabwassu laughed at the suggestion. Gerard's jaw dropped.

Jakoo looked at Arany. She caught Oludara's eye and stared for a moment, then nodded her head.

"Good idea," said Cabwassu. "We get rid of two problems at same time."

Jakoo spoke to the chiefs and they dispersed, each one towards a different longhouse. Yandir returned to his hut. Only Jakoo and Cabwassu stayed behind.

"You should leave now," said Jakoo.

Cabwassu looked at Oludara and said, "Don't try to flee. I watch you." He turned and strode off stiffly.

Oludara paddled the fifteen-foot canoe with Gerard as Arany guided them. He tried to focus on the river, but his gaze would invariably stray back to Arany. From time to time, she would look back and catch him staring at her.

Finally, she spoke. "Oludara, you should not look at me that way."

"I'm sorry," he said, "I am not familiar with your customs. Is it improper?"

"No, it is just...I cannot marry."

"Why not?"

"Do not ask," she said, with a note of finality.

"Let me ask you another question then. Why did you call the pajé to our aid, instead of speaking with the chiefs?"

"My parents died years ago, and Yandir has been like a father to me. Outside of him, the others shun me. They think I am a bringer of bad luck, and the fact that you followed me into the village helped neither your reputation nor mine."

"Is that why Cabwassu said something about 'getting rid of two problems at once'?"

"Yes. There are many who would like to be rid of me."

"When this is all over," said Oludara, "we could take you away from your tribe."

Gerard coughed at the suggestion, but said nothing.

Arany looked at Oludara, sadness in her eyes. "Do not get too close, Oludara. My name means 'foul weather'. I was born during a terrible storm. My entire life has been misfortune."

"Look!" interrupted Gerard, pointing.

A human skull lay on the shore nearby. Oddly enough, it lay in two pieces, split just above the eyes. Rowing and talking ceased as the three paused to stare at it. They floated past the skull, only to spot a pile with several more. Almost all were split at the crown, just like the first. Among the skulls lay enormous piles of dung, which, Oludara noted, rivaled the size of those left by the buffalo herds of Africa. In terms of stench, however, Oludara would have preferred the buffalo.

"We are near," whispered Arany.

"I don't think you need to tell us that," replied Gerard, nodding his head forward.

Some twenty yards before them lay a two-foot pile of cracked skulls: dozens of them.

They rowed for the bank and quietly pulled the canoe from the water. Gerard adjusted the rapier at his waist and loaded his harquebus. Oludara gathered a bow and arrows which Arany had acquired for him, and touched the ivory knife tucked at his waist. He studied the ground.

"There is a path here," he whispered, "follow my lead."

He squatted and led them into the woods, pointing out thorns, vines, and other obstacles to avoid. After a time, he stopped and motioned them to lie down. Gerard came up beside him.

At the far end of a clearing stood a ten-foot tall cave entrance. Human bones and boulders—some of them enormous—littered the ground before it.

"What is that sound?" asked Gerard.

Oludara strained to hear the muffled echo of human shouts.

"They are cries for help," whispered Arany. "It must be the lost hunters."

"The sounds do not come from the cave," said Oludara, squinting in concentration. "They seem to come from the ground. We should step with caution."

As Oludara finished his statement, a creature emerged from the cave: without a doubt, the Kalobo.

The beast walked on two legs and stood a full seven feet tall. Black hair hung in thick clumps from its body. The wide face resembled a tapir, but with an elongated snout more like an anteater's. Tiny eyes shone on the sides of its head. Instead of feet, it walked upon bull's hooves. Rough, thick claws curled from its fingers, the middle claw extending beyond the others. It walked ponderously, slouched over yet exuding power with each step.

"This won't be easy," whispered Gerard.

"Indeed not," said Oludara. He readied his bow. "First, I think we should test the natives' claim that the beast cannot be pierced."

"Wait," whispered Arany, "it is doing something."

The beast grappled a six-foot boulder and rolled it aside. From underneath, three natives jumped up and clawed their way out from a pit.

"Majui, Ipe, Uba," gasped Arany. "Those are the lost hunters!"

Oludara began to rise, but an unexpected noise froze him in place. He had never heard anything like the Kalobo's scream; it jarred his brain and pained his ears to bursting. His vision blurred; every muscle tensed and froze. All movement in and around the clearing ceased, except for the Kalobo.

Through his immobile haze, Oludara could just make out the beast grabbing one of the natives and tossing him to the ground, then kicking the other two back into the pit before replacing the stone. As Oludara felt his muscle control return, he saw the Kalobo rip off the top of the man's head, turn it over, and suck out the brains with its snout.

Arany gasped and shielded her eyes. "Uba," she sobbed, calling the man's name softly.

"God protect us," said Gerard.

"Olorun," added Oludara, speaking the name of his Yoruban God.

Gerard joggled his head and said, "Oludara, let us attack this foul beast right away!"

"Agreed," replied Oludara.

Gerard remained prone and steadied his harquebus upon a tree root. Oludara stood and drew the bow, his forceful muscles unwavering. "You for the chest," he said, "me for the head."

"On the count of three," replied Gerard. "One, two, three!"

Oludara loosened the bow and Gerard's harquebus boomed beside him. His arrow bounced off the beast's head, and he couldn't tell whether the bullet struck, but Gerard rarely missed, and the Kalobo showed no sign of impact. It did, however, cock an eye in their direction. Then it turned its snout toward them and breathed in deeply. Arany, her hands free, had time to cover her ears; the other two did not. The beast screamed again, and the sound stunned Oludara and Gerard as before. The beast lumbered towards them.

Arany shouted at the two, beating Oludara on his chest and kicking Gerard in his side. "Please," she yelled, "move!"

Oludara struggled to regain control. He became aware of the beast's hideous stench, like a pack of hyenas, as it came closer. When but five feet remained between them and the Kalobo, Oludara's head finally cleared and he said, "Run!"

Gerard took a moment more, but, as the beast's shadow fell upon him, rolled over and got to his knees. The Kalobo's claws brushed his collar as he pushed himself up and ran.

After a five-minute sprint through the woods, Oludara called his companions to a halt. Gerard, his heavy frame winded, threw himself to the ground.

Once he caught his breath, Gerard said, "We must act quickly to save the others."

"Yes," replied Oludara. "As my people say, 'He who waits for a chance, waits for a year.' We cannot linger and allow another man to suffer *that* fate."

All three shuddered at the memory of the Kalobo's terrible meal.

"Arany," asked Oludara, "your people have no notion how to defeat the beast?"

"If we did," she said, "we would have destroyed it long ago."

"What do we do?" asked Gerard. As usual, he deferred the planning to Oludara.

"Fire is always a good option for a beast which cannot be pierced," he replied. "And if that does not work, my knife has never failed me. Its enchantment is strong; it cut the skin of a dragon in Ketu, surely it will cut this beast.

"Here is my plan. First, we return to the canoe..."

Oludara approached the Kalobo's cave, stopping some ten paces before it. He yelled and hurled in a rock. He could barely hear the clatter through the wax in his ears, and spotted no movement in the darkness. When he stooped down to pick up a second stone, the beast charged out.

Oludara barely had time to duck under the Kalobo's claw. He tumbled forward and flipped himself up. As he gathered himself to run, the Kalobo released one of its terrible screams.

The sound made him shudder, but the wax deadened it enough so as not to stun him. He hobbled away in a half-run, feigning injury to draw the lumbering beast after him, but soon increased his pace when he noticed the beast gaining on him.

It took only three minutes to arrive back at the river. Oludara spotted the canoe through the trees and looked up to see Gerard standing in the crook of a large tree.

"Now!" said Oludara.

As the Kalobo stepped under him, Gerard dropped a burning torch into a pile of gunpowder-dusted kindling at its feet. The kindling ignited with a powerful "whoosh", and burned all around it. Arany, hidden nearby, gave an excited cheer.

But the Kalobo kicked away the fire, and it became apparent that only the kindling burned—the beast remained unsinged. It reached down and pulled the torch out from the remains of the fire, then looked up to search for its attacker. When it spotted Gerard, it hurled the burning brand at him with blinding velocity.

The flaming projectile slammed into Gerard's ample stomach and knocked him from his perch with a grunt. His backside snapped one branch and he just managed to grab another, holding on by his fingertips.

While the beast's attention remained focused on Gerard, Oludara drew his knife and ran up behind it. He struck an upwards thrust at its back, but the knife grazed harmlessly off its skin.

The beast turned to face Oludara and Arany charged from the other side, arrow in hand. She thrust it with both hands and struck the creature's eye, but the arrow snapped at the middle. Both she and Oludara jumped away as the Kalobo flailed at them.

"Shango take this beast," cursed Oludara, "not even its eye bleeds." He looked up and shouted, "Gerard, get down here. We need your help!"

"What?" said Gerard, still hanging from the branch.

"Take the wax from your ears!"

Gerard pulled himself up far enough to thrust his elbows over the branch, then pulled the wax out of one ear. "What of the beast's wails?" he yelled.

"Keep your eyes on its chest," replied Oludara. "If it heaves, cover your ears."

"Do it now!" said Arany.

All three covered their ears just as the terrible scream commenced. Gerard's movement, however, required him to release his grip on the branch. He crashed to the ground near Oludara and groaned.

"Are you all right?" asked Oludara.

"Nothing broken, I think."

"Then help me," said Oludara, pulling him to his feet.

The fact that its scream had no effect on the men seemed to confuse the Kalobo. They took advantage of its hesitation and ran forward, side by side. Each one grabbed one of the beast's arms and they threw their combined might against it.

The beast gave way one step, then another. Then, however, its bull's hooves found a hold and it halted their advance.

"I can't believe its strength," growled Gerard.

At that moment, the beast twisted more deftly than either expected. Oludara tripped forward and the Kalobo threw its weight at Gerard, thrusting him to the ground and stunning him.

The Kalobo appeared ready to pounce on Gerard when Oludara jumped between them and grabbed both of its arms. He pushed with all his might and for a few long seconds, held the beast in place. Then, however, the Kalobo kicked forward with one of its massive hooves.

Oludara could feel his shin split and his body collapse beneath him. He blacked out before he hit the ground.

Gerard heard the awful crunch as the Kalobo kicked Oludara's leg, and saw his companion go down. He had only one resource left: his Bolognese rapier. He stood and unsheathed the sword. The Kalobo, however, ignored him and bent over Oludara instead.

Gerard whacked the blade across the creature's back.

"You, big nose," he said, "try me first."

The creature studied Gerard for a moment with its sideways gaze, then turned to face him. Gerard pointed his rapier at the beast's chest and set himself in a *Porta di Ferro* guard, right foot forward and left hand at his waist. The beast swung at him. Gerard made an oblique step to dodge and responded with a lunge to the ribcage. Gerard's wrist jerked violently when the point made contact; it felt like striking a wall. Gerard recovered just in time to duck the Kalobo's next blow.

"Arany," he shouted, "wake him up! I can't hold this creature off for long."

Arany looked around and grabbed the only thing available: one of the skull tops lying on the bank. She filled it with river water.

Gerard continued his cat-and-mouse game with the Kalobo. He tried several thrusts and cuts, but nothing even scratched the beast. Then one of its swings grazed his sword arm, gashing his shirt and leaving three red slashes, the middle one all the way to the bone. Gerard clasped the throbbing wound with his left hand.

Using her makeshift bowl, Arany splashed water onto Oludara's face.

He shook it off and opened his eyes.

Gerard spotted the movement from the corner of his eye. "Oludara," he yelled, "this beast is invincible!"

"No beast is invincible," replied Oludara, "hold firm."

"We must flee," said Gerard. "I'm bleeding and it is only a matter of time before I tire." Gerard barely dodged a backhand swipe which sent his wide-brimmed hat flying.

"Then flee with Arany and leave me. I cannot run with a broken leg."

"Never," said Gerard. "We can drag you into the boat."

"Not with the beast this close."

Arany cradled Oludara's head in her hands. "You're brave men," she said. "I've rarely seen such courage. I am sorry to have treated you the way I did, Oludara."

"Thank you, Arany," he replied, reaching up to touch her cheek.

"Would you stop wooing and start thinking!" said Gerard.

Arany released Oludara and stood up. "Terrible beast," she said, "go away!"

She threw the skull at the Kalobo. It shattered upon impact, splattering water over the creature and matting down its fur. The Kalobo paused.

"Look," Oludara said, "the creature takes pause. Perhaps water can succeed where fire and metal have failed."

The Kalobo shook itself like a dog, spraying water in all directions, then charged Gerard again.

"So much for that idea," shouted Gerard. "What do we do next, blow on it?"

"Gerard," said Oludara, "look to the navel!"

A quick glance showed Gerard where the slicked-down hair on the beast's chest had parted to reveal a small pink hole, less than an inch across.

"Worth a try," he mumbled.

Gerard released his grip on the wound and readied his sword. Blood poured from the cut and made him giddy; he knew he wouldn't have much time. He took the *Coda Lunga* position, lowering his guard in challenge. The Kalobo took the bait and rushed forward. Gerard thrust up the rapier, but the point struck off target, two inches to the side of the navel.

Gerard didn't have time to dodge and the beast struck his left side solidly, knocking him to the ground. He rolled three times before stopping, his sword falling from his grasp.

The Kalobo let out a half-scream and charged. Even the reduced noise, heard through one ear, made Gerard cringe. He spotted his rapier beside him and knew he would have time to grab it or roll away, but not both.

He chose to grab the sword. Like an untrained child, he grasped it firmly with both hands and pointed it up.

"Giovanni would kill me for this," he said, referring to his old fencing master.

The beast dove upon him, but he held steady. The rapier struck its mark and passed through the navel. As the Kalobo came crashing down, Gerard pushed down on the hilt and thrust the point up into the beast's chest.

The Kalobo made a screech more abominable than all its previous screams put together, and Gerard could stand it for only a fraction of a second before the noise, loss of blood, and weight of the falling creature knocked him out.

Head still reeling from the hideous death wail of the Kalobo, Oludara forced himself to sit up and check on his companions. Arany lay by his side, quivering and groaning. Of Gerard, he could see only boots protruding—motionless—from under the Kalobo.

"Gerard," he shouted, "are you all right?"

Arany struggled up beside him. "Did you say something?" she asked. "My ears still ring from that horrible scream. And my head—such pain." She cupped her forehead in both hands.

"It is Gerard," he replied. "We must see to him quickly. The beast's fall smothered him."

Arany reluctantly stood and helped Oludara drag himself toward the Kalobo. His broken leg trailed behind, making every movement an agony.

With him pushing from the ground and Arany pulling from the top, they managed to roll the beast off Gerard. Oludara sent Arany to retrieve a cloth from the canoe and bandage Gerard's arm while he tried to revive his unconscious companion.

After a few worrisome minutes, Gerard opened his eyes. When he finally sat up, the first thing he did was stare at the fallen beast. He appeared thoughtful and almost sad.

"Why do you look at the beast that way?" asked Oludara. "You should be rejoicing our victory."

"It's nothing," he responded. "It will pass."

Gerard examined his companion's leg. "This is going to hurt," he said. With a couple of twists, he shoved the broken bones back into place.

Oludara clenched his teeth and let out a snort, but did not yell. When he could speak again, he gasped out, "Where did you learn that?"

"Back in the Low Countries," replied Gerard, "in the war."

"Gerard," said Oludara, smiling despite the pain, "you never told me you were a soldier."

"That's because I'm not," replied Gerard, frowning. "I spent just enough time in the war to discover that." He secured the leg using some sticks as a splint.

Oludara could see his companion did not wish to discuss the matter. With Gerard and Arany's help, he limped back to the canoe. Then they left him alone and went to the Kalobo's clearing to rescue the others. Some time later, they returned alone.

"The rock is too heavy, even with a lever," said Gerard. "We'll have to send help from the village."

Gerard shoved off the canoe and he and Arany took up the oars. Even with his injury, Oludara's spirits soared, but his companions remained in silence. While the others rowed, he lay back and enjoyed the view; birds and butterflies fluttered through the green walls of vegetation on both sides.

After some forty minutes' travel, Oludara spotted men on the left side of the stream. Cabwassu and five warriors stood at the ready, all armed with bows and arrows. Two of the warriors perched in the lowest branches of a tree, the others stood underneath.

Oludara called out to them, "Cabwassu, it is us. We have slain the Kalobo!"

Cabwassu sneered back: "It is not enough, dark one. You must also return alive!"

Cabwassu lifted his bow and shot.

Arany, without a sound, threw herself before Oludara. The arrow struck her solidly in the back.

"Arany!" he shouted. She gave him one sad look, then closed her eyes. He tried to stand, but his injured leg collapsed beneath him. He reached around, searching wildly for the bow.

Behind him, Gerard stood and roared a yell so terrifying it would have made the Kalobo proud. Cabwassu and his warriors froze.

In one skilled motion, Gerard raised his harquebus and fired. His shot struck the tree trunk inches from the head of one of the natives who stood in its branches. The man jerked sideways and collided with the other beside him, causing both to tumble. They knocked down two of their companions below with their fall.

Gerard, not pausing to watch, jumped from the canoe and swam to shore with three powerful breaststrokes, all the time looking and sounding like an angry bear.

Cabwassu and his remaining upright companion raised their bows, but Gerard rushed in and swatted them away with his gun. With a grim face, Cabwassu prepared to grapple, but Gerard, in a blind rage, boxed his arms and heaved him through the air, sending him crashing into some bushes. While Cabwassu pulled himself to his feet, Gerard picked up his bow and—screaming and straining with all his strength—snapped it in half.

The natives' wills seemed to snap with the bow. Wide-eyed, they scrambled up and ran—Cabwassu leading the way.

Gerard landed the canoe as close as possible to the village and called for help. Men and women came running. Some of them grabbed Arany and pulled her ashore, but shook their heads at the sight of her lifeless body. Others helped Oludara from the canoe and sat him on shore with his back to a tree.

A clacking sound approached as Yandir shoved his way through the crowd, his shell necklaces knocking together in his haste. He knelt down beside Arany, then said some words to a nearby woman and sent her off.

With one swift motion, Yandir yanked the arrow from Arany's back. She didn't move. Oludara trembled at the sight. Gerard knelt beside him and laid a hand on his shoulder.

Yandir bent down and blew on the wound several times. A few moments later, the woman he had sent away returned with a feathered rattle, a bamboo tube, and a ceramic jar. Yandir opened the jar and applied a salve to the wound. Then he motioned to two men and they turned Arany's body over. Yandir began a slow dance around her, chanting and shaking the rattle.

"What's does he think he's doing?" said Gerard. "Get him away from her!"

Gerard took a step forward, but Oludara grabbed his leg. "Wait, Gerard," he said. "Can't you feel it? His magic is strong."

"The only thing I'm feeling, as we call it in Europe, is 'hocus pocus'."

Yandir lit tobacco in one end of the tube, then blew smoke into Arany's face. Gerard shook his head and turned away.

On the third blow of smoke, Arany opened her eyes.

Oludara laughed heartily. "She is alive!" he said.

"What?" said Gerard, turning back to look.

Yandir smiled and bent down beside Arany. He passed a calming hand over her forehead and through her hair. Then he said something to some nearby men, and they carried her to one of the longhouses.

"The priest's magic saved her," said Oludara.

"You expect me to believe that was *his* doing?" asked Gerard. "No doubt she woke up just to clear her lungs of that virulent smoke."

"No matter what you or I believe, Arany is alive, and that is cause for rejoicing."

Yandir walked over to Oludara and examined his leg. He prodded it in several places, making Oludara wince each time. He said something in Tupi.

"What was that?" asked Gerard.

Jakoo appeared from the crowd to help. "Yandir says the bones are well placed, but your friend must rest for one moon. No walking. Yandir will make a potion to reduce the pain."

"Tell him I say thank you," said Oludara.

Jakoo spoke to Yandir who nodded. Yandir then said something and Jakoo and the other chiefs followed him.

"Well," said Gerard, "he's just the regular doctor now, isn't he? One moment a mystic, next moment a medic."

"He is what he needs to be," said Oludara, "depending on what is required. Mine is but an injury, but Arany's soul was fleeing."

"Are you trying to tell me he brought her soul back to her body?"

"And why not? Just because you believe your European culture is more enlightened, don't scorn hundreds of generations of their wisdom. Is not the reason Antonio kept you from his band his intolerance for *your* religion?"

Gerard turned red. "Well, that's different..."

"Keep an open mind, Gerard, and you will learn much in Brazil. As my people say, 'An obstinate man soon falls to disgrace'."

"We'll see," said Gerard. "That is, if they actually allow us to stay here."

Yandir and Jakoo returned.

"There are two survivors," Gerard said to Jakoo, "under a great rock by the Kalobo's cavern. You'll need at least six men to move it."

"I will send some warriors," said Jakoo. "But first, the pajé wants me to tell you a story."

Yandir spoke, pausing after every line for Jakoo to translate.

"Long ago, Maire-Monan, the creator, spoke to your father, in Europe, and to our father, here. He offered a choice of weapons. Our father chose the bow and arrow, because they are light and good for hunting. Your father chose the sword and gun, which are good for war. And that is why, these many moons later, we are no match for the Pero in war.

"Yandir says that is why we will teach you. If we fight the Pero, we cannot survive. But if we share our knowledge with you, perhaps we can learn to understand one another."

"Tell him we are honored," said Oludara. He gingerly turned over and prostrated himself.

Gerard took a knee beside him. "Do these gestures mean anything to them?" he asked.

"Who knows?" replied Oludara.

Yandir walked away laughing. The other natives dispersed.

"No need for that," said Jakoo. "You have defeated a mighty enemy, and you are Tupinambá now. Even Cabwassu accepts you. He says that you, Gerard, are a fire-haired devil. He hides in his cabin even now." Jakoo grinned. "From now on, you will be part of my longhouse," he pointed toward the same structure to which the men had carried Arany, "and I will be your chief."

"Can we be placed near Arany?" asked Oludara. "She could aid us in learning Tupi."

Gerard gave him a sideways look and grimaced.

Jakoo paused before speaking. "I suppose it is well," he said. "Of all of us, she speaks the Pero language best."

"And if you don't mind," said Gerard, "a bit of that porridge would be nice."

Within the massive cabin, lined with families from end to end, Oludara and Gerard lay in their respective hammocks, a comforting fire between them. Ten feet away, in her own hammock, Arany awoke from her long sleep. After stretching, she looked toward them and smiled.

"It appears I did not die," she said, "thanks to your courage."

"It is I who must thank you," said Oludara, "for your selfless act of sacrifice."

"You could have left me and fled," she replied. "How did you know they would let you back to the village, after Cabwassu attacked?"

"It did not matter. We could not heal you ourselves, and we would never abandon a companion, no matter what the danger. But if you feel as if you owe us something, we would not mind some lessons in Tupi while we lie here recovering."

"Of course, Oludara," she said, "whenever you like."

"But first," he said, "I would very much like to hear the story of why you cannot marry." He smiled broadly.

Gerard sighed and pulled his hat over his eyes to sleep.

A three-banded armadillo ambled along on her nighttime search for dinner. She caught a whiff of her second favorite food—carrion—and ran to investigate. She left the woods and discovered the remains of a massive, hairy creature by the river. She took a tentative nibble at its arm, but for some reason, her teeth couldn't pierce the beast's rotting skin.

She was about to desist when she spotted a pink opening in its belly. Happily, she scampered towards her next meal.

Chapter 3

The Unpropitious Return of Antonio Dias Caldas

BLACK CAPUCHIN MONKEY PEEKED into the towering human dwelling. At that hour, the hottest part of the day, the humans paid little attention to the likes of him. He glanced around the longhouse at the dozens of them resting in their hanging nets. Fires burned on the ground in several places; the monkey kept well away from those.

He spotted the object of his quest: bunches of bananas hanging on a post. He often took the humans' bananas at this time of day; it had become something of a game. Even when they spotted him, they rarely bothered to shoo him away.

But as he approached the post, a twinkle caught his eye. Over one man's face lay a strange brown covering, and attached to its side shone a piece of metal with a long, blue feather sticking up from it. The man beneath looked nothing like the rest; he was wide and pale and wore cloth over his body, where the others wore none.

All thoughts of bananas disappeared as the monkey eyed the shiny object; he knew he must possess it. He approached the resting man, coming up from behind. He climbed the post where the man's net was tied. Even though he couldn't see the man's face, he could see his chest rising and falling in measured breathing. The monkey felt sure of success.

He placed one paw after another on the net, careful not to rock it, and reached toward the metal...

In a move that had become reflex, Gerard grabbed his hat and swatted at the tiny creature behind him. He could hear the scratches as it scampered down the post and out the door. For this noonday nap at least, he wouldn't lose another hat.

Gerard sighed and swung down from the hammock, resigning himself to a day without rest. His preoccupations outweighed any hope for sleep. He walked to a bunch of bananas hanging nearby and pulled one down for a snack.

After satisfying his appetite, he returned to his area of the longhouse.

He combed his fingers through his curly red hair and straightened his linen doublet around his broad chest. Although not the most comfortable outfit for a tropical climate, Gerard had begun using his formal clothes again as an intentional contrast to Oludara's adoption of the native way of dress—or better put, lack thereof.

The smell of sweat from dozens of bodies and smoke from dozens of fires saturated the air around him. Even after spending several months among the Tupinambá, it still felt almost suffocating. Gerard didn't think he would ever get used to it.

He glanced over at Oludara, who slept in a net near that of Arany. Like the rest of the tribe, they wore nothing, not even to cover their genitalia. To the extent that Oludara had become more comfortable with the Tupinambá customs, Gerard had become less so. In fact, he had reached a tipping point.

He tugged nervously on his goatee, working up the courage to say what had been on his mind for weeks. He approached Oludara and shook his shoulder. Oludara groaned and opened one eye. After making eye contact with Gerard, he stretched his muscled arms and yawned. A smile spread beneath his wide nose.

"Gerard," said Oludara, "what can I do for you?"

"We need to speak," said Gerard. He glanced at Arany. "In private."

As if sensing something of the conversation, Arany, still asleep in her hammock, whined and turned onto her side.

Oludara pulled himself up from the hammock. Gerard motioned him through the cabin entrance, and they stepped out to the village center: the gathering place amid the five longhouses.

Once outside, Gerard looked his companion in the eye and said, "You've become too complacent here. It's time to move on."

"Why would you want to leave?" said Oludara, smiling. "We have everything we need. And," he added with a wink, "you, Gerard, could choose any wife you wish among the unmarried women of the tribe. They find you quite exotic."

Gerard blushed and replied through gritted teeth, "When the time comes, I'll have a Christian wife and a Christian wedding."

Oludara's smile faded.

"I came to Brazil for adventure," Gerard continued, "not for lying around a native village. We came here to learn the ways of the Tupinambá, and we've spent more than enough time to learn all we need. It's time to move on."

"But Gerard..." Oludara glanced back toward the cabin where Arany slept.

"Admit it, Oludara, you're as restless as I am. I know how you feel about Arany, but she's told you time and again that she won't marry you."

"That is the problem, Gerard. She is hiding something from me, and I know not what. She never says 'I don't *want* to marry you', only 'I *can't* marry you', always with sadness in her voice, but without ever giving a reason. Whenever I ask anyone else, they avoid the question. I must solve this mystery."

Gerard opened his mouth to reply, but was interrupted by a commotion from the palisade gate. A group of the tribe's warriors called out and hundreds of natives emptied from the longhouses to the village center. Men carried their bows at the ready; women shouted; and children ran around squealing, taking advantage of the commotion as an excuse to make noise.

Into their midst walked a native not of their tribe. Like them, intricate black-and-red patterns covered the man's body, but his skin was paler than those around him. He held up a hand, and when the crowd quieted, he began to dance and chant. As he danced, an intricate feather headdress swept behind him, and he shook maracas in both hands. The villagers spoke among themselves and pointed.

Something struck Gerard as familiar about the man, and he struggled to remember.

"I've seen him before," he said to Oludara. "Something about Salvador..." As the man danced closer, Gerard got a better look at his face, and saw that his features weren't native at all.

"Piraju!" he said.

The man showed no outward reaction to Gerard's outburst, yet after a few moments, his dance shifted direction and carried him closer. When he hopped but a foot away from Gerard, he shook his maracas loudly and whispered from the corner of his mouth, “Quiet, Gerard! It is not proper for anyone to speak to me before the chiefs. Which is your cabin?”

“The one to my left,” replied Gerard.

Piraju marked the cabin with a glance and nodded. Then he continued his chanting and danced toward a different group of onlookers.

“Who is that man?” asked Oludara.

“He’s the shipwrecked Spaniard I met in Salvador,” replied Gerard. “The one who told me how to find Sacy-Perey and get the favor I needed to free you.”

“Yes,” said Oludara, “you told me of him, the one who married a Tupinambá bride.” He stared at Arany, who had stepped from their cabin to join the crowd. “If only I could have such luck.”

After performing several chants, Piraju entered Gerard and Oludara’s cabin. They followed and found him lying in one of the hammocks, eyes closed. Jakoo, the cabin chief, entered and studied the stranger for a few moments. He ordered two of the unmarried women to offer him food, then strode out.

Arany came up beside Gerard and Oludara.

“Why does no one approach him?” asked Oludara.

“The man is *karaiba*,” said Arany, “a pajé who travels among tribes. The chiefs must decide whether to let him stay or to kill him. They will consult Yandir before making a decision.”

“Kill him?” said Gerard. “That’s absurd! Why would you kill a man before even speaking with him?”

“It is custom. Karaibas are powerful men, capable of cursing an entire village if they so choose. However, they must not speak until granted permission, so many tribes will kill them before taking that risk.”

“That’s barbaric!”

Gerard pulled Oludara aside. “I won’t let them kill Piraju,” he said.

“They have lived this way for many ages,” replied Oludara. “What right do we have to say what is right and wrong?”

"I'm a Christian, Oludara, and I won't tolerate murder. I'll protect him with my own life, if necessary."

Gerard stamped off to his hammock, where he belted on his Bolognese rapier, loaded his harquebus, and paced the cabin, keeping his gaze on Piraju and everyone who approached the man.

Piraju himself appeared relaxed. The women brought him a gourd of fish porridge and he scooped out balls of it with his hands and tossed them into his mouth, in the customary Tupinambá way of eating.

When he laid aside the gourd, signaling the end of his meal, Jakoo entered the cabin flanked by two warriors. Gerard tensed and edged toward them.

"The chiefs are ready to speak," said Jakoo.

Piraju rose and followed Jakoo out. Gerard walked behind them and saw that the other four chiefs sat in a circle to one side of the village center, passing a long pipe among them. When Piraju drew near, they stood but said nothing. The tribe gathered around.

Clacking noises approached and the crowd parted to make way for Yandir, hobbling toward them with a staff in one hand.

Yandir addressed the village. "The spirits tell me that the words of this karaiba bring great despair. We must not give him permission to speak."

The death sentence did not change Piraju's expression, nor cause him to utter a word; he stood straight and calm. At a sign from the chiefs, several warriors approached him with long clubs raised, ready to strike. Gerard shot his harquebus in the air and everyone turned toward him.

"No," he said in Tupi, pausing to let the word stand on its own. He had learned quite a bit of the language during their time with the tribe; not as much as Oludara, who already spoke like a native, but enough to converse. He dropped his harquebus and stepped forward to place himself between Piraju and the warriors. He crossed his arms.

"Killing is wrong," he said. "I won't fight you, but if you want to kill this man, you must kill me first."

The warriors hesitated. People whispered, but no one said a word of support.

"We know your heart is good, Gerard," said Yandir, "but this concerns the tribe. You must step away."

"Did you not make me part of the tribe? May I not speak?"

"You may speak, but this choice is made by the chiefs."

Gerard looked around for support, but none came. He caught Arany's eye and she shot him an angry look. Her relationship with the tribe still tenuous, she often admonished Gerard for embarrassing her. He looked to Oludara, at her side, who merely shook his head and stared down at the ground.

When he saw that even his friend had abandoned him, Gerard's stomach knotted in despair, yet still he stood firm. Yandir motioned to some warriors.

"Hold him," commanded Yandir. "Don't let him interfere."

Gerard braced himself as a dozen warriors converged around him.

A boisterous bellow broke the silence. Gerard turned to see Cabwassu holding his sides and laughing. The village watched in silence as the warrior took a full minute to compose himself.

"Gerard van Oost," he said, "you are a madman. You stand against your own tribe. You stand against the will of your chiefs and your pajé. Only a madman would stand alone against all."

Cabwassu turned and spoke to the tribe. "Yet perhaps it is not madness. This reminds me of a time not long ago, when two strangers came to our tribe. I would have killed them"—he passed a finger across his neck for emphasis—"but others showed them mercy. In time, I discovered them to be very brave. And today, Gerard is once again brave."

Turning back to Gerard, he said, "Gerard, I will stand by you, not because you are right, but because you are brave." He went beside Gerard and threw an arm over his shoulder. At that, many of Cabwassu's warriors joined them.

Gerard thanked Cabwassu with a Tupi saying: "I jump with happiness." Cabwassu replied with one of his overly toothy smiles.

People whispered to each other, unsure what to do, until Jakoo broke the silence.

"Perhaps Cabwassu is right," he said. "When we allowed the strangers Gerard and Oludara to speak, they saved our tribe from Kalobo. We should listen to what the karaiba has to say."

Jakoo went to Gerard's other side. Jakoo was a popular chief, and many families followed him. Gerard saw that nearly a hundred stood with him, although they were still outnumbered three-to-one. He was disappointed that no one took into account the life of the innocent man in their decision to support him, but he decided to count his blessings and leave that argument for later. Gerard knew he needed to convince Yandir. He looked the pajé in the eye.

"Let the karaiba speak," he said. "If his words bring despair, I will bear the consequence."

"And I with him," said Oludara, squeezing him in a tight embrace before Gerard even realized he had approached. "We may have our differences, friend, but we should not be divided."

Arany seemed torn, but eventually took a breath and reluctantly placed herself beside Oludara. She held his hand and Oludara smiled at her. The presence of his friends raised Gerard's courage.

Yandir seemed taken aback. "I must consult the spirits."

He went into his hut while the villagers spoke in hushed groups. Gerard had lost track of time when the pajé finally appeared again.

"Very well, Gerard," said Yandir. "The spirits agree; you and Oludara shall bear the consequences of the karaiba's words, however terrible they may be." He turned to Piraju. "You are welcome in our village. You may speak."

"I am called Piraju, and I am honored by your kindness. I bear an urgent warning for this tribe: a banner approaches."

"Which banner?" asked Gerard, dreading the answer.

"A gold-and-red one, that of Antonio Dias Caldas."

Gerard paled at the name.

"You know this Antonio?" asked Yandir.

"He's the most dangerous bannerman in Brazil, and has sworn himself my enemy, although I doubt he knows I'm here. There can be but one purpose which brings him toward us: to capture Tupinambá and sell them as slaves."

Commotion arose around them.

"It is true," Piraju shouted above the crowd. "He has already enslaved other tribes, taking them to work in the sugar mills, and he will be here in two days."

"How many are in his troop?" asked Gerard.

"At least eighty harquebusiers, and dozens of native slaves."

"We cannot fight so many, can we?" asked Jakoo.

"No," said Gerard. "A direct battle would be a massacre. Even if we attack them with traps and surprise, we could lose many in the fight."

The commotion turned into general panic.

"Gerard is right," said Piraju. "Your only choice is to flee. Even if you stop Antonio this time, at great cost of life, more will come. The tribe is too close to Salvador. You must move inland, into the Backlands."

Oludara shook his head and said, "It is a difficult land, almost as bad as the red clay plateau of my home, Ketu, where water is so scarce we say 'water becomes honey in Ketu.' "

"We know the dangers of the Backlands," said Jakoo. "But I agree with Piraju, it is better than being killed or captured by the slavers. The Tupinambá are strong. We can survive there."

The other chiefs voiced their agreement.

"But they arrive in two days," said Gerard. "It will take a week to prepare rations for a flight like that."

"Yes," said Cabwassu. "We must hold them off in battle." He seemed pleased at the idea.

"There must be a better way," said Gerard. "The responsibility is mine, I've taken it upon myself, although I don't know what to do. Oludara, you'll think of something, won't you? You always do."

"Yes," said Oludara, "I will try. Antonio is too dangerous; he will not be stopped by force. Gerard and I, however, might halt him with trickery."

"We leave this Antonio to you, then," said Yandir. "The tribe must prepare for travel."

At that, the chiefs split up, each one going off to organize the members of his longhouse. They called away their people, including Arany, leaving Gerard and Oludara alone with Piraju.

Oludara sighed and spoke. “You were right, Gerard: about letting Piraju speak, about me, about everything. You and I have tallied here too long, and now destiny forces us to act.”

“That’s all in the past now,” said Gerard. “We must deal with the matter at hand, and, as always, I will trust in your planning.”

“Antonio will not be easy to dissuade,” said Oludara, “it would take a great reason to change his course. My people have a saying: ‘No one will throw away venison to pick up squirrel meat.’ Antonio comes here for profit, but perhaps there is something he desires more than money?”

Gerard hated to admit it, but although their methods were different, he and Antonio had much in common. He knew what the man most desired.

“The chance to be a hero,” he said with a sigh.

It took mere moments for Oludara to come up with an idea. “We should send someone to tell Antonio of a beast besieging a town—a chance for him to win great glory.”

“It’s a good idea in theory,” replied Gerard, “but whom would he believe? I can’t go to him; he’d spit me and boil me like a piece of meat.”

“They know of me,” said Piraju, “and that I’ve been warning tribes of their coming. And any Tupinambá would be suspect.”

“Then that leaves only one option,” said Oludara. “I must go.”

“But Antonio saw you that day we met in Salvador,” said Gerard. “He’ll recognize you.”

Oludara smirked at the suggestion. “Gerard, you are so delightfully sincere; it is a pleasure to know a man such as you exists in this world. Antonio didn’t spare me a glance that day. To him, slaves are not people, only property. He would not recognize one African from another.”

“Diogo, however, remains his second-in-command. He won’t be so easily fooled.”

“I will disguise myself. It will be enough.”

“Where will our feigned attack occur?”

“That is an important question. He came from Salvador, so any message from there will appear suspect. Yet it must be somewhere not too far away."

"Ilhéus, then," said Gerard. "It's not too far, but he'll have to cut his way through a forest to get there. Even at his fastest, it will take him five days to reach there and five to return. That should give the tribe enough time."

"An excellent plan!" said Piraju. He clasped Gerard's shoulders. "How strange is destiny, Gerard van Oost. How could I imagine that a Dutchman I met in Salvador would one day save my life in the midst of the Tupinambá? Thank you so much. The story of how you came to live among this tribe and speak their language must be amazing, but I haven't the time to stay and hear it."

"You can't leave without at least allowing me to introduce my friend," said Gerard. "Piraju, this is Oludara. It was for his cause that I sought the aid of Sacy-Perey in Salvador."

Oludara offered a firm handshake. "Greetings and good health," he said.

"It is indeed a pleasure to meet you, Oludara," said Piraju. "Your plan will give me time to warn other tribes, saving more lives than you can imagine."

"I am glad to hear it."

"I must go now, and warn the others."

"Good luck," said Gerard.

As Piraju strode away, Oludara said, "I am impressed, Gerard. You risked your life to save a man you met only once."

"It was the Christian thing to do."

"Many call themselves Christians," said Oludara, "but I doubt one in a hundred would have done that. The bannermen who come to enslave this tribe are Christians, are they not?"

"Indeed they are," said Gerard, looking away. "Indeed they are."

Oludara squatted beside Arany in the village center, sharing a meal with a few dozen members of their longhouse. They passed around baskets filled with mangoes, cassava cakes, and roasted fish. It would be Oludara's last meal before his trip. As was customary among the Tupinambá, the group ate in silence.

When their meal ended, Oludara looked to Arany. He searched for a saying to break the silence, but the wisdom of his people failed him. Instead, he chose to be direct.

"My adventures with Gerard have waited too long," he said. "I gave him my word I would travel the Brazilian wilderness with him for five years, and four still remain."

"I know of your oath."

"We will visit again within a year," he said, "I promise."

"You may come and go as you want. You are part of the tribe."

"That's not what I mean."

Arany kept her eyes to the ground and said nothing.

"You know how I feel about you. Do you have nothing to say before I go?"

"I..." Arany seemed to struggle with the words. "Don't get yourself killed."

It was not the response he wanted. "I don't plan on it. Gerard and I are no strangers to peril."

"How very well I know *that*," said Arany. "Danger follows that man as flies are attracted to meat."

"Yet I can think of no better companion to face that danger. I would follow him to his Christian hell if he asked it, and yet it is he who follows my lead."

"Then lead him to hell and back, for all I care."

Oludara laughed. "Are you jealous? You act as though I go off to marry him!"

Arany said nothing.

"Do not be this way. A brother by blood no man can choose, but Gerard is my brother by choice. How could I abandon a brother?"

"Then don't abandon him," she said, "if you love him so much."

Oludara didn't know how to respond to that. He was relieved when Gerard and Jakoo approached and broke the silence.

"I've said my goodbyes," said Gerard. "We should depart."

"Will you return to us once you rid yourselves of Antonio?" asked Jakoo.

"No," said Gerard. "As soon as Oludara has sent him off to Ilhéus, we'll head south. I've heard tales of perilous beasts that way, and I'm curious to see with my own eyes this Rio de Janeiro of which so many speak."

Gerard turned toward Arany and stopped abruptly. Oludara followed his gaze to see her on the brink of tears. Oludara tried to think of something that might break the tension, but it was Gerard who spoke first:

"Arany..." he muttered. "I've been thinking. You've shown yourself to be quite brave. You could come with us, if you like."

Oludara almost fell over at the unexpected suggestion; Gerard had never once mentioned the thought. Arany's jaw dropped. After a few moments of awkward silence, she smiled.

"No thank you, Gerard," she said. "You are like two little boys, always needing to prove yourselves. I have no need for fame, and no desire to watch you two put yourselves into danger for it. I'll leave the little adventures for the little boys. My place is with my tribe." She gave Gerard a purposeful look. "Just make sure *both* of you come back safely, or suffer the consequences."

Gerard took a step back and said, "You know I'll do my best."

Arany laughed at his reaction, then her expression turned somber again. She gave them both quick, awkward hugs, then turned and hurried into her longhouse. Oludara wondered if he should run after her, but clacking noises drew his attention as Yandir came hobbling up.

"Gerard," he said, "it is good I found you before your journey."

"Yandir," said Gerard, nodding.

Oludara noticed the formality with which Gerard addressed the pajé. Even after their many months with the tribe, Gerard continued referring to him as a "damned sorcerer" behind his back.

Yandir held forward a gourd with a wooden stopper. Unusual symbols had been carved into it.

"I know you believe not in my magic, but please accept this. The spirits tell me you will need it."

Gerard held the gourd with his fingertips and eyed it skeptically. He shook it by his ear and it made a sloshing sound.

"It is a powerful mixture," said Yandir. "It will heal you when your wounds are dire."

Gerard opened his mouth as if to argue, but Jakoo stopped him with a hand on the shoulder.

"Your acceptance of the gift will honor us all, Gerard," he said.

Gerard sighed and shrugged. "If I must." he said. He slung down his pack and shoved in the gourd.

"There is something else," said Yandir. "You were right about Piraju. His speech had terrible consequences for us, but if he had not spoken, the consequences would have been worse. It was a cruel trick the spirits played upon is, but you saw through it."

"It was no trick," said Gerard. "Life is precious, and should never be ended lightly."

"It is a strange idea, Gerard. To us, life and death are the same, neither greater than the other. I will think on this."

Yandir turned and left.

Jakoo looked to Oludara and said, "We head northwest. As is our custom, we will burn the village when we leave. You know the signs we use to hide messages in the forest; I will leave some to show our trail. May your gods protect you."

"And may the tribe find good land," said Oludara, "filled with water and hunting."

"For many lifetimes, our people have searched for the Land Without Evil. Our ancestors came here, to the great water, looking for it, but never found it. Perhaps we shall find it in the dry plains of the Backlands."

"May we all find it someday," said Oludara.

Oludara took a deep breath before leaving the cover of the forest to emerge in Antonio's camp. He stooped as he walked, greatly reducing his height. His ivory knife lay tucked into his pants, hidden beneath his shirt. An eye patch covered his right eye. It was a great discomfort, but he took heart in the fact that, if everything went as planned, he could send off Antonio quickly and be on his way. As he hobbled into camp, all eyes turned toward him. Just as Piraju had described, dozens upon dozens of bannermen and native slaves filled the ranks of Antonio's band.

The camp itself consisted of netted hammocks stretched between trees and campfires spread among them. Packs and supplies littered the ground, most of them covered by hanging canvas sheets. Antonio's banner—red and gold split diagonally along the middle—stood in the center of the clearing. Unlike Gerard's crude sketch of the elephant and macaw, this banner had been embroidered from fine cloth.

Almost all of the bannermen wore cotton shirts and leggings. Some used boots while others walked barefoot. Many wore thick, leather vests capable of blocking a sluggish arrow, and a few even wore helmets, though most used wide-brimmed hats to protect themselves from a greater enemy: the sun. Perhaps half of the bannermen looked to be of full European descent, while *caboclos*—those of mixed native and European parentage so common in Brazil—comprised the other half.

The native slaves reminded Oludara of his adopted Tupinambá tribe. They used no clothing except for some decorative feathers and stones. Most wore their hair in a tonsure.

Oludara wondered who would address him first, until he spotted Antonio and Diogo striding forward from one end of the encampment. Antonio wore a rich, red doublet over his cotton clothes. On his belt hung a shining, fancy rapier and matching dagger. A red feather curled out from his wide-brimmed hat. In his right hand he carried a harquebus decorated with engraved metal plates. On his sun-darkened face he sported a black beard, fuller and longer than the last time Oludara had seen it. He held his head high and his eyes exuded confidence.

Diogo wore a brown, padded vest and carried a simpler rapier and harquebus. Tufts of dark brown hair curled from under his hat, and the stubble of days' old whiskers marked his cheeks. His movements were more relaxed, but still confident.

"Where did this slave come from?" asked Antonio, ignoring Oludara and looking instead to his soldiers for an answer.

"Master," said Oludara, keeping his eyes down, "I come from Ilhéus."

"Ilhéus?" asked Antonio, his voice skeptical. "Must have escaped." He motioned to some nearby men. "Tie him up!"

"Wait!" said Oludara, falling to his knees for effect. "I am not escaped; I am my master's faithful servant. He sent me to seek the red-and-gold banner of Antonio Dias Caldas and ask for his help."

"Is that so? And what help is that?"

"A terrible beast torments the town, stealing people at night and leaving them bloodied and dead in the hills. My master said that Antonio must come quickly, or we will all die. Is Antonio here?"

"I am the one you seek, but I don't go chasing around the territory at the whim of any man." Antonio looked at Diogo. "Do you believe this story? Or is this slave just trying to save his skin?"

Diogo stared at Oludara, who kept his gaze firmly on the ground.

"It's possible," said Diogo. "We should make sure. Ilhéus is but a five-day walk."

"Hmm," said Antonio, tugging his beard in a way that reminded Oludara of Gerard. "I don't think so. Ilhéus has always been a plague. The people have no respect for their leaders, even to the point of rebellion. And the Aimore Indians are a constant threat. Even if the slave does tell the truth, it's not worth it.

"Besides, we should be close to that village by now. I can't return to the coast empty-handed. We need to capture some of the local blacks first."

Oludara grimaced at Antonio's casual use of "local blacks", an insult to both his own people and the natives he had come to love. However, he controlled himself.

"My master, Francisco de Santarem," said Oludara, using a name Gerard had made up, "said that he would be most grateful for your aid. His sugar mill is the largest in Ilhéus, and his family has ties to the king."

This gave Antonio pause. With a quick glance, Oludara could see he was mulling over the invented name, but likely wouldn't mention that he'd never heard of it in front of his troop.

"Yes," Antonio finally replied. "Ilhéus may be a godforsaken rubbish heap, but if the people there are in distress, we should respond. We'll head out first thing in the morning."

From the corner of his eye, Oludara could see Diogo staring steadily in his direction, so he lowered his head even farther.

"I must return to my master with the good news," said Oludara.

"No need for that," said Antonio, "you'll be safer with us. And if something should happen to your master before we get there, I'll keep you for the trouble.

"Martim," he shouted to someone behind him, "place a collar on this slave."

Oludara gritted his teeth as the soldier approached with a heavy iron clasp.

The next night, after a long march, Oludara's neck chafed from the collar and his feet ached from the constant stubbing he suffered as he accustomed himself to the eye patch. He longed for a hearty meal and a deep slumber, and searched the camp for the means to both.

Catching the scent of cooking meat, Oludara followed it to the middle of camp, where he discovered a boar roasting over a fire. One of the soldiers had spotted the animal around dusk, and on a bet, Antonio had taken it down with a single shot. A soldier tended the meat while a native slave turned the spit. Oludara licked his lips and delighted in the musical sound of the crackling grease.

When the soldier noticed Oludara's hungry gaze, his face squeezed into a frown. He scanned the campsite and shouted to Antonio, "Hey, Captain! What do we feed to this slave here?"

Antonio shrugged and said, "Give him some green bananas. That's what everyone feeds the slaves."

Oludara's spirit sank as someone dropped a pair of bananas into his hand. He turned and slunk away, muttering, "Not again with the cursed bananas..."

When no one offered him a place to sleep, he found a patch of grass beneath a tree and leaned back to eat. He relaxed and watched the bustle around him as others took their meat and settled into their hammocks, one by one drifting off to sleep.

Just as his eyelids began to fall, a hand on his shoulder jerked him awake. He turned to see Gerard crouched in the shadow of the tree.

Oludara smiled at his friend and whispered, "I was wondering when you might show up."

"Well, I'm here now," said Gerard, "so let's flee."

"I cannot leave with this collar on; I must steal the key from Antonio first. And even so, the moment is not right. If I escape now, it will seem suspicious. It is best I accompany him all the way to Ilhéus and make sure the group does not stray off course. If Antonio has second thoughts, I will convince him to continue on."

"Then what do I do?"

"Race ahead to Ilhéus. One man can travel faster than many, and you can gather supplies there while you wait for us to arrive. Once we are close, I will escape and we can flee south."

Gerard opened his mouth to comment when a hand grabbed Oludara's eye patch and yanked it off. Oludara looked up to find Diogo staring down at him.

"Not exactly blind in that eye, are you?" said Diogo. He turned to Gerard. "I thought you might show up, Gerard. Did you think I wouldn't recognize your companion, whom I saw in the plaza that day we returned from slaying the Botat? Tell me swiftly what you're doing here, or I'll sound the alarm."

"We're saving the tribe of Tupinambá with which we spent the last six months," Gerard said. "Your troop was almost upon them."

The fact that Gerard would share the truth so quickly surprised Oludara, but he trusted his friend's judgment. Diogo, after all, had been an acquaintance of Gerard before Oludara met him.

"I wondered how you disappeared for so long," said Diogo. "Antonio always keeps an eye out for you; don't think he's forgotten the way you embarrassed him in Salvador."

"Embarrassed *him*?" said Gerard, raising his voice for a moment before recalling where he was and returning it to a whisper. "He tried to ship me back to Europe!"

"It was one of his few failures, and he won't soon forget it. Now, if you're leading us into a trap, I must tell Antonio."

"It's no trap," said Gerard. "There's no monster in Ilhéus. Antonio will lose nothing but time, and countless of our friends will be saved."

"Nevertheless, it is to his cost and I must tell him." Diogo turned to leave.

Gerard stood and grabbed him, spinning him around to face him.

"I know what kind of man you are, Diogo, and I know this mission is not to your liking. Enslaving innocent natives is barbaric. When you recognized Oludara, why didn't you tell Antonio immediately?"

Diogo lowered his eyes. "You're right, Gerard. I saw Oludara's arrival as a chance to divert Antonio from this rotten business and go back to what we should be doing: saving those in need from the ravaging monsters which plague this land."

"You are a good man," said Oludara. "Why do you follow one such as Antonio?"

"You didn't know Antonio before. When he formed the banner, his intentions were noble. We fought mighty battles and saved countless lives. Antonio always ran first into danger, with never a moment's hesitation. He was the best of us, with both sword and gun: a man to inspire. If you could have seen him like that, you would have followed him as well.

"But then his thoughts changed to profit, and the Indians. It weighs heavily on me, this business of slaving. The Indians were our allies. They fell from favor only because the sugar mills were built, and the Africans couldn't be brought fast enough to run them all."

"They aren't Indians," said Gerard, "they are Tupinambá, and Tupiniquim, and many others. And they are as much my people now as the Dutch ever were. I beg you, Diogo, don't tell Antonio. It's only a few more days, then you'll be off on your next adventure."

Diogo stood silent for a long time. With a sigh, he tossed the eye patch back to Oludara.

"Very well, Gerard. This one time, you can have your ruse. Just be off quickly, before anyone finds you here."

During the extreme midday heat typical of the Brazilian rainforests, Gerard took a welcome afternoon rest. Four days of travel had exhausted him. He sat against a fallen log and rummaged through his pack for something to eat.

The rations he had taken from the Tupinambá village were almost gone, but he had carried little enough to begin with, living off the land along the way as much as he could. Oludara had been right to insist on their spending time among the Tupinambá; the natives had imparted invaluable knowledge upon them. Where Gerard had once seen the forest as an imposing wall of green, it now felt as comfortable as a city street. Wherever he looked, he recognized plants and animals by the dozens.

He unwrapped the cloth containing the last of his cassava crackers and cut open a pineapple to accompany them. A hot meal of fish or game would have suited him better, but he hadn't risked a fire since his visit to Antonio's camp.

When he tossed his pack on the ground, it tipped over and the potion Yandir had given him rolled out. Gerard had forgotten about it after stuffing it into the bottom of the pack, but that was before he had consumed most everything else inside.

Gerard picked up the gourd and held it close to his face. He examined the strange carvings, but they held no meaning to him.

"Heathen magic," he said. He cocked back his arm to throw it.

A snap sounded from the north. Gerard absently fumbled the potion back into his pack and moved to investigate. As he walked, he caught the scent of something sweet, and the forest opened to reveal a lake surrounded by rows of sugar cane. He spotted an estate to the east, at the far end of the lake. The only buildings Gerard had seen for many months had been the Tupinambá longhouses, and the sight of brick-and-mortar constructions pleased him to no end. The white plaster walls and ceramic, salmon-colored roofs rekindled memories of the cities back in Europe.

"Ah, society," he sighed. "Has it been so long?" Since his departure from Oludara, he had ever more frequently spoken to himself to pass the time.

"Hello!" he called out several times, to no response.

Gerard circumnavigated the lake and crossed an orchard of quince and fig trees on his way to the estate. The constructions followed a similar pattern to those he had seen on other sugar plantations. The two-story building would be the owner's house. Nearby stood a private chapel with square columns in front and a wooden cross on top. A pillar with a bell stood next to it. A roofed pavilion protected the massive wooden press and other equipment used for sugar extraction. The only structure not built to last—a clay building with a thatched roof—would be the *senzala*: the slave house. Gerard estimated the structure capable of holding some two hundred slaves, based on the way the mill owners typically packed them in.

Despite a thorough search of the buildings, Gerard found no one. Drawers, cabinets, and other containers had been emptied and closed, suggesting abandonment rather than thievery. The kitchen still smelled of expensive spices like cinnamon and pepper, but none remained. Strangely enough, he found claw marks on some furniture and walls, but no trace of violence to any person.

Gerard returned to the orchard to see what he could scavenge. The quince trees held no fruit, but he would have had to cook them to make them edible, so it was no great loss. He did discover some ripe figs, so he stuffed several handfuls into his pack. He considered continuing his search of the estate, to try and find some clue as to what had happened there, but dark clouds had formed out west, the direction from which he had come.

"Glad I'm not in that," he said. "I'd best move on to Ilhéus, in case it comes this way."

He found a well-worn cart path leading east. Near the path, he spotted some tracks. At first sight they looked like overly large human feet, but gashes beyond the toes indicated claws.

"Strange," he said. "Oludara might recognize them, but they're like nothing I've ever seen."

Out of caution, Gerard loaded his harquebus.

Oludara couldn't imagine a more appropriate way of topping off four days of hard marching and banana eating than the torrential rain that now assaulted Antonio's group.

A swollen river, its water rushing by in an endless roar, halted their progress. The bank's wet clay suctioned Oludara's feet as he watched Antonio and Diogo confer with the group's principal guide, Moara.

Moara was a *caboclo*, a mix of European and native. She was taller and lighter skinned than most natives Oludara had met, with a muscular form. Her hair fell in waves, unlike the natives characteristic straight hair.

In all other respects, however, she would not be confused for a European. Her only clothing consisted of a woven band on her head with a few flowers for decoration, a leather belt, a loincloth, and green stones in her ears. Black-and-red designs colored her body, cheeks and forehead. For weapons, she carried a carved wooden club and wore a dagger at her belt. She was one of but a handful of women in the troop, and while well-respected by all, tended to keep to herself.

Oludara, pretending to examine the river, edged closer to the group to eavesdrop on their conversation.

"We can't cross," said Moara, shaking her head.

"I can see we can't cross here," responded Antonio. "I want to know where we can."

Moara shrugged. "We can follow the river back west. We can round the source perhaps ten leagues back."

"That's the wrong direction. Can't we cross farther east?"

"Yes, but..." Moara hesitated. "That will take us through the Kaa'ité."

" 'Bad Forest'? " asked Diogo.

"More like 'Terrible Forest', " replied Antonio.

Oludara had been surprised to discover Antonio spoke Tupi at least as well as he and Gerard. But Antonio used it only for yelling commands or curses at the native slaves.

"Why are you so reluctant to cross this forest?" asked Antonio.

"It is said to harbor deadly creatures," replied Moara.

Antonio scoffed at her. "I certainly hope so! We haven't had a decent battle for months." Antonio turned to the group. "Lift that equipment, laggards, we're moving on."

Moara turned to leave, but made eye contact with Oludara as she strode away. Where the others had ignored him during the march, the caboclo had been sizing him up for days. Oludara had avoided speaking with her, trying to play the part of the timid slave. Moara, however, didn't appear to believe the farce.

That one will make a great ally or a great enemy, thought Oludara. *I had best try to sway her to my side.*

The company continued its march until dusk, penetrating the forest along a thin yet discernible path. From time to time, they sent a scout south to check the river, but found only the same: a rushing, uncrossable torrent along a sticky clay bank. Exhausted, the company set up camp in the forest.

As the group hung their hammocks and lit fires, Antonio walked among his bannermen with words of: "Take heart, we'll be in Ilhéus on the morrow."

Oludara spotted Moara clearing away a bit of ground under a tree and decided to take the opportunity to speak. As he approached, however, the caboclo stood to attention.

"Captain," called Moara, "look at this."

Antonio strode over, followed by Diogo and a few others. Oludara snuck in behind the group for a peek.

Moara pointed down toward a rotting corpse. Oludara could tell there was something unusual about it; it had not decomposed naturally.

Antonio bent over for a look. “Well, that’s a repulsive corpse.” He pointed to a couple of natives nearby and said in Tupi, “You two, bury this mess.”

“Wait,” said Oludara.

When everyone stopped and trained their eyes on him, Oludara regretted his outburst, but decided it was too late to go back. He stooped down over the corpse, keeping his face low.

“There is something wrong here,” he said. “It has not rotted away; it is as if something dried it out, like a fruit in the sun. I have never seen anything like it.”

He did not add the obvious: that the corpse had not been dried by any natural cause. Anyone could see that almost no sunlight made it through the dense forest canopy.

“Slave,” said Antonio, “don’t ever speak to me unless I ask you a question.”

“He may be right, Antonio,” interjected Diogo. “This corpse is unusual. We shouldn’t make camp here.”

“Nonsense! Look at it, it’s been rotting here for ages.”

“Why should we take the chance?”

“Are you frightened, Diogo? We have a hundred strong men here, eighty of them harquebusiers. Not to mention fifty savages for fodder. What could possibly harm us?”

“I’d rather not find out.”

“Ha! We’ve slain countless beasts in our travels. If another waits nearby, so be it. It will suffer the same fate as the others. There is nothing in this forest capable of stopping Antonio Dias Caldas.”

As Antonio walked away, Diogo glanced at Oludara and frowned.

Gerard spotted Ilhéus on the horizon and breathed a sigh of relief. He examined the town as he hiked the gradual slope that led up to it.

On the far side of the city ran a massive river: navigable even by the largest of ships, from the looks of it. Out to sea, he spotted islands dotting the horizon. Only one caravel anchored in port, where he would have expected a half-dozen. As he approached, he noticed that the caravel's main mast was broken.

He had heard stories of Ilhéus's decadence, caused by many years of raiding by the formidable Aimore warriors, but the disrepair went beyond his expectations. Many buildings had been burned out and left to ruin. Most of the others were dirty, their whitewash flaking away, some even crumbling apart. He couldn't spot a freshly painted building in the lot. A wattle-and-daub fort stood on a rise with its gates open, apparently abandoned.

The only building in reasonable condition was the church: a solid, two-story structure with a bell tower at one corner. Gerard guessed that Jesuits had erected the building; it resembled others of theirs that he had seen. The whitewashing was soiled, but immaculate compared to the rest of the town.

A commotion arose when the few people walking the streets spotted him. They scattered around, calling to others. By the time Gerard arrived at the pillory in the central plaza, it seemed the entire town, perhaps a hundred people, had flooded out to surround him.

As the crowd closed in around him, a man in black, priestly robes emerged from the mob. The man was portly with a stubby nose and wore his brown hair in a tonsure. Gerard had the sensation that the priest gazed almost hungrily at his harquebus and rapier.

"I am Father Nicolau, shepherd of Ilhéus's flock," said the priest, opening his arms to encompass the crowd around him. "And who are you, kind sir?"

"My name is Gerard van Oost, and I represent the Elephant and Macaw Banner."

"God be praised!" shouted Nicolau, holding his hands toward the sky. "A banner has arrived to save us." A cheer spread through the crowd.

"Save you?" asked Gerard.

"We've been attacked," said Nicolau. "Didn't you hear? I thought you came at our summons."

"You've been attacked?"

"Yes, by a most terrible creature."

"Really?" asked Gerard. He looked skeptically at the crowd. "This isn't some type of farce?"

"Farce?" said Nicolau, almost choking on the word. "Of course not! How dare you ask a man of God such a question? What kind of person are you?"

"My apologies," said Gerard, turning red. "You have my word that I'll do all in my power to help."

"Thank you then," said the priest, more coldly this time. "Now, where is the rest of your banner?"

"The others have been detained," said Gerard. "For now, it's just me."

"Oh, terrible day," cried Nicolau. "We require a troop of hundred men. Nothing less could possibly defeat Labateau!"

A break in the rain allowed Antonio's troop time to distribute supper. Oludara collected his ration of bananas and pondered what he might say to Moara. He searched the camp to find the woman playing an intricate bone flute. She played a deliberate, melancholy melody. When she finished the song, she set down the flute and stared off at nothing.

"What is it you play?" Oludara asked in Tupi.

Moara spared a quick glance at him, then looked away again. "I was just making that up."

"I mean to ask what you call that instrument?"

Moara picked up the flute and turned it in her hand. "It is called 'thing which makes music'. "

Oludara laughed.

Moara paused for a moment, then joined in the laughter. "Yes, it seems funny once you learn the language of the white men. They have names for everything. They even name things with languages they do not speak. *Spiritus Sanctus*," she said, the Latin words rolling clumsily off her tongue.

Some of the nearby bannermen looked at them suspiciously. Most of them didn't speak Tupi.

"You are not Tupinambá," said Oludara.

"No, I was Caeté," responded Moara.

"Was?"

"My people are no more."

"What happened?"

"I was a child at the time, but my tribe captured a group of shipwrecked Portuguese and devoured them."

"That has occurred many times in Brazil."

"But one of the men we ate was a bishop," said Moara.

Oludara whistled. The bishop was the second most powerful man in Brazil, behind only the governor. While eating a few shipwrecked sailors wouldn't normally cause a commotion, the death of a bishop would have grave consequences.

"After that," said Moara, "we had no more peace. The Portuguese slaughtered or enslaved all of us...thousands." Moara used the Portuguese word to express the value, which did not exist in Tupi, then switched back. "A few were taken in by other tribes, but most wanted nothing to do with us. I was taken as a slave, and a valuable one because of my young age and European blood."

"Excuse me if it is an offense to ask, but how did you come to be born of mixed blood if your tribe hated the Europeans so much?"

"It was the custom of our tribe to offer women to our captives, before their sacrifice. A European captured by my tribe fathered me before he was eaten. My tribe would have eaten me too, eventually, for having his blood." She shook her head. "The slaughter of my people became my salvation. But I would trade my miserable life to have them back."

"Why do you serve Antonio?"

"What is my choice? I am a slave, and can hope for no better. I could run away and live alone in the wilderness, but what kind of life is that? This business of enslaving natives is wretched, but we have done good as well, killing the accursed creatures of this land which harassed my people for generations."

A nearby man drinking water from an ox horn hocked and spat in their direction. "Stop speaking like that!" he said. "Speak in Portuguese if you want to talk."

Oludara, changing to Portuguese, replied, “Sorry, I only desired to practice the language.”

The man stood and approached him. “How did a slave learn to speak like the savages, anyway?”

“From the Indian slaves in my master’s sugar mill. We work side by side with them.”

“Hmph,” replied the man. The response seemed to satisfy him, though. He turned and walked back to sit on a rotten log. Just after he sat, he scrunched his face and jerked his shoulders.

“Now what’s that?” he said. “I’ve a strange feeling in my arse.”

Someone nearby said, “Perhaps it’s from all those beans you ate at dinner!” Everyone laughed.

The man gasped for breath. He stood, but the log moved with him, firmly attached to his bottom. He got no more than half way up before the imbalance caused him to fall to the side.

The log came alive, pieces of it folding out, which Oludara recognized as limbs. It took a form reminiscent of a rotten, wooden cadaver, and embraced the man in its arms. Within seconds, the man dried to a lifeless corpse, like the one they had discovered earlier that day.

Bannerman jumped in shock on all sides. Two arms stretched out from what appeared to be a pile of sticks and grabbed hold of another man, who dried up just like the first. All around them, leaves scattered as the ground moved.

“God save us,” someone cried out, “it’s the Dry Bodies!”

Gerard took dinner with Father Nicolau in the church’s sacristy. Through the open doorway, he could hear the front doors opening and closing as people entered.

A native brought in a meal of mussels and bread. The mussels smelled of vinegar, garlic, and peppers, and Gerard downed them by the handful. He washed them down with a glass of wine made from local fruit.

“So,” said Gerard, his mouth half-full with mussels, “tell me about this Labateau.”

"It was once a man: a pirate from France. Captain Labateau captured our town, then ravished it for a month, killing many and abusing the rest. He came back a year later, greedy to raid us a second time, but the governor had a fleet ready and blocked the port behind him.

"He killed many Christian souls—God bless them—as he tried to escape, but in the end the governor's troops captured the wretch. They handed him over to us for burning, but when we lit the bonfire, the very flames refused to touch the foul man. In the end, we shot him a dozen times. But as he screamed his final curse at us, the full moon appeared through the clouds, and his body sprouted hair.

"Changed from man to savage beast, the creature split the cords which held it like threads. It fled into the woods and for many years we did not see it, although the name 'Labateau' was whispered every time a cow or goat went missing.

"Then, a month ago, the infernal creature returned for revenge. Every night it kills one man, woman, or child."

Gerard swallowed the last of the mussels and looked longingly at the empty plate. Outside the sacristy door, he could hear a rumble of conversations as people packed into the church.

"Why is everyone coming in here?" he asked.

"Labateau won't touch this sacred ground," replied Nicolau. "St. George protects us here. Also, this is the strongest building in Ilhéus."

Nicolau stood and Gerard followed him into the church proper. People crowded from wall to wall.

"It is time," shouted Nicolau. "Close the door."

Two men closed and bolted the heavy wooden doors.

"Is this everyone, Father?" asked Gerard.

"Most have already fled; there aren't so many left. Here we protect ourselves, and Labateau will take a slave for his dinner, instead of one of us."

"There are slaves here?" asked Gerard.

"The slaves are locked in some warehouses down at the docks, although many have escaped. There are still some two-hundred Indians and the same of Africans."

"What?" bellowed Gerard. "You leave them in a warehouse where the monster can find them?"

"We must save the Christian souls first."

Gerard opened his mouth to argue when a shrill scream pierced the air. He scanned the church for a vantage point, but found only stained glass.

"Are there no open windows here?" he asked.

"Only in the mezzanine," replied Nicolau, "or the belfry."

"I'll take the mezzanine."

"Very well."

Nicolau led him to a ladder at the front of the church, the crowd parting for them along the way. Gerard climbed the ladder with Nicolau coming up behind. At the top, he found two-foot square windows at the corners and opened the shutters.

"I suppose this is good enough," said Gerard. "If Labateau wants in, it'll have to come this way."

A half-scream, half-howl sounded. Everyone in the church remained silent.

Gerard looked out the window and saw the creature's silhouette framed in the moonlight. For some reason, bright points shimmered at the edges, but Gerard could tell little else at that distance. Beside him, Nicolau made the sign of the cross.

Gerard looked down and called out, "Someone hand up my harquebus!"

The Dry Bodies, when upright, looked like gangly men carved from rotting wood. Their branch arms ended in twig-like claws, and everyone they touched dried to a husk. They shuffled along, too slow to catch a running person, but what they lacked in speed they made up for in numbers. Hundreds of Dry Bodies sprouted in all directions.

Oludara observed the chaos with his uncovered eye, trying to form a plan. He watched as one man hacked a Dry Body with an axe, only to have the blade stick in the creature. As the man tried to pull the axe free, the Dry Body grasped his wrist, sucking the life from him.

Another man climbed a tree—an idea Oludara considered foolish from the start—and met his end when he grabbed a Dry Body instead of a branch. Two other Dry Bodies ambled up from below and the three of them grappled grotesquely for the rotting corpse.

Antonio's rapier caught in the side of one. The Dry Body swiped at him but he ducked and the beast grabbed only his hat in its claws, which it tossed away.

"You won't keep either of those," said Antonio.

The Dry Body lunged forward and Antonio rolled under its arm, snatching back his hat as he passed. He then grabbed his rapier and twisted around, yanking it free and sending the creature flying to one side all in the same movement.

Oludara saw Moara backing slowly toward a tree, a look of terror on her face. Then he saw bark on the tree begin to move.

"Look out!" he said.

Moara spun and pulled the club from her belt, but she was too late. A Dry Body grabbed her wrist. Moara screamed and dropped the club.

Without thinking, Oludara grasped his ivory knife. As always, the enchanted weapon tingled as he wielded it. He slashed at the Dry Body's arm and cut it straight through. The severed hand let go and fell to the ground.

Moara glanced at the knife, then raised her eyebrows at Oludara as if to say, *I knew all along you were no obsequious slave.*

A rustling sound caught their attention, and they looked down in unison to see the hand grasping its way toward their feet. Moara reached down for her club, Oludara hid his knife back under his shirt, and the two of them ran.

A group of men tried to burn the Dry Bodies with torches, but to no effect. A Dry Body grasped one of them, who promptly dropped his torch and set some leaves on fire.

"Stop it!" yelled Diogo. "You'll burn down the forest and us with it."

Around them, an inexorable circle of Dry Bodies closed in.

—◇—

Gerard sighted Labateau down the barrel of his harquebus.

"Should we be shooting from a church?" asked Nicolau.

"As long as a man of the cloth is here," replied Gerard, "he won't dare enter."

Nicolau tapped him on the shoulder and whispered, "There's something I should tell you, Gerard. I was never ordained."

"You're not a priest?" said Gerard, spinning around.

"Shh!" Nicolau looked down to see the reactions of those below, but no one seemed to have heard. "I never finished the seminary. Too much scripture and Latin for a mind to hold, don't you agree?"

Nicolau's confession both surprised and irritated Gerard, but he decided to leave the reprimands for another time. "I suppose it must indeed be difficult," he said.

"When I arrived here," said Nicolau, "the Jesuits had left to start new churches farther down the coast. The people needed a priest, and didn't ask any questions."

"Hmmm," said Gerard. "Well, as long as we're making confessions, I should tell you that I'm a member of the Reformed Church: a follower of Calvin."

"Oh, no," wailed Nicolau, "we are doomed!" He made the sign of the cross.

At the words, a commotion sounded below them. People yelled up to know what was happening.

"Don't worry, Nicolau," said Gerard. "Just hold steady, keep your cross high, and have faith."

Gerard took his shot. He watched as Labateau reeled backwards and howled. Gerard nodded and refilled the harquebus's flash pan with powder.

"At least this one bleeds," he said.

"What does that mean?" asked Nicolau.

"Just that I've met my share of creatures which don't."

Outside, Labateau performed a series of jumps and flips, all the time howling at the church. A visible sweat formed on Nicolau's brow. Gerard, now loading the barrel, noticed his discomfort.

"Hold steady, Nicolau," he said. "We'll be fine."

Gerard steadied the rifle and took another shot. A piercing howl, louder and more terrifying than the first, came from below.

"See?" said Gerard, readying for a third shot. "It's just a matter of wearing the beast down—one shot at a time."

"But look," said Nicolau, "he comes!"

Labateau's silhouette approached the church with deliberate, forced steps.

"He's never come this close before," said Nicolau. "He's going to come in. He's going to attack!"

"Courage, Nicolau," shouted Gerard, losing his patience. "Just keep faith, and the beast will hold."

The false priest screamed and raced down the ladder. He pushed his way through the crowd to the sacristy and slammed the door shut.

Gerard looked out to see the beast pause. It took on a different demeanor, standing straight and no longer wavering. It let out a triumphant howl and charged.

"Get back!" Gerard yelled to the people below. "Away from the doors!"

A pounding boom sounded on the wooden doors, and people packed away from them as well as they could. On the second slam, the huge doors came crashing apart, and Labateau's momentum brought it rolling in.

Oludara stood among the ever-dwindling group. For once, he had no plan. Standing and fighting would get him nowhere, but running through the forest meant facing a gauntlet of Dry Bodies in the darkness. The bannermen panicked around him, searching for a way through their relentless foes.

"Damn this cursed forest," said Antonio. "There must be hundreds of these rotten creatures."

"We've lost half our troop," said Diogo.

Antonio raised his rapier. "They're slow, we can break through their ranks."

"A charge through the thick of them is risky."

"The best of us will escape," said Antonio. "The rest..." He shrugged.

"Might will not save us this time," said Oludara. "We must use our minds."

"I didn't ask you to speak, slave."

Antonio slashed at an approaching Dry Body, severing an arm. The Dry Body reached down and recovered the fallen limb, which it unsuccessfully attempted to jam back into place.

"Captain," shouted someone. "We can't kill them."

"Of course you can't kill them, fool," replied Antonio. "They're already dead."

"My people have a saying," said Oludara, " 'If you place a mortar on the fire the mortar will burn, if you pound a yam in a pot the pot will break.' Each thing has its own weakness."

"Will you be quiet, slave," said Antonio. "This is no time to be talking about yams!"

"I am saying that we are trying to kill the dead as we would the living. Are they not different? How do these creatures move if they are dead?"

"They suck the life from others," said Diogo.

"Then we must cut them off from this vigor, or feed them something from which they cannot drain life."

"I don't need your advice, slave," said Antonio.

"It's an idea," said Diogo.

"There must be something," said Oludara.

"You know, slave," said Antonio, "the way you speak, you seem almost familiar. Have we not met before?"

"I am sure I would remember such an honor," said Oludara, deflecting the question. "The name Antonio Dias Caldas is praised by many."

"I'm certain it is," said Antonio, hacking at another Dry Body.

"Enough talking," said Diogo. "How do we stop them?"

"Through here," yelled someone to the south. "The way to the river is open!"

"To the river!" yelled someone else.

For lack of other options, Oludara followed the fleeing group. From what he could see with his uncovered eye, the path did appear to contain fewer Dry Bodies. The few of them that did appear were knocked aside by Diogo and Antonio, each of them having traded their rapiers for logs. Nevertheless, Oludara had the suspicion they were only stalling the inevitable.

Distracted in his thoughts, he failed to see a Dry Body drop from a tree above him. He looked in terror as it gripped his arm. Pain shot from the contact and his body froze in shock. His vision fuzzed and he felt his consciousness slipping away.

Without warning, a club caught the Dry Body solidly in the middle and sent it flying.

"Are you all right?" asked Moara.

Oludara coughed when he tried to speak, then settled for a nod.

"Good then, we're even," she said, smiling.

Staying close behind Moara, who whacked several Dry Bodies from their path, Oludara completed the nightmare run to the river. As he had feared, though, the flight was pointless. They had gained some minutes of respite, but the torrent of water remained impassable.

"This gains us nothing," spat Moara. "They will be upon us in a matter of minutes and we have no other escape."

Several men ran to the water and jumped in.

"No!" yelled Oludara and Moara in unison.

No man swam more than ten feet before being pulled under.

"If it's between drowning or fighting to death, I'm for fighting," said Antonio. "Who's with me?"

Most of the men cheered. Others, particularly the natives, hunched over in defeat.

Oludara noted how much Antonio could resemble Gerard. Not in face or bearing, for in those they were quite different. But in bravery, skill, and desire for adventure, they were kindred spirits. Oludara had no idea which of them would win in a fight, but what set them apart lay within their souls: Gerard's heart was as good as Antonio's was rotten.

Following Antonio, the men charged back toward the forest. Oludara could only shake his head at the foolish gesture. As he lowered his gaze, he caught sight of his feet sinking into the wet clay of the riverbank.

"Wait!" he yelled. His voice commanded such force that the men turned and stopped, just paces from the trees.

Oludara knelt down and desperately scraped together a pile of clay.

"In Ketu, we tell the tale of a spider," he said, "which was fooled by a pile of tar."

Looking down from the mezzanine, Gerard examined Labateau. A single, lemon-sized, furious eye dominated the middle of its wide face. A snout with tusks pointing up from both sides extended from what once had been a human mouth. The creature's muscled body stood over six feet tall. Quills poked from its back and arms like a porcupine. Its massive, human feet ended in long claws. Gerard could see two streams of blood on its chest where his shots had landed.

The creature howled at the people cowering around it, its bristles popping out to add emphasis. Gerard noticed white tips on the quills, which explained the shimmering he had seen earlier. The beast pounced into the crowd.

Gerard finished loading his gun and raised it, but failed to get a shot on Labateau as it sped out the door, a child clasped under one arm.

"Pedro!" a lady below him yelled after the retreating beast and its victim.

Gerard jumped from the mezzanine and landed heavily. It took him a few moments to shake the sting from his legs. When he finally stumbled to the door, he spotted the beast rushing toward the woods. Even with the child in its arms, Labateau ran too fast for him to catch; he needed to slow it down.

He raised his harquebus and aimed for the chest, but with the boy's head peeking out just below the armpit, he couldn't risk that shot. Instead, he fired at the creature's buttocks.

Labateau jerked at the impact and snarled in pain. It hobbled a few steps, then continued its flight, although at a slower pace.

Knowing he wouldn't have time to load again before Labateau reached the woods, Gerard threw down the harquebus and set out after the beast. In his haste, he realized he hadn't dropped his pack. He made a quick struggle to throw it off, but as he closed in on Labateau he was forced to leave it on. He caught up to the creature some fifty paces into the woods.

He tried to grapple Labateau from behind, but his hand burned when it touched the spines on the creature's back. Gerard howled at the sensation.

Still holding the child, the beast turned to attack. It grappled with one arm and tried to pull Gerard into its toothy snout. Gerard ducked and lunged as the beast's putrid jaws snapped above him. His elbow caught Labateau in the chest and sent it sprawling.

Gerard lunged down to choke Labateau, but the beast backhanded him, pricking his arm and face with its quills. Gerard could feel himself numbing and realized the spines contained poison.

The beast righted itself and Gerard pulled out his rapier. With a lightning lunge he sliced Labateau's side, but the creature swiped down on his sword arm and pricked him again, making him drop the blade.

Gerard conceded that the battle would be his last. However, Labateau bled profusely from his wounds and moved in a daze, so Gerard hoped his death would not be in vain. All that remained was to see which combatant would perish first.

Labateau finally released the child, who fell at its feet. Then it stumbled forward and struck at Gerard with a lazy backhand. Gerard, having learned to avoid the quill pricks at all costs, stepped well out of the way. In his own lethargic haze, Gerard swung off his pack and threw it at the beast's face. Labateau brought up both hands to deflect. Gerard used the distraction to charge forward and caught the beast with a punch to the chin. Labateau swayed before going down.

While Labateau tried to shake off the blow, Gerard wagged his muddled head from side to side, searching for his rapier. He found it near his feet, and on his second attempt, overcame his double vision and managed to pick it up. As Labateau finally sat up, Gerard thrust the blade toward its face. Labateau caught the point with its forearm and fell back, yanking down Gerard as well. With the last of his strength, Gerard yanked free the rapier and thrust it under the beast's chin.

This time the rapier struck before Labateau could react. The sword punctured through to the creature's brain. Labateau's head rolled back and moved no more.

"Got you first," mumbled Gerard, just before rolling to the ground beside it.

Gerard raised his arm to see purple and red lines running all along it. He shook his head and it lolled to one side. Six inches before his face lay the gourd containing Yandir's potion, dislodged from his pack when it struck Labateau.

Gerard shook his head. "No, never," he said. "I will not resort to that heathen magic."

He raised one arm, an action that whisked pain all the way to his toes, and grabbed the cross he wore around his neck.

"Holy Father," he said, "please..." He forgot his prayer mid-sentence. Rather than concentrating on repenting his sins before his imminent death, his mind raced back through his adventures.

So much mystery left unsolved, he thought. *So much left to explore.*

He thought of the potion again.

"Oh, to hell with it," he said.

Gerard struggled to remove the stopper and splashed as much of the potion as he could down his throat. Even swallowing had become a chore, and he nearly choked on the liquid. Then, everything turned black.

The Dry Bodies appeared from the woods and shambled toward the figures before them. The moment they reached the clay riverbank, their feet mired in its stickiness and their movements slowed.

They forced their way to the clay lumps—hastily erected and covered in men's clothing—and clawed at them. When their twig-like fingers became stuck, they clawed with their feet and even bit into the clay effigies. Soon, Dry Bodies piled upon each other within the mass of sticky clay, more arriving every moment. Hundreds of them crowded together in the muck, all the time churning up more clay and creating an enormous, convulsing mound. At the first rays of dawn, the grotesque movement stopped and the creatures curled back into shapes which looked like nothing more than rotting logs.

One by one, the expedition's survivors climbed their way up from the tree roots on the river's edge. Most were naked, their clothes having been employed in the trickery, and all shivered from the river's icy water. However, the hot Brazilian morning soon warmed them.

Oludara and Moara dragged themselves out last from the roots, having been the first to climb in and leading the rest behind them. Antonio, still fully clothed, pondered the mound of Dry Bodies before him.

"Let's get out of here," said one of the survivors.

"No," said Antonio. "First we bury them."

"It won't hold them forever," said Diogo. "Another hard rain and many will escape."

"It will hold them long enough. Let someone else deal with them later."

Once the creatures had been covered to his satisfaction, Antonio looked to his men and said, "Once again, I've rid this land of evil. Songs will be made of this day."

"It is easy to cut to pieces a dead elephant," said Oludara.

Diogo covered a smile.

Antonio spun on Oludara. "Was that some kind of jest?"

"Just a saying of my people."

Antonio punched him. Oludara had known Antonio might strike him and could have ducked it, but instead chose to take the blow and fall down, so as to not raise suspicion. The ache in his jaw made him regret it. Antonio stood over him.

"I'll see you well-whipped when we arrive in Ilhéus." He turned to the others. "For now, let us push on and leave this cursed forest."

Someone shook Gerard's shoulder and he struggled to consciousness. He heard a timid voice say, "Are you all right?"

With effort, he opened his eyes. He saw the boy Labateau had captured looking down at him wide-eyed, while a velvet dawn appeared through the trees. Though it felt like lifting a thousand pounds, Gerard pushed himself up.

"Why yes," he said, "I think I am."

Minutes later, Gerard left the woods, hand in hand with the child. His rapier hung limply from his other hand, the point dragging the ground behind him.

As they neared the pillory, a cry sounded from the church and everyone rushed out to greet them. The boy ran to the arms of his sobbing mother. Someone handed Gerard his harquebus, while others patted his back.

Nicolau pushed through the crowd and cradled Gerard's hand.

"Is it dead?" he asked.

"You'll find the body in the woods nearby," replied Gerard.

"Praise be the Lord for sending this most heroic and loyal man to save us!" said Nicolau.

"Gerard van Oost!" shouted someone from the crowd. Several others joined in the cry.

"A slayer of monsters," shouted another, "like the heroes of old!"

Gerard's eyes glazed over and he whispered to himself, "Like the heroes of old."

"What's that?" asked someone, pointing back to the woods.

Gerard turned to spot movement at the edge of the forest. He tensed and raised his rapier instinctively. However, it drooped to his side the moment he saw a group of men led by a gold-and-red banner emerge from the woods.

"Why now?" he mumbled to himself. Then he turned to the crowd and said, "So sorry, but I must be going."

He pushed his way through a throng of admirers and sprinted south without looking back.

Someone shouted, "Three cheers for Gerard van Oost: Huzzah!"

The crowd joined in: "Huzzah! Huzzah!"

Their cries diminished as his retreating silhouette disappeared over a hill to the south.

"What an unusual man," commented Nicolau.

Antonio—haggard and exhausted—shivered in relief at the sight of Ilhéus before him.

"We made it out alive," said Diogo.

"Some of us did," said Moara.

A cheer broke out before them. Antonio could make out a crowd in the town center ahead. "They must have seen us coming," he said, a smile breaking upon his face.

He straightened up and dusted off his clothes for the big moment. When he saw the shocked faces of the crowd and the women covering their eyes, he remembered that many of his men remained naked. He grimaced. It was not be the triumphant entrance he'd desired, but it would have to do. He reached up to wipe the sweat from his eyes and realized his head was uncovered.

"Where's my hat?" he asked to no one in particular.

His men shook their heads and shrugged their shoulders. He growled and quickened his pace towards town.

When his group arrived at the pillory, he said, "I am Antonio Dias Caldas. I've brought my banner here to rescue you."

A man shouted, "Gerard van Oost has saved us!" Many cheered at the sound of Gerard's name.

"WHAT?" screamed Antonio. "I've marched day and night to get here and you're telling me that Gerard van Oost has slain the beast?"

"Labateau is dead," said Nicolau. "Praise be to God."

"Where's Gerard?" growled Antonio, looking around furiously.

"He left just moments ago."

"Curse the day that Gerard van Oost was born. Curse the day he came to Brazil. I'll have his head yet."

"Fie!" came a cry from the crowd. "He's our hero."

Antonio spat on the ground. "Then show me to the mill owner Francisco de Santarem. I have his slave here and I expect a reward."

"We have but eight mill owners in Ilhéus," said Nicolau, "and none by that name."

"Impossible!" yelled Antonio. In a flash, he unsheathed his rapier and turned to face his men. "Where is that cursed slave? Bring him here so I can run him through."

The men looked among themselves but no one spoke. Finally, someone at the back of the troop said, "Captain, here!"

Antonio went to the man, who pointed to the ground. There, at his feet, lay two objects: an eye patch and an iron collar.

A black capuchin monkey swung through the trees, his latest acquisition held in one of his lower paws.

He screamed to his friends, calling them to show off his prize. They appeared from the branches all around him, and he waved the hat at them: the one with the shiny buckle and red feather he had taken from the boisterous man. He had hung by the tail from a tree branch and grabbed it as the man walked past. The men around him, their weary heads bowed toward the ground, hadn't even noticed.

The monkey put the hat on his head and it fell down, covering his face. The other monkeys screeched in approval at his mockery of the men who walked on two legs below the trees, and he howled along with them.

Chapter 4

A Preposterous Series of Captures and Calamities

N ANACONDA FLOATED just below the surface of the river, waiting for some unsuspecting victim to come and drink. Only her snout poked above the water, a single lump hidden among the roots and weeds. An exhausting night had passed without a single morsel, and she had almost conceded to sleeping on an empty stomach, when she sensed something. Through the murky water she spotted a large form approaching. From the way the creature moved on two legs, it had to be human.

The anaconda's first reaction was to flee. The local humans could swim like fish and run like deer, and they killed her kind for sport. They were one of only two things she feared—the other being that terrible, toothy beast which roamed the woods just upriver.

What made her pause, however, was the way this human differed from the others. It had dark, almost black skin, and wore some kind of second skin over it. Also, it smelled different than the rest.

The human bent down just above her for a drink. It all seemed too easy: at this distance, the thing wouldn't have time to react. Out of instinct, she tightened her muscles and prepared for the strike. She would latch onto the creature's face, pull it underwater, and crush it with her coils. Though large, it was surely no larger than the many deer and tapir she had slain.

At the last moment, however, she decided against it. The local men were nothing like the bumbling tapirs, and this one might also be dangerous. She hadn't lived this long by taking chances, and decided it better to swim away hungry, but safe.

Oludara jerked back from the water as a massive shape darted into motion mere inches below his face. He could just make out a spotted, serpentine form flitting away under the murky water.

"Olorun!" he exclaimed.

Gerard, one hand securing his hat upon his head, came running. "What is it?" he asked.

"A giant serpent. Even on this side of the world, they pester me. We must keep our wits about us as we travel these parts."

Gerard chuckled and sat down. "I can't recall a single day since we've met that we didn't have to keep our wits." He rummaged through his pack and tossed Oludara a half a bunch of bananas, keeping the other half for himself. "Guess what's for breakfast?" he joked.

Oludara sighed at the sight of the fruit and the two ate in silence. For nearly two months, Antonio Dias Caldas and his bannermen had chased the pair down the coast, and they had lived on nothing but the fruits and nuts they scavenged along the way. They spared no time for hunting or fishing, and wouldn't have risked a fire in any case. They'd faced too many close encounters with Antonio's band to do anything but sleep, eat, and flee.

After finishing his bananas, Oludara asked, "And now the question, Gerard. What is our next move? Do we follow this river inland, or continue our flight south?"

"I wouldn't go inland without a boat. The forest here is dense; if we get lost or bogged down, Antonio will capture us easily. In fact, I think we should do the opposite: head back to sea and follow the shore."

"I'm not sure, Gerard. The river may be our chance to throw Antonio off our trail. And if we stay to the beaches, we'll be out in the open."

"I don't think we can lose him in the woods; he has too many trackers among his men. Our advantage is our number. In the wilderness, we struggle as much as they do to progress. On the coast, we can outrun the larger group."

Oludara wasn't convinced. If anything delayed them, they would become easy prey. But he decided to show trust in his companion and nodded agreement.

"Very well," he said, "the shore it is."

They made their way downriver, and around noon the forest opened and the pair discovered a sugar mill. What Oludara saw, however, did not encourage him in the least. The houses had been torched and fences torn down. The crops and orchards had been burned to the ground. The equipment inside the sugar mill lay smashed. Oludara and Gerard searched the ruins but found no trace of anyone or any sign of where they had gone.

They followed the river the rest of the way to the coast, and all along it the scene repeated itself: houses, chapels, sugar mills and all other signs of settlement lay burned and abandoned. Upon reaching the shore, they discovered a cluster of charred buildings and docks that must have been the abandoned town's core.

"What could have done this?" asked Gerard, shaking his head in disbelief.

"I thought you'd never ask!" came a shrill voice behind them.

They turned to find a smiling Sacy-Perey. The imp hadn't appeared for months, sparing the pair from his annoying pranks.

"All this is a warning," he said. "And if you're smart, you'll take it."

"Who left it?" asked Oludara. "And why?"

"Hmmm," Sacy cocked his head at Gerard. "That, perhaps, is a story best discussed over a smoke."

Gerard removed his pack and offered the prepubescent imp the tobacco pouch he kept on hand for just such occasions. Sacy accepted it gladly and, as always, made his pipe appear with three shakes of his pointy red hat.

Once the three had settled in for Sacy's smoke, he told them, "You should travel no farther south; you've reached Wytaka land."

"And what does that mean?" asked Gerard.

"The Wytaka are the undisputed rulers here."

"Natives?" asked Oludara. "In case you forget, Sacy, we've befriended many on our travels."

"Are you talking about the Tupinambá?" asked Sacy. "Forget all you know of them, for they have little in common with the Wytaka. Their language is not at all like Tupi. In fact, they have been enemies of the Tupi nations for countless moons.

"But that is the least of it. They are fearless and strong: expert swimmers, flawless archers, and powerful warriors. They grow no food, they eat only what they capture. And many times, that means the flesh of their enemies."

"And who are their enemies?" asked Oludara.

"Everyone who is not Wytaka!"

Gerard looked at Oludara and rolled his eyes at the dramatic statement.

"Thank you for the warning, Sacy," said Oludara, "but a nearer danger troubles us. Antonio's band is close behind. So close, in fact, they almost captured us a week ago."

"Before you decide what is danger and what is not," said Sacy, dropping his pipe back into his hat, "follow me. I'll show you something that might change your minds."

Gerard and Oludara hid with Sacy within some boulders at the water's edge. Waves struck the rocks from time to time, wetting their boots and britches, but their position afforded cover on all sides. Behind them, thirty-foot sea cliffs separated the beach from the forest beyond.

"We've been waiting for hours," said Gerard, straightening himself for a stretch. "We've lost too much time with this nonsense. Oludara, we need to move on."

Oludara yanked him by the shirt and pointed down the shore, where three men descended a path from the cliffs. The men's nakedness and straight black hair left no doubt they were natives, but their similarity to the Tupi tribes ended there. They were taller and lighter complexioned than the other natives Gerard and Oludara had met. They held themselves high and walked with confidence. Their hair hung all the way to their buttocks.

"Strange," commented Gerard, "how they wear their hair in a fashion so different from the Tupi."

"The Tupi wear their hair short and bald on top so that no one can grab it during battle," said Sacy. "The Wytaka have no such worries; no enemy ever makes it that close to a Wytaka alive."

"Your drama is wearing thin, Sacy. No one is *that* dangerous."

"Gerard," whispered Oludara, "pay attention."

Gerard returned his focus to the natives and saw that one of them held a stick with a bloody carcass hanging from it. It appeared to be a rabbit, but from the distance, Gerard couldn't be sure.

"Unusual," said Gerard.

The man with the stick dove into the water and swum out with powerful strokes. He ducked the waves and advanced with amazing speed. Once past the breakers, the man stopped and treaded water.

Gerard squinted to keep focus. "What exactly is he doing?"

"Just watch," said Sacy, putting his hands behind his head and leaning back on a rock.

They watched in silence as the man treaded water for several minutes. Then, without warning, he stiffened to attention. Gerard scanned the sea and spotted a fin approaching.

"Why doesn't he flee?" said Gerard. "The man is insane. Surely he's not still carrying that bloody stick?"

"Of course he is," said Sacy. "How else is he going to attract sharks?"

Gerard watched, horrified, as the fin closed in on the Wytaka. At the last moment, the man disappeared under the water. Loud splashing ensued for several moments, then the water quieted.

"I suppose that's the end of that, then," said Gerard. "I'm not sure what you wanted to show us, Sacy, but if these Wytaka are that foolish, I'm not worried. Bravery and stupidity are two different things, you know."

Sacy flashed an evil grin. "It's not over, Gerard. Keep watching."

Gerard returned his gaze to the water. He scanned the area of the attack for over a minute, but saw nothing. Then, something near the shore caught his attention. The man emerged from the water dragging an eight-foot shark behind him. Gerard could see the stake poking from the animal's mouth, up through its head. The Wytaka's two companions smiled and slapped him on the back.

Gerard's jaw dropped.

"And *that*," said Sacy, "is how the Wytaka get their arrowheads. They use sharks' teeth."

"All that for arrowheads?" asked Gerard.

Sacy nodded, smiling.

"Well, Sacy, I owe you an apology. You're right about the Wytaka;

I'd rather take my chances with Antonio. I've never seen *him* spear a swimming shark."

"My people have a saying," said Oludara. " 'Don't flee the sword by hiding yourself in the scabbard.' Our flight has led us into terrible danger, but we can't just run back into Antonio's arms, we must head west and take our chances inland."

"Into the unknown, then," said Gerard. "We may escape the sword and the scabbard, but who knows where the third path will take us?"

"We don't have to go far, just far enough to get around Antonio's men. Then we can circle back and return north."

"What a shame," sighed Gerard, "I was so hoping to visit the famed Rio de Janeiro."

"Better to pay a traveler's fare on a ship from Salvador than pay with our lives to cross by way of this cursed shore."

Oludara, his nerves already on alert, jumped at the sound of a shot.

Sacy had parted ways at the beach and he and Gerard had plunged into the wilderness. The travel was punishing, as they had to manage the dense, unexplored woods, all the time trying to maintain a decent speed and not alert their enemies of their passage. While Gerard seemed almost oblivious to their danger, keeping a measured pace, Oludara agonized over every step. Every branch, every vine, every patch of ground could leave sign of their passage. A thousand things demanded his attention, and the exploding shot sent those thoughts whirling, making his head reel.

"A harquebus," Gerard stated simply, as if pointing out the name of a flower. "Should we investigate or avoid it?"

Before Oludara could answer, three more shots echoed through the woods, and someone screamed in agony.

"I suppose that answers your question?" asked Oludara. Already distressed for their safety, he would have preferred avoiding any encounter, but he knew his Protestant companion wouldn't abandon people in danger.

"You're right about that," said Gerard. He pulled his pack tight and ran toward the commotion.

For the next few minutes, they followed the sound of screams and shots, interspersed with an unusual noise, which to Oludara, sounded eerily similar to a gorilla's roar. As they made their final sprint toward the combatants, Oludara caught glimpses of a revolting scene.

Three Portuguese men valiantly battled an enormous creature. They appeared to be all that remained of a contingent, because bodies littered the ground around them. One corpse lacked head and shoulders, another had been ripped in half and the parts tossed in two different places. Four others, their bodies contorted beyond repair, lay wrapped around trees or broken upon the ground. Oludara recognized the men from Antonio's troop.

The sight of the carnage, however, was nothing compared to that of the monster. The hairy creature was some eight feet tall and six feet wide, with muscular arms so long they almost reached the ground. The beast's enormous, spindly hands ended in lizard-like claws, and hooves supported its massive legs. But the creature's strangest feature was its face, which looked like it had been stretched down and around its broad chest. A small knob over the creature's torso held its eyes. Next came an oversized nose, the size of a papaya, on its upper chest. Where the creatures' belly button should have been lay its most distinguishing feature: an enormous, toothy mouth, almost three feet wide. Blood covered its huge teeth and lips.

Oludara grabbed Gerard's shoulder just as his companion began forward. "Careful," said Oludara, "these are Antonio's men."

"Nevertheless," replied Gerard, "we can't leave them like this."

"Are you certain?" asked Oludara. "Antonio could arrive any moment looking for them."

"I'll risk it," said Gerard, kneeling to load his harquebus.

Oludara crouched beside him, unsheathing his ivory knife and studying the beast for some weakness. One of the fighters poked it with a rapier, which seemed to have no effect. Another whacked it with a log, which drew the beast's attention, if nothing else. The third man struggled to load his gun, but the powder horn slipped through his trembling fingers.

One of the broken men on the ground craned his head toward Gerard and Oludara and rasped out, "Save me!"

Gerard spared him only a glance before returning his attention to his harquebus. "That's what we're trying to do," he replied.

"You can't beat it. Flee and take me with you."

"I'll be the judge of that."

"If you must fight, shoot for the mouth."

Oludara watched tensely as the beast grabbed the man with the log and dashed him to the ground. Bones snapped and the man went limp.

"Gerard," said Oludara, "whatever you're planning, do it now!"

Gerard raised his gun in a fluid motion and shot for the creature's gaping maw. The beast took a step back and let out an enraged scream, then focused its gaze on Gerard. The two remaining bannermen took advantage of the distraction to flee.

The creature charged, and Gerard and Oludara separated, ducking behind trees for cover. The creature chose to follow Gerard, knocking over an eight-foot *pitanga* tree in its haste to reach him. Oludara raced up behind it, slashing at the point on the torso where a man's kidney would lie. Unlike the bannerman's rapier, his enchanted knife sliced the beast's hide. The creature screamed and leapt away, into the brush, without so much as glancing back.

Gerard tensed to run after it, but Oludara said, "Leave it. Antonio could come at any moment."

Gerard nodded and knelt by the man who had spoken to them. He pulled a water skin from his pack and said, "Here, drink."

The man could barely crack open his mouth. Gerard poured a sip through his lips.

"What is that creature?" asked Oludara.

"Magwhar," croaked the man. "Will you take me back to my banner? I serve Antonio Dias Caldas."

"I'm afraid we can't do that," said Gerard. "But we'll make you comfortable. Two of your companions got away. I'm sure they'll be back soon with help."

"Don't be so sure," said the man, frowning.

Thudding footsteps boomed nearby and they turned to see a tree flying at them. Magwhar charged close behind, bellowing in rage. Branches struck both of them, knocking them apart, and the creature landed heavily in their midst. Its smell washed over them: a bitter, coppery stench of squalid fur matted with gore. It grabbed the injured man and shoved him into the enormous mouth on its chest, where its giant teeth crunched off the man's head and shoulders.

Gerard yelled "Run!" and Oludara needed no further urging. The two set off in different directions.

Oludara ran his fastest, dodging branches and leaping roots in a dance through the woods. Hearing no sign of pursuit, he paused and stooped over to catch his breath. A flash of color caught his eye and he looked up to find a man, mouth agape, standing just beside him. Looking around, Oludara discovered he had run into a line of men walking double file through the woods. To his dismay, he recognized the group immediately. He turned to run, but someone struck his back with the butt of a harquebus and he fell. He turned over to find five guns trained at him.

The line parted down the middle and a man wearing a rich, red doublet came striding toward him.

"Well, well," said Antonio Dias Caldas, grinning. "If it isn't Gerard van Oost's meddling slave."

Gagged and bound to a tree, Oludara considered his bleak situation. Around him, Antonio's men scampered amid the jumble of trees and brush, setting up camp as best they could. The group, much reduced since their encounters with Magwhar and the Dry Bodies, now consisted of some thirty riflemen and a dozen native slaves.

Diogo approached Oludara with a water gourd in one hand and knelt beside him. He loosened the gag and offered Oludara a sip of water.

"It is good to see you again," said Oludara.

"Good to see you as well," said Diogo. "Although I suppose the circumstances could be better. I find you all too often bound in ropes or iron when we meet."

"True enough. Perhaps I'll try a more conventional outfit at our next encounter. But I must ask you something. We met a beast with an enormous mouth, one of your bannermen called it Magwhar. Do you know of it?"

Diogo nodded.

"That beast was the cause of my flight," said Oludara. "It slew many of your companions."

"I know," said Diogo. "Two men escaped and returned to us shortly before you appeared. They're off recovering from the fight."

"Did they mention it was Gerard and I who intervened and allowed them to escape?"

"They left that part out," Diogo replied with a wry smile. "I doubt it would sit well with Antonio in any case. Truth is, when your trail passed into Wytaka land, Antonio gave you both up for dead and called off the search. Even in his greatest rage, he's too smart to venture into that territory. Instead, he decided to go after Magwhar. He offered a reward of a two-hundred silver *tostões* to anyone who can bring it down; that's more than most of these men see in a year. Now that he's captured you, however, his attention has returned to other matters."

"Gerard?" asked Oludara.

"The one and only."

"Why does he hate Gerard so? Just because he is a Protestant?"

"No." Diogo sighed and shook his head. "That's what he tells everyone, but he doesn't care about that. Truth is, he sees Gerard as a threat."

"Really?"

"Antonio is astute. He recognized Gerard's potential the moment he met him. Antonio worked his way from poverty to become the greatest bannerman in Brazil. He wasn't about to let some stranger come and take that away from him. That's why he worked so hard to have Gerard sent away, and why he hunts him now with such fervor."

Oludara looked to where Antonio lay in a hammock, rocking leisurely back and forth. "He knows his enemy is near, yet he just lies there."

"Of course," said Diogo. "Why risk going into Wytaka territory to look for Gerard, when Antonio knows he'll come after you eventually?"

"No doubt. My people say: 'Once the tree falls, you can reach the branches.' My presence here puts Gerard in great danger; he will not abandon me. Where is Moara? She and I became friends when I travelled with you last. She could warn Gerard."

"Antonio sent her scouting days ago. There's no way to know when she'll return."

"It's a shame. she is a good woman, and competent."

"In any case," said Diogo, putting Oludara's gag firmly back in place, "I'll do what I can. But for now, it's better to keep our conversation short and not raise suspicion."

Diogo walked off to oversee the men setting up camp. Oludara, with no idea what to do, decided to rest and conserve his strength. He settled himself as best he could within his bindings. Just before he closed his eyes, however, he spotted movement to one side. He looked over and saw a snake slithering toward him.

This snake he *did* recognize. The Tupinambá called it *surucucu*, and its bite was fatal. He struggled to pull away, but his bonds held firm. When he attempted to call out, the gag muffled his shouts.

He fought with all his might to free even a hand, but made no progress. He then tried keeping as still as possible. The snake, however, did not deviate. It flicked its tongue as it slithered ever closer, never taking its gaze from Oludara. Oludara could do nothing but clench his muscles in expectation as the snake reared up to strike.

The surucucu's head shot forward at blinding speed, but just as quickly slammed to the ground. Oludara, wide-eyed, saw that a rapier had pierced it just behind the eyes and pinned it to the ground, dead. Still trembling from fear and disbelief, he led his gaze up the rapier's blade to stare into the smiling eyes of Antonio Dias Caldas.

Antonio jerked back the rapier, tearing it out so cleanly that the snake's head didn't even move. He pulled a rag from under his doublet and cleaned the tip.

"Don't think I did that out of kindness," said Antonio. "I'll spit you through the eyes just the same, once I'm done with Gerard."

Antonio sheathed his rapier and returned to his hammock, where he resumed his gentle rocking as if nothing had happened.

Oludara, calm even in the face of the African dragon, had felt true panic for one of the first times in his life. It took him many deep breaths to regain his nerves. Gerard had studied swordplay under European masters, but Oludara had never seen him do anything close to spearing a serpent in mid-strike. Oludara no longer knew which threat was the greatest: the Wytaka, Magwhar, or Antonio. Oludara had taken the man too lightly, and made a silent prayer to Olorun that Gerard would not do the same.

It had taken most of an hour for Oludara to calm down enough to sleep, only to be awoken by the sound of gunfire. The bannermen jumped to attention and grabbed their weapons.

Antonio leapt from his hammock. "That was Gerard's gun," he said, "I'd know that sound anywhere." He pointed to a group of men. "Francisco, Luis, Pedro, Mateus, you come with me. Diogo, guard the camp."

Antonio charged off with the group and Diogo chanced a glance at Oludara before shouting to the remaining bannermen, "You heard him! Spread out, guard the perimeter. I don't want Gerard sneaking up on us. I'll check on the prisoner."

As the men took up their positions, Oludara could see that Diogo had dispersed them cleverly; Gerard would have his chance to slip through. Once the camp had cleared out, Diogo knelt beside Oludara. Shortly after, Oludara could feel his bonds loosening.

"I have a feeling your friend is on his way," said Diogo.

The gag still in his mouth, Oludara could only nod in response. Then he caught a glimpse of movement in some bushes and Gerard peeked his head into view. Oludara grunted and pointed with his chin. Diogo turned and spotted Gerard, then motioned for him to keep down. Gerard complied.

Diogo nudged a rock toward Oludara with his foot.

"You'll have to strike me down," he said. "Hard enough to bruise, but not to break, if you don't mind. And don't forget your dagger; it's tucked into my belt."

Oludara eyed the dagger and nodded, just as his bonds gave way. He grasped the rock and hit Diogo solidly on the temple, spinning him around. He pulled his knife from Diogo's belt and ran in Gerard's direction.

"The prisoner," Diogo groaned out, softly enough that only the closest of the men would hear.

Two perimeter guards, however, had spotted Oludara's movement and closed in on him quickly, blocking his path with harquebuses raised in challenge. They failed to see Gerard, however, who jerked into motion behind them.

In an attempt to hold the men's attention, Oludara raised his arms and said, "Don't shoot!" Moments later, Gerard came running from behind with a log. He leveled it and knocked both men down. Oludara leapt over them and ran.

As he and Gerard fled side by side into the woods, he chanced a glance back to see two other men running at them and shouting. When they reached the middle of the camp, however, Diogo lurched into them and brought all three down in a heap. Oludara could just make out his yelling: "You imbeciles! Can't you run around me and not over me?"

Oludara grinned and returned his attention to their escape.

Gerard, exhausted, threw himself on the ground beside Oludara, who had collapsed moments before.

"Thank you, Gerard," Oludara said between staggered breaths. "How did you make the shot go off from so far away?"

"I used a counterweight and running water—set a drip in a pan to fill up and pull the trigger. Wasn't easy, but it worked.

"Problem is, that trick cost me my harquebus, the best gun I've ever had. It's a dear loss, but I'd trade a thousand of them for your life."

Oludara grinned in response.

"Even so," continued Gerard, "it would never have worked without Diogo's help. Too many remained in camp for me to free your bonds and get away."

"It is true," said Oludara. "My people say, 'Wherever a man dwells, his character goes with him.' Diogo has remained a good man, even among Antonio's scoundrels, and we are lucky to count him as an ally."

Oludara's expression turned serious. "Gerard, we need to talk about Antonio."

"It can wait," said Gerard. "Rest here, and I'll get you some water. We should refresh ourselves and be on our way. We'll have time for stories soon enough."

"You're right. For that long, at least, it can wait. And a bit of water will soothe my voice for the tale."

Oludara lay on the ground and Gerard took up his pack and set out. After a half-hour of roaming, he heard the sound of running water and followed it to a brook: its water chilled and crystalline. He took a water skin from his pack and knelt to fill it when a splashing sound upstream alerted him. He looked up to see a disheartening sight: Magwhar, no more than fifty paces away, had leapt into the stream for a drink.

Gerard, trying to remain inconspicuous, reached slowly for his rapier. He had it halfway unsheathed when a rustling sound on the opposite side of the river caused Magwhar to look up. The creature, scanning around, spotted Gerard. It squinted its eyes in recognition before howling and leaping to the bank.

As the beast bounded toward him, Gerard whipped out his rapier and readied it for impact. Just before Magwhar's final lunge, however, arrows whistled over from the other side of the river. Two of them flew into the creature's howling mouth and it screamed in rage. Eight of the long-haired Wytaka warriors emerged from the trees. Seven of them carried bows while one—the tallest and strongest of the group—wielded a sharpened stone axe.

Magwhar changed direction and headed towards them, lurching through the water as best it could. The tallest warrior signaled for the others to hold position and rushed forward alone, engaging the creature as it emerged on the riverbank. Magwhar lunged for him but he slipped under its swiping claws and swung the axe toward its mouth in an underhand motion. His blow shattered both the axe and a couple of Magwhar's teeth.

The creature screeched and clutched its mouth, then turned and—legs pumping so hard it resembled a jester's farce—ran into the cover of the forest.

Gerard, dumbfounded by the warrior's fearless attack, could only stand and watch as the man and his companions crossed the river in his direction. As they approached, Gerard sheathed his rapier and held up his hands in greeting.

"Thank you, great warrior," he said in Tupi, hoping the man might understand the tongue. "I am called Gerard van Oost."

The warrior showed no sign of recognition. He sneered at Gerard and shouted one word, "Kandl'o!", backhanding Gerard for emphasis. The powerful slap sent him sprawling. Gerard couldn't believe the man's strength.

The warrior turned and said something to the others. Two of them pulled Gerard to his feet and two others prodded him with their bows, leading him back across the river and away from Oludara.

The Wytaka marched Gerard for most of the day before emerging from the woods into an open, marshy area. The sunlight gave Gerard some small comfort after spending so much time in the confines of the forest.

The Wytaka village stood in the middle of the marsh, and Gerard judged that the chance of him sneaking out or Oludara sneaking in was close to none: the marsh afforded ample visibility in every direction.

The village could not be more different from those of the Tupinambá that Gerard had come to know so well. Instead of massive longhouses, the Wytaka used tiny huts built on stilts that kept them above water. Each hut contained a single entrance, no more than three feet high.

When Gerard reached the village with his warrior escort, the men called out and dozens of families crawled from the huts to look at him. Like the Tupinambá, they wore no clothing, at least in the conventional sense. Some wore feather decorations or had painted themselves with red dye from the *genipapo* trees, although the patterns differed from any he had seen. Many shouted at Gerard, but he couldn't understand a single word.

One man grabbed Gerard's hat and put it on, causing a great commotion as others gathered around and pointed. Another man pulled Gerard's sword from its sheath and stabbed at an imaginary foe, attracting a group of laughing, clapping children. Many of them danced and threw themselves to the ground, pretending to faint at the sight of the sword.

A group of women pulled off Gerard's pack and upended it, emptying its contents upon the ground. One of the women unfurled the banner and others pointed and laughed at Gerard's drawing of the elephant and macaw.

"It's just a rough idea," he said.

Several of the natives turned and shouted "Kandl'o!" at him. Like everything else they said, Gerard had no idea what it meant, but decided it best to keep his mouth shut for the time being.

When the tall Wytaka who had faced Magwhar came strutting into their midst, the other natives deferred to him. Gerard deduced he must be the chief. The chief watched in silence for a while, but when the others grew tired of taunting Gerard and playing with his things, he said something and pointed to a nearby woman. He then turned and walked off.

A group of warriors grabbed Gerard and hauled him toward one of the huts, then bent him over and shoved him through the tiny opening. The woman whom the chief had indicated crawled in after. After that, the men dispersed, leaving the two of them alone.

Gerard looked around the hut, but the only furnishings were a woven mat and a few containers. He looked to the woman, who sat staring at him. She was young, probably about seventeen, with high cheekbones, sunken eyes, and a straight nose.

"I know how this works," said Gerard. "I've heard the stories. First, I'm offered a woman to couple with."

The woman didn't appear to understand a word he said, but he blushed anyway.

"But don't think it's going to work." He waved a finger at her for emphasis. "I spent almost a year with the Tupinambá, and never once engaged in carnal pleasure. And don't think they didn't offer. I swear I shall remain celibate until marriage."

The woman said "Kandl'o!" then lay down and spread her naked legs open. Gerard gasped and looked away. After a few minutes, when it became apparent he wouldn't do anything, the woman made an angry clacking sound and rolled into one corner to sleep. Another woman brought in a wooden tray and set it on the floor. She looked quizzically back and forth between Gerard and the woman.

Gerard examined the tray to find a cooked piece of meat—venison from the look of it—some honey, and a pile of a tiny, yellow fruit he'd never seen before.

"I know this trick as well," he said. "You're here to make sure I get fattened up for your cannibalistic feast. The bigger the better, right?"

Gerard noticed the Wytaka woman staring at his belly. Gerard, robust even by European standards, was already much wider—and he feared, meatier—than any of the natives. He gulped.

"Maybe that won't take so long after all," he groaned. "I hope Oludara thinks of something quick."

Oludara awoke with a start. Without meaning to, he'd fallen asleep when Gerard set off in search of water. He looked around but noticed no sign of his companion. From the fading light, he knew that hours had passed.

Worried, but not panicked enough to call out and alert their enemies,

Oludara set out in search of Gerard. It didn't take him long to find his friend's trail, or to follow it to a stream. At the water's muddy edge, he startled to find Gerard's tracks surrounded by those of at least a half-dozen sets of bare feet. The bare feet reminded him of the Wytaka and he became truly worried for his friend's safety. The tracks seemed to come from and return to the stream, so Oludara crossed it.

What he found on the other side of the river bothered him even more. Signs of battle lay everywhere: blood, arrows, a shattered axe, and the remains of two huge teeth. Oludara's heart sank, imagining his companion crushed by Magwhar, or worse. He rushed around, looking for any sign of escape, until, greatly relieved, he discovered Gerard's boot prints heading away, surrounded yet again by tracks made from bare feet. The trail proved difficult to follow in the woods, and he lost it after only half a league.

For the next two days, Oludara wandered the woods looking for signs, while at the same time trying to avoid calling attention to himself. For the first time in his life, he couldn't find a single clue to guide him, and his worry grew with every passing moment. At the edge of breakdown, trembling in despair, he squeezed himself into the hollow of a tree and hid there to think. After several minutes of deep breathing, when he almost felt he had regained enough calm to continue his search, a strident voice cried out: "How did you ever make it this far into Wytaka land?"

Oludara first felt a pain in his chest, followed by one in his head when he jumped and struck it within the tree. Sacy-Perey stood just outside, a devilish smile upon his face.

When the pains subsided, Oludara said, "Be quiet, Sacy! I've spent days sneaking through this cursed forest. The enemy could be hiding anywhere."

"Well, I did warn you not to pass through here."

"I had no choice. The Wytaka captured Gerard and I must find him."

"Finding him isn't your problem," said Sacy. "Surely they've taken him to their village. They're probably fattening him up for a feast as we speak."

Oludara almost reached out to strangle the imp, but realized that would probably just make him disappear. Instead, he took a few more breaths to calm himself before speaking.

"Do you know where this village is, Sacy?"

"Of course! It's in a marsh, not too far from here. A mere two hours' walk that way." Sacy pointed southeast. "But as I said, finding him isn't your problem. Saving him, that's another matter. The Wytaka don't take kindly to anyone robbing their meals."

"It won't be the first time I've rescued Gerard."

"They live in an open marsh. There's no cover, no way to sneak up on them."

Oludara considered this for a time. Then he climbed from the tree and stretched his limbs.

"In that case," he said. "I will not sneak."

Two warriors unceremoniously tossed Gerard into a three-inch deep puddle in the middle of the village.

The chief and a dozen warriors had spent the last two days parading him around the neighboring villages, which, for some reason, induced dancing and feasting at each stop. They had finally returned to their own village and—as Gerard couldn't help but notice—were preparing a feast of their own.

Everyone had decorated themselves with red dye. Women prepared food and drink while men played drums and flutes. People danced whenever it took their fancy. A large fire had been lit in the middle of the village, but no meat was anywhere in sight.

"Looks like feast day," Gerard said with a sigh, "and I have a feeling I know what they're having for the main course."

Gerard had attempted escape on two occasions, once by day and once by night, but had failed utterly both times. He could neither fool nor outrun the Wytaka warriors, and had run out of ideas. When Oludara had not appeared, Gerard had resigned himself to playing his part in their feast.

When all was ready, four warriors wrapped a cord around Gerard's waist and held it tight. The chief—so covered in feathers, he looked more bird than man—appeared from his hut. He approached Gerard, shouting and pumping his fist in the air. In his other hand he held a carved wooden mace, also decorated in feathers.

The warriors holding Gerard tightened the cord, squeezing the air from his lungs and holding him in place. The chief shouted ever louder and the villagers joined in a frenzied dance around him. Everyone cheered shrill screams as the chief raised the mace above Gerard's head for the killing blow.

At that moment, however, the drummers stopped. People turned their attention away from the chief and everyone fell silent, save for whispered hushes. It took all Gerard's nerve to open his eyes and not stare at the mace hovering over his head, but he followed the natives' gaze to see Oludara standing tall at the edge of the village.

Once the initial surprise passed, the natives sprang into movement. Curious children circled Oludara at a distance. Warriors rushed to grab their bows.

"Run, Oludara!" said Gerard. "There are too many."

"I need defeat only one," said Oludara. He raised a finger and pointed toward the chief.

The chief remained with his feet planted and chest held high as Oludara, his finger never wavering, approached him. Once he stood ten feet from the chief, Oludara pulled his shirt over his head and tossed it to the ground, then removed the ivory dagger from his belt. He pointed to himself and back at the chief.

The chief scoffed at the challenge, as did most of the tribe. He said something, almost casually, and his men lowered their bows and backed away. He spoke again and one of his men came running with a stone axe, which he traded for the ceremonial mace. He motioned for Oludara to approach.

"Don't!" shouted Gerard. "He's inhuman. You don't know—"

Someone yelled "Kandl'o!" and slapped Gerard mid-sentence, silencing him.

Oludara and the chief circled each other several times before Oludara finally chanced a feint. The chief didn't even wince, even though it halted just inches from his torso. Instead, he returned the feint with a lightning cut which Oludara barely dodged.

Gerard watched in anguish as the two battled, trading lunges, slashes, and feints. The chief took a couple of cuts to his arms, but Oludara had the worst of it: a deep gash bloodied his collarbone and nicks glistened in half-a-dozen places. His movements had slowed visibly, while the chief continued confident. Gerard had almost given up hope when he spotted smoke rising from one of the huts.

"Fire!" he shouted, and a dozen Wytaka shouted back "Kandl'o" without even taking the time to look away from the fight. Two more lines of smoke filled the sky before others finally took notice and shouted "Boteh!" People ran to grab bowls and jars of water. The men holding the rope around Gerard's waist ran off, leaving him free.

A stilt gave way on another hut, causing it to crash into a puddle beneath.

"What's going on here?" Gerard asked himself.

Then he heard shrill laughter and spotted a red hat bobbing up and down beside a hut. The next moment, the hat disappeared.

"The little devil," he said, smiling.

Sacy appeared at Gerard's side with his rapier and pack in hand. He tossed them to Gerard and said, "Don't just stand there you fools, run!" Then he disappeared again.

Gerard looked back to see Oludara and the chief still focused on each other. It appeared that Oludara had heard Sacy's advice, however, because he lowered his knife and ran. The chief took a step after him, but paused after finally taking in the chaos around him. He lowered his axe, stood up straight, and shouted commands at his villagers, organizing their efforts to quench the fires.

Gerard followed Oludara and said, "Are you all right to run?"

"I'll manage," said Oludara, though Gerard could see he was obviously weakened from loss of blood.

The two of them sprinted toward the woods, and to their relief, no one followed. As they ran, the Wytaka yells and Sacy's laughing grew ever fainter.

Just as they reached the edge of the woods, however, Sacy's laugher changed to a shriek. Gerard paused to look back and spotted Sacy at the edge of the village, frantically patting his bald head, searching in vain for his pointy hat. He turned to see the chief just behind him, holding it triumphantly in the air. Sacy tried to run, but the chief sent him sprawling with a swift kick, then grabbed him by his neck and carried him back to the village like a kitten.

Yet again, Oludara and Gerard lay panting side by side in the woods. Once he'd caught his breath, Oludara sat up and found some bandages in Gerard's pack, offering silent thanks to Sacy for recovering it. He staunched his wounds as best he could.

"A third capture?" gasped Gerard. "This is preposterous!"

"It is difficult to believe," replied Oludara. "Unfortunately, we must go back. We can't leave Sacy with the Wytaka."

"As tempting as the idea is to move on and free ourselves forever from that prankster, I have to agree. He saved our lives today. Although I can't for the life of me say why; he's never risked his neck for us before."

"Perhaps he thought saving us would be easier than finding someone else to pester."

"Perhaps," said Gerard. "But what can we do? As creative as your idea was of walking straight into their village, I don't think I'd risk it a second time."

"Neither would I," said Oludara, shaking his head. "If Sacy hadn't intervened, it would have been the end of me. That chief is incredible. Rarely have I seen such a great fighter." Oludara gave an exhausted sigh. "We have faced too many trials this week. I am too tired even to think."

"And I'm tired of running. It seems we've done nothing else these past days."

"We are surrounded on all sides by the most dangerous enemies we have ever faced. What can one do in a situation like this?"

"No plan?" asked Gerard, appearing genuinely surprised. "No saying from your people this time?"

Oludara looked down and shook his head.

"In that case," said Gerard, "I believe *I* recall a saying." He grinned slyly as he spoke.

Oludara raised an eyebrow. "Really? What is it?"

"An old Greek named Aeschylus once said, 'there is no disgrace in an enemy suffering at an enemy's hand'. We face three foes who hate each other as much as they do us. Why are *we* the ones fighting them all?"

Gerard heard Oludara's signal: a fox howl. He took a deep breath, then ran toward the camp. A man on guard duty, some hundred feet away, spotted him first.

"It's him!" shouted the man. "It's that van Oost fellow."

Gerard slid, pretending to slip. He took his time straightening up, wobbling around until Antonio and a dozen men armed with harquebuses came running. Diogo wasn't among them.

"Stay back, Antonio!" yelled Gerard, waving his hands. "It's dangerous."

"Take him!" Antonio yelled at his men. "One hundred tostões, dead or alive."

At that, Antonio's men gave a cheer and charged. Gerard turned and fled.

As the first shots rang out behind him, Gerard knew his run would be short. He had spent the last day leaving a trail for Antonio, and, even with the man's fear of the Wytaka, his rival couldn't resist the bait. Antonio had set up camp no more than a quarter mile from the Wytaka marsh. In the next moments, Gerard would either reach his destination, or take a bullet trying.

Nevertheless, it seemed an eternity before Gerard finally broke from the woods and into the marsh. The moment he did, he was greeted by the scene he had desired: the Wytaka chief, alerted by the harquebus fire, led some forty warriors straight in his direction.

The chief didn't slow his pace when Gerard came into view, but when the first of Antonio's men appeared from the woods, he called out an order and his warriors lined up, bows drawn.

At least one of Antonio's men had enough sense to scream a terrified warning of "Wytaka!" before turning tail to flee. The other men, however, continued pouring into the marsh from sheer momentum. After spotting the Wytaka line, they quickly joined in the retreat. Gerard fled just behind them.

With another command, the chief sent his men sprinting into the woods. Great runners, they closed quickly with the bannermen. Antonio bellowed orders, calling for his men to stand their ground, and through sheer force of will managed to put some order into his retreating troop.

At that, the two sides paused to organize into jagged lines among the trees. Then, the combat began. Gerard, caught in the middle, dropped to the ground and pulled the brim of his hat down over his ears as arrows and shot whistled overhead. Both sides ignored him for the moment, locked in their own deadly duel. He made a silent prayer for Oludara to arrive quickly. As much as he had the right to bear a grudge against both sides, he had no desire to see the affair turn into a bloodbath.

Moments later, thudding footsteps and a familiar gorilla-like bellow answered his prayer. Oludara passed him on one side while Magwhar came crashing after.

Shouts of "Magwhar!" echoed from both sides. That word, at least, shared the same meaning and terror for everyone involved. For the moment, Wytaka and bannermen forgot each other and trained their fire on the beast. The Magwhar, finding itself assailed on both sides and unsure where to flee, screamed and ripped trees from the ground to toss at its attackers.

Gerard scouted through Antonio's men and spotted the object of his desire—his harquebus—in the hands of a skinny Portuguese man. The man knelt upon the ground for a shot at Magwhar and Gerard rushed in his direction. The man took his shot and, in the ensuing cloud of smoke, Gerard yanked the gun from his hands and sent him sprawling. The man looked up, flabbergasted.

“Thanks for holding on to that for me,” said Gerard, already sprinting for the marsh.

As he ran, he spotted Oludara sneaking up on the chief. The chief noticed and readied himself for an attack. Oludara lunged and the chief hacked at his head, but Oludara ducked the blow and side-armed a hand toward his true objective: Sacy’s hat, stuffed into a feather band on one of the chief’s arms. Oludara yanked the hat free and didn’t stop moving as he made his own dash for the marsh. The chief roared in fury and almost went after him, but regained his composure and returned his attention to his men and Magwhar.

Jupi-açu, the Wytaka chief, surveyed the remnants of the battle. Magwhar lay unmoving. It had withstood hundreds of arrows and gunshots, but the dreaded beast—a longtime enemy of the Wytaka—had finally fallen. Many of Jupi-açu’s men had been injured, but he saw no dead among his own. The Portuguese cowards had fled during the confusion.

One of his men called him back to the marsh. When he reached the clearing, he spotted movement in the distance. In his village, he could just make out the two strange men trying to undo Sacy-Perey’s bonds, until the dark one had the idea of placing the devil’s hat upon its head, at which point it disappeared and reappeared nearby, leaving the coils of rope to collapse on their own. The three ran off, Sacy in the middle, hopping deftly on his one leg.

Several of his warriors gathered around Jupi-açu, awaiting orders.

“Do we chase them?” asked a warrior at his side.

Jupi-açu considered, then laughed heartily.

“You can catch and hold one devil,” he replied, “perhaps two if you are lucky. But, as we have seen, never three at one time.

“These men are not our enemies. They fight the invaders, just as we do, and unlike the cowards who come to take our land, these possess the spirit of the Wytaka. Send word to the other tribes to let them pass. Make no contact with them, just leave them on their way.”

Jupi-açu turned back to fetch Magwhar's corpse. His captive had been lost, but the tribe had a new reason to feast.

Antonio looked at his men in disgust. It had taken the better part of a day to regroup them, and he wasn't sure they were worth the time after their debacle with the Wytaka. He called over Diogo, who had single-handedly tracked down many of the stragglers.

"What are our losses?" he asked.

"Many of the men took an arrow or two during the fight," said Diogo, "but only one, Everardo, died from his wounds. Magwhar crushed Bartolomeu and Domingos."

Antonio removed his hat and made the sign of the cross, then put it back on.

"It could have been worse, I suppose," he said.

"What will we do now?"

"We won't be traveling through Wytaka land, that's for sure. Gerard will have to wait. We have business down in Santos, so we'll go inland and skirt around their territory."

"That will take time," said Diogo. "And who knows what lurks there? It might be better to double back to Victoria and hire a ship."

"Perhaps," mused Antonio. "By land or by sea, it doesn't matter; I'll get there all the same. And if Gerard van Oost somehow survives the Wytaka, he won't last for long. I swear I'll find him on the other side."

Gerard, Oludara, and Sacy rested on a wide beach which—and Gerard gave silent thanks for this—ended in dunes that hid all sight of the forest behind them. Gerard sat watching the waves while Oludara and Sacy lay with their hands behind their heads, looking up at the sky.

"A shame we could not take the hide of that Magwhar," said Oludara. "It's leather would make a fine, protective vest."

Gerard's stomach turned at the thought of anyone wearing a piece of that malodorous, abominable creature.

"Yes," said Gerard, "what a shame..." Then he turned to Sacy. "One question, Sacy. Do you happen to know what 'kandl'o' means in the Wytaka tongue? It is a word they spoke often, at least to me."

Sacy rolled on the ground, holding his sides and laughing. "Shut up!" he gurgled out between laughs.

"Why are you telling Gerard to shut up?" asked Oludara.

"No, the word means 'shut up' in Wytaka."

"Much as I suspected," Gerard said with a frown.

Sacy hopped up and looked at them with a rare, somber expression. Then, he stared down the shore to the south.

"I've quite enjoyed watching your bumbling travels," he said, "but I must travel no farther. My domain ends here."

Gerard, his heart soaring at the notion of traveling unimpeded by the imp's unending nuisance, bit his lip to keep a smile from breaking across his face.

"That's too bad," he said. "It won't be the same without you, but I think we'll get on all right."

"Perhaps," said Sacy. "But if you should chance upon some other Sacy, be sure to tell him that Sacy-Perey is the only *true* Sacy."

"*Other* Sacy?" said Gerard, almost choking on the words.

With a final giggle, Sacy disappeared.

Gerard, crestfallen, looked to Oludara.

"What did he mean by 'other' Sacy?" he asked.

Oludara could do no more than chuckle in reply.

The smell seemed too good to be true. Abandoning caution, the anaconda slipped from the stream and approached the corpse. Her senses hadn't lied: the Magwhar had indeed been slain.

Readying herself for the meal of a lifetime, she unhooked her jaw and slithered toward the beast. She knew it would stretch her to the limit to swallow the giant creature, but refused to relinquish such a glorious treat.

That's when she sensed movement and rocked her head from side to side, flicking her tongue. She caught a scent which made her turn back in panic. The Magwhar's stench had masked that of something even worse.

Turning, she discovered she had nowhere to run. Wytaka, bows raised, surrounded her on all sides. One of them, taller and broader than the rest, approached her with axe in hand, his lips curved up in a smile.

Chapter 5

A Tumultuous Convergence of Misfits, Monsters, and Frenchmen

A BLUE TANAGER STOOD upon a clay wall, waiting—along with many others of her kind—for the daily snack provided by the humans who lived within. One of the humans appeared, carrying the tanager's favorite food, papayas, and she added her happy chirping to the chorus that broke out around her.

The man, one of the ones that carried the booming sticks, split four papayas and laid them out. The tanager and her companions trilled at each other, establishing eating order for the day.

Just as she picked her first nibble from the tasty fruit, a thunderous crack echoed from the woods. The tanager cocked her head and looked out over the forest, where a tall tree shook in time with a second crack, this one nearer. The tanager, used to such things, returned to her pecking.

A third crack, this one very close, brought a tree crashing down. The tanager, nervous, thought it best to take her leave and come back when things quieted down. Just as she took flight, she spotted two men—one light-skinned and one dark-skinned—burst from the edge of the woods and into the clearing below.

Gerard panted as his flight led him zigzagging through the forest. He had lost sight of Oludara, and no longer knew if he continued intact or had been gored by their pursuer: an abnormally large, black bull with glowing red eyes.

Gerard's dodging had successfully caused the bull to strike several trees—and completely topple a few of them in the process. Each strike to the head bought Gerard precious moments of flight, and the continued pounding seemed to be taking a toll on the bull, which required a bit more time to recover after each blow. At the same time, Gerard didn't know how much longer he could keep up the pace himself.

Without warning, he broke from the trees and into a clearing of stumps, where the forest had been cleared away. At first, he was dismayed at seeing his cover break, thinking he would have to dive back in. However, he looked up the rise to spot a ten-foot clay wall some hundred yards before him. Atop the wall, far to his right, he spotted a bastion manned by two soldiers, and, just below it, a closed wooden gate. Gerard knew he had but a heartbeat to make a decision: run for the gate or return to the woods.

"Open the gate!" he yelled as he charged toward the bastion. "Open the gate!"

Oludara broke from the woods off to Gerard's right, paused to look where Gerard was headed, then joined in his flight.

Gerard's lungs burst with the effort. He could hear the hooves thudding ever closer, could imagine the bull lowering its head for the gore and knew he had no chance.

A volley of shots rang from the bastion and the hoofbeats paused, substituted by a ferocious bellow. Gerard chanced a look back to see the beast shake its head, then stubbornly continue the chase. Looking forward, he saw the gate opening, but knew he would never make it in time. He decided on a different course of action.

"Oludara," he said, "keep to the gate."

Oludara continued for the gate and Gerard veered away from it, heading instead for the nearest section of wall.

"Try me, you overgrown steak!" he shouted at the bull.

To his satisfaction, the bull followed him. He reached the wall and turned around to face his pursuer.

Oludara, arriving at the gate, turned back and yelled, "Gerard, get out of there!"

As Gerard rummaged through his pack, he shouted back, "I know what I'm doing. I think."

The bull charged him at full speed, and Gerard's hand finally brushed his target: his banner. He yanked it from the pack with a flourish and waved it to one side.

The bull, still charging, looked back and forth between Gerard and the banner, as if unable to make up its mind. Gerard braced for impact, but at the last moment the bull swerved, tearing through the banner and smashing into the packed clay beyond. The impact caused the beast to flip up and strike the wall, back first. A crack radiated out from the bull until an entire ten-foot section collapsed upon it, leaving only rubble between the two wooden supports on either side.

Gerard wasted no time in pulling out his rapier and stabbing at the only patch of skin he could spot under the rubble: the rump. The bull let out a half-groan, half-squeal and jerked itself from the wreckage. It looked Gerard in the eye and snorted. Gerard leveled his rapier at the bull's head and prepared to meet its attack.

A second volley rang from the bastion and interrupted the confrontation. The bull—bleeding all over from cuts and punctures—snorted and raced back to the woods.

Gerard sheathed his rapier, dusted off his doublet, and adjusted his wide-brimmed hat. He then climbed over the rubble to pass inside the wall. Oludara rushed toward him.

"Gerard," said Oludara, "that was brilliant. How did you think of such an idea?"

"A Spaniard once told me you could fool a bull that way," responded Gerard, "though I hardly believed him."

"Why not?"

"You don't know many Spaniards, do you?"

Oludara didn't seem to understand the jest, so Gerard let it pass.

"Are you injured?" asked Oludara.

"Escaped without a cut," replied Gerard. He held up the crudely-drawn banner, now with two jagged rips down the middle. "This will need some stitches, though."

At that moment, the two soldiers from the bastion joined them. Both bore harquebuses and appeared to be Portuguese, so close in appearance they might be brothers. One wore his hair long and sported a thick black mustache pulled out to paintbrush-like tips. The other wore his hair shorter and used a full beard. Both wore cotton pants, simple leather vests, and iron helmets.

"Ironic," said the first man. "That's the same section of wall we fixed last time the bull smashed into it."

"Although that time," said the other one, "we had to clean up what was left of Afonso as well."

The two men made the sign of the cross at the words.

"I thank you both for your timely shots," said Gerard. "My name is Gerard van Oost, and this is my companion Oludara."

"Welcome to Saint Sebastian of Rio de Janeiro," said the first man. "My name is Luis."

"And mine Duarte," added the second.

"Rio de Janeiro," said Gerard with a sparkle in his eye. "We finally made it."

"A strange trio you formed with the bull," said Luis, "but not the strangest thing we've seen running out of those woods."

"Nor the most dangerous," added Duarte, "not by far."

"What was that creature?" asked Oludara.

"That one?" said Luis. "We just call it 'The Bull'."

"I'm sure the Indians call it something like 'bulgawalagali'," said Duarte. "They always come up with long, bizarre names for things."

"What do you mean, 'that one'?" asked Gerard. "There are others?"

"Well," said Luis, "there's the giant snake."

"And the black pig," added Duarte.

"And don't forget the humongous crocodile with poison breath."

"Well," said Gerard, "it appears there is much we could do here."

"How so?" asked Duarte.

"We've conquered many perilous beasts on our journeys."

"Like you conquered that one today?" asked Luis, causing both soldiers to snicker.

"Well," said Gerard, embarrassed, "we do have better days, to be sure."

"You *enjoy* fighting those creatures?" asked Duarte. "How ludicrous."

"Absurd," said Luis. "What kind of person goes looking for trouble like that?"

"In any case," said Duarte, "if you *are* looking to get yourselves killed, you've come to the right place. Rio de Janeiro is the worst post in Brazil."

"Because of the monsters?" asked Oludara.

"Because of the monsters, the pirates..."

"And the French," added Luis.

Both soldiers shuddered at the word.

"Why the French?" asked Oludara.

"They used to have a settlement here," said Luis.

"'Antarctic France' they called it," said Duarte. "That is, until we booted them out."

"And let's just say they weren't too happy about it."

"They must have put a curse upon this bay when they left. It's the only explanation for the constant convergence of pirates, monsters..."

"And Frenchmen," completed Luis.

"What an unusual place, Gerard," remarked Oludara. "Perhaps there *is* a curse.

"Gerard?" came a voice from behind them. "A French name if I've ever heard one."

They turned to see a dark-skinned man with an eye patch eying them suspiciously. He appeared to be caboclo, of mixed European and native blood. He wore his hair cropped short and his face shaven smooth. He used a yellow-and-green doublet and a fine hat.

"Luis and Duarte," he said, looking Gerard and Oludara up and down with his one eye, "what did you drag out of the woods today?"

Gerard offered the man a hand, "Gerard van Oost, if you please," he said. "From Brabant, not France. And this is my companion Oludara, a free man."

The man continued to eye him suspiciously. "Mercenaries, then?"

"Of sorts. We're bannermen, by allowance of the governor."

"I suppose that's document enough. If the governor is giving banners to Frenchmen, he's either given leave of his senses or given up on Brazil entirely. I'm Simon Santo, captain of the guard. I'll need to see your papers, of course, and your banner."

"Our banner is the Elephant and Macaw." Gerard held up the tattered banner.

Simon held a fist over his mouth to stifle a laugh. The two soldiers snickered openly.

Gerard frowned and stuffed the banner back into his pack.

"Oludara and I would like to stay here for a time," he said.

Simon considered before responding. "No one stays here for free. As long as you remain in Rio de Janeiro, you'll have duties, including patrol."

"It's dangerous work," advised Luis.

"We've lost five men this year," added Duarte.

"And it's only March."

"We'll take our chances," said Gerard.

"Fine then," said Simon. "Go to the barracks for a meal, then find these two for your first patrol."

Rio de Janeiro's fort stood upon a hill overlooking the bay. Oludara didn't pay much attention on his way up, but at the top, Gerard paused to sweep out his arm in an exaggerated gesture.

"Just look at this," he said.

Oludara followed Gerard's movement and found the sight indeed impressive. A massive, island-filled bay stretched out before them. Rock formations covered by lush greenery stretched toward the sky on all sides, like the fingertips of a giant cupping the bay in its hands.

"This port is astonishing," said Gerard, speaking excitedly. "I can see why the French covet it so. It's not only beautiful, but ample. There are a half-dozen landmarks recognizable from leagues away at sea. It will be almost unconquerable, once it's properly established." Gerard paused and looked back at the city. "Although it appears they're a long way from that."

Oludara could see what he meant. The city, if you could call it that, was formed by no more than thirty low buildings, almost all built from clay. The wall was buttressed clay, with four bastions and some cannon spread around the perimeter. The unfinished fort was being pieced together from clay and stone.

"Nothing here is built to last," said Gerard. "It's no city, not yet, just the promise of one. It will make a jewel of a port one day, though—beautiful and powerful."

After a few minutes admiring the scenery, they entered the barracks, which turned out to be nothing more than a dining hall with some long tables, a kitchen, and a row of hammocks for sleeping. Too late for breakfast and too early for dinner, they only found one person inside, a peg-legged man with wispy black strands of hair surrounding a bald crown.

Gerard held out a hand to the man and said, "I'm Gerard van Oost and this is Oludara. We've just joined the garrison here and were sent by Captain Simon for a meal." The man shook Gerard's hand but didn't even glance at Oludara.

"You've come to the right place," he replied. "My name is Pedro Galo and when I'm not soldiering, I'm cooking. I'll see what I can round up."

They followed Pedro to the kitchen and he grabbed two plates. He ladled out some white meat with onions from a pot.

"You're lucky," he said, "still some left from last night."

"This is fine fare for soldiers," said Oludara, his mouth watering at the sight.

"Wild pig and wild onions, the wilderness here provides a bounty. If food and water alone could win wars, this would be the most powerful city on Earth. Unfortunately for us, powder and shot don't grow on trees."

Pedro added figs, quince cheese, and two slabs of bread to the plates.

As the two walked back to the tables, Gerard exclaimed, "Can you believe this feast? They even have wheat bread here. We've been eating that cassava hardtack for so long, I've forgotten what it tastes like."

Oludara held out an arm to silence his companion. An old native sat at one table with a meal of his own before him. The man used his hair in a tonsure, like the Tupinambá natives they knew so well, but it shone white. A crow perched on his right shoulder.

"Did you see that man when we came in?" asked Oludara.

"No, can't say I did."

"Don't you think you would have noticed him?"

Oludara would have given the strange man a wide berth, but Gerard shrugged and sat down across from him. Oludara sat beside Gerard and wrinkled his nose when he spotted the old man's plate. It contained a meat he didn't recognize, raw to the point of bloody. The man pulled off a dripping hunk and slung it into his mouth. Oludara looked away from the grotesque display and returned his attention to his own plate, although the better part of his appetite had disappeared.

Gerard took in a sharp breath before regaining his composure. "My name is Gerard van Oost," he said, "and this is my companion, Oludara. We're bannermen, come to join the garrison for a time."

The man looked back and forth between the two. The crow mimicked the movement, looking them over.

"I know of you and your banner, Gerard van Oost," the native replied in Tupi.

Oludara noticed his companion flushing red. He knew how much Gerard desired recognition. It appeared that word of their adventures had spread.

As if reading his thoughts, the native turned toward him and said, "I didn't say I've *heard* of you, Oludara. I said I know who you are."

Oludara and Gerard looked at each other but said nothing. Instead, they returned their concentration to the food and ignored the unusual man. The native stared at Gerard, as if studying him. When he next spoke, he switched to Portuguese, causing them both to look up in surprise.

"Your actions will decide the fate of an empire, van Oost."

Gerard choked on his food and had to gulp down some water to clear his throat. When he could finally speak again, he asked, "Empire? What empire?"

"The Empire of Brazil!"

Oludara and Gerard laughed in unison.

"Hah," said Gerard. "Brazil is barely a colony."

"It is now," said the man, "but not forever. And *you* will decide who is to rule."

Gerard snorted. "Even if I did believe that this 'Brazilian Empire' might someday come to pass, it's none of my concern who rules it. I came here for adventure, not politics."

"Perhaps you will change your mind, before this day is done. Choose well."

The man pushed his plate toward Gerard. "I'm not hungry for this anymore," he said. "Would you care for a bite?"

Gerard couldn't hide his disgust. "No thank you," he said. "I'm fine with what I have."

"That's what I figured. You see? You've already made one choice. One more awaits."

Without another word, the man stood and left, leaving Gerard and Oludara to shrug their shoulders and, after removing the plate of disgusting meat from their sight, return to their meals.

Out for their first guard duty, Oludara and Gerard followed Luis and Duarte along the coast. As they passed from the city and into the surrounding farms, Oludara spotted hundreds of natives, some living in their own villages, others dispersed among the European families settled there. He was thankful not to spot any African slaves, but noticed with distaste that many of the natives served the same purpose.

When they passed beyond the farms and into the forest, Gerard grabbed Oludara's arm and broke his attention. Gerard pointed up to a tree from which hung bunches of an enormous, orange fruit.

"Look at the size of those!" he said. "They're as big as the famed gourds of Cyprus."

"Don't ever sleep under one of those trees," said Luis.

"We once found a soldier with his neck broken," said Duarte. "One of those things fell on his head."

"Like we said, this is the worst place in Brazil to be a soldier."

"Even the fruit here is dangerous," agreed Duarte.

"We must be careful," said Oludara. "What if that enraged bull returns?"

"Don't worry about him," said Luis. "He'll lick his wounds for at least a month before he comes back."

"Yeah," agreed Duarte. "By then, we'll have the wall patched."

"You should be worried about all the *other* creatures around here."

Oludara recalled the old man they had met in the barracks. “I have a question,” he said. “We met an old native in the barracks today, one with white hair.”

“And his diet is somewhat unusual,” added Gerard.

“Is he part of the garrison?”

“A white-haired native?” asked Luis. “That’s a rare sight. And we certainly don’t have anyone like that back at the fort.”

“A crow was perched on his shoulder,” said Oludara.

Luis and Duarte looked at each other with wide eyes.

“Stay away from that one,” said Luis.

“Why?” asked Oludara. “Who is it?”

“Better to ask ‘what’ than ‘who’. If you think the bull is dangerous, you should...”

Duarte, his gaze focused on the ocean, interrupted Luis with a “Hush!” He pointed out to sea.

“Oh no,” said Luis.

Squinting, Oludara could just make out three ships on the horizon.

“Pirates?” asked Gerard.

“Worse,” said Luis.

“Frenchmen?” asked Oludara, chancing a joke.

“Worse,” said Duarte.

“What is worse than that?”

Luis and Duarte responded in unison, “French pirates.”

“I am most certainly *not* a pirate,” came a strongly-accented voice behind them.

Dozens of soldiers filed out from the woods. A robust, confident man stepped to the front.

“In fact, I am the new governor of Antarctic France.”

The Frenchmen bound Gerard and the others and forced them to march back toward the city. The soldiers, most of them harquebusiers, wore simple cotton clothes suitable to the climate. Their leader, however, who called himself Guy de Coullons, was the very picture of extravagance.

A thin mustache and goatee accented the man's long face. He wore a hat with a huge brim curling up on one side. He used a golden yellow jacket and doublet, and carried a rapier with a hilt so decorated Gerard had no idea how the man handled it. His vest sported an enormous cross. The man sweat in the tropical heat and appeared disgusted by everything around him.

Luis and Duarte walked in solemn silence until Luis finally asked Guy, "What are you doing here?"

"Isn't it obvious?" he replied. "We're here to destroy your pathetic settlement and build a glorious city in its place; the kind of city a port like this deserves."

"You're nothing but pirates," said Duarte.

Guy stopped and turned on Duarte, furious. "I, fool," he said, tapping at the cross on his chest, "am a Knight of Malta! And if you don't show respect, it will cost you your head."

Gerard decided to intervene and perhaps develop some rapport with the man by speaking to him in French. "My name is Gerard van Oost," he said. "I'm originally from Brabant, but had the pleasure of living in France for many years."

Upon hearing Gerard speak French, Luis and Duarte both cast him hate-filled stares. Guy's face, on the other hand, turned to delight.

"Oh," he replied in French. "I can't believe I found someone cultured in this province. I really didn't think it possible. This coast is crawling with Portuguese scum, not a gentleman among them. It's like the king of Portugal decided to clean out the prisons and send all the riffraff here. Even worse, of course, are the savages." The man shuddered while saying it.

Gerard also shuddered, at Guy's use of the word "savages". *Bad enough the Portuguese call them 'Indians'*, he thought.

"How this terrible place exhausts me," continued Guy. "Nicolas!"

A clean-shaven soldier with a wide jaw stepped forward.

"Bring me some cheese," ordered Guy.

Gerard noticed the soldier's lips tighten at the request, but he nodded curtly and strode off toward the supplies.

Guy looked back to Gerard. "Would you care to join me for a bit of cheese?"

Gerard looked down at his bonds. "Well, yes...but..."

"Please pardon my manners." Guy motioned to some soldiers, "Untie this man immediately."

While a man removed Gerard's bonds, Nicolas returned with two other soldiers. One set out a sheet and Nicolas filled it with fruits and cheeses. Another soldier brought a jug and two goblets. The French soldiers scowled at being treated like menservants, but Guy seemed oblivious. Guy sat down and motioned for Gerard to join him. Out of the corner of his eye, Gerard noticed Luis and Duarte, furious. Oludara, on the other hand, gave Gerard the slightest of nods, pleased with the turn of events.

Gerard rubbed his wrists to get the blood flowing and sat down. Guy handed him a goblet and toasted. Gerard took a whiff and inhaled a scent so rich—when compared to the local wines—as to be almost dizzying. The smell brought back memories of blackcurrants and the fields of France. He took a sip and enjoyed the caress of the tart, hearty wine along his tongue.

"A Burgundy, I presume?" he asked.

Guy's wide smile confirmed his suspicion. "Only the best, of course. None of that upstart vinegar from Bordeaux."

Gerard's family had at one time traded wines from Bordeaux, but he knew better than to mention that fact.

"I see I was right about you, Gerard," said Guy. "You're a man of culture." He sliced off a piece of cheese and offered it to Gerard. "Isn't it nice to have a taste of Europe in the middle of this waste?"

"Most excellent indeed," said Gerard, happily accepting the firm, yellow cheese. He took an over-eager bite, and saw Guy's nose crinkle in disapproval. After gulping down the mouthful, he tried to turn attention away from his *faux pas*. "This land is far from a waste, Guy. It has much to offer."

"I hope so," sighed Guy, "or it will be simply unbearable to rule it."

"Might I ask your plan?" asked Gerard.

Guy looked at Duarte and Luis and shrugged. "I suppose it doesn't make any difference now. By land and sea, tonight we make a two-pronged attack. The town's defenses are laughable: less than forty soldiers and no more than a hundred colonists capable of bearing arms. They are low on guns, powder, sulfur, and shot. I have three armed galleons and over three-hundred men. I'll take the city in a matter of hours."

"How do you know so much of their defenses?" asked Gerard.

"We captured two patrols. I'm sure they assumed some deadly creature devoured them; this land is crawling with them."

"So I've heard."

Two of Guy's men approached with baskets. Nicolas exchanged some words with them, then brought one of the baskets to show Guy. It was filled to the top with oysters.

"The soldiers found these oysters in the trees. They must have washed up there."

"Well, boil them," said Guy, dismissing Nicolas with a curt wave. He returned his attention to Gerard. "Oysters on trees! Perhaps this land won't be so bad after all. Once we deal with the savages, of course. They're sure to put up more of a fight than that Portuguese rabble."

"I have lived among the Tupinambá," said Gerard. "They are not so savage as you might think."

"Not savage?" Guy scoffed. "They walk as naked as newborn babes, kill each other for no reason, and like the anthropophagi of Scythia, devour their enemies. Their only resemblance to humans is the way they walk on two legs. In all other respects, they are nothing but animals.

"But like dogs," continued Guy, "they have their uses. There are still a few thousand of our old allies, the Tamoio, hiding away inland. Those boors will build us an entire city for no more than a crateful of fishhooks."

Gerard gritted his teeth. "I think you should get to know them better before you make judgment."

"What, like the Portuguese do? They go so far as to breed with the savages. Disgusting. But enough of that, let's talk about matters at hand."

With a snap of his fingers, Guy called forth a soldier bearing Gerard's rapier and harquebus. He held the harquebus in his hands and admired it.

"I see you know your weapons, Gerard. A wheel lock harquebus," he said, referring to the gun's mechanism, "a gentleman's weapon; none of that shaphaunce rubbish used by bandits. And the ironwork is exquisite."

"It was forged in Genoa by Galeazzo Calvo. The barrel contains grooves which make the shot spin, giving it an accuracy far beyond the norm. I've never found its equal."

"A fine gun, Gerard, but take a look at this."

Guy pulled a pistol from his belt and handed it to Gerard, who held it gingerly. Exquisite goldwork decorated the gun, but even more amazing was its mechanism: the gun contained two barrels and two triggers. Gerard had never before seen a gun capable of taking two shots.

"That gold work was done by Benvenuto Cellini himself," said Guy, "and the pistol presented to me by Jean de la Cassièr, head of my order."

Gerard whistled. Cellini, who had died just a few years before, had established himself as one of Europe's greatest goldsmiths. Many of his commissions had come from kings and queens. The gun was worth a fortune, for both its composition and its origin.

"I've never seen its like," said Gerard. "But with such a short barrel, how can you guarantee your shot? It can't be accurate to any great distance."

Guy grinned and placed the pistol back into his belt. "I keep my enemies close, Gerard; I need not shoot far." Then he leaned in to speak more privately. "I like you, Gerard. You're more useful than anyone from this rabble that came with me from France. Fight with me today, and I'll make you an officer in the city. Believe me, you can rise quickly in my service. Who knows? You could replace Nicolas as my second-in-command someday and help me rule Brazil."

"Truth be told," said Gerard, "I'm no soldier. Conquest and war are not in my blood. I've never killed a man, nor do I ever plan to."

Guy raised an eyebrow at the revelation. "Why own such fine weapons if you don't put them to use?"

"I put my harquebus and rapier to use battling the ferocious monsters of this land, not slaying its people. I'm sorry, but I must refuse your offer."

Guy shook his head in disgust. Gerard thought it best to placate him quickly.

"I may not help you," said Gerard, "but neither will I hinder you. I bear no allegiance to the Portuguese. There are those among them, in fact, who hold me as an enemy."

"Very well," said Guy. "I will let you go on your way, as long as you swear not to interfere."

"I must ask that you release my companion as well."

"The nago?" he asked, using the French word for the Yoruban peoples.

"Yes," said Gerard.

"Very well," said Guy. He motioned some of his men toward Oludara. "Release that one." He tossed Gerard his weapons.

When Duarte saw this, he said, "What's going on? You've betrayed us, Gerard."

Before Gerard could respond, Guy shouted to one of his soldiers, "Shut that fool up!"

The man walked to Duarte and punched his nose, breaking it.

"You will one day regret your decision not to serve me, van Oost," said Guy. "People will remember this day as the beginning of French dominance in the New World. Brazil is just the start; who says we can't conquer America all the way from Canada to the Land of Fire, and create an empire?"

After hearing the strange native speak of empire that same day, Gerard startled at Guy's use of the word.

"When our conquest of Brazil is complete," said Guy, "this glorious day will become just as famous as St. Bartholomew's Day, when we rousted the heathens from France!"

"What?" said Gerard. "You speak of the massacre?"

Gerard's voice carried a coldness that caused everyone to stop what they were doing.

"Killing worms isn't massacre," said Guy.

Oludara, even though he didn't understand the language, had also caught the coldness in Gerard's voice. Not yet free from his bonds, he tried to interrupt and make Gerard realize his folly.

"Gerard," he said, "whatever it is, please calm down..."

Gerard, however, ignored him. Through clenched teeth, he said, "I am a follower of Calvin. Many of my friends were slain during that senseless massacre."

Guy looked at him with disgust. "Then no doubt I had the pleasure of killing many of them myself, you pathetic heretic."

"You villain," screamed Gerard. "Brazil will never be yours!"

"Seize him," said Guy.

Gerard snatched up his weapons and ran.

"Kill him!" yelled Guy.

At least twenty men took up Guy's order to chase Gerard. He zigzagged through the woods as shots rang out behind him.

Gerard rested against a brazilwood tree. He pressed his right hand to a chest wound—the worst of three—and watched as the blood seeped through his fingers.

To die like this, he thought, *murdered by a scoundrel. After facing so many worthy foes, to fall to the worst and weakest of them all.*

A tear rolled down his cheek and his vision blurred. Unable to hold up his head any longer, it drooped to his chest. He closed his eyes and listened as at least a half-dozen of his pursuers closed in on him.

"Here he is," one of Guy's soldiers said in French.

"Do we carry him back?" asked another.

"He's almost dead. Better to finish him off and take the head back. Less work. You do it."

Gerard heard the second man snort in displeasure at the command, then the reluctant footsteps as he approached to carry out the task. In his head, Gerard recited a silent, final prayer.

Three distinct notes, played by some kind of wind instrument, broke his thoughts.

"What was that?" asked the second man, his voice so close that he must have been almost on top of Gerard.

A tramping sound approached, accompanied by rustling bushes.

"Look," said a different soldier.

Shots rang out around Gerard, but, to his surprise, none were aimed at him.

"*Sacrebleu*!" shouted another soldier. "Our shots do nothing."

"Flee!" yelled the first soldier.

Gerard could hear the men crashing through the woods, replaced by the sound of heavy steps clomping toward him. The steps paused just before him, and the stench of mud and filth filled the air as something snorted into his face. Using the last of his strength, Gerard opened one eye.

A massive, black snout wedged between two yellowed tusks sniffed a mere inch from his face. The mouth opened and bellowed a porcine squeal.

The three notes played again, this time in reverse order, and the massive pig turned and shuffled off. Gerard blacked out.

The touch of a hand on his cheek startled Gerard awake. His eyes fluttered on his first attempts to open them, but he finally managed to keep them open. Through the haze, he could barely make out a man with reddish-brown hair and white skin. Gerard didn't recall seeing him among Guy's men, but he certainly had the look of a Frenchman.

"Please," Gerard said in French, "kill me quickly."

"Why would I do that?" the man asked.

Gerard felt the man's hands pressing upon his chest. He felt warm and, curiously, better. Gerard squinted at the kneeling man and noticed a crow perched on his right shoulder, staring back at him.

"Is it fashionable to keep crows as pets these days?" he asked.

"I'm the only one in these parts," replied the man, now pressing his hands against Gerard's leg.

"So you think. I saw an old Tupi with one this very day."

The man only smiled in response.

"Who are you?"

"You may pretend not to remember me, Gerard van Oost, but I remember you."

The words hinted at Gerard's nagging doubt, that this man could somehow be the native he had met that day, but he found it difficult to believe. The age difference alone was tremendous.

"Have you made your choice yet?" asked the man.

"What choice?"

"Must I repeat myself? The choice of empire, of course. The choice between Portugal and France."

"Strange choice, coming from a Frenchman."

"I am neither the Frenchman you see now nor the old Tupi you saw before. I am whatever the Land tells me to be. But you ignore my question. Have you made your choice?"

"Curse your choice. I failed my companion, Oludara, and that's all that matters. If I would have kept my mouth shut, we would both be safe and on our way."

"Interesting," said the man. "But you did not keep your mouth shut, did you? And *when* you did not keep your mouth shut, did you not tell Guy that he would never take Brazil?"

Gerard searched the man's blue eyes, but they revealed no emotion at all. "How do you know that?"

"I know what the Land knows."

"What's that supposed to mean?" Gerard felt stronger, and he let his frustration fuel his words.

"Answer me, Gerard. Did you not tell Guy he would never have Brazil?"

"I suppose I did."

"You did. But you did not mean what you said."

"And how would you know that?"

"Look at me," the man said, grabbing a tuft of his red hair. "If you had meant it, would I look like this?"

"I have no idea why you look like that."

"Why must you be so dense today?"

The sound of cannon fire rang in the distance.

"Is that what I think it is?" asked Gerard.

"Yes. Those are the sounds of Guy's 'glorious victory'. The battle will be brief; Simon's men are far overpowered."

"Then it doesn't matter anymore. Brazil will be French."

"Not if you choose otherwise."

"Me? What choice can a dying man make?"

"Who says you're dying?"

Gerard looked down to see that his wounds had closed.

"What have you done?" he asked.

"Enough of your pointless questions. The only question that matters is: what will you do now?"

"My only concern is Oludara."

"Saving him, you may save others."

"I don't care for the others."

"Very well, then," said the man. "Then Guy will conquer Brazil. He won't be satisfied as a mere governor, though, he will eventually name himself king. Perhaps it won't be so bad."

Gerard scowled. "What would you have me do? I'm weak. I'm alone. I lost my gun and sword in the flight."

"This sword?" The man placed Gerard's rapier in his hands.

"Yes," said Gerard. Just holding it made him feel better. "Do you have my gun as well?"

"Will you use it?" asked the man.

"Probably not," said Gerard. "No matter what I decide, I won't kill Guy or his men. I have no desire to become a murderer like him."

"Then take this instead." The man waved a rustic, four-piped bamboo flute in front of him. "Have you ever played?"

"You ask me to stop an invasion of hundreds with a sword and a pipe flute?"

"Empires have been won with less."

"Have they?"

"Probably not," the man admitted. "But this is no simple instrument. If you don't repeat a note, there are twenty-four ways to play these four notes in sets of three."

"Thank you for the music lesson," Gerard replied.

The man seemed unperturbed by Gerard's sarcasm. "Those twenty-four three-note sets can be grouped into twelve pairs: each set and its opposite."

"Fascinating," said Gerard.

"So there are twelve calls, and twelve counters. Just make sure not to repeat a note. And never, *ever*, play all four notes in order."

"Why not?"

"That will bring them all."

"Bring who all?"

The man whacked Gerard across the bridge of the nose with the flute, then pressed it into his hand.

"Don't be daft, Gerard. It is time to be wise."

The man stood, and Gerard thought his features appeared blurry, even though his vision had returned almost to normal during their conversation. The man headed off.

"Where are you going?" asked Gerard. "I'm going to need all the help I can get."

The man replied without turning back. "I've done too much already. The choice must be yours, van Oost."

During the battle, Oludara and a half-dozen other prisoners had been left tied-up in the woods. The next morning, a group of French soldiers led them to the city.

As they entered the gate, Oludara could spot little sign of battle. Cannon fire had left a few holes, and one building had been burned, but he didn't see any bodies. The most conspicuous change were the blue French flags with the triple *fleur-de-lis* fluttering along the walls and the three galleons anchored in the bay. As he ascended the hill, Oludara spotted Simon, his soldiers, and some forty male colonists in a line at the top. They were bound at the wrists and guarded by Nicolas and a dozen French soldiers. Oludara reasoned that the city must have been taken by surprise.

Nicolas lined Oludara up with the other prisoners, where they waited in the hot sun for almost an hour, their only company a group of blue birds bouncing along the wall and chirping.

When Guy finally arrived, his men stood at attention and Nicolas stepped forward to speak. "Here are your prisoners, Governor."

Guy walked along the line, sizing them up. Behind him, one of the prisoners mumbled, "Dirty pirate."

Guy, furious, turned and screamed, "I'm not a pirate!" Then, composing himself, he said, "From the look of this pathetic lot, I'm not sure I should even bother asking, but are any of you worth anything? I will happily ship any gentlemen back to Portugal for ransom."

Simon stepped forward and replied, "You won't find any nobility here. Most of us were born in Brazil and most of us will die here."

Guy strode up to Simon and said, "Most of you certainly will. Who are you?"

"I'm Simon, captain of the guard."

Guy looked him up and down. "With a one-eyed, half-breed in command, no wonder no one of any worth lives here."

Simon turned red and said, "This eye was the price I paid to drive the French out of Rio de Janeiro the first time."

Guy ignored the comment and looked around. "What is that infernal noise?" he asked.

Duarte spoke, his voice thick from his broken nose, "Those tanagers are waiting for fruit. We give them some every day."

Guy grabbed a harquebus from one of his men and shot at the birds, dispersing them. "I hate birds," he said, sneering.

"Then you've probably come to the wrong place," said Luis.

Guy turned to him, mouth wide to yell, when Gerard's voice interrupted from the gate below.

"Shooting at songbirds, Guy? Finally found an opponent of your stature?"

"Who left that gate open?" yelled Guy. "Why is no one guarding the bastion?"

Below, Gerard waved the elephant and macaw banner, stitched roughly back together after their encounter with the bull. "Remember this, Guy. This symbol will mark the end of your plans for Brazil."

Many of the Frenchmen, including Guy, pointed and laughed. Guy yelled down, "Your banner has me quivering in my boots, Gerard. Did a five-year-old draw that for you?"

"Hey," shouted Gerard, his face turning red, "it's just a rough idea!"

"Enough of this nonsense. Come up here, and I'll show you how worthy an opponent I am."

"In the Low Countries, we're well aware of the French battle prowess." Gerard broke into a song:

"Oh, the grand old King of France,
with forty thousand men,
marched them up to the top of a hill
and so came down again."

Many of the prisoners snickered at this, and several received cuffs to the head or groin. The song so infuriated Guy that Oludara could see the veins in his neck.

Guy screamed down, "You will regret your words, frog!"

Oludara turned to Duarte and asked, "Why does he call Gerard a frog?"

"In Europe, they call the Dutch frogs because they live in a marshy land."

Guy pointed at Gerard and said to Nicolas, "Shoot him."

"Too far," he replied.

Guy judged the shot and nodded. He shouted to everyone present. "Whoever captures that man will receive a hundred *ecus d'or.*"

With a chorus of hollers, the French soldiers charged down the hill. Guy looked around to find himself alone with over fifty prisoners.

"Come back here, you fools!" he shouted.

Gerard sat high in the crook of a tree, watching as a group of six French soldiers searched for him below.

"I'm up here," he said.

They turned to look up at him.

"I have an offer for you," he said. "Leave Brazil and no harm will come to you."

"Come down, imbecile," one of them replied, "or we'll shoot you down."

"You don't really care about Brazil, do you? And even less about Guy, anyone can see that. Just take your ships and return to France."

The men grumbled, neither agreeing nor disagreeing, until one of them raised his gun. "Last chance," he said.

"All right," replied Gerard, "I suppose I must. But please allow me to play you a tune first." Under his breath, he mumbled, "Three notes, all different."

He placed the flute to his mouth and played three notes.

The Frenchmen looked at each other and shrugged. The one who had spoken said, "Enough nonsense. Get down."

"You might want to look behind you first."

"No stupid tricks."

One soldier, however, did turn around, alerted by a rattling noise behind them. Mouth open, gasping for air, he could only grab the sleeve of the one speaking and spin him around to face an alarming sight: a diamond-backed pit viper of enormous size.

One by one, the soldiers turned to see the danger. They backed away as the serpent lifted its head eight feet off the ground and stared down at them. Its rattle vibrated in anticipation.

Not one of them daring to open fire, they broke and ran. Two of them even dropped their guns in their haste.

From his perch in the tree, Gerard chuckled.

⟜◇⊸

Guy grabbed a soldier and pointed down to the bay, where only two of his galleons remained.

"Where's my other ship?" he shouted.

"Some hundred men set off in the middle of the night."

"And no one told me?"

"They said they had orders from you."

Guy wailed in frustration and searched out Nicolas, who he practically dragged back to the office he had set up in what had been the governor's house.

"A group of men stole one of my ships during the night. I want them hanged. Any and all deserters will be shot."

Nicolas took a deep breath and replied. "This place is cursed, Governor. There seems to be no end to the creatures Gerard can call down with that flute. Every day morale gets worse. Why don't we move on to some other port, before more men desert?"

"Coward!" yelled Guy. "Why don't you try fighting those monsters instead of running from them?"

"Most of them we can't even wound."

"Why does Gerard plague me so? Why does he care so much about this town?"

"Perhaps it is because of his companion?"

"What companion?" asked Guy, puzzled.

"The nago."

"The slave? Ha! Don't make such jests. An educated man like Gerard make all this fuss over him? Nonsense." Guy scratched his hair. "But there is something here he wants. Perhaps that slave might know. Bring him to me."

Five minutes later, Nicolas returned with Oludara. Guy looked him up and down and had to admire his proud stature, better than many of his soldiers.

"Help me capture your old master, Gerard," said Guy, "and I'll give you your freedom."

"I am a free man already."

"Really? Then why do you travel with Gerard?"

Oludara seemed about to say something, then stopped.

"If you won't tell me that, at least tell me of his flute."

"Flute?"

"The one he plays to call monsters upon my men. Don't pretend you've never seen it."

Once again, Oludara remained silent. Guy was impressed by the man's dedication. Perhaps Nicolas was right, after all. If so, he would use it to his advantage. He chanced a test.

"Tell me anything that will help me capture Gerard, and I will set you free. Otherwise, you hang at dawn."

Oludara hesitated, then spoke. "I must ask your forgiveness. I lied to you not because of my loyalty to Gerard, but rather my fear of him. My people have a saying, 'When the shin bone is not hurt, it says it has no flesh to protect it.' "

"Um...I'm not sure I understand. Perhaps it is an error of translation?"

"It means I will never know what I can do unless I try. I will overcome my fear of Gerard and stop him for you. Give me back my knife and I will go into the woods to call on him, pretend to negotiate in your name. He will trust me enough to come out, and I will kill him. If I succeed, I want fifty of the gold coins you promised to your men."

A poorly told lie, mused Guy, *and everything I needed to know.*

"A tempting offer," he said. "Let me sleep on it."

The precarious, clay building which served as the brig contained just two cells, both of them packed with exhausted prisoners who didn't even have room to sit. Even with the cell crowded beyond capacity, however, Oludara stood alone. Since he had returned from his meeting with Guy, the others looked upon him with open suspicion. They had shoved him to the back of the cell and isolated him, not even daring to speak where he could hear. Oludara could do nothing but worry as the long hours passed.

In the middle of the night, a commotion began. Some of the prisoners gasped, others hissed, and still others spit loudly. He could heard Simon say, somewhere from the front of the cell, "What are you doing here?"

"I'm here to free you," replied Gerard's voice, "and take back Rio de Janeiro from Guy."

Oludara pushed forward through the crowd, his fellow prisoners not easing his passage in any way.

"It is a trap," said Oludara. "Guy knew you would come back for me."

"Nonsense," said Gerard, unlocking the cells. "He thinks of you as nothing but a slave."

"Then how did you get in here so easily?"

"I came through that hole in the wall the bull made."

Gerard tossed Oludara his enchanted ivory knife, which tingled in his hands as he held it. He noticed Gerard had recovered his own weapons as well.

"And after that?" asked Olduara. "Why do you think there are no guards here? How did you get those keys and our weapons? As we say, 'When the spider intends to attack you, it encircles you with its web.' "

That made Gerard pause, but he shook it off and cut the bonds of those around him with his knife. Oludara joined in with his own.

"It doesn't matter," said Gerard, "this is our only chance. Over half of Guy's men have fled, and the others are panicked. There's not one among them who doesn't hate the man. If we capture him, the others will desist. We can avoid bloodshed if we take him quickly."

"All right," said Simon. "What's your plan?"

"You and your men create a distraction down by the bay while Oludara and I surprise Guy in his quarters."

"Only if you take Duarte and Luis with you."

"Agreed."

Oludara shook his head. He knew he hadn't convinced Guy during their meeting. Quite the contrary, he was sure Guy had discerned the bond between the two, but nothing he could say now would convince Gerard.

"You lead the way?" requested Gerard.

Oludara agreed reluctantly. Trap or no trap, they had no choice but to go forward.

He pushed the brig door open to peek out, and found himself face to face with a half-dozen harquebus barrels.

Gerard lost all hope as he spotted the mass of French soldiers just outside the brig. He had fallen into the very trap that Oludara had predicted.

Guy's voice called out from beyond the soldiers. "Bring them out."

Dejected, the men walked single file from the jail and formed a line in the moonlight.

Guy pointed toward Gerard, "Take his weapons, and find that cursed flute."

One soldier took Gerard's rapier and harquebus, and three others searched him roughly until they found the flute hidden in his shirt. A soldier carried it to Guy, who turned it over in his hands, studying it. He held it up before his men.

"Is this toy what caused you all so much fear?"

Guy dropped the flute to the ground and crushed it beneath his boot.

"Cowards," he said, eliciting reactions from his men which ranged from embarrassment to anger. "Your ridiculous plan is finished, Gerard. Did you think you could take me unawares?"

A crow landed on a wall near Guy and cocked its head. Only Gerard seemed to notice it.

"Don't ignore me, Gerard!" screamed Guy. His hand trembling in anger, he pulled his double-barreled pistol from his belt and aimed it between Gerard's eyes. "You should listen when someone better than you is speaking."

At that moment, a long note whistled through the air. To Gerard, it sounded reminiscent of the flute. The French soldiers who had heard Gerard's perilous melodies cringed at the sound. All heads turned in unison toward the source: the crow.

"I've never heard a crow sing like that," commented Luis.

The crow whistled three more notes.

"*Four* notes?" Gerard mumbled under his breath.

"Someone shut that thing up!" yelled Guy.

The crow repeated the four notes. They were, unmistakably, the same notes as the pipe flute.

"Four notes..." said Gerard, this time louder.

Guy turned the pistol away from Gerard and shot at the bird. With a flutter of wings, the crow leapt just before the shot went off and flew away. In the distance, a thunderous crack sounded and a tree fell.

"Four notes," shouted Gerard, "take cover!"

A crash echoed below them and a section of the perimeter wall collapsed. Through the gap rushed a menagerie of enormous creatures. Gerard recognized the bull, snake, pig and several others he had summoned with the flute, accompanied by many he had never seen before.

A general panic ensued. Guy berated his men, but most of them ignored his insults and fled for the docks. One of them dropped Gerard's weapons, and he ran to recover them.

Simon shouted orders, and most of his men shook off their panic and obeyed. He began organizing a defense against the invading monsters.

"Look to the bay!" yelled one of the Frenchmen.

Down below, a galleon pulled anchor and raised sail. Gerard could just make out Nicolas on the deck, waving a cheeky goodbye to Guy. The remaining French soldiers redoubled their speed toward the last ship.

Gerard saw Guy blanch, finally realizing just how desperate his situation had become. He put his pistol back into his belt and chased after his fleeing men. Gerard started after him, but Oludara grabbed his shoulder.

"We must help Simon against the creatures," said Oludara.

"No! If Guy escapes, he'll come back with more men; I know it. I have to stop him." Gerard pulled away and ran after Guy.

Behind him, he heard Oludara shout, "Since when do you take sides?"

Gerard ignored the comment and raced on, zigzagging through the battles which raged between monsters and men. He rounded a group of four Frenchmen facing a huge, ape-like creature. It picked one of the men up like a doll and used it to batter his companions. In the distance, an enormous crocodile breathed a cloud of greenish gas upon a group of Portuguese soldiers, causing them to grab their throats and gasp in agony. When Gerard returned his attention to his chase, he was shocked to find the giant rattlesnake just before him, rearing up to strike.

With no time left to think, he threw himself to the ground and rolled downhill. The serpent's strike passed just above him, and his momentum carried him past the creature before he stumbled back to his feet.

He looked behind to see Oludara and the black bull rushing straight at each other. His breath caught in his throat as they approached impact, but Oludara vaulted over the animal's lowered horns at the last moment, bounced off its back, and rolled to a stop. Gerard paused, ready to race back and help his friend, but the bull didn't stop charging; it simply changed course toward a different target.

Gerard scanned for Guy and spotted him approaching the docks. The only thing left between him and the last galleon was an enormous capybara, calmly grazing and ignoring the commotion around it.

"That won't hold him," muttered Gerard.

As Guy neared the beast, however, it stared up at him with eyes of fire. It opened its mouth a full one-hundred and eighty degrees to display an immense pair of fangs. Guy skidded and fell, his pistol rolling from his grasp.

Gerard had no time to set his gun; he threw it aside and drew his rapier. The creature and Gerard both lunged for Guy, and Gerard's rapier struck true, passing through the capybara's mouth and impaling its brain. They swiveled in the air, the creature landing on one side of Guy and Gerard crashing just as heavily on the other. Guy scooted back from them, toward his pistol.

Gerard scrambled back for his gun, then spun towards Guy. Guy, pistol already aimed at Gerard's head, strode toward him.

"You're a fine warrior, Gerard," said Guy, "and you would have done well to join me. But this game is ended. As you yourself said, you won't kill me. You see, walking around with that big gun of yours doesn't mean a thing if you're not willing to use it."

Gerard considered shooting Guy's legs, but he knew the thought had come too late. With Guy's pistol pointed at his head, he would never have time to get off a shot.

As Guy tightened his finger on the trigger, a shape emerged from the darkness beside him, and an ivory blade flashed into view at his neck. Guy turned his eyes to stare straight into Oludara's teeth, shining in the moonlight.

"I, on the other hand," said Oludara, "do not share my companion's scruples. If you do not lower your gun, I will pass this blade through your throat."

His beaming smile left no doubt he would not only do it, but enjoy it.

In the rising dawn light, Oludara looked out over Rio de Janeiro and the aftermath of the battle. The monsters' attack had taken a far heavier toll than the French invasion. Buildings lay in crumbled heaps. Several men had been killed, both French and Portuguese, and Simon's soldiers were busy at work digging graves. They also had to dig three oversized graves for the enormous capybara, pig, and rattlesnake. The rest of the creatures—most of them heavily wounded—had wandered off when, out of the nighttime darkness, four notes had sounded, in opposite order of the ones which had summoned them.

The final French ship never left port. A group of soldiers led by Luis and Duarte had reached the ship first and captured the French as they straggled on, one by one.

Nearby, Guy and twenty French prisoners sat bound on the ground. Gerard sat off by himself, oiling his rapier and cleaning his harquebus, lost in his own thoughts and ignoring all else around him. Luis and Duarte led another twenty prisoners up from the bay. The two soldiers were dressed in colorful, extravagant clothes.

"Simon," said Luis, "look what we found in Guy's cabin on the ship."

Simon chuckled and said, "Guy, did you come here to set up a city or a tailor's shop?"

Simon's men all laughed at the joke and even the Frenchmen

snickered. Guy turned red but said nothing. Besides him, only Gerard remained silent. Oludara watched his companion with concern.

Finally, Gerard put away his equipment and approached Simon.

"What will you do now?" asked Gerard.

"Send a letter to the governor," responded Simon. "He can't ignore this problem anymore. Soon we'll have the funds to erect a true city."

"I mean with them," said Gerard, motioning toward the prisoners.

"I haven't decided yet."

"Ransom them, put them to work. Whatever you do, just make sure they come to no harm."

Gerard's words came out like a command, and Simon stared him in the eye before responding. "Very well. But you and your friend must leave."

Gerard nodded as if he had expected it, but Oludara was offended. "Gerard rescued us all," he said.

"And that's the only reason you two aren't tied up like them. I'm convinced you didn't betray us to the French, but I don't trust you, either. I think Gerard would have abandoned the city if you hadn't been taken prisoner."

Oludara, angered, looked to Gerard, waiting for his friend to offer some rebuttal. Gerard, however, merely adjusted his pack and tipped his hat to Simon in a wordless goodbye. Then he turned to Oludara.

"Perhaps it's time we returned to our Tupinambá friends for a while," he said. "We've travelled a thousand miles down this coast."

Oludara didn't understand his friend's reluctance to defend himself, but nodded in agreement and followed him in silence as Gerard set off for the north gate. He waved goodbye to Luis and Duarte, and he couldn't be sure, but thought he spotted wetness in their eyes.

"Wait, Gerard!" screamed Guy. "Don't go. Explain to this man that he can't keep me tied up like this. I'm a Knight Hospitaller. I fought at Lepanto. I met the Grand Turk!"

"Really?" said Gerard, turning to face him.

"Yes!"

Gerard turned to Simon and said, "Then that should make the

ransom all the sweeter."

Simon responded with a smile and a nod, and Gerard continued down the path.

Returning to French, Guy screamed, "*Le mond va de pis en pis*!"

"What does that mean?" asked Oludara.

Without turning, Gerard replied, "He said: 'The world goes from bad to worse.' "

"And what do you think?"

"What do I think? I think the world goes on."

Guy's ranting continued behind them, but Oludara neither looked back, nor asked any more questions.

A half league from the city, Gerard and Oludara passed a small rise to find a man standing on the path before them. The man appeared to be a caboclo, a mixture of Tupi and Portuguese, like Simon, but if Gerard wasn't mistaken, he could swear he had some African features as well. His black hair was cut short and parted to one side. A crow perched upon his right shoulder.

Gerard stopped several paces from the man and looked him up and down before saying, "Hail!"

"Hail, Gerard van Oost and Oludara," replied the man.

"Why do you change so?"

"I told you, Gerard, I am whatever the Land tells me I am. Although, this time, I believe I shall remain this way for quite a while."

Gerard paused to ponder those words.

"What is your name?" asked Oludara.

"My name is whatever the Land calls me."

"If you ask anything of this one," said Gerard, "get used to answers like that. Nevertheless," he said, returning his attention to the man, "I hope you'll give me at least one clear answer. You said you wouldn't interfere, but your crow called down the monsters. What made you change your mind? And don't tell me 'the Land told me to do it'."

"You made the choice, Gerard. Once you had saved your friend, you chose to go after Guy, not run away. If my bird here decided to sing a little song, so be it."

"I don't think your bird just 'decided' to do anything."

"Very well, Gerard, if you demand an answer, I'll give you one. I couldn't stand that pompous ass any more than anyone else could."

"I thought that might be the reason."

"You were a native when we first met," said Oludara. "Why would you help the Portuguese to rule this land?"

"It may appear strange to you, who have lived for so short a time, but the Land is more ancient than you can imagine. I love the Tupinambá, and Tupiniquim, and Tamoio, it is true, but they are not the first to inhabit this coast. Those who lived here before, I loved them as well. The Tupi nations came and made war and drove them away. And even before them, there were yet others whom I loved. The world goes on, and we live as best we can within it."

Gerard, not at all surprised to hear his earlier words echoed, nodded in agreement.

"At least, in this form," said the man, holding out his arms for emphasis, "the blood of the Tupi tribes still flows within my veins. They are not gone, just changed. Brazil will be neither Portuguese nor Tupi, but something unique." He looked at Oludara. "Something very unique indeed."

"An empire?" asked Oludara, raising an eyebrow.

"Not in your lifetime, but Brazil will have its day."

"And I suppose that will end as well?" asked Gerard.

"It is the nature of this world. But I can only see so far. A path has been laid, and it leads to empire. I fear that our paths, however, shall never cross again."

"Then I wish you luck," said Gerard, tipping his hat.

"And a long life," added Oludara.

"That," replied the man, smirking, "you can be sure of."

The man left the path and disappeared into the woods. Gerard and Oludara continued on their way for several minutes before Gerard finally broke the silence.

"Empire..." he said, shaking his head.

At that, they shared a long chuckle.

In what had become a daily ritual, Luis and Duarte dragged Guy, screaming and biting, from his prison cell to a low clay wall. Duarte returned a few minutes later with an armful of papayas, which he cut up and laid around the man.

Before Duarte had even cut the second fruit, blue tanagers filled the air around them. Some of them, perhaps by accident, brushed Guy with their feathers as they passed by. Others, very unlikely by accident, took time out from their feast to alight on his head and peck at his scalp.

"Birds," he cried, "cursed birds!"

Chapter 6

A Torrential Complication

WARA, A SMALL RED FOX, approached the hut to scavenge the remains of that day's meal. She spotted the refuse strewn behind it, in the same place Conte and Mayara left it every day. The pile consisted of bits of banana and boiled manioc, and a few fish bones with some scaly bits of meat still hanging from them. However, it was far from the simple fare it appeared—it was the refuse of immortals. The meal would do little to nourish Gwara's body, but it would be a feast for her mind. Every day she ate there, every meal she consumed, opened her to new thoughts. She had partaken of the food for so long, she had come to understand and even replicate human speech.

As the fox chewed up the remains, she could hear Conte and Mayara speaking from within the hut. The building, with its walls of packed earth and roof of palm leaves, appeared to be a modest construction. However, it had been raised by the same immortal hands that had prepared her food, and for that, was a building more solid than stone.

Gwara peeked through the hut's entrance and spotted Conte in a squatting position, his elbows upon his knees and his muscles tense. From his looks alone, Conte appeared to be nothing more than a Tupinambá warrior, a fit adult with a single green feather sticking up from the band upon his head. His skin was perfect, without a single mark of his battles from ages past, and covered with designs in a green dye that Gwara had seen nowhere else. His hair was shorter than most, as was his temper, but beyond that, he appeared nothing out of the ordinary.

Mayara sat cross-legged on the ground beside him. While Conte had the appearance of someone in his thirties, his wife Mayara looked at least a decade older. She wove an intricate cloth, full of colorful designs. Gwara had seen her working on this particular piece for years, always with a hint of sadness upon her face.

Without looking up from her work, she asked, "Why don't you tell me what troubles you, my falcon? You haven't relaxed since you returned."

"If you'd seen what I have, you'd be troubled as well."

Conte stood abruptly and paced back and forth.

"These foreigners come from across the sea in their overlarge canoes, the ones with cloths pushed by the wind. They bring disease and war, and no good will come of them."

Mayara didn't look up from her work, only nodded.

"The Tupi nations are no better. They take sides with these foreigners and fight their wars for them."

"Men will always fight wars," said Mayara.

"I've had enough of men." Conte's voice had worked up to a shout.

"I spend my days near our hut," she said. "And I have not seen these things with my own eyes. But tell me your plan, and whatever it is, I will help you."

"It is time to put an end to all this. To repeat what we did so long ago. To start over."

Mayara laid aside her weave.

"If that's what you think is best, Conte." She stood and lay a hand upon his shoulder. "I am with you."

At that, he nodded. "Then let us begin."

Gwara ducked away just as the two of them turned toward the entrance. She hid behind the house as they set out together.

That doesn't sound good, thought Gwara. *I should see what he's planning.*

Cautiously, she set off behind them.

Oludara strolled through the woods near the village of his adopted Tupinambá tribe. After fleeing their old village, the tribe had taken up residence on the farthest edge of the forest: the last refuge before the dry, inhospitable Backlands. They lived well enough for the time being, but everyone shared the unspoken fear that one day, the roaming groups of bannermen—who prowled ever farther into the wilderness in search of native slaves—would leave them no choice but to move once and for all into that fearful land.

When Oludara had returned to the village, Aray had been overjoyed to see him. However, they had soon taken up their old arguments again, her refusing to even discuss the possibility of marriage without ever giving a reason. In the hope of smoothing things over a bit, he searched the woods for some small token of his affection: a pretty rock, a special flower, or whatever might catch his eye. He examined everything around him with that single goal in mind.

He was surprised, however, when a native couple emerged from some brush before him. The man's body was painted with an unusual green dye. The couple also seemed surprised to find him there, but quickly regained their composure.

"I jump to meet you," said the man, using a typical Tupi greeting.

"Greetings and good health," replied Oludara. "My name is Oludara."

"I am Conte, and this is my wife, Mayara. It is unusual to find one from across the sea this far into our land."

"I live with the Tupinambá nearby, who have taken me in as one of their own. But I've never seen the two of you before. Are you travelers?"

"We live not far from here," said Mayara, "but we live alone."

"Let me take you to my tribe. Our village is not so far from here, and you will both be welcome."

"No need," Conte replied curtly.

"What my husband means," said Mayara, "is that we would like to visit, but first, we have an important task. It would be a great boon if you could accompany us."

"You think he'll do?" asked Conte.

"Yes, I'm sure."

Oludara felt something unusual about this couple from the start; he disliked the way they weighed his worth right before his face.

"Why don't we share a meal at my village, and you can tell us what you need," he said. "There are many there who could help."

"No," replied Conte. "What we need is nearby, and your aid will be enough."

"Please come with us," said Mayara. "We can reward you with a great gift."

Oludara didn't trust them, but the offer of a gift gave him pause. It was exactly what he'd been looking for, after all, and he rarely dared to ignore destiny.

"Very well," he said. "Lead on."

Conte pulled back some of the thicket they had stepped out of and Oludara saw a two-trunked tree growing up in a 'v' shape from the ground.

"Walk through this tree here," said Comte.

"We don't need to pass through this thicket," said Oludara. "I know a way around it which is much faster."

"Believe us," said Mayara. "This is the way."

Oludara felt foolish, but stepped through the tree and worked his way through the brush beyond. After about a minute of thrashing through the thick vegetation, he stepped into a clearing with a small lake.

"What is this?" he asked. "This can't be."

"Shh," advised Mayara, stepping from the brush behind him. She pointed to the other side of the lake, where an enormous, ogre-like man sat fishing with a long pole. "We don't want to interrupt Agnen."

"What is going on?" asked Oludara. "There should be no lake here. Where are we?"

"Sometimes," said Conte, "men don't see what is right before their eyes. It is one of their many faults."

"What do you mean, 'their' faults?" asked Oludara, taking a step back. "What are you?"

"We are nothing more than a simple Tupinambá couple looking for help," said Mayara.

"We need the hook from Agnen's line," said Conte. "He doesn't trust me, so it's up to you."

"I don't trust you, either. My people have a saying, 'A hog that wallows in the mud seeks a clean person to rub against.' I don't know what you want, but I doubt it is good."

Oludara turned to leave.

At that, Conte grabbed his arm and Oludara felt a dizzying jolt through his body. He could feel himself changing, shrinking, and he fell to the ground, landing upon his clothes. To his horror, he had eyes on both sides of his head: one to the ground, and one to the air. He flopped around and choked on the air.

Conte picked him up and looked into one of his eyes.

"Don't come back without the bait and hook."

At that, Oludara felt himself tossed through the air and landed in the water. The water entered through gills on his neck and returned his breath. His fish body jiggled from side to side and propelled him clumsily through the water.

Arany was worried about Oludara. She had grown accustomed to his antics with Gerard, with whom he might disappear for weeks or months at a time. This time, however, she had argued with him in the morning and he had set off alone, saying he would not take long. Now it was well into the afternoon.

She searched the village and to worsen her fears, found Gerard and Cabwassu sitting and laughing in the middle of the village. They played one of Gerard's European games with black and white stones. If Oludara were anywhere within the village, he would almost certainly have been with the two of them, but he was nowhere in sight.

"Do either of you know where Oludara is?" she asked.

Focused on their game, they didn't even look up.

"Haven't seen him all day," replied Gerard, lifting his hat to scratch his head as he concentrated on the game before him.

"We should go look for him," she said.

"Why?" said Cabwassu, also without looking up. He tugged a pointed stone jutting from one of his cheeks. "If you don't know where he is, where will you look?"

Arany turned and stormed off to her longhouse. She grabbed Gerard's big gun, then headed to Cabwassu's longhouse for his bow and arrows. After a moment's thought, she retrieved a bow for herself as well.

She returned to the village center and tossed the men's weapons between them, scattering the stones and finally getting their attention. Open-mouthed, they gaped up at her.

"Let's go," she said, in a voice that left no room for questions.

At first, Oludara moved up, down, and in circles, desperately trying to get used to his fish body. He rammed into roots, fish, and dirt as he grew accustomed to his wide field of vision. After what seemed like hours, he finally gained enough control to concentrate his attention on a plan.

He knew his best chance lie in retrieving the hook. If he could get that and have Conte turn him back to his normal form, he could then turn his attention to stopping the couple, for whatever plan they had in mind, he doubted it was benevolent. He might even seek the ogre's aid against them.

However, he first had to concentrate on the hook. His fish form possessed exceptionally sharp teeth, so his best course of action would be using them to cut the line. He moved closer to Agnen for a better look.

Agnen was somewhat human-like, but with an exaggerated body. His arms and legs were the size of tree trunks, his head the size of a boulder. Two rounded tusks jutted up from the corners of his mouth. Just below the water, Oludara could see that Agnen had baited the hook with an enormous piece of meat, one he didn't recognize. Oludara had no idea what attracted the fish to it, but they came by the dozens to sink their teeth into the meat, at which point Agnen would yank them from the water and toss them into a massive clay pot, all the while humming a dreadful tune.

To Oludara's dismay, Agnen never took his eyes off the bait, never even blinked. He kept his line so close to the shore that he could easily reach in and grab Oludara if he came too close. Oludara could do nothing but circle and wait for an opening.

Apparently, Conte noticed his hesitation, because Oludara spotted him approaching Agnen from one side. Moving close to the surface of the water, he could make out their conversation.

As Conte approached, Agnen gave him one wary glance, then returned his attention to his bait.

"Didn't I rip you to pieces once?" Agnen asked in a booming, tired voice.

"That is no proper greeting for one you have known for so long, Agnen. And in any case, I think you confuse me for my brother."

"Do I?"

"Perhaps. That was a long time ago, too long to remember. Countless generations of men have come and gone since."

"Indeed. My cave is ever more crowded with their souls, and I must work that much harder to feed them."

"It sounds tedious," said Conte.

"It is. But without my hook, it would be much worse. Which is why you should keep well away from it."

"I wouldn't think of it."

"You wouldn't? Why would you be here, who have not spoken to me for ages, if not for my hook?"

"Because I need to show you something."

With that, Conte chanced a quick, knowing glance at Oludara, leaving no doubt it was almost time to act. Oludara tensed and waited for the right moment. Conte held up his hands toward Agnen and said, "Take a look at this."

Agnen turned to look and Oludara shot towards the bait.

Just as his sharp teeth approached the line, however, a wave crashed into him, hurling him away from it. Agnen, waist deep after splashing into the water, grabbed him with both hands and pulled him up.

"Don't think I didn't expect a silly trick like this, Conte. You won't fool me so easily a second time."

At that, Agnen turned back toward the shore. Both Conte and his fishing pole were gone.

Agnen roared in fury as he stepped from the water. He screamed "Conte!" several times, but received no response.

His hands squeezed down and Oludara thought his fish body would burst. At the same time, his torture was doubled as he gasped for water to fill his lungs. After a final terrifying scream, Agnen appeared to remember he was holding something and lifted Oludara to his face.

"I'll rip your friend to pieces once again," said Agnen. "This time, it will be for good. But first, I'll serve you to the dead."

Oludara felt himself falling and landed in the clay pot, crowded to the brim with squirming fish. He gasped a merciful blast of water into his lungs and could do nothing but await a fate he had no hope of changing while inside that squirming, maddening prison.

Gwara watched from the brush as Agnen fished the black piranha from the lake with his bare hands while Conte ran off with his pole and line. Gwara snuck toward the place where Mayara awaited her husband.

"Very good, my falcon," said Mayara.

Conte smiled. "I didn't expect it to be so easy. That demon has grown even stupider over time."

"Are you ready?"

"Yes. You head for the High Place. I will head for the Spout. It is time to flood the Earth and destroy mankind. We will start over once again, as we did so long ago."

The two of them strode away.

Gwara, panicked, ran one way, turned around, then ran the other. She spun in circles multiple times before realizing she had no idea what she was doing and stopped to think of a plan.

What could I possibly do to stop Conte from creating a flood? The answer came easily. *Nothing. I can do nothing.*

Then she remembered Narre.

He's the only one who could stop Conte, she thought. *I must go to him.* She tensed to run before another thought gave her pause. *I can't reach him alone, I'll need help.*

She considered Agnen, but the demon was too big to help where she needed to go. She knew of no one else nearby. She would have to pass through the split tree, to that other place. She ran, unsure what she would find, but desperate to find something.

Arany walked through the woods alongside Gerard and Cabwassu, the three of them calling out at intervals for Oludara. With every passing moment, she became more nervous.

"Wait," said Cabwassu, holding up a hand and squatting down to look at something.

"What is it?" asked Arany.

"Some tracks. More than one person."

"I don't think he left with anyone," said Gerard.

"But he might have met someone," said Arany. "Can you tell where they're headed?"

Cabwassu scratched his head. "It looks like they went into that brush over there, maybe?"

"That goes nowhere," said Arany, frustrated. "What kind of a tracker are you?"

"Wait," said Gerard. "Something's moving in there."

Arany turned, desperate for any sign. "Oludara? Is that you?"

As she spoke, a fox's head peeked out from the brush. She gnashed her teeth in frustration.

"Oludara could be in danger, and you lead us to a fox? What good are the two of you?"

"I'm sorry to interrupt," came a nearby voice, "but I need your help."

Arany looked into the brush for the voice's source, but could see nothing.

"Down here," said the voice.

She stared down at the fox.

"By all the saints!" said Gerard. "You can talk?"

The fox stepped out of the brush. "I don't have a lot of time for explanations. I'm Gwara, and I need one of you to help me."

"Gwara, have you seen a dark-skinned man around here?"

"As a matter of fact, I have, but what I need to tell you..."

Arany grabbed her by the scruff of his neck and lifted her up.

"Where is he?"

"It's more of a 'what is he' at the moment. Conte turned him into a black piranha and Agnen has him."

"Agnen?" The demon's name shocked Arany.

"Conte?" asked Cabwassu. "You mean Ariconte?"

"Yes."

Arany and Cabwassu gave each other knowing looks. She couldn't believe her ears, but the mere thought those immortals might be involved multiplied her fear tenfold.

"Impossible," she said, unsure.

Cabwassu shrugged. "It's just a fox. It probably doesn't know what it's talking about."

"I'm not an 'it', I'm a 'she', thank you."

"Can anyone explain to me what you're all talking about?" asked Gerard.

"Quiet!" said Arany. "Tell me where he is."

"Let me go," said Gwara, "and we can talk."

"Not until you tell me where he is."

"If you don't help me, we'll all die anyway."

"Listen," said Gerard. "Gwara, is it? I'm Gerard, and this is Arany and Cabwassu. Tell her where to find Oludara, and I'll help you."

"Swear it?" asked the fox, struggling to turn her head towards him in Arany's ever-tightening grip.

"By my life, I swear it."

"Very well, Agnen is taking your friend to his cave to feed..." The animal paused.

"*Feed*?" exclaimed Arany. "Feed what?"

Her shout made Gwara cringe. "Uh. I don't remember. Something about feeding."

Arany didn't believe the fox, but didn't want to waste any more time finding out.

"Where is he?"

"Walk through that split tree over there." Gwara pointed with her snout. "On the other side, you'll find a lake. Agnen is massive, his tracks should be easy enough to find. If you save your friend, come back through that same tree, or you'll never find your way back. There is a stream that springs from the ground near here. Do you know of it?"

Arany nodded. Her people considered the place sacred.

"That's where Conte is headed," said Gwara. "Your friend and I will meet you there, once we're done."

"And what exactly are you going to do?" asked Cabwassu.

"We're going to find Narre."

Cabwassu shook his head in disbelief.

"Who's Narre?" asked Gerard.

"Enough talking," said Arany. She ran into the thicket, not waiting for a reply.

The group passed through the unusual tree, arrived at a lake that couldn't have possibly been there, then Arany and Cabwassu split up from Gerard and Gwara.

Agnen's tracks were indeed easy to follow, and led them to a wide trail. Arany and Cabwassu followed the well-worn path at a run.

The trail led them to a massive cave entrance. Beyond, Arany could see a passage, dimly lit by intermittent torches, leading off into the distance. A cold sensation gripped her as she took the first step into the cave. From the dark depths beyond, she could hear wailing voices. Countless voices. Arany had faced terrible things in her life, but she didn't think she could face this. She had never been so terrified.

Cabwassu came to a halt beside her. She had never seen him so pale.

"You know what this place is, don't you?" he asked.

Arany nodded. It took her some time to speak. "Can you go?"

"Into this cursed place?" The question hung in the air, with no answer.

This was a place of souls. Not the paradise, high in the mountains, where the valiant souls enjoyed pleasure and bounty. This was the place of cowards.

"Ariconte and Tamendonarre? Agnen? These things are beyond us, Cabwassu. We shouldn't be here. We can't be here."

"I know. It's not right. But don't blame me. Your darling is the one who got us into this."

"My...darling...?"

"Oludara."

Hearing his name lessened the chill. Arany couldn't abandon him, not even if it meant entering the worst place in the world.

Which is what she did. She took the hardest step of her life.

To her relief, Cabwassu did the same. Then they both took another step. In moments, the two of them were once again running, side by side, into a place no living soul should ever go.

It wasn't easy keeping up with Gwara, who didn't always take Gerard's height into account as she chose their path through the woods, causing him to smack into countless branches and spider webs along the way.

As he chased after the little fox, Gerard asked, "Who is Conte? And what does he want with Oludara?"

Without slowing down, Gwara shouted back, "He used him to get something he needed. Something to create a flood."

"A flood?"

"A flood that will wipe out the world."

"That's ridiculous. No man could start a flood like that."

"Conte is no man. And he's done it before. Or at least his brother has."

"And who is his brother?"

"The one we're going to find."

At that, they reached a stream seeping out from a rock cliff.

"Stay there," said Gwara.

The fox ran to the other side of the stream and stood upon a flat rock. When she did, the rock wall before Gerard parted, leaving an empty space before him.

"What is going on here?" asked Gerard, open-mouthed.

"There should be a flat rock in there, like the one I'm standing on. Go stand on it, and don't move until I tell you."

Gerard did as she said, and at his side, in front of Gwara, another space opened in the rock.

"Don't move," said Gwara.

The fox ran forward and stepped on another rock, causing a new space to open in front of Gerard.

"Now it gets tricky," said Gwara. "You need to be quick. Run forward and find the next stone."

Gerard took a breath and jogged toward a stone some ten yards before him. Rocks closed the space behind him. If he had hesitated, he would have been crushed. The two of them were now completely encircled by walls of stone.

"What is this place?" asked Gerard.

Gwara rushed forward to the next stone on her side, creating a new opening for Gerard.

"It is known as Itha Irapi. It is the only way to reach Narre, and it can never be traversed alone."

As Gerard ran to the next stone, he asked, "Remind me why we're trying to find the one who you say created a flood in the first place?"

"He and Conte are twins, though they look nothing alike. They were born of different fathers."

"Twins from different fathers? Ridiculous."

"When you meet them, you might just stop calling my stories ridiculous. In any case, they have been rivals since birth. We can use that against Conte."

Gerard and Gwara repeated the pattern with the stones several times, until Gwara stepped on one that parted the rocks before them into a clearing. In the middle of the clearing stood a wattle-and-daub cabin.

"Well I guess that's that," said Gerard, stepping forward.

"Wait!" shouted the fox.

All around Gerard, the rocks began closing in. He rushed forward and made it into the clearing just as the rock wall slammed shut. However, a miserable yelp screeched behind him.

He turned to see Gwara with her tail caught between the rocks.

Not far into the cavern, Arany came upon the first soul. At first, she thought it to be a reflection upon the rock wall, but as she came closer, she recognized it as a translucent, human form: that of an elderly man. He stared sadly off into nothingness until they came close, then, without warning, moved toward them. His legs moved as if walking, but the weightless form simply floated through the air. He stretched his arms toward them.

"Do you have any food?" he asked. "Feed me, please!"

The words, coupled with the desperate look on the man's face, made Arany cringe in terror. Cabwassu also jumped back, but kept his composure enough to reply.

"We have no food," he shouted at the man. "Get away from us."

The soul, however, didn't stop. Arany lunged away from his grasp and ran down the hall.

The scene repeated itself ever more frequently. Souls came floating toward Arany and Cabwassu from all directions, begging for food. They became more persistent as the passage carried on. Not a second passed that Arany didn't feel compelled to turn around and flee. She was on the edge of panic, and only managed to carry on because of Cabwassu's presence at her side. However, even he—the greatest warrior of their tribe—faltered from time to time. When Arany chanced a glance at him, she could see the terror in his eyes.

The passage opened into an enormous cavern, and the sound of hundreds of pleading voices echoed around them. The damp cavern was lit by a dozen flickering torches. Clay pots littered the floor and filled crude shelves upon the walls. On the far end of the cavern, Agnen stood before a multitude of souls. Every time the crowd pushed in too close, he would shoo them with his arms and an angry "Get back!" He reached into a clay pot beside him and pulled out a catfish, which he threw into the crowd. Ravenous souls fought over it, yanking and biting at it and shredding it bit by bit. Arany felt sick at the display.

As she worked up the courage to face the demon, Agnen reached into the bucket once again, this time pulling out an unnaturally black piranha.

—<>—

Gwara, her tail crushed between the rocks, squealed in pain. Gerard ran to her.

"What should I do?" asked Gerard.

"Pull me out! Pull me out!"

Gerard planted his feet firmly on the rocks and grabbed the fox just behind the shoulders. He yanked with all his strength and the fox jerked out, collapsing on top of him as they both fell.

Gerard untangled himself from the animal and stood up. Gwara remained on the ground.

"How is it?" asked the fox.

"How is what?"

"My tail. I can't stand to look."

Oddly enough, the end of her tail had turned completely white.

"It doesn't look so bad. If it still hurts, go dunk it in that stream over there."

That seemed to animate Gwara. "Good idea," she said, jumping up and running to the stream that emptied under the rock wall from which they had come. She dunked in her tail and sighed in relief.

Gerard looked to the cabin for movement. It was a simple hut, just big enough for a single family, if that. Gwara joined him at his side.

"We don't have time to waste," said Gwara.

"What should we do?"

"Best to call out to him."

"All right then." Gerard cleared his throat and shouted, "We're looking for Narre. Narre, are you here?"

A woman's face peeked from the entrance, then ducked back inside. A few moments later, a man stepped forth. He was a tall native, taller even than Oludara, and held himself calmly and proudly, as if the two before him presented no possible threat. A band of blue feathers stood up from his head like a crown, and designs in blue dye covered his body. He held a bow horizontally, with two arrows notched and ready. From what Gerard could tell, one was aimed directly at him, the other at Gwara.

⤙◇⤚

"Stop!" was the only thing Arany could think to say as Agnen prepared to feed Oludara to the dead.

Agnen turned toward them, a look of surprise on his face.

"What are you two doing here? Get out! This is no place for the living."

Unsure whether she was more terrified of Agnen or the dead, Arany mustered her courage and took a step forward. Cabwassu followed her lead and advanced beside her.

"Agnen," she said. "Please don't feed that fish to the dead. He is no fish, but a person disguised as one."

"Well that I know. This rascal helped Conte steal my hook."

Arany and Cabwassu advanced a few more steps as she spoke.

"He is my beloved. Please have mercy and return him to me."

"I don't think so," said Agnen. "He deserves no better."

With that, Cabwassu rushed forward and grabbed the ogre's arm. Cabwassu's muscles strained to move the demon, but Agnen simply tossed him aside with a shrug. Cabwassu thudded to the ground on one side.

Arany knew that force would get them nowhere, so she scanned the cave for another solution. Her eyes fell on the clay pot full of fish. In a flash of inspiration, she ran forward and kicked it over. The fish splayed to the ground and the souls rushed forward greedily.

Agnen, waving Oludara's fish body back and forth in front of him, yelled, "Back! All of you back!" Arany tried to sneak up on him but he swung the fish at her as well, making her stumble back and fall down. She could see the black piranha's gills flapping, gasping for air.

The souls cowered back and Agnen bent over the fallen vase. He placed Oludara on the ground and grabbed the vase with both hands to right it.

Cabwassu, now recovered, vaulted onto Agnen's back. Agnen, furious, turned and tried to grab him, but Cabwassu leapt off. He raced to one side and Agnen followed after.

The souls rushed back in at the fish and Arany, overcoming her revulsion, grabbed Oludara just before a hungry soul did. She rushed for the exit, but Oludara thrashed in her hands and she remembered he needed water. She looked into the clay pots and found one of the few small enough for her to carry, thankfully with a bit of water in the bottom. She tossed Oludara in, grabbed it, and continued her run.

Agnen noticed the movement and paused his cat-and-mouse game with Cabwassu to shout "Come back here!" He took a first step toward her, until he noticed the souls once again thrashing about the fallen fish. After a moment's hesitation, he ran back toward them, shouting curses as he went.

Arany and Cabwassu wasted no time in rushing back down the corridor.

The clearing remained in eerie silence as Gerard and Narre sized each other up. Gerard would normally laugh at a man trying to shoot two arrows at once, but if all that Gwara had told him was true, Narre was no man.

It was Gwara who broke the impasse. "Greetings, Narre."

"Greetings, little fox," replied Narre. "You should know better than to bring anyone here."

"It was the only way to cross the Itha Irapi, you know that."

"Indeed I do."

"This man is no threat to you."

At that, Narre lowered his bow. "Indeed he is not."

Gerard cleared his throat and said, "Gerard van Oost, from Brabant. Pleased to meet you."

"Greetings, man from across the sea. I am Tamendonarre, born in this land, hundreds of generations before you set foot here."

"Narre," said Gwara, "we need your help. Conte stole Agnen's hook."

"Really? His courage surprises me. The last time he did that, Agnen tore him to pieces."

Gerard wondered how a man could be torn to pieces and still be alive, but decided to leave that question for another time.

"He plans to flood the world," said Gwara, "as you did so long ago."

"Flood the world again? Why would he do that?"

"He wants to destroy mankind. Start over."

Narre pressed his lips together, thinking. Then he turned back toward his hut.

"Jassyara!" he called out.

The woman who had first peeked from the hut looked out again.

"Go to the High Place," said Narre. "Stay there until I come for you."

She nodded and headed off without a word.

Narre turned back to Gwara and Gerard. "We must find Conte immediately."

"Back through the rocks then?" Gerard asked, looking back.

"Not like that. Like this."

At that, Narre clapped his hands. A boom sounded and washed over Gerard with a blast of air. His head spun and everything went black.

Gerard opened his eyes to find himself in a different clearing. He and Gwara lay upon the ground, and Narre stood proudly, as if nothing had happened. Gerard recognized the place, where a spring spouted up unexpectedly from the ground and formed a tiny stream. Beside it, a man who looked very much like Narre, except with green designs on his body instead of blue ones, sat upon a stump. He was using some kind of stone-bladed knife to skin an enormous tapir, and a long, bamboo fishing pole lay beside him. He looked up in surprise at the group.

In the next moment, Arany and Cabwassu came running from the woods to the south, along the stream. Strangely, Arany carried a large, clay pot in her arms.

Conte put down his knife and stood up. "Are we having some kind of celebration? I would have prepared cauim if you'd told me," he said, referring to a traditional Tupinambá beverage.

Narre smirked at his brother's comment. "Good to see you, brother. It has been many moons."

"Many indeed," replied Conte. "If you've come all this way, you must have heard of my plan." He looked at Gwara, who had just picked herself up from the ground. "Little Gwara, did you hear something while you nibbled on my refuse today?"

Gwara looked down and said nothing.

"Where is Mayara?" asked Narre.

"She is well," replied Conte. "She has gone to the High Place."

"She will have company there. Jassyara has gone as well."

"In that case, you most certainly have heard of my plans."

"I have heard you plan to flood the Earth."

"It is true. I have tired of these invaders," Conte said, glancing at Gerard. "And those who welcome them." He motioned toward Arany and Cabwassu. "Have you come to stop me, brother?"

Narre strode toward him. "And what if I have?"

"Then we will settle our differences once and for all."

Narre stopped just in front of Conte, who stood firm and met his gaze. Everyone held their breath in expectation.

"Always foolish, brother," said Narre. "I haven't come here to stop you. I've come here to help you. You can't do this alone."

At that, even Conte looked surprised. Narre clasped arms with him at the elbows, and the two embraced.

When they separated, Narre said, "I am tired of men as well. Let us bury the past, and do this together. Not in anger, as we did the last time."

Conte smiled.

"So, Gwara," Gerard asked dryly, "do you have another plan?"

While everyone around her seemed shocked by Narre's declaration, Arany wasn't surprised. She didn't trust these strange, timeless men. They had flooded the world ages past, during an angry quarrel, as the stories told.

First Agnen and the land of the dead, she thought, *now we face the sons of Soomeh himself. Could this day get any more hopeless?* They faced powers mentioned only in legends, passed down for generations. Her foolish suitor had gotten them caught up in schemes of which no mortal should dare take part.

Nearby, Gerard drew his sword. Cabwassu rushed to grab his arms and Arany put herself between him and the twins.

"Don't do it," said Cabwassu.

"That won't help," said Arany. "These twins are not like us. They are like gods."

"There is only one God," Gerard replied through clenched teeth, "and that God is nothing like *them*."

"Then think of them like those heroes you talk about in your stories: Heracles and such. They are far beyond our powers."

Narre looked back at them. "Call me what you wish, but your friend is right. I have lived for moons beyond counting. If you think you can kill me by poking me with that, go ahead and try."

Gerard sheathed his sword and Arany whispered a sigh of relief.

"We can't just let them do whatever it is they're planning," he whispered.

"First things first," she said. She held forward the clay pot. "Conte, won't you please change back my beloved? If we are to die in this flood, at least allow me to die with him."

Conte had already returned to skinning the tapir, and appeared to be almost finished. Without looking up, he replied, "Don't you think he'll be better off as a fish?"

Arany saw Cabwassu gripping his bow, and Gerard's hand twitching at his sword. Fighting the twins, however, would lead to nothing but their deaths. Arany could think of but one option, a path without hope. Nevertheless, it would gain them some time to think.

"If you think we are unworthy," she said, "then we challenge you. We will prove our worth."

Gerard's jaw dropped at Arany's daring challenge. He looked to the twins, who—much as he suspected—laughed at the suggestion.

In their travels through the Brazilian wilderness, they had faced everything from invulnerable, brain-sucking monsters to enchanted pranksters, but Gerard knew they had gotten wrapped up in something far beyond their usual dose of the extraordinary. With every minute that passed, he had less of a grasp on what was going on. Of one thing he was sure, though; when Narre said he had lived for ages, Gerard believed him. No simple challenge would solve this situation.

"It is a good idea," said Narre. "This will be fun, finding out who is best to decide what happens to the Earth. What do you think, brother?"

"Fine with me," replied Conte. He pointed to Cabwassu. "I see you brought a bow. Do you know how to use it?"

Cabwassu gave one of his toothy smiles, but Gerard could tell the man was tense.

Conte pointed to a quince tree some forty yards away. "How fast can you bring down three fruits from that tree?"

Cabwassu held the bow and five arrows in one hand, leaving the other free to fire. He grabbed the first arrow and shot, then grabbed a second arrow and nocked it before the first had even reached the tree. Gerard had never seen anyone shoot so fast. Cabwassu sent off five shots in a matter of seconds.

Conte pointed to Gwara. "Go check."

Gwara trotted off past the tree to find the arrows. She came back and reported, "Three of the arrows brought down fruit!"

Cabwassu smiled and Gerard breathed a sigh of relief. Perhaps this challenge could work, after all. When he looked at Arany, though, she didn't seem at all convinced.

"My turn," said Conte.

He retrieved the longest, heaviest bow Gerard had ever seen. He drew it back with ease and shot a single shaft at the tree, then rested the bow on the ground.

"That's that, then," he said.

"What do you mean?" asked Gerard.

"Go check."

Gerard took the long walk to the tree and, just beyond it, found the arrow stuck deeply into the trunk of another. The arrow held three quince on it.

"Good lord," said Gerard.

Shaking his head in disbelief, Gerard returned to the group. Cabwassu's face fell.

"Don't look so down," said Conte. "You're pretty good. But I am obviously better prepared to protect this land."

"My brother thinks only of war," said Narre. "But there is more to the world than fighting. You," he pointed to Arany, "we'll see who can plant the fastest. A test to see who is best to feed this world. I'm not as quick as Jassyara, but I think I'm good enough."

Narre pulled a pouch from his belt and poured seeds into his hand.

"Planting?" said Arany. "I brought a bow as well." She held up the weapon for emphasis.

"You challenged, the choice of competition is ours."

Arany bowed her head in acquiescence and Narre counted twenty seeds into her palm. He counted the same into his.

"Let us begin," he said.

Arany used a stick to break the ground and plant the seeds as quickly as possible. However, her face showed her defeat from the start, and the entire exercise turned out to be pointless. Narre had planted all his seeds before she even reached halfway, and—amazingly enough—the plants had already begun to sprout from the ground.

"Heathen magic," muttered Gerard. "How can we compete with that?"

"Magic?" asked Narre. "It is no more than the wisdom passed down from our father, Soomeh. You can use whatever talents you have at your disposal."

"Soomeh saved people," argued Arany, "he didn't massacre them."

"You're right," said Conte. "It was one of his many faults. Now, brother, can we begin the flood?"

"Not yet," said Narre. "I'd like to give them one more chance: a test of wits."

Gerard stepped forward. "Oludara would be better at this, but I'll do my best."

"Not you," said Narre. "That wouldn't be interesting. I challenge her." Narre pointed to Gwara.

"What?" asked Gerard.

"Very well," said Gwara.

"You," said Narre, pointing to Cabwassu. "Choose one of the nearby banana trees. Whoever counts the number of bananas first, wins."

"That one," said Cabwassu.

In a matter of seconds, Narre said, "There are seven times twenty, plus four."

Gwara took a quick run around the tree and held down her head. "Narre's right," she said.

"Unbelievable," said Gerard. "So, what is my test?"

"No more tests," said Narre. "Are you better with the bow, or at planting, or at counting than your friends?"

"Well, no, but..."

"Enough," said Conte, attaching the enormous, skinned tapir to Agnen's hook. "How can we leave the world to you, you who cannot best us in the simplest of tasks?"

Arany looked at Gerard pleadingly. "You have overcome so many trials with Oludara. Please, do something."

"Against these two? What can I do?"

Conte lifted the fishing pole and carcass as if they weighed nothing, and held them over the stream's source. The pole didn't even bend with the weight.

"Are you ready, brother?" he asked.

Gerard looked at Arany, who could only return his glance with despair. Cabwassu raised his bow.

Without looking back, Narre said, "Don't make us kill you now. Save your strength for what comes next."

Cabwassu considered and then lowered the bow.

With that, Narre stamped his foot at the stream's source. The impact sent a shock wave through the ground that knocked everyone down except for the twins. When Gerard managed to sit up, he could see that Narre had opened an enormous crack, where the former trickle of water now jetted out.

"What are they up to?" asked Gerard.

Beneath him, he felt the earth shake. For fifty yards in every direction, the ground heaved up in a hill. Seconds later, an impossibly large worm broke forth, snapping at the tapir with a toothy mouth more suited to a shark than a worm. Conte and Narre jumped away as the creature's mouth shut upon the carcass, and the others managed to roll far enough away to avoid the gaping opening.

The worm then descended back into the ground. Instead of falling into the humongous hole the creature had created, however, Gerard was lifted by a cold mass of water rushing up and over him.

The crashing wave submerged Arany and tumbled her over so many times, she no longer knew which way was was up or down. Then it gave way to a steady, pulsing flow of water, pushing her ever farther away from the hole. Something grabbed her arm and flipped her around. She looked to see Cabwassu pointing up toward sunlight reflecting on the water's surface far above.

She shook her head, however, and searched the water for Oludara. It turned out to be no easy task, however, for the Great Worm—yet another legend that Arany had never expected to see with her own eyes—had brought up not only the water, but also a black, sticky substance. There was so much in the water that Arany couldn't spot Oludara within it.

Cabwassu gave another tug on her arm, insistent, but Arany pulled away from him. Fish or not, she would die with her beloved. Cabwassu shrugged and swam toward sunlight.

She scanned the water again and this time, spotted the black piranha rushing toward her. She grabbed the black fish in her arms and kissed Oludara upon his toothy mouth. As strange as it felt, she didn't mind.

In some way, she was glad to die like this; glad they would never face the terrible moment when they must part ways; glad she would not live to see the day that he would return to Ketu, a place she would never go, and leave her alone.

With that thought, her breath gave out and the water rushed in to fill her lungs. She had never felt such pain.

Gerard oriented himself in the rushing water and tried to get his bearings. He spotted Arany to one side. Cabwassu tugged on her arm, trying to make her swim for the surface, but she pulled away from him. Narre and Conte swam to the surface like a pair of eels, where they treaded water, high above.

Gerard was about to follow their example when a flash of red caught his eye. Gwara had gotten caught in one of the wads of tar that had come up with the enormous worm. The tar stuck to her snout and feet, and a patch clung to her back. The fox struggled in vain to shake it off.

With the water rising every second, Gerard had to make a decision. He decided to dive for Gwara.

He grabbed the fox and heaved them both toward the sunlight—the tar would have to wait. With his lungs bursting, he swam as hard as he could. He concentrated on holding his breath, taking one stroke at a time, but with the fox weighing him down, he knew he would never make it. He was still twenty feet below the ever-rising surface when the water entered his lungs.

Oludara's fish eyes refused to shed tears as he stared at the his friends' lifeless bodies floating in the water. He could only watch in despair as they perished, one by one. Arany cradled him and gave him a final kiss before she died. Cabwassu tried to make it to the water's surface, but failed. Gerard chose to save the fox, but his choice cost him his life.

Oludara spotted Conte and Narre treading water high above. He rushed up to attack them. It was a futile gesture, one that would certainly cost him his life, but he felt little desire to continue living.

Something, however, tugged at him. He looked down to see that a whirlpool had emerged from the massive hole below. Its circumference grew quickly, sucking back both water and tar at an astonishing rate. Oludara couldn't escape the tug, and found himself whirled around at dizzying speed. He slammed into the limbs of a tree and the water crashed against him relentlessly until, without warning, its level dropped below him.

Oludara's fish body flapped as it tried to breathe the air, to no avail. He fell from the tree and smacked down on the ground, which was no longer covered with water, merely damp.

Breathing or not, his body had taken such a beating that he could feel his life escaping. His last vision, from the fish eye facing up from the ground, was that of Narre standing over him, staring.

The water receded, depositing Conte and Narre back on the ground, along with the bodies of Gerard, Arany, Cabwassu and Gwara. The retreating dirt and tar had refilled most of the hole. When the last of the water disappeared below, the man-turned-fish fell from a tree and flapped on the ground. Narre walked over and watched him take his last breath and go still.

Conte came running up behind him and demanded, "What have you done, brother? Why did you stop the flood?"

Narre knelt down and touched the dead fish, changing Oludara back to his human form. With a word, he filled the man's lungs with air. Oludara spit up water, but his eyes remained closed.

"What are you doing?" asked Conte.

Narre walked to Gerard and repeated the procedure, putting air into his lungs.

"This one here passed his test," he said.

"What test?"

"The only test that mattered: that of compassion. He chose to give his life to save a tiny, insignificant fox. Can you truly say, brother, that they all deserve to die?"

Narre filled Arany's and Cabwassu's lungs with air. The four humans lay with their eyes shut, breathing deeply, as if sleeping.

Conte stomped around, and Narre thought he might attack him. Narre stood to face him. They locked eyes, until Conte's anger slowly receded.

"Not today, then," said Conte, "but their day will come."

"Today we awoke the Great Worm. Their day might come sooner than you think."

"They know where we live."

"When I awaken them, they will forget."

Conte nodded, satisfied. "Until next time, then, brother."

"Until next time."

Conte clapped his hands and disappeared.

Narre touched Gwara. The fox spit the water from her lungs and took a breath. Unlike the humans, she opened her eyes and wearily lifted her head from the ground.

"I never want to be under water again," she said, in a weak voice.

"Then you never shall, little fox. You've earned that right."

Narre laid a palm on Gwara and her body grew. Her legs extended to the point where they almost looked like stilts. Narre studied her. The tar had left her snout and feet black, as well as a patch on her back. The point of her tail shown white. She could no longer be called a fox.

"Look upon yourself. You shall never be so low again, but forever above the water."

Wobbling at first, Gwara righted herself upon her extended legs and walked to a puddle of water left over from the flood.

"Look at me," she said, excitedly. "I'm huge!"

"The little fox Gwara is no more," said Narre. "You are now Gwara-wassu, queen of the wolves. Your name and your form shall pass on to your descendants."

Gwara-wassu wagged her tail happily.

"Eat my brother's scraps no more," said Narre, "and forget the language of the humans. It is time to take care of your own."

Gwara-wassu lowered her head in acknowledgment.

"There was something else," said Narre, looking around until his eyes fell upon Oludara. "Oh, right."

Narre pulled a feather from his headband and placed it in Oludara's hand, closing the fingers gently around it.

"Give this to your fiancé. She has suffered much, and will face a great trial if she marries you. Treat her as she deserves."

With that, Narre clapped his hands and disappeared.

A clapping noise woke Gerard. He looked around, confused. Arany, Cabwassu, and Oludara all sat up around him.

"What on Earth is going on?" he asked. "Why am I all wet?"

"I'm not sure..." said Cabwassu. "We went looking for Oludara and then, did we fall asleep?"

Oludara crawled toward Arany.

"I have no idea either," he said. "I went to find you a gift and..."

As he spoke, something wiggled in his hand. He opened it to reveal a tiny, blue bird hopping there. Oludara's mouth dropped in surprise. The bird chirped happily and jumped from his hand to Arany's shoulder.

"Amazing!" said Arany. "Where did you find it?"

"I..." Oludara started, but allowed the phrase to die away as Arany embraced him.

"I was so worried, when you were lost. I...I will marry you, Oludara."

"You will? I have never felt such joy."

Oludara's face lightened up, but Gerard could swear that a cloud passed over Arany's. He looked away from their intimate moment and a flash of red from the nearby woods caught his attention. He spotted some kind of canine looking out at them. It stood on spindly legs and had a gorgeous red coat of hair, complemented by a black tuft on its back. Gerard felt as if he somehow recognized the creature and tugged on his goatee in thought. After a few seconds, it turned and headed off into the woods.

Gwara-wassu followed the humans at a distance, making sure they reached their homes safely. The massive longhouses in their village had been damaged by the flood which had come and gone and left everyone puzzled. Their only certainty was that of long weeks of work ahead, repairing the damage.

Now a proud maned wolf, Gwara-wassu headed to a gathering spot deep within the forest. She howled, and at her call, wild dogs and foxes came pouring from the forest. They marveled at the white spot on her tail, her black legs, and her mane with black fur. Little Gwara had indeed become the Queen of the Wolves, champion of her kind, and she knew she had much to do.

Chapter 7

The Discommodious Wedding of Oludara and Arany

BREEZE TICKLED THE PUMA'S WHISKERS as she emerged from the brush. She raised her nose for a few sniffs, which brought nothing more than the scent of orchids. A twirl of her ears located only the rustling of leaves and occasional plop of a leaping fish. Confident of her solitude, she sauntered toward the riverbank.

Habit dictated a nap by her favorite muddy river after a meal, and a chance encounter with an agouti at dawn had provided the repast. She circled a sunny patch of grass and tossed herself down. Just as she began to lick her haunches, a noise alerted her. She spotted two figures—human—emerge from the forest on the other side of the river.

To her surprise, one of them bore black skin, a coloring she had never before seen on a human. However, she recalled her many jaguar cousins with black hides, who were no different from their yellow brothers, so she assumed the man's skin made no difference. She found more astonishing the covering he used *over* his skin. The humans who lived nearby at most hung a few feathers and shells from their bodies; this one had covered most of his.

The other human, a female, *did* appear to be from the local pack, those who lived within the circular wall of tree trunks. Her skin, naked from head to foot, matched their usual tanned tone. For some reason, the woman did not seem entirely unfamiliar to the puma, although she could not remember why.

The two humans seemed pleased, both smiling at each other. The man placed a hand upon the female's. She shook her straight, black hair and it whirled briefly before settling back down, falling all the way to her waist. Then the man said something and she assumed a more hostile pose.

That gesture jogged the puma's memory. She raised herself cautiously, to avoid attracting attention, and crept back to the woods. Once the brush closed around her, she raced off to seek the Master of the Forest.

He would find this news most interesting.

⤙◇⤚

Oludara, staring over the muddy waters of the Black River, noticed movement on the other side. It appeared to be an animal, possibly feline.

"What was that?" he asked, pointing. "Did you see something move?"

Arany yanked his muscled shoulder, turning him to face her. "Don't change the subject," she said, her voice stern. "What did you just say about our marriage?"

"I said I that I spoke with Jakoo, to mark the ceremony," replied Oludara.

Arany gasped. "And what did he say?"

"He attempted to put it off, much like you, but I demanded my right. In the end, Jakoo said that I can take you as my bride when the caju ripens." The Tupinambá often used fruit ripening and other natural events as measures of time.

"And you didn't think of asking me?"

"What is the point? Every time I ask to choose a date, you make up some new excuse. Are you not ready to marry?"

Arany lowered her head. "It's not about being ready."

"It is time to begin our life as man and wife. How strange is destiny? To believe I was brought to Brazil as a slave! I thought it would be the end of me, but I was freed by Gerard, the most steadfast friend I've ever had, and then I met you, my true love. Who would believe so much good fortune could blossom from such evil? Olorun works in mysterious ways.

"So stop punishing yourself, whatever the cause. The caju should ripen in no more than two weeks, and we will be married. When this is all over, you will thank me for taking action." At that, he turned and walked away.

Arany waited for Oludara to disappear in the distance, then whispered, "Destiny may be your friend, Oludara, but it has never been mine. I do love you. And that is why I fear."

Gerard returned from his fishing trip carrying three trahiras on a line. He held the catch proudly before his stout chest as he walked among the group of natives he had accompanied on the outing. He could never entirely get over the contrast between himself and those around him: his palm-length goatee against their lack of facial hair; his short red curls against their mushroom-cut black hair with shaved crowns; and, most of all, his cotton shirt and knee breeches against their nakedness. Nevertheless, Gerard felt every day more at home among them.

Gerard received an unexpected slap on the back and turned to face Cabwassu's teeth jutting forward in an overly enthusiastic smile. As usual, Cabwassu wore pointed stones in his earlobes and lower lip, and the blue and green feathers which marked him as a chief fanned out from his armbands.

"You fished well today, Gerard," he said. Then, without warning, he noticed something and said, "Stop!"

Gerard tensed and spun around, looking for danger, which caused him to accidentally smack Cabwassu in the face with the fish.

Cabwassu wiped off his face and grinned. "Sorry, I did not mean to frighten you," he said. "I just wanted to show you something. Do you know this fruit?" He pointed to a red fruit with a strange brown curl growing from the bottom.

"I've seen it," replied Gerard, "but never knew it's name."

"It is called 'caju'," said Cabwassu. "The fruit is tasty, as is the nut which grows from it."

"Cashoo" repeated Gerard. Even after his many months speaking Tupi, his accent remained strong.

Cabwassu laughed. "Try again, 'caju'," he said, pronouncing the "j" with a strong "zh" sound.

"Caju."

"Good," said Cabwassu, nodding his head in approval. "You almost speak our language like a native now."

"Not that well," Gerard replied with a sigh, "not like Oludara. Would you believe I could speak six languages when I arrived in Brazil? Oludara knew but two: Portuguese, which he learned while a captive of the slavers, and his native Yoruba. You would think I would have been the one to master Tupi first, but Oludara picked it up much faster.

"I suppose it shouldn't come as a surprise, though, Oludara is the most intelligent man I've ever known. Except perhaps for that Tyge Brahe fellow I met at the university in Mecklenburg, the gentleman with the funny nose. Now *that* man could talk about anything."

"Are you done speaking?" asked Cabwassu.

"Why...yes."

"Good," replied Cabwassu, "because I have no idea what you are talking about." He turned and continued down the path.

Gerard sighed and pulled one of the cajus from the tree before following. Minutes later, they arrived at the village to find Oludara and Jakoo speaking in the center common. Jakoo wore an elaborate headdress of yellow-and-red feathers, and little else.

Oludara's eyes widened when he spotted Gerard. "Gerard," he said, "what is that?"

Gerard held up his fish proudly.

"Dinner!" he replied. "Caught them myself, I might add."

"No," said Oludara, "in your other hand."

"A cashoo," he replied, going back to his first, incorrect enunciation.

Cabwassu rolled his eyes, a gesture he had picked up from Gerard.

"The caju," said Oludara. "It is ripe!"

"Well you certainly seem excited about it," said Gerard. "I was going to eat it, but if you want, I'll give you this one and go find another for myself. There's a tree just five-minutes' walk from here."

"It is not that, my friend. Now that the caju is ripe, it is time for my marriage to Arany. I will tell her immediately."

Cabwassu's eyes went wide at the declaration. He looked at Jakoo. "Marry Arany?"

Jakoo shrugged and said, "The decision is theirs."

Cabwassu shook his head in disbelief.

Gerard found the exchange a bit unusual, but returned his attention to Oludara.

"Just don't expect me to participate in this farce," he said. "I told you before, marriage is a sacrament. What you're talking about is nothing more than a pagan ritual."

"You know I love Arany," said Oludara, "No matter what the custom, she will be my bride."

Gerard crossed his arms. "Unless that means sharing religious vows, it's not marriage."

"Gerard, the Tupinambá do not practice wedding ceremonies the way you know them. They do not worship your Protestant god, and neither do I."

"It is true," said Jakoo. "When we lived among the Jesuits, they taught us about Christian weddings, but our customs are simpler."

"And what customs are those?" asked Gerard.

"We throw a party," offered Cabwassu. "We drink and dance all night long. Then, the next day, we roast an enemy and eat him!"

Another nearby native added, "Good idea, we can go to battle and find a warrior to eat!" Several others perked up at the suggestion.

"Well isn't that exceptional?" said Gerard, mocking. "Let's replace wedding vows with war and cannibalism."

"Gerard," said Jakoo, "you know that Cabwassu speaks in jest. Our tribe stopped those practices long ago. The day after the party, we meet in the village center to perform the marriage."

"And who performs this marriage?"

"Yandir, of course."

"The village sorcerer?" Gerard shook his head.

"Please, Gerard," said Oludara. "You know how much Arany means to me. You are my closest friend. If you do not participate..."

"For your friendship, I'll go to your party. But don't expect me at your so-called wedding." He strode away to their longhouse.

Oludara turned to Jakoo. "The time has come," he said, "just as you promised."

Jakoo appeared distressed, but nodded. "I will speak to Yandir," he said. "You will have your party, you and Arany deserve it." He motioned to a nearby native, one of his men. "Alert the other chiefs, tonight we celebrate."

Then he spoke to Oludara again. "I have one favor to ask. Please wait until tomorrow, after we have all recovered from our drinking, to take Arany as your bride."

"I have waited many days," replied Oludara. "One more night will be nothing."

Everyone in the village, almost four-hundred people, had crowded into one of the five longhouses for the party. Many had donned elaborate feather decorations on their arms, heads, and backs, and almost all had painted designs on their naked bodies.

At the center of the crowd stood a three-foot tall ceramic vase filled with *cauim*, an alcoholic beverage. Beautiful red, black, and white decorations covered it. The women would go to the vase from time to time to fill gourd cups with cauim, which they would take to the men or drink themselves. No food of any kind was served, as was the Tupinambá custom for a drinking celebration.

As always, fires burned throughout the dwelling, one for each family housed in the cabin. From time to time, people circled the vase: dancing, singing, and playing flutes and drums. People relieved themselves near the walls whenever they felt the need, and Gerard felt nauseated every time a draft carried the sour scent to his nose.

He sat glumly beside the bride and groom, trying to drown his concerns about the wedding with drink, but the powerful beverage and the sight of people emptying their bladders not fifteen feet away from him had only compounded his unease. He spent much of the night averting his gaze from the women's nakedness—a habit ingrained by his Protestant ethics—but their dancing, bouncing bodies made it a dizzying task.

Turning to Oludara, he commented dryly, "Quite the party, isn't it? I imagine the bacchanalia of Rome didn't surpass it in decadence."

"It *is* a wonderful party," agreed Oludara, completely missing the sarcasm.

Gerard noticed Arany sitting upright, her face filled with worry. Before he could say anything to her, Cabwassu staggered over and slapped him on the shoulder.

"Having a good time?" he asked, an alcohol-exaggerated smile across his face.

"I've had better," responded Gerard.

Cabwassu laughed. He turned and shouted, "I would like to say words to our honored couple!"

The room silenced. Cabwassu held up his gourd before him and said, "I hope we are not all slain tomorrow."

Gasps wheezed around the room.

Jakoo jumped up and grabbed Cabwassu's shoulder. "Think what you're saying!" he said.

"I know what I'm saying," replied Cabwassu. "I am saying that tomorrow, during the wedding of Oludara and Arany, I hope our heads are not caved in, and our bodies not cooked for meat."

Gerard leaned over to Oludara and asked, "Is this normal for a wedding toast?" With the Tupinambá, former eaters of human flesh, it was difficult to know for certain.

"I have no idea," replied Oludara.

Both of them turned toward Arany in askance, but she grimaced and looked away.

Everyone stared at Oludara.

"I think they want you to say something," whispered Gerard.

Oludara rose deliberately and took a deep breath. "Thank you all. I also hope that tomorrow is a propitious day."

Everyone waited until it was obvious he would say nothing more. Finally, Cabwassu shrugged his shoulders, grinned, and took a drink from his gourd. A collective sigh sounded around the room, and everyone went back to their revelry.

From the middle of the room, a woman exclaimed, "The vase is empty!"

Gerard, relived, took a final swig from his gourd. "I'm glad that's over," he said.

"Over?" said Cabwassu. He almost fell over with laughter. "It is time to move to the next hut, and open another vase."

"There'sh more?" asked Gerard, his voice slurring. "I'm feeling a bit fuddled. Moderation ish important for a Christian."

Arany smiled for the first time that evening. "Gerard, we will drink cauim from all five longhouses this night."

"Oh my!" exclaimed Gerard. He frowned at his empty gourd, his head swaying as he tried to concentrate on it. "Where does thish cauim come from, anyway?"

"Have you not seen the women making it?" asked Oludara. "They chew cassava and spit the juice into these vases, where it is left to ferment."

"What?" Gerard squinted at the vase in the middle of the room, trying to focus his double vision into one. Then came a sudden recognition; he *had* seen the vase some weeks before, a group of women doing exactly what Oludara had described.

He slapped a hand over his mouth and ran from the hut.

Oludara chuckled and took another drink, and Arany, by his side, did the same.

Oludara, anxiously awaiting the ceremony in the village center, spotted Gerard emerge from their longhouse. Gerard had dressed his finest. As always, he wore his wide-brimmed hat with the feather on top, but instead of the cotton shirt, vest, and breeches he used for traveling, he wore a dark blue doublet with ruff collar and stockings, an outfit much too warm for the stifling heat of the forest. Oludara recalled the first time he had seen Gerard in those clothes: the first time they met in Salvador's central square. On that occasion, Oludara had worn chains.

Gerard had also cleaned and shaven himself, leaving his goatee trim and cheeks smooth. But the fine clothes could not hide the green tint of his face and grimaces from a headache: consequences of the previous night's revelry.

"Gerard," said Oludara, "you've come for my wedding!"

"No," said Gerard. "I put on my Christian finest to go off and pray for your soul. Are you certain you won't desist? Just give the word and I'll go in search of a priest."

"I'm sorry, Gerard. My ways are not yours."

"Very well." Gerard turned to leave but stopped. "Oludara, have you noticed that everyone is carrying weapons?"

Oludara examined the crowd and found that most of the men did, in fact, hold bows or wooden clubs. Many in the crowd sweat visibly, despite their nakedness.

"Indeed I had not noticed," he replied. "I've been lost in thoughts of my bride."

"Is it custom here to arm oneself for a wedding?"

"I've not seen it before, perhaps we should ask."

They were interrupted when Arany appeared from her cabin. Her body had been painted with elaborate black and red designs. Gerard shook his head and walked away. Oludara frowned at Gerard's back, then returned his attention to his bride.

Arany approached Oludara with slow, careful steps, nervously glancing from side to side the entire time. When she stood just one step before him, she took one last look around. Satisfied, she let out a breath and reached out to grasp his hand.

A shrill scream interrupted her movement.

Not five feet from Oludara and Arany stood Sacy-Perey. As usual, he wore his pointy red cap and short leggings. His abrupt appearance did not surprise Oludara, even though the imp hadn't shown himself since he and Gerard had returned to the Tupinambá village. Sacy did, however, surprise the natives, most of whom had never seen the imp before.

"What are you doing?" yelled Sacy in his high-pitched voice.

Gerard came running. "What was that scream?"

"It appears our friend Sacy has finally returned, come for my wedding," replied Oludara.

"I'm here to save your life, you fool," said Sacy. "You can't marry *her*!" He pointed at Arany. "Curooper placed a curse on her. If she does not marry him, she must remain unwed forever. He heard of this marriage and is on his way."

"Who is Curooper?"

Sacy lifted his red cap and scratched his bald head. "Well, he is much like me, a lord of the wilderness. The animals serve him."

"Why did no one tell us of this curse?" Oludara asked the crowd.

"They can't," replied Sacy. "The whole village is cursed, and anyone who speaks of it will die."

At those words, the tribe relaxed. Many wiped sweat from their brows.

"Finally," commented Cabwassu to a nearby group. "Now that he knows, we can cancel this wedding. I'm glad we don't have to worry about *that* anymore."

"I will marry her anyway," said Oludara.

"Oh, no!" said Cabwassu.

"You can't disobey Curooper!" yelled Sacy. "If he arrives here and the two of you are married, he'll kill you on the spot."

"You said he's like you, didn't you?"

"Well, mostly."

Oludara looked up and down Sacy's prepubescent body.

"I think we can handle a child, even a magical one. Gerard, are you with me?"

"If there's danger about, I'll stay by your side," replied Gerard. "Just let me retrieve my weapons."

Before he could move, a rumbling sound like a bull charging came from the woods. Screams of "Curooper!" erupted around the village.

Riding upon a giant boar, what at first sight appeared to be an adolescent male came rushing through the front gate of the village palisade. However, Oludara soon discerned that Curooper was not a man. A thick red mat of hair splayed out from his head. Other, tinier hairs bristled along his entire body, and his feet turned backwards at the ankles. Sinewy muscles rippled from head to toe. With one hand, he grasped the spiky fur on the boar's neck, and with the other, he carried a spear with a bone-white, sharpened tip. On each side of him ran a jaguar: one yellow, one black.

"Who speaks of the curse?" he said.

Oludara stepped forward. "It was I, Oludara. I wish you no ill, great Curooper. Only now I heard of your claim on Arany, but in truth, I plan to make her my wife."

Curooper spat on the ground and turned to Sacy. "What are you doing here, cousin?" he asked. "Colluding with dark-skinned," then he motioned toward Gerard, "and white-skinned invaders of our land?"

"Please spare them!" said Sacy. "They're friends of mine. They don't understand the laws of the wilderness."

"They'll learn soon enough. Arany, you would dare accept this marriage?"

"I love him," she said, "with a love stronger than your stupid curse. Leave us be."

"Enough!" said Curooper.

With a word of command, he put his jaguars in motion. They charged Gerard. Without his weapons, Gerard could only hold up his arms as they pounced. They knocked him to the ground, where one of them placed an open jaw over his neck and the other roared in his face. Its carnivorous, noxious breath coursed around him.

Oludara rushed to help his companion, but Curooper shouted and the boar charged. Holding his spear as a lance, Curooper aimed for Oludara's chest. Oludara placed his feet in a wide stance and held his position. At the last moment, he dodged and grabbed the spear as it passed.

The jolt dragged Curooper from his mount. He fell spine-first on the ground and released his hold on the weapon. Oludara deftly spun the spear around and touched the point to Curooper's chest, pinning him down. However, he heard hoof beats behind him and jumped to avoid the boar's tusks.

Curooper sat up, opened a palm toward Oludara, and cried out a word in a language Oludara had never heard. As Curooper spoke, an invisible blow struck Oludara's chest, knocking him to the ground and sending the spear clattering away.

Curooper stood and dusted himself off. He walked deliberately to his spear and picked it up. Oludara could do nothing but grip his chest and try to breathe. As Curooper approached Oludara for a final blow, Arany ran before him.

"Spare him," she said, "and I will marry you."

Her words made Curooper pause. He pulled back his spear and rested the butt on the ground.

"Very well," he said. He mounted his boar and held out a hand to her. "Let us go."

Arany looked around, as if asking for support, but no one said a word. "Please," she said, "give me time to prepare myself for marriage. You know that if I am to leave the tribe, I must honor the spirits first."

Curooper squinted at her, then nodded. "You say that to give yourself time, but I cannot deny that it is true. In any case, you only delay what you know is inevitable." He shouted to the tribe, "I will return in two days time. If she has been touched, I will raze this village. And those two," he pointed to Oludara and Gerard, "I will feed to my jaguars."

He turned his boar and rode off. The jaguars roared a final time before releasing Gerard and following after.

Gerard stood and lent a hand to Oludara. "Why does it always come down to something devouring us? Is there no other way to kill a man?" He looked at the tribe. "You could have helped, you know."

"No, they could not," said Sacy. "Curooper laid claim to Arany long ago, and bound the warriors to never interfere. If any of them had attacked, he would have slain them all and burned the village to the ground."

"What he says is true," said Cabwassu. "We bear weapons only for defense."

Gerard turned to Oludara. "Well," he said, "if you needed another reason not to marry Arany, I think you have one."

"Even if he kills me," said Oludara, "I will not allow him to take Arany."

"Then you'd best think of something brilliant if you plan to defeat an enemy who can toss you down with a word."

A clattering of shell necklaces alerted them to Yandir's approach. A waist-length red-and-white feather headdress waved in the breeze behind him.

"Gerard is right," said Yandir. "You cannot defeat Curooper; he is immortal. Even if slain, his body revives at the next new moon and he soon after takes revenge."

"I felt the power of his magic," said Oludara, rubbing his neck. "He struck me with a force greater than a lion's pounce." Then he lowered his voice and whispered. "But before we speak, I must warn you that someone watches us. Look behind that longhouse."

Gerard turned and saw what appeared to be a child peeping out from behind one of the village longhouses.

"I'll take a look!" said Sacy. He disappeared, transporting away. Almost immediately, sounds of struggle erupted from behind the hut.

Gerard and Oludara ran toward the fight, followed by most of the village. They discovered Sacy pinning down a girl by her wrists.

The girl looked like one of the native children, except for her long, golden hair—permeated with colorful flowers—and her homely features. An unbroken, dark eyebrow and an unsightly nose dominated her face.

"Do you know this girl, Sacy?" asked Oludara.

"Yes," he said, "this is Wildflower. She is a friend of the animals, like Curooper."

"Wildflower," asked Oludara, "why have you come here today?"

"I heard you challenge Curooper, and I came to protect him."

"Protect him? Why?"

"Why? He is the most beautiful, powerful man in the world! Someday I will be his bride."

Sacy stuck his tongue out and said, "Bleh, forget about that. Curooper will never touch you."

Wildflower scowled at him.

"Hmm," said Oludara, "but why not? What if we could make Curooper fall in love with her and forget Arany?"

At that, Wildflower gasped. She threw Sacy to the side as if he weighed nothing, and he rolled away grunting. She heaved herself up and ran to Oludara, her face bright with emotion.

"Is that possible?" she asked.

"Perhaps if his brains were splattered by a club," said Sacy, deftly vaulting up to stand on his one leg.

Wildflower punched Sacy in the arm.

"Exactly, Sacy," said Oludara. "We must find a way to confuse his mind."

"Hey!" said Wildflower. "Don't you mean *clarify* his mind? Show him his true feelings?"

"Yes, of course" said Oludara, fighting back a grin. "Yandir," he said, turning toward the pajé, "what you do think?"

"We should not discuss this out here," Yandir replied. "Come with me."

Oludara, Gerard, Jakoo, Arany, and Wildflower followed Yandir into his hut. Sacy came hopping behind. Gerard and Oludara both had to bend down to keep their heads from hitting the ceiling. The group crowded in shoulder to shoulder, carefully avoiding the many containers, items, and roots lining the shelves and hanging from the walls. Yandir sat comfortably on the ground with his legs crossed.

Before speaking, Yandir peeled a banana and pinched off a piece, which he placed on a shelf beside him. A tiny, black bat hung just above the outcropping.

"I am no charmer," began Yandir, "yet it makes little difference. I have no magic which would compel Curooper; he is magic itself."

"What if we found someone more powerful than him?" asked Gerard.

"Yes," said Oludara. "My people have a saying: 'He who is pierced with a thorn must limp off to him who has a knife.' We have been pierced and must find one with the power to help us. Does some such creature exist? One with enough power to sway him?"

Yandir rubbed a hand over his bald head as he thought. "You could call upon Yara," he said. "She lives not far from here. But you would do better to face Curooper himself—her magic makes even his appear childish."

"Nevertheless," said Oludara, "if she is the only option, I will face her."

"Oludara," said Jakoo, "we can equip you with whatever you need, but no warrior from our village can go. We cannot interfere."

"I understand," responded Oludara, placing a hand on Jakoo's shoulder. "You have shown us your courage time and again, but it is right that I face this task alone, and decide my own fate."

"Alone?" snorted Gerard. "I'm going with you, of course. No heathen curse bars me, and a thousand of them wouldn't keep me from your side."

"You argue against my wedding but you risk your life to make it happen?"

"This has nothing to do with your misguided affair. I won't allow you to face danger alone."

"It doesn't matter," said Yandir. "Yara can enchant any man. You will both be helpless against her."

"But I'll be with them," said Arany. "Her charms will have no effect on me." She grasped Oludara's hand. "We should decide our fate together."

"You may go where the others may not?" asked Oludara.

"Like the others, there is much I cannot say, but a curse to never lay a hand upon Curooper would not serve very well for one he intends to have as a wife."

"Yara's charms may not affect you, Arany," said Yandir, "but her other magics will. Do you really hope to face her and live?"

Wildflower grabbed Oludara's hand and stared up into his eyes. "I'll go," she said in her girlish voice. "I'll do anything to help Curooper realize his love for me."

Oludara shook his head but Yandir interrupted. "Don't refuse her offer lightly, Oludara. Wildflower has powers you do not know, and you will need magic to fight magic. Don't be fooled by her childish appearance; all those who enter the forest are cautious of her. Yet even so, I fear she is still a girl at heart. Where Wildflower is innocent, Yara is cunning. And Yara's powers are far greater; it will not be an even match."

"Then we require more magic," said Oludara.

Everyone turned toward Sacy.

"Hah!" he said. "Plot against Curooper? Confront Yara in her lair? No thank you, I'd rather keep my skin intact. But I do wish you the best possible outcome: a quick death and proper burial." He bowed and blinked out of sight.

"If only he would disappear as quickly when we *don't* need him," sighed Gerard.

Yandir, rubbing his head, examined the companions one by one. "It is not enough," he sighed. After a moment's thought, he opened a clay pot and removed a necklace of polished red rocks. "Take this," he said. "It may offer some protection."

"What is it?" asked Oludara.

"It will protect your body from magical harm. It is the greatest treasure of the village."

"Thank you for your trust in me," said Oludara. "I swear I will return it."

"But beware, not all magic is direct. If Yara's magic causes a tree to fall upon your head, it will kill you just as surely."

Oludara nodded.

"And Gerard," said Yandir, "I may be able to prepare something for you."

"No thank you," said Gerard, "I have an amulet of my own, much better than any heathen witchcraft." He pulled a cross from under his doublet.

Gerard had never admitted to using the potion Yandir had given him before their trip to Ilhéus, but Oludara had his suspicions.

Yandir frowned. "At least take this," he said, pulling down a string of garlic bulbs from the ceiling. "It is said that Yara can't stand the smell. Eat some before your encounter."

Oludara stepped from the hut and raised himself to his full, imposing height. "We have no time to lose," he said. "Let us be on our way."

After hours following Arany through the dark forest, batting away vines on a rarely treaded path, the sudden expanse caught Oludara by surprise. They had arrived at the edge of a lake. Grass-covered islands peeked above its surface, and lily pads with violet-tinged flowers formed floating, green bridges between them. To the left, spray sparkled in the moonlight as a waterfall caressed a mossy rock wall. A mist filled the air, thick enough to obscure the far side of the lake in a cottony blanket of air.

"Is this it?" asked Gerard, coming up behind them.

"Yes," replied Arany. "We must wait here; Yara comes every night to bathe."

"Oh," whispered Gerard, covering his mouth, "should we be silent?"

"Don't worry," said Arany, "we are here to bargain with her, not surprise her. Our voices will attract her, so feel free to speak."

"Fine with me," said Gerard, throwing himself to the ground. "Conversation is better than that march through the forest."

"A toilsome journey," agreed Oludara, "but necessary. I only hope we made it in time."

Oludara and Arany sat side by side, staring out over the water. Wildflower sat behind them. No one spoke for several minutes.

"You tell us to speak," said Oludara, "but it appears no one is the mood for conversation."

"These lily pads remind me of a story," said Arany. "If you wish, I can tell it while we wait."

"Please do," replied Oludara, "I would like that."

"There was once a woman named Naya," said Arany, "daughter of a powerful chief and the most beloved of her tribe. She fell in love with the moon, but became distraught when she found she could not call its attention. One night, she came to a pond, much like this one, to admire it. When she saw the moon's reflection upon the water, she thought it had come to swim with her, so she jumped in. She was never seen again, but the lily pads grew in the spot of her dive. They always look up from the water, catching the moonlight.

"So you see, I am not the first woman to be cursed by a magical love beyond her control."

"It is a nice story," said Oludara. "Although I hope ours has a happier ending." After a moment, he stood up and said, "We waste our time here. Is there no way to call this Yara to us?"

As if in response, a voice sounded. One soft, steady note called out in the night, and gradually escalated in volume. Then the note changed, and a song began. The words sounded familiar, yet at the same time unrecognizable, like some long-forgotten language. Everyone's eyes were drawn toward a shimmering silhouette in the mist, sitting upon one of the lake's tiny islands. The glow obscured details, yet the form appeared to be human, female.

Without speaking, Gerard stood and walked toward the water.

"Oludara," shouted Arany, "stop him!"

Oludara followed in his own measured pace.

"No!" said Arany.

She ran in front of Oludara and pushed him back. He shoved her away, but she grabbed onto his arm.

"Please," she screamed, "I love you!" She repeated the words several times, stumbling backwards as Oludara pressed forward. A few paces ahead of them, Gerard took a first step into the water. Arany threw her head into Oludara's broad chest and cried.

Oludara paused and stared down at her. He touched one of her tears, then shook his head to clear it. He spotted Gerard knee-deep in the river and still moving.

Pushing away Arany lightly but firmly, he ran forward and grabbed his comrade. Gerard struggled against him, managing a few inches of progress with each step. As Oludara fought to halt him, Arany dashed back for her bow. With a fluid movement, she raised the weapon and shot at the shimmer. The light disappeared in a puff, leaving no trace of the form within. Arany let out a sigh and relaxed. Gerard, waist high in the water, stopped his movement.

Oludara loosed his grip on Gerard and asked Arany, "What do you think happened? Did she leave?"

Something like a fish with arms jumped from the water and grabbed Gerard at the throat. The two forms disappeared below the water with a splash.

"Olorun!" yelled Oludara. He plunged his hands into the water but found nothing. He readied himself for a dive.

"No," said Arany, "you'll never keep up."

Wildflower ran up beside them, arms waving. "I can follow!" she said.

"And I can take one of you with me."

"I'll go," said Arany.

"No," said Oludara. "The spell is broken; I will forget your love no more."

Arany raised a hand in protest, but deferred. She was too practical to waste time arguing during a crisis, and Oludara silently thanked her for it.

"Hurry up," said Wildflower, kneeling on all fours in the water. "Grab on to me."

Oludara grasped her tightly around her neck and chest. Under his arms he could feel a change, as her skin became coarse and tough. A fin rasped along his face as it grew from her back.

He sucked in a breath as the pink river dolphin dragged him under.

Lungs bursting, Oludara felt the dolphin jerk upward. They leapt from the water and crashed to the ground, the dolphin form of Wildflower squeaking at the impact. Oludara rolled off her and gasped air into his lungs. Beside him, Wildflower returned to her own form and did the same.

Oludara regained his breath and rubbed the water from his eyes to find himself in complete darkness. Echoes of dripping water filled the space around them, and he felt around to discover water on all sides of the small patch of dirt on which they rested.

"Wildflower," he said, "we have reached an underground cave, and I fear we must navigate through the water. Can you carry me a little farther?"

She gave a tired nod and transformed back into a dolphin. Oludara fell off the leathery back twice before finally getting the hang of the unusual mount, and they set off along the underground waterway.

Beneath Oludara, Wildflower turned her dolphin head from side to side and made low clicking sounds. In this fashion, she unerringly located passage after passage. After searching several dead ends, she reached a tunnel which caused her body to tense. She rushed down it and Oludara could soon tell why: the tunnel echoed with distant music, and they soon spotted a faint glow. The light grew brighter as they raced down the tunnel, which ended in a sumptuous cavern.

Rough, unrefined gold spotted with sparkling rubies and emeralds formed the walls. Narrow shores rose on the sides and back of the cavern, with a myriad of objects littered upon them: from simple clay pots to golden dishes. The collection favored musical instruments and apparel such as discarded armor, clothes, and boots—all masculine. The objects varied so much in style and wear that Oludara assumed they came not just from different places, but different ages. A glow from the ceiling—Oludara couldn't discern the source—illuminated everything.

At the back of the cavern, upon a bed of fine pillows, lay the unmoving body of Gerard van Oost. A woman who could only be Yara lounged near him at the edge of the water and strummed a golden harp. Her human upper half reclined just out of the water, her naked breasts half-submerged and floating. Her lower half was that of a fish, and it swayed back and forth, making perfect ripples in time with the music. Voluminous hair spread around her like a nest, and matched the color of the rubies. Her eyes, in contrast, sparkled the color of the emeralds. Her white skin appeared more European than Brazilian.

When she spotted Oludara and Wildflower, she struck a discordant note on the harp.

"What is this?" she shouted. Even shouting, her voice reverberated deep and seductive.

Yara snapped her fingers and Wildflower transformed back to her true form, dunking both her and Oludara in the process. The two of them swam to shore on one side of the cavern, while Yara picked up a nearby goblet and took a drink.

"Wildflower," she said, "how dare you enter my lair. Although—" she swam closer to them and eyed Oludara up and down, "—I must say I like what you bring. Tall, with an onyx skin I've not seen for a hundred years, and deep, lush eyes to match. And those muscles!" She stared just below his waist and gave a hungry smile.

"I am not here to pleasure you," said Oludara.

"Really?" she asked. "Are you certain of that?" She swam back to a corner of the cavern and picked up a hollowed out turtle shell. "I'd be remiss if I didn't entertain you. One from Guinea probably doesn't care for the harp. But this..." she picked up a handful of grape-sized conchs and cascaded them into the shell, "might be more to your pleasure."

Yara shook the turtle shell with a deliberate rhythm. She sang with the swish of the shells, in the same incomprehensible tongue as before. Her torso rocked from side to side as she swam ever closer.

Visions of Ketu filled Oludara's mind, and he longed for home. Yara swam to his feet and motioned for him to jump in. He reached down to her.

"Oludara!" said Wildflower, her voice an angry child's tantrum. "Remember Arany."

Oludara's eyes focused. He grabbed Yara by the neck and pulled her up from the water.

"Yes, Wildflower," said Oludara, "I swore to my love I would not forget. Your enchantment is broken, Yara, your spells will work on me no more."

Yara wiggled in his grip, but he held firm.

"I am more than a simple charmer," she said with venom in her voice, "and you are nothing but a toad!"

With a glowing finger, she reached out and touched his chest. When she made contact, however, the amulet around his neck crackled and she pulled back in pain.

Without warning, Yara turned into an eel and fell from Oludara's grip. He grasped down for her, but his fingers closed just behind. She slithered through the water to Gerard's side and returned to her womanly form.

"Do not dare touch me again," she said. "And if you think a pajé's trick amulet will save you, you're mistaken." She turned to Gerard and said, "Wake, my dear."

Gerard sat up and blinked his eyes. "Yes, my love," he said.

Yara laid back and retrieved her goblet. With her other hand, she pointed to Oludara. "Kill that man," she commanded.

Gerard stood and unsheathed his rapier. He strode around the cavern toward Oludara.

"Gerard," shouted Oludara, "it is I, Oludara!"

Gerard ran at him full bore. Oludara unsheathed his ivory knife and used it to parry Gerard's first thrust. Although Gerard's over-aggressive lunge left his side open, Oludara did not attack.

"Wildflower," he said, "to my disadvantage, I cannot strike. Can you not do something?"

"I can't transform!" she said. "Yara has negated my power."

Yara laughed and took a drink from her goblet.

Oludara dodged another of Gerard's thrusts. Gerard had been trained in swordplay by Bolognese masters, but much to Oludara's relief, he attacked clumsily, not at all like his usual, precise self—most likely, an effect of the enchantment.

A fist-sized ruby spun through the air and struck Gerard in the head. He rubbed the spot and turned to where Wildflower stood with a smug look on her face. Oludara used the distraction to flip behind Gerard and wallop the back of his head with the knife butt. Gerard collapsed without a sound.

Yara gasped, choking on her drink. She set down the goblet and lay back.

"Perhaps we can come to an understanding," she said, "unless you would like to continue our game?"

Her skin turned green and scaly. In seconds, she transformed into a sea serpent with foot-long fangs. Just as quickly, she returned to her original form.

"That is why I came," said Oludara, "to speak." He sheathed his knife and sat cross-legged on the ground.

"Only to speak?" she asked. "If you wish to possess me, you need only ask." Her mouth curved into a sensual, inviting smile.

"I have no wish to be your lover," he said. He pointed to the discarded clothing and armor in the cave. "I can see what happens to them."

"I can make an exception," she said.

"The offer is tempting, but I fear my companion's Protestant beliefs are beginning to affect me. I save myself for my true love."

"How tedious," replied Yara. "But if you didn't come here for me, then you must have come for my jewels."

"The white men are the merchants, who trade even human lives for gold. I know, for I myself was sold in this way. But for me, these treasures have little worth. My people have a saying, 'Desire for money is the father of disgrace.' "

"If you seek neither my caress nor my jewels, then you surely came here for my magic."

"I did indeed come for a boon," said Oludara, "a magic which will make Curooper fall in love with Wildflower."

"Make Curooper fall in love with Wildflower?" She laughed in her sumptuous voice. "That would be entertaining. But charming Curooper is no small magic." She paused. "Since you intrigue me, I offer you this: leave your companion with me, and the spell is yours."

"I will never sell a man, especially one so dear to my heart. If there is nothing else you desire in trade, I will leave with him and find another way to defeat my enemy."

"Then go."

"No!" shrilled Wildflower. "Please, you are the only one who can help us, Yara."

"Letting the fat one go is favor enough," said Yara. "Leave before you anger me."

Wildflower fell to her knees. "Give us the charm, and I will do anything."

Yara stared hard at Wildflower. "Would you be my servant?" she asked.

"Yes, but only if I may still see my love, Curooper."

"Then the bargain is this: you will spend every other moon here with me, doing whatever I require. The other moons you may spend with Curooper, if any magic is indeed powerful enough to make him love one such as you."

"Oh, thank you!"

"Leave my realm now, both of you. I will prepare your charm and deliver it to you above. No one may witness the secrets of my power and live."

Oludara bowed.

"And don't forget to take your friend," said Yara. "He reeks of garlic."

Coughing, Gerard snapped out of his trance. Yandir stood over him, blowing smoke into his face from a bamboo tube.

Gerard sat up and flailed his arms. "Get those demonic fumes out of my face!" he said. Then he burped, launching a blast of hot air putrefied by old garlic.

"Phew!" said Wildflower, waving a hand in front of her nose.

Oludara, Arany, and several others stood around Gerard with expectant faces. "How did we return to the village?" he asked.

"*We* walked," replied Oludara. "*You* we carried stumbling along, wasting what little time we had to spare."

"Perhaps you should have worn an amulet," said Yandir, holding up his chin.

"I'll not bind myself to heathen sorcery," said Gerard.

"Please, Gerard," said Oludara, "we have no time to argue. With Wildflower's help, I attained from Yara a crown of leaves enchanted by her magic. If we place it upon Curooper's head, he will fall in love with the first woman he sees." Oludara held up a finely woven garland for Gerard's inspection.

"More magic," Gerard said with a scowl. "What happened to winning the day with might and wit?"

"A beast immortal like Curooper requires more than might to dissuade from his path," said Yandir.

"Then what's your plan for putting the garland on his head?" asked Gerard. "Is your sorcery of any assistance there?"

Yandir shook his head.

"I can ask him to put on the crown," said Arany. "He would do that for me."

"No," said Oludara. "You would almost certainly be the first woman he sees. In fact, we cannot allow him to come near the village; he could spot any woman here and fall in love. Gerard and I must go alone with Wildflower. We will find Curooper in the woods and separate him from the jaguars. We cannot handle all of them at once."

"And how would we do that?" asked Gerard.

"What do jaguars fear?" asked Oludara.

"Nothing," said Arany. "The jaguar is prey to none, and those two were raised by Curooper himself. They are the most powerful in the land."

"Hmm," said Oludara. "Then what do they *desire*?"

A capybara, wailing miserably, dragged itself through the forest on its two front legs. Its back legs trailed uselessly behind.

Two jaguars—one black and one yellow—appeared nearby, searching for the source of the commotion. They crept in, bodies low, but relaxed when they spotted the prey. They glanced at each other, as if not believing their luck. The capybara wailed louder and thrashed ahead.

The jaguars strolled behind it leisurely, drawing out the beast's suffering. When they came within a few paces of the capybara, the giant rodent turned toward them with an anguished expression. Then it transformed into a blond-haired child with an unsightly nose.

"Got you!" said Wildflower.

A net jerked up under the jaguars and hoisted them toward the canopy above.

Oludara walked into the clearing; Gerard dusted his hands and followed closely behind. They looked up to examine their handiwork.

"That worked easily enough," said Gerard.

"Yes," agreed Oludara. "I was worried the trap would fail, and we would have to fight the beasts."

Above them, razor-sharp claws poked out from the bottom of the net.

"Surely they can't..." said Gerard, backing away.

The net snapped, and the two jaguars crashed to the ground in a pile of skin and muscle. Oludara unsheathed his ivory dagger and Gerard whipped out his rapier. The jaguars untangled themselves and stood, rage in their eyes. The black one strode toward Gerard and the yellow one toward Oludara.

"Be careful," said Wildflower, hiding in a bush behind them. "They can crush a skull in their jaws!"

"Pleasant image," said Gerard.

The black jaguar reared up and came at him. Gerard made a half lunge, stabbing for the beast's face. The jaguar, however, showed its bluff when it dove under the blade. Its pounce caught Gerard in the knees and sent the two rolling.

Oludara spotted the movement from the corner of this eye.

"Gerard!" he yelled.

The yellow jaguar used the distraction to attack, leaping for Oludara's head. Oludara dodged right and slashed out with his blade. He scored a nick on the beast's front leg. The jaguar turned and roared.

From out of the bushes, a third jaguar appeared and pounced on the beast's back.

"Wildflower," said Oludara, "do not fight the beast in its own form."

The true jaguar rolled and threw off Wildflower, then lunged and bit her on the shoulder. She yelped.

Oludara closed in, searching for an opening, but the two creatures danced with their attacks and left no opportunity to strike.

"Wildflower," said Oludara, "change to a porcupine."

With a powerful swipe, the jaguar slapped Wildflower to the ground.

"Trust me!" shouted Oludara.

The jaguar leapt for a death blow, its maw aimed at her skull. As the jaw bit down, Wildflower transformed into a porcupine.

The jaguar, mouth filled with quills, let out a high-pitched half-roar, half-scream. In rage, it struck with its front paw, only to dislodge another set of quills into its skin. It squealed a sickly yelp and ran off on three legs.

Oludara ran to the fallen girl-turned-porcupine. He reached down to grab her but thought better.

"Change back," he ordered.

Wildflower returned to her true from. Cuts covered her arms and face, but were nothing compared to the awful bite on her shoulder.

"Wildflower, are you all right?"

Between gasps, she squeaked out, "I'll live."

"Stay here, I must help Gerard."

Oludara spotted his companion on the other side of the clearing. The jaguar balanced on its back legs while Gerard, behind it, pulled the scruff of its neck with both hands, his stout arms bulging under the strain.

"Gerard," said Oludara, running toward him, "what are you doing?"

"An old cat trick I learned as a child," he said. "But if you don't mind, could you please stop talking and tie this animal up?"

Gerard and Oludara arrived at a sunlit clearing to discover Curooper waking from a nap. They dropped behind some scrub to watch and plan their attack. Wildflower, bandaged and resting, had stayed behind with the bound jaguar.

Curooper stretched himself up from where he had lain against the sleeping boar. He scratched his scalp and whistled, calling for his jaguars. When they didn't appear, he placed his hands on his hips and looked around. His boar remained asleep.

"We must strike now," said Gerard. "He has awoken, and is suspicious."

"Yes," said Oludara, "we have no time for a more elaborate plan."

"So what should we do?"

"First we should deal with the boar."

"And how do you propose that?"

"Much like the warthog of Africa, its anger can be used against it."

Oludara walked into the clearing. He stood with a tree to his back and notched an arrow in his bow. He sent the shaft flying into the boar's haunches. It jumped up and spun around, huffing. Oludara waved at it and smiled. The beast charged.

"Stop, you hairy pig," commanded Curooper, "it's a trick!"

Oludara loosed another arrow, striking the boar in its hump, and it raced even faster. At the last moment, Oludara dodged.

The boar saw the ruse and managed to turn its head in time to avoid the trunk. Its body, however, slammed into the tree, knocking the air from its lungs. Gerard bounded from the brush and struck its head with a log. His blow seemed to have no effect, so he whacked it again, then a third time. The beast wavered for a moment before falling to its side.

At that, Curooper yelled and raised his spear in challenge. Gerard picked up his harquebus and circled to Curooper's right. Oludara drew his bow and walked to Curooper's left. The three formed a triangle in the middle of the clearing. Curooper shifted his eyes left and right, watching his foes carefully.

Oludara raised a hand. "Mighty Curooper," he said, "we wish to parlay."

"Speak your words," said Curooper. "They will be your last."

Oludara paced forward.

"We have a present for you," he said. "A crown for your wedding day." Oludara passed bow and arrow to one hand and removed the garland from his belt.

"What foolishness is this?" said Curooper. "Do you think me a stupid beast, to accept a present from my enemies? Waste no more of my time; die and be done with it."

Curooper raised a palm at Oludara and cried out a word. The amulet on Oludara's neck crackled and the magic had no effect. Curooper squinted at the sound.

Oludara lunged forward with the garland, but Curooper leapt and struck Oludara's side with the butt of his spear.

"Let us settle this in a fair fight then," said Oludara. "The amulet protects me from your magic."

Curooper straightened and scoffed at him. "Do you think I have but one power?" He whistled a shrill, complex tune. "I am the master of the wilderness, not a childish imp like your friend Sacy!"

A tapir appeared from the brush at the edge of the clearing. Birds of every color flew in and circled overhead. The grass wiggled in all directions.

"Beware, Gerard," said Oludara, "snakes!"

A group of crocodiles came waddling in the far end of the clearing.

"Will you fight the entire forest?" asked Curooper.

Gerard winked at Oludara and both of them charged. Curooper shouted a word and dropped to one knee, striking the ground with his fist. His blow caused the earth to heave out around him and throw Gerard and Oludara to the ground. Gerard's gun slipped from his hands and the round bullet was dislodged from the barrel. The garland flew from Oludara's grasp and landed several feet away.

Oludara reached for the garland but Curooper spoke another word and roots shot up from the ground, binding him from head to foot. Curooper sauntered towards him.

"You have injured my animals, attacked me, and tried to take what is mine. Any one of these is an offense for which I would kill you, but for all three, I'll feed you to the piranhas and laugh as they bite the flesh from your bones." He clasped the spear with both hands and raised it.

A green-and-yellow parrot squawked and made a shaky plunge toward them. It passed within inches of Curooper's face, distracting him, then dove and snatched the garland in its beak.

"What is this?" said Curooper. "A drunken parrot?"

Gerard pulled himself to his knees and took stock of the situation. Oludara lay tangled in vines, unmoving. A strange parrot flew a wobbly spiral around Curooper, each pass bringing it closer. Gerard noticed that an injured wing caused the bird's erratic flight.

"Why that little sneak," he whispered. He recovered his harquebus from the grass.

Curooper spun around to watch the bird's flight. The movement seemed to make him dizzy.

"Drop that crown and leave here," he commanded. When the bird continued to circle, he drew back his spear.

With no time to reload, Gerard grabbed the barrel of his gun with both hands and hurled it end over end. It struck Curooper's arm just as he released the spear. The parrot transformed mid-flight into Wildflower, crown held tightly in her mouth. She dropped from the air.

The spear, nudged off course by Gerard's gun, sliced through a lock of her golden hair. Curooper unwillingly broke her fall; she landed on his chest and knocked the breath out of him.

Before Curooper could move, Wildflower plucked the garland from her teeth and jammed it upon his head. Then she grabbed his face on both sides and smothered him in a kiss.

Curooper struggled under the romantic assault, but when he opened his eyes and looked upon Wildflower, his body relaxed. He shut his eyes and grabbed her, returning the passionate kiss.

When they separated, both sucked in a breath of air. Wildflower stood and pulled Curooper after her.

"Sweetest honey," she said, "let us be off to someplace more private."

Gerard stood and dusted himself off. Oludara untangled himself from the roots, which had come loose during the kiss.

Curooper caught sight of the movement. "All right," he said, "just let me kill those two first."

"Oh, forget about them," said Wildflower.

Curooper scrunched his eyes in confusion. "Really?"

She nodded.

"And Arany?"

"Forget her too. I want you to swear her off this very moment, and that horrendous curse you placed upon her village. You will do this as a gesture of love to me."

Curooper made a face, then sighed and said, "All right. I swear that the oath and curse bind no longer. Arany and her people can do as they wish."

With those words, the gathered animals dispersed, each in its own fashion.

"Very well," said Wildflower. "Your jaguars are a short ride from here. Let's go find them and be on our way."

Curooper kicked his boar in the ribs and it grunted and wobbled to its feet. It snorted at Oludara but Curooper grabbed the spiky hair on its neck and pulled it around. He mounted the animal and helped Wildflower up behind him. As they rode off, Wildflower looked back toward Gerard and Oludara and winked.

As the couple disappeared into the woods, Oludara said, “Goodbye, Wildflower. I will not forget your bravery, which saved my life more than once. You held your ground at times when many warriors would have paled in fear.”

“I’ll second that,” said Gerard, “quite an amazing little girl.” Then he looked down and said, “I suppose we’d best get back to your...marriage.”

Oludara touched his shoulder and said, “Gerard, if it means that much to you, I will go to Salvador and find a priest.”

“It’s not that,” said Gerard, shaking his head, “it’s *this!*” He motioned to the forest around them. “We’ve been through so much: seen wonders, battled foes—everything I came to Brazil to do. This has been the best time of my life. I didn’t want to give that up...to give you up. I’ve been selfish, Oludara, and I’m sorry. I shouldn’t put my happiness before that of others. I’m glad we at least had this last adventure together.”

“And what makes you think our adventures have come to an end?”

Gerard looked up, surprised. “Because you’ll stay in the village now, of course. Raise a family with Arany.”

Oludara laughed heartily. “Do you think I am so old as to settle down and never leave my hammock? The Tupinambá warriors leave their families for months at a time on their war campaigns, why can’t I?

“Our time together has been the best of my life as well, and we have much left to do. My people say, ‘A father’s honor makes his son proud,’ so before I begin fathering children, let us perform deeds worthy of them!”

Gerard sighed in relief. “Then I suppose we have a wedding to attend. But let me speak with Yandir first, and try to give this ceremony at least some semblance of a Christian wedding.”

“Whatever you wish, my friend.”

Gerard, again dressed in his finest, stood beside Oludara in the village center. Yandir stood before them, wearing a headdress of red feathers which hung to his knees, and several collars of polished stones. Gerard’s cross also hung among the collars, an addition which had required no small amount of arguing.

"Well," said Gerard, "here we are. I hope this wedding is worth it."

"My people have a saying," said Oludara, " 'He who marries beauty, marries trouble.' I knew from the first time I saw Arany, she would bring me much trouble." Both of them smiled.

Arany came from her cabin and approached. She stopped a pace before Oludara and looked left and right nervously.

"You need worry about him no more," said Oludara.

She smiled and took his hand.

"Now," said Gerard, motioning toward Yandir, "we can start."

"What was it you want me to say?" asked the pajé.

Gerard turned to Arany and asked in Portuguese, "How do you translate 'dearly beloved'?"

Arany shook her head.

Gerard said to Yandir, "Just say 'husband and wife'."

"Husband and wife," repeated Yandir.

"Now, 'kiss your wife'," he said, coming as close as he could in Tupi to 'kiss the bride'.

"Kiss your wife."

Oludara and Arany came together awkwardly, first striking noses, then making disjointed movements to make their lips meet. They finally connected for a quick smack.

"A bit strange for the both of us," said Oludara. "It is not our custom."

"And in the way of the Tupinambá," said Yandir, "we present the wedding bed." He held out a newly fashioned hammock.

"Now *this* will come more naturally," said Oludara as he reached out to take it.

He picked up Arany in his muscular arms and carried her off to their group's longhouse.

Gerard clapped. The natives glanced at each other and shrugged. Yandir slapped his hands together one time, then another, and soon the others joined in, clapping and cheering for the newlyweds.

"Well," commented Cabwassu to a nearby group, "I'm glad we don't have to worry about *that* anymore."

A puma rolled onto her back and stretched out, enjoying a nice bit of sun beside her favorite muddy river. After making a snack out of a caiman earlier that day, she had felt the urge for a nap.

A noise from downriver alerted her and she flipped over. She spotted the same dark man and native woman she had seen weeks before.

She thought it curious to see the two together again. Knowing that Curooper had claimed the girl long before, she had warned her cousins, the two jaguars which served him. Perhaps he had tired of the woman.

When the two humans lay down beside the river and mashed their faces together, the puma lay back down, unconcerned. After a few minutes, however, they began performing other actions, and she was forced to leave and find someplace quieter.

Chapter 8

The Minacious Appearance of the Headless Mule

POTOO PERCHED in the crook of a branch, his feathers blending perfectly with the wood around him. He stared at a small fire in the clearing below, a rare sight in his part of the forest. Two men, one white and one dark, slept in nets hung between trees, close to the fire. They didn't worry him, though, as no man—not even in the brightest daylight—ever spotted him so high among the trees.

So, he dismissed the fire and returned his attention to something more important: his nightly song. He opened his beak and called out the first note.

A shrill blast jolted Gerard from his sleep. The sound was followed by a series of whistles, each one lower in pitch and volume than the last. The song gradually faded away before beginning a second, identical series with another shriek. As the cry repeated, Gerard searched in vain for the source. Oludara also jerked awake in his hammock.

"Any idea where that blighted noise is coming from?" asked Gerard.

Oludara yawned and placed a hand behind his neck to stretch. Then he motioned toward some trees.

"Over there, I think," he said. "An owl, perhaps? Yet I see none."

"That song is awful. It sounds like the creature is crying."

"Indeed," said a child's voice from near the fire, "they say the potoo's song foretells death."

Gerard, already on edge from the doleful melody, jerked around and flipped over his hammock. He fell face first on the ground. He righted himself to see the silhouette of a child sitting on a log near the fire—a one-legged silhouette.

Certain that Sacy-Perey had appeared to plague them, he pulled himself to his feet and prepared a tongue-lashing for the imp. However, as his eyes adjusted to the firelight, he realized that the child was not black like Sacy, but a native. The child also lacked Sacy's cap and pants; he wore nothing but three brown feathers in a headband that passed beneath his black hair. Oludara stood at the ready, knife in hand.

"Who are you?" asked Oludara. "And what are you doing in our camp?"

"My name is Sacy-Taperey," replied the child, his eyes squinting a warning at Oludara, "and what are *you* doing in my forest?"

Gerard gulped at the name. *Just what we needed,* he thought, *another Sacy to plague us. Can't say the other one didn't warn us; he mentioned something about other Sacys once.* He decided to placate the creature as quickly as possible.

"We mean no inconvenience," said Gerard. "I have some fine tobacco if you'd like some."

Sacy-Taperey, or 'Sacy Number Two' as Gerard was already beginning to think of him, stuck his tongue out in reply.

"Disgusting. For all the good they say it does for the health, I find the flavor appalling." Then his face brightened. "But perhaps you have some sweets on you?"

"As a matter of fact, I do."

Gerard rummaged through his pack for his box of crystallized fruits. The chief magistrate of Victoria had gifted them to Gerard after he and Oludara had rid that city of a trio of monsters which plagued it, just one of many adventures the two had shared in the year since Oludara's wedding. He took a few from the box and offered them to the imp, who snatched them from his palm and tossed them up into his open mouth.

"Delicious," he gushed out while still chewing. "I've never had anything like them."

"These came from far away," said Gerard. "You won't find too many around here." The sweets, imported from Madeira Island, were worth a fortune in Brazil, but Gerard considered them well spent if they appeased the demon.

Sacy-Taperey locked his fingers behind his head and leaned against the log with a smile. Gerard saw something which appeared to be a snake move behind him, and he opened his mouth to shout a warning, but slapped his hand over it mid-gasp when he realized the movement was Sacy-Taperey's wagging tail. It whipped back and forth like that of a contented cat.

"I suppose we can be friends now," said Sacy-Taperey. "That is, if you care to tell me your names."

"I'm Gerard van Oost," Gerard said with a tip of his hat.

Oludara put his knife away, but remained standing. "I am Oludara. You never answered my question, Sacy-Taperey. Why did you come to our camp?"

"The potoo's song brought me here. As I told you, it foretells death."

"Whose death?" asked Gerard, pulling nervously at his goatee.

"That remains to be seen. And you never answered *my* question: what are the two of you doing here?"

"We are headed toward Santos," said Oludara.

"And what do you plan on doing there?"

"We'll see if they need help battling any foul creatures," said Gerard. He made the comment off-hand, then realized who he was speaking with, and stifled back another gasp. He had become too casually accustomed to Sacy-Perey, and felt as if we were speaking with his old acquaintance. Oludara frowned and shook his head at him, and Sacy Number Two's eyes widened in surprise.

"You two go in search of creatures to battle?" he asked. His voice had changed, but Gerard couldn't quite interpret the sentiment.

"Only the dangerous ones," said Gerard, feeling hot in the face, "those which murder people."

Sacy-Taperey gave him a grin which he definitely didn't like.

"That's quite a coincidence," he said, "because a creature has been terrorizing Santos for years. And I can lead you to it."

At that, Sacy-Taperey jumped up and placed his hands on his hips, as if waiting for them.

"What is this creature?" asked Oludara.

"You should see for yourself."

"Umm," said Gerard. "Best to leave that for morning."

"We need to go now," said Sacy-Taperey. "The creature only appears at night."

Oludara looked none too convinced, but Gerard decided that *not* following the demon could turn out even worse than following him. "All right," he said, "lead on." He grabbed his weapons and pack and lit two torches.

"Right this way," said Sacy Number Two, hopping into the woods.

Oludara frowned at Gerard. "My people have a saying, 'The spoon, seeing death, ventures his head into it.' "

"I'm not quite sure what that means."

"It means don't stick your head into boiling water!" Oludara rasped under his breath.

"You're right," said Gerard, "but isn't it better to play along with his game than go back to sleep? If he's anything like *our* Sacy, he'll just play some prank and leave us alone."

"I don't know, Gerard. This is not 'our' Sacy."

"I know. Just watch my back."

"You need not tell me that."

Oludara felt none-too-comfortable as Sacy-Taperey led them through the forest. Although Gerard seemed to think him no more harmful than Sacy-Perey, Oludara had his doubts. The creature's name and, principally, his one-legged hopping did remind Oludara of their former tormentor, but this one was different.

In the torchlight, they followed the bouncing silhouette for hours. By the time Sacy-Taperey finally paused, the black sky had already begun its transformation to dark blue.

"The creature is in the clearing ahead," whispered Sacy-Taperey. "Be careful!"

Oludara readied his bow and Gerard his harquebus, and the two crawled forward and peeked through the trees. The clearing held a pond, and as far as Oludara could tell, only a single creature: an equine animal bent over for a drink. From the size, he judged it to be a mule, but from their vantage point, he could see no more than the beast's haunches.

Gerard stood up, furious.

"Sacy-Taperey," he shouted, "you brought us all the way out here to look at a donkey's arse?"

Sacy-Taperey snickered and his tail flicked as he replied. "That thing is no more a donkey than I am a boy."

Oludara, expecting trouble, hadn't taken his eyes off the clearing. The mule, alerted by the noise, lifted its head from the water and turned toward them. Only, to Oludara's surprise, it had no head.

"Gerard," Oludara said, calling his attention.

"What is *that*?" came the astonished reply.

"That," said Sacy-Taperey, "is the Headless Mule."

The mule whinnied from a face not there, and flames shot from its neck.

Oludara felt a strange sensation at his side and Sacy-Taperey, shrieking with laughter, turned into a whirlwind which rose into the trees above them. Oludara had little time to consider that, however, when a second blaze erupted from the mule's neck and it charged them. He and Gerard fell back into the woods. Gerard threw himself behind a bush and Oludara hid behind a tree trunk. The mule stopped at the edge of the clearing, then came pacing into the woods after them.

Oludara could see Gerard motioning toward his harquebus in askance. Oludara shook his head and pointed toward his own bow. Gerard would only get one shot, so Oludara thought it better to test the creature first with an arrow.

As the Headless Mule stepped ever closer, Oludara took a deep breath and notched an arrow. He pulled it back and swung out from the tree, aiming at the mule no more than thirty paces before him. Oludara could see the beast's organs through the hole in its neck and shot for that, but the mule turned at the last moment and the arrow struck its shoulder instead, burying itself deep into the flesh.

The Headless Mule uttered a cry of pain accompanied by a furnace of flames so strong, Oludara could feel the heat even at that distance. The stink of sulfur washed over him.

The mule lunged toward him, flames blazing, and Gerard sprang from his cover. Instead of the shot Oludara expected, however, Gerard threw a double handful of dirt at the beast's flames, which, if anything, appeared to make them stronger. A shrill laughter echoed in the trees above them.

Oludara, running out of options, climbed up the nearest tree. The mule reared under him and shot flames which burned through his pants from his ankles to his backside. The laughing intensified and as he pulled himself painfully up the tree, where he found himself face to face with Sacy-Taperey.

Between laughs, Sacy-Taperey muttered, "What a pleasure! You two are the best thing to come through this forest in years."

Oludara scanned for Gerard in the flickering light cast by the mule's flames and discovered he had also chosen to climb a tree. The mule raged below him, circling the trunk. When Gerard looked to have settled in, Oludara called to him.

"Why did you throw dirt at the creature?"

"Plinio wrote of the Chimera," responded Gerard, "a monster whose fire could be doused by volcanic ash. I thought I could smother the flames in a similar fashion. What do we do now?"

"Wait until sunrise. If indeed the creature appears only at night, it should leave us soon."

At that moment, the Headless Mule belched flames at the lower branches of Gerard's tree, which caught on fire.

"I don't think we have that long!" shouted Gerard, drawing his rapier.

"Wait!" said Oludara. "Let me retrieve my bow and distract it first."

Oludara scuttled down and ran toward the bow, but the mule noticed him and charged. Its hooves cracked the bow and Oludara skidded to a halt before it, his burned haunches scraping the ground in agony. Gerard leapt from the tree but tumbled as he landed; Oludara knew he wouldn't arrive in time. The mule bent down its headless neck and aimed a blast at Oludara.

"Begone!" bellowed a commanding voice.

Oludara and the mule turned in unison.

A barefoot man with a stout walking staff strode toward them. He wore only a simple cotton cassock, tied at the waist with a ragged sash. The robe had probably been black once, but had faded to a motley gray.

"By the grace of Christ our Lord, begone!" he yelled.

The mule took a few steps back, then turned and ran into the forest. A whirlwind descended from the trees and transformed into Sacy-Taperey, who rolled with laughter upon the ground.

Gerard ran to Oludara. "Are you all right?"

"A bit burned," he replied, never taking his eyes off the stranger.

The man wore his dark hair cropped short. His blue eyes blazed out from skin tanned dark by the sun. His round chin showed only the slightest hint of stubble.

"Are you a priest?" asked Oludara.

"I am Father Miguel Samperes," replied the man, "Provincial of the Society of Jesus here in Brazil."

"The leader of the Jesuits," Gerard added in explanation.

"Thank you, Father," said Oludara. "Your magic is strong."

"Magic?" Miguel's lips turned up in the slightest of grins. "Leave it to a Guinean heathen to call that magic." He knelt down beside Oludara and examined his leg. "What you saw was the power of the Lord; I am but its vessel. I wield not magic, but faith." He pulled a canteen from his sash and applied water to Oludara's burns.

"I'm Gerard van Oost," said Gerard, "a member of the Reformed Church and a follower of Calvin."

"Calvin?" asked the priest, gently wrapping Oludara's wounds in a bandage. "That's a venom I would gladly free from your soul by means of a holy baptism."

"Venom?" challenged Gerard. "You'd clean my blood as the Huguenots were cleaned from France on St. Bartholomew's Day?"

"By the grace of God, nothing like that." Miguel finished his bandaging and looked Gerard in the eye. "Do you think the Society of Jesus had something to do with that bloody massacre? Be careful where you cast your stones, van Oost. Do you know that Calvinists captured and killed forty members of the Society two years before that?"

Gerard flushed red but did not respond.

"They were on their way here, to Brazil, to help us." Miguel sighed. "We could have used them."

Gerard started to mouth a protest, but the priest stood up and stared at him, and he kept quiet.

"Why don't we leave the sins of others behind us?" said Father Miguel.

"Fine by me," said Gerard. "But I believe any man should be free to worship as he wishes."

"We can leave that question for later, but I refuse succor to no one, not even a Calvinist like yourself." He returned his attention to Oludara. "Those burns aren't so bad, but sitting will pain you for a day or two. And what is your name?"

It was so rare a white man to ask his name, Oludara almost choked on the words. "I am Oludara, from Ketu."

"Interesting indeed," said Miguel. "A white heathen traveling with a black heathen," then he looked toward Sacy-Taperey, "and led by the devil himself. God give me strength, for it appears my work has no end."

"You know this Sacy?" asked Oludara.

"I'm well aware of Sacy-Taperey's antics."

Sacy-Taperey hopped up and bowed. "Always at your service, Father Miguel."

"Enough. You be gone as well," said Miguel, waving a hand at him.

Sacy-Taperey turned into a whirlwind and zagged off through the forest.

"Oh, how I wish I could do that," sighed Gerard. "And I should add my own thanks for saving us from the monster."

"Monster?" asked Father Miguel. "You refer to the Headless Mule? In that, you are mistaken. That animal is no monster, it is a tortured soul. Can you not see it?"

"A tortured soul which breathes fire from its headless neck," grumbled Gerard.

"A tortured soul, nonetheless. Now, what brings you two here, besides following demons through the forest?"

"Oludara and I are partners," said Gerard. "We form the Elephant and Macaw Banner."

Miguel scowled. "Providing aid to heathens is one thing, but bannermen slavers are quite another."

"We take no slaves," said Oludara. "Gerard and I lived among the Tupinambá; they are like brothers to us. I even took one as my wife."

"I would never take a man as a slave," said Gerard, his distaste apparent. "It is a foul practice."

"Bannermen who stand against the enslavement of the natives? I thought, on that subject, we Jesuits stood alone. You two are different indeed. Wait! In Rio de Janeiro, just two weeks past, I heard the tale of an unusual Dutchman who repelled the French pirates last year. I should have realized sooner with whom I spoke."

As Oludara expected, Gerard glowed at the mention of people discussing his exploits, but Oludara was more interested in something else the Jesuit had mentioned.

"You walked here barefoot?" he asked. "In two weeks? With no equipment?" He and Gerard would have taken six weeks of hiking to cover the same ground.

"I have walked all the way from Salvador, and the Lord provides all that I need along the way. I came to visit my flocks along the coast. That in Sao Paulo of Piritininga will be the last." This made him pause, thinking of something. "Where are the two of you headed?"

"To Santos."

"Perhaps it is no mere chance which makes our paths cross. Why don't you come with me to Sao Paulo instead?"

"Why?" asked Oludara.

"My flock there consists of two Tupiniquim villages, good Christian souls who have found God. However, they live in danger. They have been harassed by demons and warring tribes. With mere hundreds, they held off five thousand Carijó gentiles who came to destroy them. Through their faith, they have survived all that, but now face a threat more ominous than all those others combined."

"And what is that?"

"Bannermen."

⟡

The trip through the highlands exhausted Gerard. In the valleys, they passed through mud and frigid rivers. Along the hillsides, they navigated thick jungles. Father Miguel marched them up and down the hills at an extraordinary pace, and while Gerard pushed himself to the limit to keep up, the priest showed no sign of tiring.

Relief came at midday on the second day of their march, when the hills descended into a lightly wooded plain which stretched to the horizon.

"Isn't it magnificent?" asked Father Miguel. "A land blessed by the Lord, where we can live close to the tribes. This is a gateway to the heart of this vast land. If you head west, you will soon reach a river you can navigate all the way to the Spanish city of Asunción, or take south to the La Plata River."

As they descended the final ridge, a village came into view: a few dozen packed clay buildings and a wooden church.

"Is that Sao Paulo?" asked Oludara.

"Indeed," replied Father Miguel. "I spent many years here, before I became Provincial and had to install myself in Salvador. Back then, we had neither chalices nor linens for the altar, not even a corporal for the Eucharist. The town has come a long way since them."

Gerard didn't think it had progressed all that far, but he kept the thought to himself.

When they reached the outskirts of town, a native child saw them and ran toward one of the buildings, yelling, "Father Miguel! Father Miguel is here!" Within seconds, dozens of children, all of them natives or mixed blood, came rushing out. Unlike the other natives Gerard had met, they wore clothing. They surrounded Father Miguel, pulling his cassock and screaming welcomes at him.

He greeted every one of them by name, then said in a gentle but firm voice, "My presence here is no excuse for missing your lessons. But we have guests here today, so I expect you to play your instruments for them at lunch."

The children ran off as fast as they had come, and in their place formed a line of novices and priests. Europeans—Portuguese and

Spaniards by the look of them—compromised half the group, while the other half consisted of natives. Some walked barefoot while others wore sandals woven from coarse strands: espadrilles, as Gerard had heard them called in Spain. One of the priests stepped forward with an outstretched hand.

This priest contrasted Father Miguel in many ways. He wore his black hair slicked back in perfect lines. His small nose and wide forehead sported far less tanning and wrinkling than those of his superior.

"Welcome back, Father," he said. "May the Lord be with you."

"And also with you," replied Father Miguel. He turned to Gerard and Oludara. "Gregorio is rector of the school here and in charge of all our undertakings in Sao Paulo."

The priest introduced himself as "Gregorio Bras" and shook their hands in turn as they introduced themselves.

"Did you receive my letter?" asked Gregorio.

"Yes. I pondered long upon the problem, but found no solution. As the days brought me closer, I prayed to the Lord for a sign..." He glanced toward Gerard and Oludara. "And then I met these two. They have their own banner, that of the Elephant and Macaw."

"It is strange to seek succor from bannermen in this matter," said Gregorio, sizing them up.

"Strange are the ways of the Lord," replied Miguel. "Why don't we have lunch before we speak? We can eat out here in the open while the children perform."

Gregorio brought out food while Miguel introduced them to the others. The meal consisted of a light rice porridge, cooked vegetables, and mustard leaves—and it left Gerard's stomach growling.

"Here are some napkins," said Gregorio, handing them a pair of banana leaves. "Here in Sao Paulo, we can't afford linen for our napkins; we use only what the Lord provides us."

"Fortunately," added Miguel, "here the Lord provides well."

During their meal, the children played instruments and sang kyrielles: some in Latin and others in Tupi. Their Tupi differed from that which Gerard had learned among the far away Tupinambá, but he found he could understand it well enough.

"What instruments are those?" asked Oludara. "There are some I have never seen."

Gerard pointed them out one by one: "That's a shawn, the flutes you know, that one's a trumpet, and the two on the end are a cornett and a dulcian."

Shouting broke out in the village and the children stopped playing. Gerard turned to see hundreds of natives, most of them clothed, pouring into town. The women, shouting and crying, fell to the ground before Father Miguel. Gerard could make out phrases like: "You are our good friend," and "How much work it must have been to come visit us." It reminded him of the Tupinambá village; the women there would also make a great-to-do every time someone they knew came to visit.

Father Miguel took it all in stride, greeting and blessing all who came before him. He spoke a Spanish-tinged Tupi in a voice so measured and calm that even Gerard felt relaxed by it. After a time, Miguel led a native couple, aged around sixty, toward Gerard and Oludara. Gerard caught a bit of their conversation as they approached.

"And the pains in my head have returned," said the man.

"I'll let some of your blood tonight," replied Father Miguel.

"Thank you, Father!"

"But for now, I'd like to introduce you to these men here. Gerard and Oludara, meet Isabel and Pasquale. Pasquale is the great chief of the Tupiniquim tribes here."

Pasquale embodied the mixture of Christian and Tupi present in Sao Paulo. From his Tupi side, Pasquale wore a single feather in a band on his head and a modest shell collar—much more modest than the decorations Gerard had witnessed on other chiefs. From the Christian influence, he wore cotton pants and a leather vest. Isabel wore a skirt but left her chest bare, save for a wooden cross.

"You have Christian names?" asked Gerard.

"We take them upon holy baptism," replied Isabel.

Oludara gave a slight bow and said in Tupi, "We jump with happiness."

"We are content you have come," Isabel replied.

"They speak our language!" shouted Pasquale, his smile rounding his cheeks all the way to his ears.

Gregorio, nearby, said, "You two speak the *lingua brasilica* also? Indeed, we are well met."

Father Miguel nodded in approval. "I believe the six of us should discuss our problem. Let us retire to the school."

Pasquale's smile faded and a grim nod replaced it. "Yes, we must speak."

Gerard and Oludara followed the two priests and the native couple into one of the clay buildings. The house, much like the natives, mixed Tupi and European. On the one hand, hammocks hung throughout with fires spaced between them, just like the longhouses Gerard had become accustomed to. On the other hand, cabinets packed with all types of objects and desks littered with papers crowded the walls.

"Please pardon the modest accommodations," said Gregorio. "This building is our school, our infirmary, our pantry, our refectory, and our home. We are tithed but a tenth of the rice grown in this captaincy, and that is all we receive for our buildings, food, clothing, and anything else we need to spread the word of God to the gentiles."

The group made themselves comfortable. Gerard and the natives chose to relax in the hammocks, Gregorio took a chair, and Miguel and Oludara sat upon the ground.

"Gregorio," said Father Miguel, "enlighten our guests to the complication at hand."

Gregorio nodded and said, "The bannermen have become a far greater threat than ever we imagined. They sack the native villages, take slaves, and turn over the ones they don't want to enemy tribes to be devoured." Then he gave a nod to Gerard. "Present company excluded, of course."

"No offense taken," said Gerard. "We're aware of these practices and condemn them, same as you."

"They take our land," shouted Pasquale. "They take our wives and daughters. They sell us as slaves!"

"I know not what to do, Father," said Gregorio. "After defending our flock from so many evils, we must now face a Christian threat?"

All sat silent for some time, until at last Father Miguel spoke. "God tests us, and God sends us the means to overcome. Meeting these two on the way here was no coincidence. Who better to help us against the bannermen than bannermen themselves?"

He turned to Gerard and Oludara. "Would you aid us, find a way to defend the tribes against the bannermen?"

"Yes," said Oludara. "The Tupinambá made us one of their own. The Tupiniquim are like brothers to us."

Pasquale and Isabel smiled at him.

"I am a Calvinist," said Gerard, "with no great love of Jesuits. But in this matter, I will do all I can."

"Good," said Father Miguel. "And in return, once this matter is resolved, I will help you face the Headless Mule."

The next morning, an insistent shoving awoke Gerard from his sleep. His body felt none too eager to arise from the hammock after the long march through the highlands. He opened his eyes to discover Oludara with an over-eager smile.

"You are too long in bed," said Oludara. "As my people say, 'the sieve never sifts meal by itself'."

Gerard peeked through the window to see a dark blue sky. Oludara had awoken him on the cusp of dawn.

He rolled back over and closed his eyes. "I think the sieve can wait a little longer."

"Can it? I am eager to plan the defense of Sao Paulo. Many years have passed since I have been involved in the stratagems of war. I relish the challenge. They say that a sharp wit is the best medicine for old age." When Gerard didn't move, he added, "And if you don't get up now, you'll miss breakfast."

Gerard needed no further encouragement—only his hunger trumped his exhaustion. His enthusiasm, however, eroded quickly when Father

Gregorio served them, once again, rice porridge.

"Is it lent?" asked Gerard, not trying to hide his disappointment.

Gregorio laughed. "You refer to the lack of meat in our diet? Sometimes the children bring us a fish or an alligator to cook, but as we teach them from morning to late afternoon, they rarely have time for it. Speaking of which, they should arrive at any moment."

Right after he spoke, the echo of far-off gunfire sounded from outside. Gerard opened his mouth to ask if someone had gone hunting, but closed it when the concern on Gregorio's face told him otherwise. Gregorio ran from the house and Oludara chased after. Gerard stuffed a spoonful of porridge into his mouth and grabbed his harquebus before following.

Outside, they met Father Miguel.

"Did you hear where the shots came from?" asked Gregorio.

"Unfortunately, yes. From the same direction as Pasquale's village. We must leave immediately."

They set off at a fast pace along a worn path. After a quarter of an hour, they heard a commotion: drums and horns playing.

"What is that?" asked Gerard.

"The Tupiniquim are preparing for war," said Father Miguel. "Something terrible has happened; we must move with all haste."

They covered the last three minutes at a run, and came upon the source of the commotion: a group of fifty Tupiniquim. Some cared for an injured native, bleeding profusely from a gunshot wound. Others held down two people while their companions held clubs over their heads—poised for a killing blow. Gerard was shocked to find he recognized the two on the ground: Moara and Diogo.

Gerard, Oludara, and Father Miguel all said in unison, "Stop!"

Pasquale came running towards them, waving one of the wooden club-swords the natives called *bordunas*. Beside him, Isabel wielded what looked to be a long sack weighed down with rocks on one end.

"They took my grandsons," wailed Pasquale, waving the wooden sword in the air, "to use as beasts of burden!"

"Bring those two here," said Miguel.

Pasquale nodded reluctantly and some of his warriors dragged Moara and Diogo toward them.

"You know these two?" Miguel asked Gerard.

"Yes, they serve Antonio Dias Caldas's banner."

"Not anymore," said Diogo. "Not after today."

"What happened?"

"Antonio came looking for slaves, and found the children. There was but one guard with them, and one of Antonio's men shot him when he resisted. We stayed here to help him, but these warriors came running from the village and captured us."

"I know Antonio," said Miguel. "I didn't think him fool enough to do this."

"Antonio dared because he thought you were in Salvador," said Diogo. "I'm sorry, Father, I didn't know it would come to this...enslaving Christian children."

"We'll kill them all!" yelled Pasquale. "We'll roast them!"

"Enough!" shouted Miguel. "Do you forget our teachings so swiftly?"

Pasquale held his head in shame.

"We will go after them," said Miguel, "and we will resolve this without bloodshed."

"I know the path they take," said Moara. "I can lead you to them."

"But can we trust you?" asked Gregorio.

"We can vouch for these two," said Oludara, and Gerard nodded agreement. "They're two of the finest people I know."

"But I still don't know if we can trust the two of you. What if this is all some elaborate ruse to help them get away?"

"We can trust them," said Miguel, in a voice that offered no rebuttal. Gregorio bowed his head in deference.

Father Miguel addressed the crowd in Tupi. "We must march hard. Any who cannot keep up should stay behind."

Only a few natives stayed behind to care for the wounded man; the rest lined up behind Father Miguel. Isabel, sack in hand, stood side by side with Pasquale.

"Father Miguel," said Gerard. "You should know, this Antonio has sworn himself my enemy."

"Will that be an issue?"

"If he sees me, he could take offense."

"It doesn't matter. You must come with us; that is the reason you're here."

As the group jogged through the highlands, Oludara spoke to Pasquale and Isabel.

"Isabel," he said, "do the Tupiniquim women always travel with the warriors?"

"It is our custom for the chief's wife to follow him into battle," she replied.

"Our ways are different from the Tupinambá," said Pasquale. "Even more so from our time with the Jesuits." He pointed toward Miguel running barefoot at the front of the group, leading without pause. "You can have faith in that one. He is their greatest pajé. He has power far beyond any of the others."

Gerard heard the comment and scoffed. "A priest, even a Catholic one, is nothing like your sorcerers."

"Believe what you want; I have seen him perform miracles."

"I also saw," said Oludara. "At his command, the Headless Mule fled before him."

Gerard made a "hrumph" sound, but said nothing.

"Look at how he runs," said Pasquale. "These priests are strange. They serve us, they die for us, but they refuse to marry our daughters!"

Oludara couldn't help but smile, both at the earnestness of the comment and at Gerard's reddening face.

"They are strange indeed," agreed Oludara.

His smile disappeared as they crossed a ridge and Antonio's band came into view. Some twenty men led a line of dozens of children tied together at the neck. Oludara's own neck tingled at the remembrance of his chains.

"The children!" yelled Isabel. She raced forward, Pasquale at her side.

The other natives screamed a war cry behind them.

"Halt!" said Father Miguel.

The charge ended all at once, even though, from the faces, none were happy at the command. However, the force of Miguel's voice left no room for challenge; even Oludara froze at the sound of it.

Antonio's men turned at the commotion and lined up for battle, readying their harquebuses upon braces and aiming at the approaching group. In response, Father Miguel strode forward and held his arms wide. Antonio spotted him and called down his men. Miguel continued forward confidently, and the others followed behind.

As they came closer, Antonio spotted Gerard amidst the group and bellowed, "Van Oost, what are you doing here?"

Miguel ignored the comment and addressed him. "Antonio, what do you think *you're* doing with these Christian souls?"

A thin-nosed, moustached man wearing a black bandana stepped forward. Oludara had never seen him before among Antonio's men.

"Shouldn't you be off scourging yourself somewhere?" he asked Father Miguel.

"Watch your tongue, Grilo" said Antonio. "Don't you know who that is?"

"I know," replied Grilo, "but I don't care much."

Pasquale leapt forward, but Miguel restrained him with a hand to his shoulder. Unperturbed, Miguel replied to the man with a smile, "We save the lashings of our disciplines for Saturdays."

Diogo whispered to Oludara and Gerard, "After your last escape, Antonio demoted me. In my place, he put that man: Belchior Grilo. If you thought Antonio was bad, Grilo makes him look like a saint."

"He makes quite a first impression," agreed Gerard.

Antonio looked to Diogo and Moara. "I hope you've brought me these natives as captives."

"We follow you no longer, Antonio," said Diogo.

"Good riddance, then. You went soft long ago. The two of you are more hindrance than help. See how long you last on your own."

"If Gerard and Oludara can travel alone," said Moara, "we can at least try to be as brave."

Antonio turned red and said, "I'll allow you to live this time only because of the service you've done me in the past. But you'd best hope our paths never cross again."

Father Miguel interrupted, "Enough. Antonio, hand over the children. Release them quickly, and I won't inform the governor of this transgression."

"We took these fair," replied Antonio, "by the governor's own law."

"The law states that only natives taken in lawful battle can be enslaved. What battle did these children wage against you, I wonder?"

Antonio scratched at his beard. "Tell you what, Father. I'll turn them over if you give me van Oost."

Gerard released the slightest of squeaks.

"I'm not here to bargain," said Father Miguel.

"What difference does one Protestant make to you?"

Miguel didn't even pause before saying, "He's a Protestant no longer. He recently converted to Catholicism."

Oludara could see Gerard about to protest, so he squeezed his arm in a crushing grip. Gerard composed himself and nodded.

"I don't believe that for a second," said Antonio.

"I baptized him myself," said Father Miguel. "Do you doubt my word?"

When Antonio hesitated, Miguel raised his voice, "I am Provincial of the Society of Jesus. You will obey my command. Release the children now!"

Antonio gave in with a shrug and said to his men, "Release them." Then he added, "Father Miguel, you can be sure that Governor Veiga knows that, without slaves to work the sugar mills, Brazil will be lost. You may take these now, but it's only a matter a time before all of them are ours."

"Not while the Society of Jesus remains," said Miguel.

The children ran back to the natives, calling to their parents and grandparents.

"Don't think I'll forget this, Gerard," said Antonio. "Time and again you rob my fame and ruin my livelihood."

Gerard said nothing, so Oludara spoke for him, "If this is how you make your livelihood, ruining it is a pleasure."

Antonio huffed and turned away. Before leaving, Grilo mimicked holding a harquebus and shooting at Oludara.

Miguel turned to Diogo and Moara. "What will you do now?"

They looked at each other and Moara shrugged. Diogo said, "Who knows? We've been travelling the wilderness with Antonio for a long time."

"Would you be willing to stay in Sao Paulo for a while? Help shore our defenses from those such as him?"

"Yes," said Moara. "That is the least we can do."

"Anything to atone for this terrible deed," said Diogo.

"Good," said Miguel. "If you don't mind, please help Pasquale and Isabel escort everyone back. Gregorio, you go as well."

"You're not coming with us?" asked Gregorio.

"No," said Miguel. "I have unfinished business with these two."

For some reason, Oludara felt a chill as Miguel made eye contact with him and Gerard.

Once again, Father Miguel led Oludara and Gerard through the forest highlands. This time, however, he allowed a more casual pace.

"Where are we going, Father?" asked Oludara. "To look for the Headless Mule?"

"Toward the mule, yes. Toward destiny, I suppose you could say."

"Destiny?"

"Call it my way of thanking you."

"We haven't done a thing!" said Gerard.

"Perhaps not today, but you have done much, and you will do much. Leave it at that."

Oludara looked to Gerard and he shrugged.

When they reached a clearing, Father Miguel looked around and said, "This is the place. We can rest here."

The three of them sat down. Gerard unsheathed his rapier and oiled it.

"Can a priest tell a lie?" Oludara asked Miguel.

"Hmmm?"

"When Antonio asked for Gerard, you said he had converted."

"Oh, that. Telling a lie is a sin, but not saving a life is a greater one. I will ask for God's forgiveness for that untruth, along with my other sins."

"Other sins?" asked Gerard. "Like what, forgetting to cross yourself before supper?"

Miguel grinned at the remark. "Much worse than that, I'm afraid. I was once much like Antonio."

"What?"

"I sacked the Tupiniquim villages, then sold them by land and by sea. From their suffering, I made a fortune."

Oludara's eyes widened. Gerard dropped his rapier.

"But how long can a rational man do such a thing?" continued Father Miguel. "How long can a man tell himself that what he does is right, knowing in his heart it is wrong?"

"That thought has never occurred to Antonio," said Oludara.

"Perhaps one day it shall. In my case, I awoke one day and my sins weighed so heavy upon me, I couldn't breathe. At that moment, I swore the rest of my life to God. Many days I pray to Him to strike me down, to end my worthless existence. But the sublime glory of a martyr is reserved for heroes.

"Instead, my life is penitence. I will serve the Tupiniquim until I die, that I may gain some redemption."

At that, Father Miguel stopped and looked around.

"What is it?" asked Oludara. Knife in hand, he scanned the area, but could see nothing. Gerard, at his side, did the same.

Father Miguel focused his eyes on one spot in the woods, then stood and, arms outstretched, placed himself between that point and the two men.

Shots—at least three of them—rang from the woods, and Father Miguel collapsed. Gerard lunged to the priest's side. Oludara looked toward the shots, but could not spot their attackers.

"Gerard," he said, "we must seek cover!"

Gerard, however, didn't move. Oludara looked down to see him cradling the priest in his arms. Father Miguel had taken a shot to the chest and one to the neck. He clutched both hands to his neck and blood gurgled from his mouth as he tried to form words he could no longer voice.

"Gerard!" yelled Oludara.

He knew the time it would take their enemies to reload their harquebueses—and that time was almost up. He yanked at his companion, but it was no use.

Another volley sounded, and Oludara raised an arm to cover his face. He felt a wind and looked to see that a whirlwind had formed in front of him, whisking away the shots.

"What was that?" came a voice from the woods.

"I don't know, forget the guns," came Grilo's voice. "Let's just skewer them and be done with it."

The whirlwind flew off into the woods and in its place Oludara saw Grilo, a long knife in his hand, lead two other bannermen out of the woods. One wielded a machete and the other an axe.

Oludara stood between Gerard and the men.

"Gerard, please," he begged. "I cannot fight them alone."

Gerard remained in shock.

Oludara planned his attack. Grilo stood in the middle, so going at him first would leave him open to attack on both sides. He decided to make a lunge for the man with the machete, try to take him out quickly, then deal with the other two. It was desperate, impossible even, unless Gerard took hold of his senses and joined the fight.

As Oludara prepared his attack, a yell interrupted his thoughts.

"You fool! What have you done?"

Antonio, followed by the rest of his bannermen, strode into the clearing. He knelt by Father Miguel, opposite Gerard.

"It's not my fault," said Grilo. "That stupid priest got in the way."

Father Miguel stared up at Antonio, who said, "I didn't mean for this to happen. Grilo was supposed to capture van Oost, that's all. Please forgive me, Father."

Father Miguel took a blood-covered hand from his throat, mouthed some words, and with his thumb, drew a cross on Antonio's forehead in his own blood. He then held his hand toward Grilo, who sneered and turned away. At that, Father Miguel closed his eyes and slumped down, dead.

After a long silence, Antonio shook his head and said, "This was a terrible deed."

"What's one dead priest?" said Grilo. "They line up like lambs for the slaughter. There's nothing they like better than taking a bullet in the name of God."

"Enough!" said Antonio, standing. "I'll have your service no more. Leave me."

Grilo reached for his knife and Antonio glared at him through squinted eyes, daring an attack. After a short pause, Grilo thought better and relaxed.

"Fine by me. You've gone just as soft as the others."

At that, Grilo motioned to the other men who had aided in his ambush, and the three set off down the path. Once they disappeared from sight, Antonio turned his attention to Gerard.

"This is all your fault, van Oost."

Those words finally snapped Gerard from his trance.

"My fault?" he retorted.

"You always have to meddle where you don't belong." Antonio unsheathed his rapier. "Draw your sword, van Oost, and let's be done with it."

"I won't fight you, Antonio."

"Then you'll die."

Antonio struck, but Oludara lunged at the last second to parry the blade, angling it mere inches from Gerard's face. They pulled back their weapons and prepared for a second engagement when a command of "Enough!" stopped them both.

Gregorio stepped between them and pushed back their blades. He knelt before Father Miguel, spoke words of Latin which Oludara could not understand, and made the sign of the cross. He reverently removed from Miguel's neck a rosary made from grape-sized wooden beads, which he hung at his own side in the sash he used as a belt. Then he turned toward Antonio.

"You would dare shed blood here, on ground sanctified by *his*? With his blessing written in blood on your forehead?"

Antonio held his ground, but said nothing.

"Begone!" yelled Father Gregorio.

"No," said Antonio. "You're not Father Miguel, and I'm not leaving without van Oost."

"Begone forever! Return here again and I'll have you excommunicated."

"You don't have that authority."

"Now that Miguel is gone, who do you think will be the next Provincial?"

Antonio looked the priest up and down, considering, before finally saying, "Very well." He looked down at Gerard. "Your day will come, Gerard. Next time you won't have a priest around to protect you, and nothing less than your head on a pike will satisfy me. Consider us in first encounter."

Antonio motioned to his group and they walked away in silence.

"What is first encounter?" asked Oludara.

Gerard said nothing as Gregorio removed Miguel from his arms and laid him gently on the ground.

"Gerard, what is first encounter?" Oludara asked again.

Gerard, not taking his eyes from the dead priest, said, "It is a call for a duel. It means that the next time we meet, wherever it may be, only one of us leaves alive."

Gerard studied the massive group which had gathered for Father Miguel's funeral. Dozens of priests had come, along with hundreds of European settlers: everyone from landowners to tradesmen to scribes.

Most impressive, however, were the thousands of natives. In their best clothes, they roamed the area, shouting everything from Christian phrases like "God, protect his soul!" to the more traditional Tupi, "We also want to die with you!"

After an open air mass, a crowd gathered behind the church for the burial. The children played a nocturne, and Gregorio gave a eulogy.

"Father Miguel was a light of kindness," he said, "the glory of our Society. He chose poverty over riches, penance over pride. He suffered hunger and thirst, braved both wilderness and sea. Uncountable are the rivers he crossed and the mountains he climbed in service to his beloved Tupiniquim."

Few eyes remained dry, and Gerard shed his share of tears. Beside him, Oludara commented, "And so the 'sublime glory' of the martyr is his after all. Did he truly believe that death could be a reward?"

"I don't know. We've met many on our travels through Brazil, but none such as he." Gerard looked at Oludara. "I'm sorry I froze that day, during the ambush."

"Indeed," said Oludara, "it was the first time I have seen you so, although I did not wish to press the matter afterwards."

"It was as if I saw the very sun dimming away before my eyes. He tried to tell me something, but I couldn't make out the words."

Gregorio approached them. "Gerard," he said, "I have a favor to ask. Seek no revenge on Antonio and Grilo; Father Miguel forgave them of their sins."

"I seek no revenge, Father," said Gerard. "I've never killed a man, and never will. Our soul is the only thing we don't receive on loan in this world."

"Well said, Gerard. For a misguided Protestant, you're not a bad man."

"Gregorio," said Oludara, "how did you know to come back to us?"

"Call it divine inspiration, whatever you wish. A vision, Oludara. I saw him dying." At that, tears fell from Gregorio's eyes and he had to pause to compose himself. "At that moment, I knew he was destined to die, but that by going back, other lives could be saved."

"I believe he had a vision as well," said Gerard. "He led us to that spot. He stepped between us and the shots, without warning."

"Two visions for the same purpose. It was God's will that he should die in your stead."

"I never asked him to..." Gerard stammered.

"I don't mean to burden you, Gerard. God's works are not to be questioned." He wiped away his tears and stared off. "But one thing God has not shown me. How do you replace someone who is irreplaceable?"

They stood in silence for some time, before Oludara finally spoke: "My people have a saying: 'If you are not able to build a house at once, you first build a shed.'"

"Thank you, friend. There is wisdom in those words. And now that you mention it, I believe we have unfinished business to attend to."

"What is that?" asked Gerard.

"The Headless Mule."

"We couldn't possibly think about that at a time like this."

"It was his final task. If it is my burden to replace him, that is where I must begin."

Back in the woods where they first met the Headless Mule, Oludara shared a fire with Gerard and Gregorio. They dined on roasted tubers, and Oludara knew the time for hunting drew near. He lifted his bow and tested it.

"You won't require that," said Father Gregorio. "In fact, I'd prefer you leave your weapons here."

Oludara and Gerard looked at each other.

"You ask us to go against a fire-breathing beast with no weapons?" asked Gerard.

"This isn't a fight," said Father Gregorio. "It's more of...an intervention."

"I think it's time to tell us what you know of the beast," said Oludara.

"I know only what Miguel told me." He pulled Miguel's wooden rosary from the sash, where it had hung since he had first taken it. "You must have thought it strange when I removed this from his neck. He wore it for this very task. He told me that the only way to stop the mule is to place this upon its neck. He also told me that we should not harm the mule in any way."

"Unusual," said Oludara.

Gregorio, after one last look at the rosary, handed it to Oludara.

"Miguel told me all of this before he set out with you. I thought it strange, at the time, but he must have known, even then, that he would not live to see the task done."

"I'll leave my gun," said Gerard, "but I'd as soon go naked as leave my rapier behind."

"As would I with my knife," added Oludara.

"All right," said Gregorio. "But unless your lives are in peril, try to keep them sheathed."

"What do you think, Oludara?" asked Gerard. "Any ideas for getting this rosary on its neck?"

"Does the Mule ever sleep?" asked Oludara.

"Not that anyone has ever seen," replied Gregorio. "By all accounts, it simply disappears when the sun rises."

"I don't think sneaking up on it is an option," said Oludara, "not so close as to collar it. Thus, our choices are capturing it or confronting it."

"And if we confront it?" asked Gerard.

"Coming at the mule from the front would be suicide," said Oludara, "and trying to reach it from the sides or back not much better; mules are notorious kickers. So our best chance is coming from above. One of us hides in a tree with the necklace and the other lures the beast under it."

Gerard pulled at his goatee. "Sounds reasonable," he said. "Let me act as bait, I'd as soon not jump from another tree this week."

"And what would you have of me?" asked Gregorio.

"Stay nearby," said Oludara, "but don't let the beast see you. Your presence might cause it to flee. If our situation becomes desperate, try to send the beast away, as did Father Miguel."

"As Antonio said so eloquently, I'm no Father Miguel, but I'll do my best."

Oludara knelt in the crook of a tree, rosary in hand. The three of them had rubbed themselves down with plants and dirt to mask their scent, and taken up positions around the same lake where they encountered the mule the first time. Oludara thanked his god Olorun for the full moon, which provided as much light as they could hope for in the middle of the night. He prayed their strategy worked as planned, but from past experience, that rarely happened.

Oludara shifted his tired legs in the tree as the better part of an hour passed, but froze when he spotted a dark shape approaching the water. The mule's headless neck turned from side to side, scanning the area around it in a way Oludara could not fathom. After a short pause, it went forward to drink from the water.

Gerard snuck from his hiding spot and set himself halfway between Oludara and the mule. He called out, "Hey, you, son of a mare!"

The saying was a common insult in Brazil, but seemed to Oludara a little silly using it on a creature that was, in fact, born to a mare. And from what Oludara had seen—or better yet, not seen—the mule was female.

Nevertheless, the phrase had the desired effect. The mule turned and whinnied, flames blasting from its neck. Gerard didn't wait; he turned and ran. After his first few steps, however, he tripped and fell.

"For Olorun's sake!" said Oludara. He leapt from the tree, knowing he had no other choice but to reach Gerard before the mule.

The mule charged as Oludara recovered from the fall. Oludara waved his arms, trying to make the creature pause. Gerard scrambled to his feet. Faced with the two men, the mule reared up and shot its flame skyward.

For a moment, all three stood in silence. Oludara shuffled toward it, hoping to sneak close enough to place the collar, but a shot of flame singed his hair and he knew it would be next to impossible without a distraction.

Gerard seemed to have the same thought, and bent down to grab a branch. He waved it toward the creature, then threw it. This indeed drew the Mule's attention, but it turned its body in such a way that Oludara could no longer easily reach its neck.

Gerard unsheathed his rapier and swished it in front of the creature, holding its attention. Oludara crept around towards the beast's haunches, hoping to mount it from behind. He ran forward, but spotted the Mule's legs bending for a kick.

Nothing left to do, Oludara slid and the hooves whisked past his nose. The beast spun on him and, in desperation, he threw the rosary toward its neck. For a moment, he thought it might catch, but it failed to encircle and slipped off. Gerard rushed in with his rapier, but too late. What looked like red-hot coals burned within the creature's neck. For a second time, Oludara found himself helpless before the flames of the Headless Mule.

"Stop!" shouted Gregorio, as he stepped into the clearing. It sounded as if he tried to mimic Miguel, but lacked the force of his voice.

The Mule paused, but it's flames still pointed at Oludara.

"Stop," he said again, this time softer. What his voice dropped in volume, it gained in surety.

The mule spun away from the priest and tightened its muscles for a gallop.

"Wait," he said, in a quiet voice which asked instead of commanding.

The embers in the mule's neck died down, and it turned to face him. Gregorio, trembling, paced toward the mule, which tensed up. Gently, he rested a hand on its shoulder.

"We're here to help," he said.

At that, the Headless Mule relaxed and lowered its neck. Gregorio bent down and recovered the fallen rosary. He hung it around the creature's neck. The mule shuddered, dropped to its knees, then fell over completely. In a grotesque transformation, digits sprouted from its hooves and splotched skin replaced its coat. Gerard started forward, but Gregorio waved him back. After more agonizing thrashing, the form settled into that of a woman.

The woman looked to be around forty, with the light skin of a Portuguese but the straight black hair of a native. Gregorio removed his cassock, revealing white linen undergarments beneath, and covered the woman's nakedness. She sobbed and he laid a comforting hand upon her shoulder.

She cried for a several minutes before composing herself. "So long, so terrible," she said.

"You need say nothing," said Gregorio.

"No," she said, grabbing his undershirt but then thinking better of it and pulling her hand back. "I must confess."

"Very well." He made the sign of the cross and said, "In nomine Patris et Filii et Spiritus Sancti. Amen."

"My sins are terrible. I had a relationship with a priest, we...became lovers."

Oludara heard Gerard suck in a breath.

"We sinned together so many times. Then he turned me away, told me he could no longer bear his conscience. I felt betrayed; I mocked him. His heart gave way and he died, and shortly after, I..."

Father Gregorio nodded and said many words in Latin which Oludara could not understand, ending with, "Ego te absolvo a peccatis tuis in nomine Patris, et Filii, et Spiritus Sancti. Amen."

The woman made the sign of the cross.

"For your penance," said Gregorio, "would you not take the cloth, and be a nun for the rest of your days? Much good can still be done."

She sobbed and fell at his feet.

"Yes, Father. Thank you."

Gerard, packed and ready, awaited Oludara on the outskirts of Sao Paulo. Father Gregorio walked out to meet him.

"Your face is heavy and it saddens me," said Gregorio. "You are not the same confident man who came here mere weeks ago."

"These last days have been trying," said Gerard. "I need to rest and contemplate."

"Then do not be so quick to leave. There are few better places to rest."

"I would put this place and its memories behind me," said Gerard. "My conscience is heavy."

"Why? Because you came, a woman's soul was freed. And if you had not been present, would we have followed Diogo and Moara to the children?"

"If we had not been present, would Father Miguel have died?"

"That was his choice. With his blood, Father Miguel bought the freedom of the children, perhaps the entire tribe. Antonio will not dare return here."

Gerard could only shake his head. To his relief, Oludara joined them.

"Are you sure you don't want to stay longer?" asked Gregorio. "There is much you could do here."

"Diogo and Moara told us they'll stay until the village defenses are ready," replied Gerard. "The two of us would just be more mouths to feed."

"And it is time for me to return to my wife," said Oludara. "It has been months since I have seen her."

"Whatever you do, don't lose faith. Allow God's divine grace to guide you along extraordinary and miraculous paths."

"Even if that faith is Protestant?" asked Gerard.

"Yes, even then."

With a tip of the hat, Gerard turned and headed out.

"Funny," he said to Oludara, "Father Miguel saw my faith as a disease, but Gregorio doesn't seem to mind so much."

"Cannot a priest have his own opinion?"

Gerard grimaced. "Not usually."

"Travel this Earth from one side to the other, you will find no two people alike," said Oludara.

"Is that one of your sayings?"

"No, just an observation."

They hiked in silence for some time, until Gerard said, "You remember what Antonio said? That Brazil can't be sustained without slaves?"

"I remember."

"There are many who share his view. If they can no longer make slaves of the natives, don't you worry they'll look even more to Africa?"

"Perhaps, Gerard. But those are two different battles. Here, we fight for the Tupi tribes. When I return to Ketu, I will fight slavery there as well."

"Is that the only way to stop it, fighting?"

"You think you can turn men like Antonio and Grilo from their paths? I do have a saying for that: 'He who waits for a crab to wink will tarry long upon the shore.' "

Gerard opened his mouth to reply, but a rustling from the bushes alerted him.

"Dear God, another ambush!" he said, raising his harquebus.

Sacy-Taperey stepped onto the path before them.

"Please put that thing down," he said. "I like the smell of gunpowder even less than tobacco smoke."

"Sacy-Taperey," said Oludara, "you protected us from the gunfire that day. Why?"

Sacy-Taperey hopped toward them, grinning. "You two make me laugh, the way you're always getting into trouble. If you got killed, what would I do with my time?"

"You mean you've been following us?" said Gerard.

"Oh yes! I saw you almost get killed by the Headless Mule again. Shame she won't be here to make you bumble around anymore."

Gerard had a thought. "Well, if you want to follow us, we're headed north."

"North? Don't do that! There's nothing worth visiting there."

"Funny," said Gerard, "someone like you said there's nothing good down here."

"Like me?" squealed the demon. "There is no one like me."

"Really? Because Sacy-Perey told us that *he* is the only true Sacy."

"What? You're friends with that...that!"

Sacy-Taperey screamed and turned into a powerful whirlwind, which knocked Gerard and Oludara to the ground before spinning away into the woods.

As the two stood and dusted themselves off, Gerard commented, "If only they could all be that easy to get rid of."

For the first time in days, they both found reason to smile.

A potoo sat on his favorite tree, ready for his nighttime song. That night, only darkness and moonlight engulfed him; gone from the forest were the flames of men and mules.

He opened his beak to sing his same descending tune, but at the last moment, his song changed. That one night, when he sang, his song did not sound mournful. Instead, it sounded almost like the children's kyrielles.

Chapter 9

The Dolorous Birthing of Taynah

BROWN-THROATED SLOTH HUNG from a jacaranda tree and stared at two unusual figures below him. The sloth had grown accustomed to the tall creatures who had come to his forest years before and built up massive piles of dirt and wood covered with palm leaves to live in. He found their tiny claws amusing and their lower arms bizarre, the ones they used for moving perpendicular to the ground. The two below him, though, were even stranger than the rest. One had a tone much lighter than the others, and the other a tone much darker.

He did, however, appreciate the fact that they didn't move around as haphazardly as the others. In a more dignified fashion, they had lain on the ground for hours, looking up at him as he hung from the tree. Others of their kind could learn much from these two.

Oludara lay on the grass beside Gerard. For hours, they had watched a sloth hang silently in a tree above them.

He couldn't imagine a more perfect day for doing nothing. The jacarandas surrounded them in magnificent spring bloom, looking like giant balls of violet cotton. Every light breeze caused a rain of the colored petals, bringing with them their sweet, slightly spicy perfume, and causing an occasional sneeze as well.

These days, the two of them did little. After Father Miguel's death, Gerard had lost much of his taste for travel. That, and their return from São Paulo had also marked a huge surprise: Arany was pregnant. Her belly had grown much in their months of absence.

So their adventures had become few and far between, and they spent almost all their time in the village, still poised precariously between Antonio's bannermen on one side and the arid land known as the Backlands on the other. After months of waiting, Oludara would soon be a father. The break had been nice, but Oludara couldn't help feeling restless from time to time.

"I think you are going to lose your bet," he said to Gerard. "That creature obviously does not eat, or it would have had something by now."

"Nonsense," replied Gerard. "It must eat something."

"Activity causes hunger. That creature does nothing."

"It's one of the strangest animals I've ever seen, to be sure. It has the face of a child and the claws of a lion. Yet all it does is hang in trees."

Baiting Gerard, Oludara said, "The Tupinambá do not hunt the creature, because anyone who eats its meat will become just as slow."

Much as he suspected, the remark riled Gerard. "That's even more absurd than claiming the creature doesn't eat!"

Oludara grinned as he stood up and brushed away the violet blanket of flower petals which had accumulated on him.

"We have been here most of the day," he said. "I am beginning to feel as slow as that creature. We should do something."

"It's not so bad to take a day of rest every once in a while."

"A *day* of rest? We've done nothing but rest for months! You are not like yourself, Gerard. You used to run from one adventure to the next."

Gerard looked off in the distance and said nothing.

"My people have a saying," continued Oludara. "'Laziness is the partner of fatigue.' It is time to recommence our travels. Do we not still have a year and a half left of our pact? My son will not be born for another two months, more than enough time for some exploring." Oludara paused for thought. "I know what to do! We can find a gift for him."

At that moment, a whistling approached and Cabwassu emerged from the woods. A bright green parrot perched on his shoulder, a good match for the pointy green stones which protruded from his cheeks, earlobes, and lower lip.

"Hey you two," he said, "look at my new pet. I've been teaching him our traditional war cries. Watch."

Cabwassu took a piece of cassava cracker from a pouch and held it up near the parrot. In perfectly intellegible Tupi, it squawked, "I'll chew the meat from your bones!"

"Good parrot," said Cabwassu, giving the bird the snack and flashing his toothy smile.

"Interesting," said Gerard, finally lifting himself from the ground.

"Cabwassu," said Oludara, "what would be an appropriate present for a warrior?"

Cabwassu thought for only a moment before replying. "A good bow."

"No, it must be something out of the ordinary. Something...legendary." Oludara had to change to Portuguese to find the word.

Cabwassu's tongue stumbled on the word as he repeated it. "Legendary?"

"One of a kind," said Gerard. "Unique."

"Oh," said Cabwassu, "wait, I..." He paused and his eyes unfocused, as if digging into the deepest corners of his memory. "I just remembered something. A magnificent bow. One which never misses its target."

Oludara beamed. "An excellent idea! Where can we find it?"

"Inland, somewhere in the Backlands."

"*Somewhere*?" asked Gerard.

"How long to get there?" asked Oludara.

Cabwassu shook his head and his eyes seemed to clear. "A few weeks there, a few back. I can take you. We'll need to pass through Tupinaé land."

"Aren't they enemies of the Tupinambá?" asked Gerard.

"Yes," said Cabwassu, picking at one of the stones protruding from his cheek. "But just let me handle it. I can talk us through anything." He punctuated the remark with another of his terrifying smiles. "I'll just give them a few compliments, like..."

"You are worth nothing!" screeched the bird, interrupting him.

"Perhaps it would be best to leave the bird behind for this journey," said Gerard.

Oludara ignored the remark. "We should set out immediately."

"Are you sure about this? You're going to walk through hostile territory for weeks to look for a bow which may or may not exist based on Cabwassu's vague notion of its location?"

"Do you have something more important to do?" challenged Oludara.

Gerard seemed ready to protest, but choked back the words,

resigned. “I suppose not.”

“Then let us waste no time. Say your goodbyes and let us be on our way. Is that all right with you, Cabwassu?”

“Fine with me. What do you say, bird?”

“You deserve to die!” it squawked.

Following the seemingly endless ups and downs of the canyon, Gerard huffed breaths through his parched throat with every step. The group had spent the first twelve days of their journey crossing the dry plains of the Backlands, through an endless sea of rocks, scrub, and cacti. Since then, they had navigated sparse woods through a corridor of plateaus. Birds circled overhead constantly, their screeches echoing back and forth between the canyon walls. The orchids which dotted the landscape with color might have filled Gerard with wonder at some other moment, but the dry air sapped his strength and ruined the charm.

At a small pool, Oludara called the group to a halt. The watering holes were frequent enough, but Gerard felt almost constant thirst between one and the next. He knelt and dunked his head into the water. Only after washing his face and taking a long drink did he take time to examine their surroundings.

Shrubs and ferns—some a light green but many more brown and dry—surrounded the watering hole. The water which filled the pool came by way of a long, low waterfall made of slates of red stone. It formed a kind of natural staircase down to the pond.

“I don’t know how much more of this I can take,” said Gerard. “I feel like I’m going to shrivel up and die.”

“Today I eat you!” the parrot squawked from nearby. Cabwassu howled with laughter, as he did every time the bird spoke.

“Can you shut that thing up?” snapped Gerard.

“Why would I?” Cabwassu replied between laughs.

Gerard, famished, pulled a bag of nuts from his pack and set to cracking them open. When he looked up, Oludara stood over him, an enormous smile upon his face. To the same extent Gerard felt miserable,

Oludara seemed energized. Gerard had begun to tire of Oludara's unbridled optimism, especially when faced with the fact that they still didn't know exactly where they were going or how long it would take to get there. Cabwassu, however, led them with a purpose, as if some internal compass pointed the way.

"How can you smile in this heat?" Gerard asked Oludara.

"How can I not smile when I think of my son? Can you believe it, Gerard? In just over a month, I will be a father, and we will offer him a magnificent present to begin his life."

Gerard could believe it, if for no other reason than the fact that Oludara had spoken of little else during the trip.

"Arany will provide me with a fine, strapping son to follow in my footsteps. I will call him Kayode, which means: 'He who brings joy'."

Oludara's insistence of referring to the unborn child as a son bothered Gerard. The man would accept nothing else, and Gerard worried what would happen if the child were born a girl. He had not mentioned this to Oludara, but decided to dare a hint at the subject.

"Any healthy child would be a blessing," he said.

Oludara shot him a puzzled look that ended the conversation.

"Look over there!" said Cabwassu.

Gerard looked to see something hobbling toward them. As the figure neared, Gerard made it out to be a bent over native man, walking with the help of a stick. Unlike most natives Gerard had seen, he used a cloak which covered most of his body. His face was mostly hidden, except for an enormous, hooked nose which jutted out from the hood.

The man said nothing as he approached the pool and bent down to splash water in his face. Then he stood slowly, holding his back with the strain, and finally acknowledged them with a hearty "I jump to meet you" in Tupi.

The trio introduced themselves and the man replied, "I am Sokoy, of the Tupinaé."

"I'll chew the meat from your bones!" screeched the bird.

Embarrassed, Gerard pulled down the brim of his hat, but Sokoy took the taunt in stride.

"That is a funny bird you have," he said. "It is rare to see a Tupinambá warrior here, and much less two men from across the water. Why have you come to these dry lands?"

Gerard thought it best to not mention their quest to a stranger, but before he could make something up, Oludara spoke out:

"We seek a bow which never misses its target. It is to be a birthday present for my son."

"A worthy quest for three warriors," said Sokoy, "and a worthy present."

"You know of it?"

"Know of it? I know where to find it!"

Oludara slapped Gerard on the back. "See, Gerard? You worried we would search these lands forever, but when your course is true, fortune favors you."

Gerard decided to reserve judgment.

"We are well met," said Sokoy. "I can lead you to the bow, if you will in return retrieve something for me."

"Name it," said Oludara, "and it shall be done."

"You see, some years ago, in my arrogance, I went looking for the bow myself. However, a terrible creature guards it, a dog made of iron!"

"A dog made of iron?" asked Cabwassu.

"Do you not believe me?" asked Sokoy.

"We believe you," said Gerard. "An iron dog is almost mundane compared to the creatures we've seen."

Gerard could just make out Sokoy wrinkling his eyebrows and studying him up and down from beneath his hood.

"This dog is called Massone," continued Sokoy. "Be wary, he hides in the shadows and attacks when you least expect."

"Shadows?" asked Oludara.

"Oh," said Sokoy, chuckling, "I forgot to say. The bow is in a cavern: the longest and deepest I've ever seen."

"And where do we find the bow in this cavern?"

"I don't know. Massone attacked me, and I was forced to run. He bit my old walking stick from my hand; I'm glad that's all he got. Massone was too much for me to handle, but I'm sure he'll be no problem for three sturdy men like you."

"And what is the item you seek?"

"I want my walking stick back."

"Your walking stick?" asked Gerard.

"Yes," said Sokoy, holding up the gnarled branch in his hand with a sigh. "I've looked, but I've never found another like it. It is hard to walk these canyons without it. Please help an old man."

"As you wish."

"I almost forgot, the stick looks much like a club." At Gerard's quizzical glance, he added, "Makes the wild cats think twice about attacking me."

"How much farther do we have to go?" asked Gerard.

"Almost there," replied Sokoy, the same reply he had given Gerard for an entire day as he hobbled along, leading the group through the canyon.

This time, however, he veered from the canyon and led the group up a wooded path between two plateaus. When they entered the shade of the towering cliffs, Gerard sighed and removed his wide-brimmed hat to wipe the sweat from his forehead.

Sokoy pointed to a spot some thirty feet up a cliff. "Up there," he said.

Even squinting, Gerard couldn't make out anything exceptional on the rocky face. Sokoy, however, approached the cliff and started up some uneven steps in the rock, each around three feet high. Gerard couldn't be sure if they had been carved there long ago or were an accident of nature. On the third step, Sokoy slipped and cut his leg. Oludara and Cabwassu took to either side of him and carried him the rest of the way.

At the top of the steps, they discovered a fissure behind the rock face. Gerard could see why he hadn't spotted it before; from the angle it entered the rock, it was nearly impossible to spot from below.

Just beyond the fissure was a larger opening, curving in between two walls of layered rock. Above the opening hung a dozen horned skulls. Gerard could recognize skulls from deer, oxen and goats, but some he couldn't recognize at all—and didn't much care to.

To one side, a green mantis hung on a wall at eye level and stared straight at him.

"Pleasant place you've got here," Gerard said to the insect.

"What was that?" asked Sokoy, huffing with exhaustion.

"Nothing," said Gerard. "Please lead on."

Sokoy nodded and led them through the opening into a deep cavern with a bowl-shaped lake at the bottom. A shaft of sunlight found its way in from above to illuminate the water with an eerie blue glow, one which darkened into blackness at its lowest depths. Massive, fallen boulders lay to every side.

Sokoy hobbled slowly toward one of the boulders and sat down.

"This is as far as I go," he said. "I need to rest. But if you dive over there," he pointed to the far corner of the pool, "you'll find a way to reach the main cavern."

"I'll go," said Oludara.

He dove into the lake and disappeared into the darkness. He came up for air and dove another three times before staying under for quite a long time. When he finally reappeared, he announced, "I've found it! A passage some ten feet down, leading into a dark cavern."

Gerard took his harquebus and powder and offered them to Sokoy.

"Mind keeping an eye on these while we're gone? Won't be much use if I get the powder wet."

"Not at all," said Sokoy. "And good luck!"

The enormous, complex cave impressed Oludara; he had never seen anything like it. By torchlight, they searched dozens of rooms and corridors formed naturally from the rock. The cavern led them up and down, through stalactites and stalagmites and over massive piles of fallen rock. Most of the corridors were ample and easy to traverse, but crawl spaces connected some. Gerard got stuck in one, and to his embarrassment, Cabwassu and Oludara had to pull him out and find a larger opening.

The three walked with weapons at the ready: Oludara with his knife, Cabwassu with his bow and Gerard with his rapier. The stress of expecting an attack at any moment wore on all of them. Any movement caused them to spin in anticipation, and with beetles and bats everywhere, there was no lack of it.

The cavern descended into yet another massive space, this one covered in knee-deep water. When Gerard yelped, Oludara, nerves on edge, jerked his torch nervously from side to side.

"There's something in the water," said Gerard.

Oludara ran toward him, ivory knife in one hand and torch in the other, scanning the water for movement. Indeed, he spotted ripples all around—something circled them. He lunged at one movement but it spun away, like a fish. Oludara lowered his torch to see the movement was just that: a group of eyeless catfish.

"Calm down, Gerard," he said, relaxing. "It's just fish."

Cabwassu, however, eyes wide, screamed, "Behind you!"

Oludara turned just in time to see something shiny leap at him from a crevasse in the ceiling. He lifted his knife too late, the creature crashed into him, knocking him back into the water.

Oludara surged up for breath, and a shiny snout lashed at his throat. Just in time, Cabwassu slammed into the beast and splashed with it to one side. The parrot circled overhead, screeching furiously and weaving through the stalactites.

As he struggled to stand, Oludara glanced at the beast. At first sight, the creature looked like a metal wolf, but Oludara quickly realized that "armored" might be a better word. It was not made of metal; instead, bronze plates covered most of its body—Oludara could see black fur poking out at the gaps. Its legs bent in awkward directions and its eyes glimmered with tiny blue fires. As Cabwassu wrestled the beast, Gerard lunged at it with his rapier, which clinked harmlessly off the metal.

Finally getting to his feet, Oludara sloshed toward the creature. Faced with three foes, the wolf spun off Cabwassu and raced through the water.

As it passed Oludara, he aimed a strike below its snout and felt the blade nick flesh. The creature howled in pain and continued running.

"After it!" yelled Oludara, and the other two followed without comment.

The chase came to an abrupt halt, however, when a woman's voice shouted "Stop!" in Portuguese.

The three came to a halt just before an old woman in a ragged robe. Oludara could see the wrinkles on her face in the flickering torchlight, but little else. The wolf's glowing blue eyes peeked out from behind her, and she patted its bronze-plated head with a gentle hand as it whimpered.

"I'm sorry," she said. "Is my doggy bothering you?"

"Unusual pet," said Gerard.

"Many come here on foolish quests, seeking treasures which never existed. Massone here is the only protection I have."

"We search for a bow, rumored to lie in this cave," said Oludara.

"A bow which never misses its target? That's the kind of nonsense I'm talking about. Nothing but a child's tale."

"An old man told us we could find it here," said Cabwassu.

"I suppose he told you to get his club while you're at it?"

"Yes, how did you know?"

"No good will come of that one, to be sure."

"What do you mean?" asked Oludara.

The woman sighed. "Come, have a seat and I'll tell you the whole story."

She walked toward a boulder on one wall. To Oludara, her gait seemed inhuman; her strides were far too long and her robe bowed out at the knees. When she sat down, she held out a hand to one side, offering them a row of stones on which to sit.

Oludara accepted her offer and sat down. Cabwassu followed, and his parrot returned to his shoulder, all the time keeping one eye cocked toward Massone. Gerard did not sit, but stood in place, eying the old lady cautiously.

"Where do I begin?" she said. "Oh, I know."

She muttered a few words which Oludara could not understand.

"What did you say?" asked Oludara.

"I said goodbye." She waved, and below her hood, Oludara could just make out a smile.

At that, the water below his feet was sucked away, and all the water in the cavern collected into one massive column. Oludara reacted far too late, as the column descended and a powerful wave crashed into him. His last sight, as the water carried him over a ledge and into darkness, was of Cabwassu's parrot flying away, screeching.

The initial shock over, Oludara found himself underwater. He opened his eyes to complete darkness. Jerking himself forward in a search for air, he instead struck rock with his hands. He spun around and pushed up, breaking the surface of the water. His legs wobbled, but he managed to get them under him and find that the water reached almost to his armpits.

"Gerard!" he said. "Cabwassu!"

"I'm here," Cabwassu responded from the darkness.

"And Gerard?"

"I don't know."

"Find him!"

Oludara scrambled through the water, until his foot struck a body.

"Here," he said. "Help me!"

Cabwassu's hands slapped back and forth, searching for him in the complete darkness, and Oludara guided them down to Gerard's body. The two of them lifted and pulled his head above water. Oludara slapped his back several times until he vomited a lungful of water.

"Are you all right?" said Oludara.

Gerard hacked out a series of coughs, but Oludara could feel him nodding.

"We're lucky to have survived that fall," said Cabwassu.

Oludara heard a sound from above and shushed him.

"Are they dead?" came a slavish, unusual voice.

"Soon enough," responded the old woman's voice.

"Now we can go find the dark one's baby?"

"Yes. I have waited long to devour that child."

Oludara's muscles froze. He couldn't believe what he was hearing. He wondered if he was asleep, in the midst of some terrible nightmare.

"You promised me a piece!" said the unusual voice.

"A foot will be yours, my pet. The rest is mine."

Oludara realized the second voice could only be Massone's. He could picture the foul creature wagging its tail as it spoke.

"That thing can talk?" said Gerard.

"Shh!" replied Oludara.

He listened, but the voices spoke no more. Oludara's breath felt short. Lost in the darkness, he had never felt so helpless.

"She wants my child," he said. "We must find a way out.!"

Gerard's hands fumbled at him in the darkness, then gripped him firmly. "You must keep your wits. Calm yourself."

"She said she would eat my baby!"

"We'll never get out of here by panicking. Don't your people have some saying about that?"

"Gerard, I have no time for sayings."

"We're in a pit," said Cabwassu. "I have walked all around and can find no opening. The walls are too slick to climb."

"There must be a way out!" said Oludara.

He searched around frantically, while Gerard and Cabwassu made a more methodical search.

"Worst thing is," said Cabwassu, "my bird is gone!"

"Thank God for small favors," said Gerard.

Oludara almost struck them both. "This is no time for pets and jokes! My child's life is at stake."

"That's why you need to calm down," said Gerard. "We must think our way out of this."

Oludara knew his friend was right. He stopped and took ten deep breaths. However, images of his unborn son passed through his mind and his eyes flashed red with anger. He again thrashed around, looking for a way out.

After what felt like hours, but couldn't have been more than thirty minutes, a voice came from above, saying: "Psst!"

The sound caught his attention and he looked up in vain for the source.

"Grab the rope," came the voice.

"What rope?" asked Gerard.

"Search around, you'll find it."

Oludara swung his arms around and sure enough, slapped against a hanging rope. He tugged on it and found it to be firmly tied.

"Over here," he said to the others.

Oludara climbed up first, followed closely by Cabwassu and Gerard. Once the three had reached the top, a torch lit. As Oludara's eyes became accustomed to the darkness, he could make out Sokoy standing before them.

"How did you know to find us?" asked Oludara.

"I heard that parrot of yours squawking. It had found another way out of the cavern, one not filled with water. I decided to investigate."

The parrot flew from the darkness to alight on Cabwassu's shoulder. "You are worth nothing!" it screeched.

"Once I descended," said Sokoy, "I heard that crazy witch gloating how she'd dropped you all into a hole."

"You know who she is?"

"Yes, her name is Kooka. I didn't know she'd be here or I would have warned you."

"Oh," said Cabwassu. "I've heard of her. Terrible witch."

"She eats babies," said Sokoy, looking at Oludara. "And from what I heard, she wants yours."

"We should set a trap for her," said Oludara.

"No," said Sokoy. "If there are two exits, there may be be more. You have no way of knowing where she might leave. You should hurry and surprise her in her lair, while she prepares for her journey." He pointed down a large tunnel. "She headed that way."

Oludara considered, then nodded. "You are right. Let us move."

"If you don't mind," said Sokoy, "this is all a bit much for someone my age. I'll wait back outside."

Oludara spared only a moment to take in the magnificent cavern. The walls sparkled with the reflections of thousands of pin-like crystals. Water covered one-half the floor; the other half formed a kind of workshop and living space. It contained a table, some chairs, a wooden bed, a pile of rags on the ground, and, most importantly, Kooka.

Kooka stared into a round, violet amethyst the size of a melon. Within the stone, Oludara could make out a face he knew well: Arany.

All at once, Oludara gasped and Massone leapt out from the pile of rags, barking and causing Kooka to lose her concentration and the image to disappear.

Massone paced toward his master, growling at the trio the entire time, and Kooka turned to face Oludara. Time seemed to stop as they silently studied one another. Gerard and Cabwassu came to stand on either side of him. Kooka finally broke the silence.

"How did you escape?" she asked.

Instead of answering, Oludara demanded, "Why do you desire my child?"

"There is greatness in that one."

"Greatness? My son will be great?"

Kooka cocked her head to one side as if puzzled, then let out a cackle.

Oludara ignored the mad laughter and asked, "How did you know we would come?"

"I brought you here," she said. "All I had to do was slip a thought into that guava-brained savage over there. I made him tell you to look for the bow."

"Hey!" shouted Cabwassu.

"But I suppose our game is over," said Kooka. "Please have mercy on an old woman."

Kooka looked down in resignation, but Oludara spotted her muttering words under her breath. He charged at her, only to have

Massone, barking, block his path. He attempted to cut under the creature's snout again, but it maneuvered and bit his arm instead. He dropped his knife in agony.

Kooka finished her incantation and Oludara heard Gerard yelp in pain behind him. He glanced back to see his friend grab his stomach and drop to the ground. At the same time, Cabwassu grabbed Massone and—muscles straining to the utmost—tossed him to one side. Kooka ran for one of the shelves.

"Oludara," Gerard gasped through clenched teeth. "The bow! Don't let her get it."

Oludara looked to the shelves and indeed, Kooka reached for a bow. He lurched up and ran full speed toward her. She grabbed the bow, readied an arrow, and turned to aim just as he crashed into her. The bow and arrow flew from her hands and the two of them fell. To Oludara's horror, Kooka's robe flipped up to reveal a pair of insect legs flapping beneath.

Massone raced at Oludara's prone figure, but Cabwassu launched a shaft from his own bow and pierced the creature through a gap between the plates on its head and neck. It paused and howled in pain, but forced itself toward Oludara, one painful step at a time. Cabwassu, arrows in hand, released four more shots at incredible speed. Two of them bounced from the creature's plates, but the other two struck true, and Massone fell.

Kooka righted herself and cried, "Massone! What have they done to you, my pet?" She crawled toward the dog's limp body.

Oludara watched in disgust as Kooka wept over the body of Massone, her insect legs twitching behind her. Cabwassu recovered one of his fallen arrows and readied the bow at Kooka, looking to Oludara for guidance. Oludara shook his head.

"As she asked," said Oludara, "we shall be merciful to an old woman."

"Oh, thank you!" she said, turning and crawling toward him.

She seemed about to kiss his feet when Oludara noticed her hand make a quick motion into her robe. He pulled away just as she struck out with what looked like a palm-length thorn.

"Enough!" he said, kicking it from her hand.

"This isn't over!" she screamed.

Before Oludara could react, she spoke a word of command and her body transformed into an alligator. She took a snap at his feet, but he backed away just in time. The Kooka-alligator rushed on its squat legs toward the water and disappeared within. The ripples from its movement led toward the wall, then disappeared.

Gerard, recovered from whatever magic Kooka had used against him, stood and joined Oludara.

"Where is she?" he asked.

"She fled through some passage under the water."

"Should we follow?"

"I think not. In that form, she has the advantage underwater. Better to leave her here to lick her wounds and be on our way."

"Here's the bow," said Cabwassu, holding it out to Oludara.

Oludara took the magnificent bow: a thick, six-foot weapon criss-crossed with delicate carvings.

"And don't forget Sokoy's walking stick," said Gerard.

A quick search of the shelves turned up a club. Cabwassu also noticed a passage leading up and out of the cave, toward light.

Gerard's eyes burned from the brightness at the end of the tunnel. The sun blazed through the opening, lighting up the rocks in yellows and oranges so intense, they looked like the coals of a blazing forge. Once outside, they worked their way back to the entrance and Sokoy.

Along the way, Cabwassu beamed at them. "Did you see how I shot Massone? I don't need a 'legendary' bow."

Oludara rubbed his bandaged arm, still burning from the creature's bite.

"Indeed," he said. "That was the most amazing feat of archery I've ever seen. You saved my life."

"You deserve to die!" said the parrot.

They found Sokoy at the bottom of the stairs they had used to enter the cavern.

"How did you fare against Kooka?" asked Sokoy. Before they could answer, his eyes grew wide at the sight of the bow. "You found it."

Oludara held it toward him. "Indeed. But we have not yet put it to the test."

"Then what are you waiting for?" Sokoy looked around. "Shoot that red rock up there." He pointed toward the top of one of the plateaus.

"That shot is impossible," said Cabwassu.

"Exactly!"

Oludara looked doubtful, but accepted an arrow from Cabwassu and aimed at the target. The arrow fired with unbelievable speed and struck the target above.

"Amazing!" he said. "This will make a fine present for a boy who will one day be a great warrior."

"I could think of no better present," agreed Sokoy.

"And I believe this is yours," said Gerard, presenting Sokoy with the club.

Sokoy handed Gerard his harquebus, tossed his own staff aside, and picked the club gingerly from Gerard's outstretched hands. He caressed the lumpy wood as one might touch a long lost lover.

"Oh," he said. "That is better. Much better."

As he spoke, his back straightened up.

"It's like that club has taken off ten years of your age," remarked Gerard.

"More than that," said Sokoy. He threw back his hood they could finally see his face properly, one much younger than the old man Gerard had expected.

Next to him, Oludara tensed. Gerard could see him reaching for his dagger, but he wasn't sure why.

Sokoy also noticed the movement and tossed the club into the air, saying, "Strike Oludara!"

At that, the club swung through the air and caught Oludara on the side of the head, knocking him down.

Gerard went for his rapier, but had barely unsheathed it when Sokoy said, “Strike Gerard!” The club whacked his hand and he dropped the weapon. Then the club struck him in the stomach, knocking the wind from him.

With a yell of “Strike Cabwassu!” the club changed directions and knocked Cabwassu’s bow from his hands. It next whacked his arm, causing the parrot to fly up and screech, “You are worth nothing!”

Gerard recovered enough to lunge at Sokoy and grab his throat, but not before he rushed out another call of “Strike Gerard!” The club battered Gerard in the neck and ribs, sending him painfully to the ground.

Sokoy alternated the enchanted club between the three, pounding them mercilessly. They could do nothing but writhe on the ground and protect themselves as best they could from the blows. Overhead, the bird circled and chanted “You are worth nothing. You are worth nothing.”

Finally, Sokoy shouted, “Enough!” The club returned to his hand. He reached down and picked up the enchanted bow.

“And thank you for this wonderful present. I mean, what would a baby do with a splendid bow like this, after all?”

Cabwassu looked up with one eye, his other bruised and shut. “You must be...but you couldn’t...”

Sokoy grinned down at him. “You may have heard of me before. I am called Way-Krig.”

“Oh no,” said Cabwassu. “I should have known.”

As Way-Krig marched off, he waved and said “Send my regards to the baby!”

The three lay gasping for several minutes, until Gerard finally managed to squeeze out some words.

“We must get him,” he said.

“Yes,” responded Oludara. “My people say, ‘Two rams cannot drink from the same calabash’. This Way-Krig has humiliated us, but I will not let him steal glory from my child.”

“You talk of rams,” said Cabwassu, “but Way-Krig is no sheep. He is a fox. He makes a fool of all he meets, and has never been fooled in return. Besides that, he now has two enchanted weapons.”

"I don't think we'll forget that club any time soon," said Gerard.

"I will come up with a plan," said Oludara.

The parrot returned to Cabwassu's shoulder. "You deserve to die," it said.

Oludara watched breathlessly as Way-Krig strode down the path below them. They had watched him for days, discovering his patterns, and prepared a trap.

Just steps before their hidden pit, Way-Krig paused. He cocked his head to one side and studied the ground.

Beside Oludara, Gerard and Cabwassu froze, unsure what to do. Oludara, however, refused to lose the opportunity. He snatched Cabwassu's bow away from him and notched an arrow. Then the stepped boldly out from their cover.

"Make no move!" he shouted toward Way-Krig.

"I have a bow that never misses, you know."

"Yet I will shoot first. Will you bet your life that I miss?"

"I suppose not."

Oludara walked toward the path, never taking his aim off the man. "Come forward," he said.

"Why would I be so stupid as to walk into a pit?"

Oludara paused. "Then drop the club and bow and walk away."

Way-Krig nodded and threw down the bow. Then he grabbed the club and allowed it to slowly slip from his fingers. Right before it dropped, however, he gripped it firmly and said, "How about I toss it to you instead?"

He launched the club high in the air and yelled, "Strike Oludara!"

Oludara had only a second to react, and decided to raise his bow and shoot at the club. His shot passed just below it and the club came crashing down, snapping the borrowed bow in half. It then spun behind him. He turned to meet it just as it rushed into his chest and sent him sprawling through the camouflage and into the pit.

Gerard and Cabwassu rushed down to help, but faired no better. Way-

Krig ordered the club to batter them and one by one, sent them rolling into the pit beside Oludara.

Way-Krig gave only a cursory glance into the pit before walking off, laughing.

Gerard, his face more purple than white, said, "I think it is time to quit and head home."

"I warned you," agreed Cabwassu.

"No," Oludara said, furious. "I will not disgrace my child with failure."

Almost every part of Oludara ached from the beatings, but still he grinned as his enemy snored beneath him.

They had caught Way-Krig during one of his customary afternoon naps. He slept against an unusual tree whose branches curved back and forth in a way Oludara had never seen. Instead of a typical crown, it looked more like a woven nest. The bow and club were nowhere to be seen, but Oludara had no doubt they were hidden nearby.

Oludara looked to his two companions, who nodded. He nudged Way-Krig with his foot. With a final snort, Way-Krig stretched and opened his eyes. He jumped at the sight of the three men looking down at him.

"I came for my son's present," said Oludara, knife in hand.

Way-Krig's eyes grew at the sight of the knife and sweat formed on his forehead.

"It's in the tree," he said.

"Pull it out," said Gerard.

"If you insist," said Way-Krig, reaching toward a hole in the tree. Oludara spotted him pursing his lips to hold back a grin.

"Stop!" shouted Oludara. "It's another of his tricks. He will turn the club upon us the moment he lays his hand upon it. Get back!"

Way-Krig looked longingly toward the hole, opened his mouth as if to say something, then held his head down and backed away. To Oludara's delight, his grin had disappeared.

Oludara reached into the hole. He dug around, feeling for the bow, when he felt movement around his arm. In the next instant, pain shot through him. He screamed and ripped his hand from the hole, a horde of wasps flowing out behind it.

The wasps surrounded him and his companions, stinging them without remorse. Way-Krig scooted around to the other side of the tree, where he recovered the bow and club from a different hole. He tossed the club in the air and shouted, "Strike Oludara, Gerard and Cabwassu!"

Oludara and the others stumbled for a nearby stream under the relentless attack of the wasps and club. When they finally made it, they collapsed into the water.

After staying under as long as possible, the three surfaced to find the wasps had left. Cabwassu's parrot sat in a squat tree and Way-Krig, club and bow in hand, looked down on them from the edge of the lake.

"I'm beginning to think the three of you enjoy these beatings," he said. Then he added, more seriously, "It has been funny pounding you three fools, but the game is starting to lose its delight. If you come after me again, I'll use the bow. And you know what happens then, don't you, bird?"

"I'll chew the meat from your bones!" it said.

"Right," said Way-Krig. Then he strode off, not bothering to look back.

Oludara began to crawl after him, but Gerard and Cabwassu held him back.

"It's over," said Gerard. "He has bested us three times. It's time to get back to Arany."

"We defeated Massone and Kooka," said Cabwassu. "There is no need to be ashamed."

Oludara, pain flaring through every part of his body, clawed his way forward, even as his friends struggled against him.

"This isn't over," he said. "There is no 'nearly' catching a rabbit. You can't cook a 'nearly' in a stew."

At that moment, an arrow pounded into the ground, inches from his nose. The powerful strike threw dirt in his face—and snapped his will.

He dropped his head in resignation.

When they reached the village, Cabwassu departed with a wave and Gerard and Oludara continued on toward their longhouse.

Gerard worried for his friend. The return trip had been long and lonesome—three weeks to feel the ache of their wounds and think upon their defeat. Hardly a word had been spoken, except by the parrot, which had jeered at them the entire way. Even Cabwassu had stopped laughing at its antics.

The few times Oludara had spoken, he voiced concerns over the terrible things which could go wrong with the birth of his baby, its tiny body deformed by the failure of the father. Gerard had tried to assuage him, but to no avail. Now, entering the village, Oludara's anxiety seemed to triple.

"Don't worry," said Gerard. "Everything will be fine."

"Our failure does not bode well for the birth of my boy," replied Oludara.

"That's just superstition."

"What if she loses the child? What if she lost it three weeks ago? Will you still call it superstition?"

"Quit languishing over it and go find out."

"Hey!" screeched a voice beside them.

They turned to see Sacy-Perey beside them, grinning broadly.

"Where have you two been?" he asked.

Oludara scowled and Gerard shook his head, advising against taking the subject any further.

"Well, what are you standing out here for?" continued Sacy. "Don't you want watch the birth? I've always been curious what they're like."

Oludara's eyes grew wide and he rushed to the longhouse, Gerard following closely behind. They entered to find Arany squatting near the ground, surrounded by women. No one even blinked when Sacy hopped in; they had grown accustomed to his frequent, annoying visits. As the women held Arany, she grunted and pushed the baby. She opened her eyes between pushes and spotted Oludara.

"What happened to your face?" she asked. They still bore scabs and welts from their encounter with Way-Krig.

"That story can wait," said Oludara, kneeling behind her and gripping her firmly.

After a few more pushes, the baby's head appeared. The baby's dark skin contrasted with Arany's tan complexion, and the child let out a healthy bellow which made Oludara smile. After a few more pushes, the child slid into the waiting arms of the women. Oludara peeked back and forth over Arany's shoulders, searching with terrified eyes for some defect. The child lacked nothing, except for the one organ Oludara had most wanted to see: the one which would have marked the child as a boy. Gerard could see the disappointment on his face.

"She's beautiful!" said Sacy, with a type of reverence Gerard had never before heard in his voice.

At the mention of the word 'she', Arany's gaze shot to Oludara. She didn't seem at all pleased with what she saw there.

One of the women held the girl up to Oludara's face. "It is custom for the father to chew through the cord with his teeth," she said.

Even Oludara, normally comfortable with the strangest of Tupinambá customs, flinched at the request.

"Just cut it," Arany said through clinched teeth.

Without a word, Gerard rummaged through his pack and removed a knife. Oludara accepted it with a nod and cut the cord. Several of the women took up the baby and left the longhouse with her. Sacy, his eyes still wide with amazement, bounded out after them.

"Where do they go?" asked Gerard.

Arany opened her eyes and replied weakly, "They go to the river for washing." She looked back at her husband. "How is our child?" she asked.

Oludara paused before replying, "Healthy."

Gerard was worried how his friend would react, but letting out that one word seemed to relieve him.

With a sigh, he repeated, "Healthy."

He sat beside Arany and cradled her in his arms.

"Have you thought of a name?" she asked.

"Yes," he said, "but not one which fits. I think you should choose."

Arany, still resting against Oludara's chest, nodded and sighed.

The next day, Gerard found Oludara and Arany laying side by side in their hammock, cradling their daughter between them. A pile of crudely woven objects of all shapes and sizes lay beneath them.

"Hello," said Gerard. "What are all these things?"

"Sacy keeps popping in and leaving these as presents," said Arany. "He's quite fond of Taynah."

"Taynah? So you've chosen a name then?"

"Yes," said Arany. "It means 'shining star'. I will not have my child plagued with a foolish name like mine."

"It's a beautiful name," said Gerard.

"For a beautiful child," said Oludara, gently passing a finger over her.

"Look how he dotes over her," said Arany. "Even though he still craves a son."

"It has nothing to do with craving," said Oludara. "I must continue my line."

"That story of continuing your line."

"It is no story, it is my duty to my ancestors. In any case, it doesn't matter. In less than two years, we'll be back in Ketu, where we can have a houseful of children."

"If you go back to Ketu," said Arany, "you go alone."

Oludara appeared ready to explode, and both Gerard and Arany pulled back. However, at the last moment, he deliberately stood from the hammock, careful not to disturb Taynah, and strode off to the far side of the longhouse.

Gerard looked at Arany, but she only shook her head and returned her attention to the baby.

As the days stretched on, Gerard's worry for his companion grew. Tupinambá custom required the father to remain in his cabin until the

baby's umbilical stump fell out. Oludara dutifully followed this custom, however, when the cord fell out, he remained there, spending the days in his hammock. He spoke with no one, not even Arany.

After a week of Oludara's moping, Gerard decided to take action. It was no easy choice for him. He had thought much upon their travels since the death of Father Miguel, and had lost most of his stomach for them. He had surely changed the future of the colony, for better or worse, though he knew not which. He had saved many, but perhaps doomed others. He had gained much fame, the whole reason he had come to Brazil. Now, he no longer knew if he desired it.

Nonetheless, he could not deny that Oludara had invited him on the quest for the bow to rescue him from his doldrums; he could do no less for his friend.

Gerard dressed in the same clothes he had worn on the day the two of them first met, and went to stand beside Oludara's hammock. Oludara did his best to pretend Gerard wasn't there.

"Taynah grows by the day, doesn't she?" said Gerard.

Oludara replied with a weak, distant, "Yes."

"You needn't worry about Kooka coming after her. Cabwassu and I spoke to Yandir of our journey, and he set wards around the village. Kooka can't come near without him knowing. Leave witchcraft to fight witchcraft, fine by me."

Oludara grunted in reply.

"You should speak to Arany, she's worried."

Instead of answering, Oludara said, "I envy you sometimes, Gerard. You owe nothing to your ancestors. You are free to go wherever you choose, do whatever you want."

"We all owe our ancestors. We just choose to honor them in different ways."

"That is right. I must return to Ketu, and Arany must stay here. What have we done? Perhaps we should never have been married."

"Don't say that. You both followed your heart, and that is never wrong."

Oludara didn't seem convinced.

"The problem is, you're too much alike: stubborn as mules."

At that, Oludara nodded in agreement.

Gerard changed his tone, making his next statement sound like a command. "In any case, it is time to be off on our next journey."

"Hmm?" Oludara replied.

"You still owe me more than a year, remember?"

"I suppose," said Oludara.

"You know, someone once told me that 'laziness is the partner of fatigue'. Ever heard it?"

"Perhaps," said Oludara, without even a grin to acknowledge the reference.

Gerard paused, unsure what to say, and to his surprise, Oludara filled the silence.

"There was a time I thought we were invincible," said Oludara. "That no matter how great the task, we would find some way to surmount it."

"So did I," Gerard agreed with a sigh. "That time is long past. We're no longer as young or as foolish...but I believe we could still do much good."

"Or much harm. Do you wish to add to our failures?"

Oludara had put Gerard's greatest fears into words, and it gave him pause. When he searched deep, however, he remembered the Tupiniquim children, and the town of Ilhéus, and the garrison at Rio de Janeiro, and so many others. When he thought on them, he finally found the answer.

"I would sooner fail than not try!"

Oludara's eyes widened at Gerard's spirited response. To Gerard's relief, he stood up from the hammock and stretched his arms into the air.

"I will think on it," he said.

He walked from the longhouse and Gerard followed close behind.

In the village center, they found Cabwassu cooking some meat on a spit. He looked up at them and flashed his demonic smile.

"You look sad," Cabwassu said, looking at Oludara. He grabbed the spit from the fire and handed it to him. "Eat some of this. It will make you feel better."

Oludara took the spit and examined it. "What is it?"

"It's a dish I created," said Cabwassu. "I call it roasted, deserves-to-die parrot."

Gerard and Oludara's eyes looked to Cabwassu's shoulder, where, indeed, the ever-present bird was gone. For the first time in a month, Gerard saw Oludara smile.

"Yes," he said. "That would definitely make me feel better."

Gerard, pack filled and weapons by his side, waited for Oludara in the village center. Arany, Taynah suckling at her breast, approached him. He turned his eyes down in embarrassment.

"You're going off?" she asked.

"Yes," he replied. "Oludara didn't tell you?"

"He has spoken to me little these last days."

"I'm sorry."

"No, it's good you're going away. There's nothing worse than men getting in the way when a woman is trying to raise a baby."

From the cracking in her voice and the way she looked away, Gerard was certain she didn't mean it.

After a long, awkward pause, Gerard said: "He'll come around. The two of you are everything to him."

"I hope so, because neither I nor my child have any place in Africa. She will stay with our tribe, same as I."

Arany pulled the baby from her breast and held it in front of him.

"Gerard, could you hold her for a moment while I relieve myself?"

Gerard awkwardly cradled the baby and Arany headed off. He rocked Taynah back and forth, studying her. The child combined features from both her parents. The first dark hairs already curled upon her head. Her skin shone a dark brown, lighter than her father, but much darker than her mother. She looked up at Gerard with unfocused eyes as he rocked her.

"Looks like everyone has their own expectations for you, Taynah," he said. "This is no easy world for a woman, but I hope you follow your own path. There is much that others will say you can't do, but back in the Low Countries, the women study whatever practice they choose, and some are even soldiers in the war against Spain. I've met my share of women poets and pirates, and many who do a better job at it than men. Even mighty England is ruled by a fine queen. Kooka said there is greatness in you, and I don't doubt it."

Gerard jumped as Arany's voice came from behind him.

"Poets and pirates?" she said. "Don't put such silly notions in her head, Gerard." She took the baby from him and added, "Tupinambá women do not care for writing or sailing. And queens are a thing for white men."

Gerard nodded and tipped his hat. "You're right, of course."

As he walked away, he added, under his breath, "But then again, there is more to her blood than Tupinambá."

The sloth looked down at the dwelling of the strange, upright creatures. The two lazy men had lost their calm and become agitated, and had long since left the village. In their place, however, someone even calmer had appeared.

The sloth made the slow climb down the tree, then made his way between the large, mud dwellings. The tall creatures cast looks at him as they passed quickly by, some of the smaller ones pointed at him and giggled, but none made a move to stop him.

Step by step, he headed toward his destination: a woven stack of branches which contained—bundled within a set of rags—the tiny creature he sought.

He climbed up the branches, careful not to tip them over, and cuddled up beside the tiny, dark creature. This one, without a doubt, was quite calming.

Chapter 10

An Audacious Engagement in Olinda

HE JAGUAR PROWLED through the woods, searching for an elusive quarry: a new, unknown female in his territory. He had first smelled her scent a few weeks back, and found her trail almost every night, but would somehow lose it at dawn. The hunt had become an obsession, and he forgot even nourishment in his quest to find her.

This night, however, he sensed she was close. He yearned to possess her, and rushed without caution through the woods, pausing only to make sure he kept on her trail. Her scent led along a wide, dirt path, one of those which the humans cleared through the woods. Even though the scents of the humans stank all around, her scent stood out. Once he realized her trail did not deviate from the path, he raced ahead.

It wasn't long before he spotted haunches on the path before him. She walked with a limp; her right front paw was crooked. His body ached in anticipation of catching her. As he approached, however, his senses bristled in alarm. The jaguar before him was too large: oversized for a male and immense for a female. He realized her smell wasn't mixing with the smell of humans, instead, part of her own smell was human.

The female sensed him and turned. She crouched menacingly on her front paws. The jaguar tensed himself for a fight. He had never run from a male contender, and wouldn't be scared away by this female.

As she edged closer, however, the extent of her humongous size became apparent. She dwarfed him, perhaps doubled his weight. She let out an echoing roar and he trembled.

He hissed at her once for show, but knew he had no choice. Step by step he backed away, before bolting into the woods.

Oludara followed Gerard up a steep hill which marked Olinda's city center. Halfway up, a humble clay building marked their destination. At a knock from Gerard, an elderly nun answered the door. She squinted at them from under her black hood.

"Good day," said Gerard, tipping his hat. "I'm looking for Sister I. Leite."

"And who may I ask, would like to see her?"

"My name is Gerard van Oost. I came at her summons: a letter speaking of a problem here in Olinda."

The woman examined the two of them with an air of mistrust, but finally nodded and said, "Just a moment."

She disappeared into the building, to be replaced minutes later by a much younger nun, one around thirty years of age. Like the other, she wore a black cape over a white robe. Oludara had no idea how the nuns could stand the tropical heat in the heavy clothes. Her face—thin with a nose which rose up at the tip—broke into an enormous, beaming smile when she looked at Gerard.

"I am Gerard van Oost," he said, "and this is my companion, Oludara."

She greeted Oludara with a nod and a genuine smile, a courtesy few had shown him during his time in Brazil. The woman exuded an aura of such gentleness that it almost made him uncomfortable.

"You came!" she said to Gerard. "I can't believe it. I don't know how I ever had the courage to send that letter."

"Your summons surprised me, Sister Leite," said Gerard, "but I could hardly refuse them."

"You shouldn't be surprised. Father Gregorio Bras of the Society of Jesus recommended you: 'Gerard van Oost, magnanimous man and possessor of high virtues.' He told me you of your brave deeds, and that although a Protestant, we could trust you in any matter."

Gerard's face reached a cherry red Oludara had never seen before.

"Thank you so much for coming. I never expected you to travel so far at the request of a humble nun."

"It's nothing, Sister Leite," stammered Gerard.

"Please," she said, "call me Inocencia."

"Inocencia?" said Gerard. "What a lovely name."

It was the nun's turn to blush.

Gerard, likely looking for any excuse to change the subject, fumbled through his pack and pulled out a box, which he handed to her.

"I didn't want to come all this way empty-handed," he said.

When she opened the box, Oludara could see multi-colored candies inside.

"Crystallized fruits?" she said. "Are these from Madeira Island?"

Gerard raised his eyebrows.

"You recognize them?"

"Of course," she said, "they're worth a fortune! I can't possibly accept them."

Oludara noticed, however, that she didn't make any move to give them back.

"It's nothing," said Gerard, "I received them myself as a present. Please accept and enjoy them."

She moved toward him, as if to give him a hug, then caught herself and pulled her hands back.

"Thank you," she said, eyes turned down. Then she stepped aside to let them in. "Welcome to our humble house: Our Lady of the Immaculate Conception. Men aren't allowed beyond the reception, but we can sit and talk at a table here."

The front room was packed with women and children; Oludara spotted natives, whites, and mixtures of the two. A few women offered a table to Inocencia and went on their way, not taking their eyes off of Oludara and Gerard.

After the three of them sat at the table, Oludara asked, "What is this place?"

"It's a women's refuge," she responded. "We accept all those who need our help and guidance. The house originated as a place to take in native women—Christians who had been abandoned by their white lovers. It's a shame how often that happens. These days, however, even women from highborn families come to us, those who choose to eschew marriage and follow the religious life. We seek donations to amplify our house, but they have been scarce recently, in part from the problem we face."

At that moment, a nun carrying a plate of bread approached their table. Oludara guessed she couldn't be older than twenty. She had the look of a caboclo: a cross between native and European. She had black hair, although not completely straight. Her tan skin was lighter than that of the pure natives. Her square nose could only come from European decent.

"I brought something for our guests," she said. "May I join you?"

"Of course," said Inocencia.

As the woman placed the plate on the table, Oludara caught sight of her hands. Both were splotchy, with mottled white and tan skin, and her right hand twisted into itself and appeared almost useless. She sat opposite them, beside Inocencia.

"This is Sister Catarina Castanha," said Inocencia. "Catarina was one of the first to come to our house, taken in as a child. She went away to become a nun, and recently returned to join us as a sister. It's such a joy to have someone grow up here and then come back to serve."

Catarina smiled at the compliment. "Please, accept some of our bread," she said. "It's a poor meal for esteemed visitors, but we have nothing better to offer."

Oludara accepted a piece of the bread and bit through the hard crust. The nun hadn't exaggerated about its quality; the taste was even worse than the texture.

Gerard made no move toward the bread, speaking to Inocencia instead. "Tell us of your problem."

"Something terrible is preying upon Olinda," she said. "Many have been killed, always at night. I called you because I believe it to be something uncanny. The bodies of the victims look like they've been slain by some kind of animal, but none I've ever heard of. Some victims are ripped apart, others burned. Whatever it is, it ignores slaves and workers, instead preying on the rich and important: mill owners and officials. Even then, it targets the most charitable of Christians. The worst ones, the corrupt and unscrupulous, it seems to leave alone."

Catarina nudged her. "Speak of the devil and he's sure to appear. Look who just walked in."

Oludara followed her her gaze to see a towering man approach them. He wore an expensive red doublet with a huge ruff and a black cape. A red cap folded down over one ear and covered slicked-back, black hair.

His goatee consisted of a tiny triangle beneath his broad lips and flat-fronted nose. Two men carrying halberds flanked him.

"I hear someone called a banner to town?" he asked, his tone confrontational.

"That would be my banner," said Gerard.

"And where are your bannermen?"

"It is just the two of us," replied Gerard, motioning toward Oludara.

The owner gave them a confused look. "We don't need anyone meddling here," he said.

"Aren't you worried that something is killing the town's wealthy?" asked Gerard, eying the man's fancy clothes for effect.

"I've hired soldiers to look into it."

"Apparently, they're not doing a good job," commented Oludara.

The man looked at Oludara and his eyes narrowed. When he spoke, he returned his gaze to Gerard.

"I see you own a slave, so you must be a man of some means. I, however, own three-hundred of them. My mill earns me twelve thousand cruzados a year. If you think you can do alone what I can do with all my resources, I wish you luck, Mister..."

"Gerard van Oost," said Gerard, tipping his hat. "And I own no slaves; Oludara here is a free man."

Oludara noticed the man's eyes widen at the mention of Gerard's name, but he quickly caught the lapse and returned his expression to its former arrogance.

"Good luck, then, Mr. van Oost."

The man turned and strode out, followed promptly by his guards.

"Who was that?" asked Oludara.

"Sibaldo Romani," responded Inocencia. "A Florentine gentleman and owner of Saint Peter's sugar mill."

"Florentine?" asked Gerard. "What's he doing here?"

"Why does any gentleman come to Brazil?" asked Catarina. "Money. You heard him, twelve thousand cruzados a year. There are princes who don't earn as much."

"Business appears to be good in the sugar mills."

"And getting better. He's been purchasing mills from some of the recently deceased." Catarina's face left no doubt she thought the two facts had something in common.

"Don't go making insinuations," said Inocencia. "It was no man that killed those mill owners."

"How did someone from Tuscany earn an estate here?" asked Gerard.

"He's a friend of the captain general and some say of the king himself. I've heard he's related to the grand duke of Tuscany."

Oludara had no idea what that meant, but Gerard seemed impressed.

"But for once," said Catarina, "I agree with Sibaldo. You shouldn't have called these two here, Inocencia." She looked at Oludara and Gerard. "Don't endanger yourselves for our cause. Sibaldo's mercenaries and the local militia are more than enough to stop whatever is behind this. They number hundreds to your two."

"We didn't come all this way just to turn and go home," said Gerard. "We'll have a look tonight, see what we can discover."

"So soon?" asked Inocencia.

"My people have a saying," said Oludara, "'If a matter be dark, dive to the bottom.'"

—⟡—

From atop the city wall, a guard called out, "Nine o'clock! Who's in is in! Who's out is out!"

Gerard looked back towards Oludara. "Well that's that, then. We won't get back in there until daylight."

"Be wary," responded Oludara.

"Of course."

They kept to the roads, where most of the killings had taken place. As Oludara studied everything around them carefully, Gerard found his mind slipping back to Olinda.

"Nice nuns, aren't they?" he asked.

"What?" asked Oludara.

"Those nuns back in Olinda."

"We need to concentrate on finding this creature, not on nuns."

"I'm just saying."

Oludara shook his head. "First the Jesuits and now these nuns. For all you complain about Catholics, you certainly seem to like them."

Gerard grumbled in reply.

"Now, please focus," said Oludara.

They crested a hill and Gerard spotted a torch far down the road below them, someone walking in their direction.

"Gerard, do you see it?" asked Oludara.

"What, the man down there?"

"No, behind him."

Gerard had to squint, but sure enough, a silhouette followed the man, sneaking through the shadows. From its movement, it appeared feline, but it paced awkwardly, as if with a limp.

"What do we do?" asked Gerard.

"Get down there before the creature strikes. But try not to alert it too soon. We want to confront it, not frighten it off."

Gerard followed Oludara through the brush beside the road until they came even with the man. Oludara stepped from the bushes to alert the man to their presence, and he panicked at the sight of them, scrambling to unsheathe a basket-hilted sword at his side.

"We are not here to harm you," said Oludara, "but I do suggest you run."

At that, Oludara drew his ivory knife and turned toward the beast. The man looked back, gave one terrified gasp, then ran off down the road as instructed.

Gerard stepped beside Oludara and raised his harquebus, primed and ready for a shot. From this distance, he got his first good look at the creature: a jaguar of enormous size. The jaguar's right front paw curved in, causing its awkward movement. At the sight of them, the jaguar crouched menacingly and roared.

"Wait no longer," said Oludara. "Attack while you have the chance!"

Gerard shot and the creature screamed, but he could spot no mark from the ball. The jaguar leapt past Oludara, who gashed it with his knife. The jaguar didn't look back; instead, it sprinted down the road.

"After it!" yelled Oludara.

As the two set off running, Gerard asked, "Did your blade cut it?"

"A nick on the cheek, nothing serious."

"More than my shot."

At the crest of the next hill, they spotted something laying on the road below them. They ran down to find the bloodied body of the man they had passed on the road. Of the jaguar, they found no sign.

At midday, Inocencia led Oludara and Gerard to a garden behind the shelter, where they sat at a wooden table.

"I'll be right back," she said.

Trees with pink flowers which hung like colored bells filled the garden with a pleasant scent. Oludara found it relaxing after a taxing night.

Inocencia returned carrying a tray with three glasses of water. Oludara took his and noticed an unusual scent.

"This water has a fruity smell," said Oludara. "Perhaps something contaminated it."

Inocencia smiled. "It's orange-blossom water. You have no need to worry, I prepared it myself."

Gerard took a gulp and nodded in approval. "A delicacy," he said.

"I'm glad you like it. It has been years since I've prepared it. Our work here leaves little time for such frivolity."

"And where did you learn the making of orange-blossom water?"

"Portugal, or Spain. Perhaps someplace else. I moved around Europe much before I came here."

"So did I!" said Gerard. He placed his elbows on the table and rested his head between his hands. "Tell me where you've been."

"Shouldn't we discuss last night?" interrupted Oludara.

"What happened?" asked Inocencia. "I heard Fernando Leitão was murdered on the road. He was a good man. Did you see him?"

"Yes," said Gerard. "We were too late to save him. I'm sorry."

Inocencia bowed her head and made the sign of the cross. "I thank

God the two of you are all right. My conscience would weigh heavy if I called you here only to die."

"We were indeed too late to save him," said Oludara, "but we discovered his killer. It is a jaguar of uncommon size. The creature appears to have an enchantment of some sort."

"My shot bounced off its hide," added Gerard.

"It sounds terrible," said Inocencia. Her hands moved toward Gerard, but stopped just short of touching him.

"We've faced worse," said Gerard.

"Like what?" she asked.

"One time, for instance, near Santos, we faced a creature known as Epoopar."

Oludara sighed as Gerard dove into the story. Bored, he looked around the garden and spotted Catarina. When she noticed him, she turned away and headed back into the shelter. Just before she turned, Oludara noticed a scratch upon her cheek.

Oludara interrupted Gerard with a tug. "May we have a moment?" he asked Inocencia. After pulling Gerard out of earshot, he said, "Did you notice Catarina?"

"No," said Gerard, looking around. "Is she here?"

"Not anymore, but I saw her, and she has a scratch on her cheek—the same cheek I scratched on the jaguar last night."

"Probably just a coincidence."

"And is it also a coincidence that her hand is deformed, same as the jaguar's front paw?"

"Her hand is deformed? I hadn't noticed."

Oludara shook his head at his companion. "What if it is her?" he asked. "Perhaps she wishes to revenge herself on the mill owners for past wrongs."

"Are you suggesting that a nun turns into a giant, man-eating jaguar at night?"

"We've seen stranger upon our journeys."

"Yes," said Gerard, scratching his chin. "I suppose we have."

Gerard turned back toward Inocencia. "Which reminds me. One time, we met a most unusual creature called Curooper. His feet are turned backwards, and he rides a giant boar."

Oludara could only sigh and roll his eyes.

Gerard, face hooded, walked the road carrying a torch. Oludara followed through the woods beside him. They had roamed the roads for hours, trying to bait the jaguar, but with no luck so far. The long night wore on Gerard's patience.

"Psst," came Oludara's voice from the woods. "Be ready."

Gerard responded with a nod and fought to keep from looking back until he heard his companion crash from the woods and yell "Now!"

Gerard spun around and unsheathed his rapier. He doubted the blade would pierce the jaguar's hide, but a hit to its mouth or eyes might work.

Some twenty paces away from him, Oludara leapt at the hindquarters of the jaguar, which in turn reared back and roared at him. He aimed a strike at the creature's neck and it avoided the blow, rolling below him at the last moment.

Gerard charged and the jaguar looked in his direction, eyes wide. It raced forward, ignoring Oludara's next attack and taking a cut to its haunches in the process.

A flickering light appeared and cast Gerard's shadow on the ground before him. He felt a warmth on his neck which grew with every passing second, but he ignored it to face the danger before him. Rapier and torch firmly in hand, Gerard readied himself for the onslaught.

At the last moment, however, the jaguar dashed to one side and leapt behind him. Gerard turned to see a three-foot tall, flaming skull—its mouth open and ready to bite—hovering in the air just inches from his face. He threw himself to the ground as the jaguar crashed into it.

The two bizarre creatures rolled on the ground, biting at each other until the jaguar, its hide singed from chest to face, could no longer stand the flames and pulled away. The skull took the opportunity to float back up in the air.

Gerard paused, unsure what to do, but Oludara came running and stabbed at the skull. The skull flew to one side to avoid the blow and bit at him, barely missing, yet burning his hand nonetheless. He pulled it back in pain.

The jaguar got to its feet and prepared for an attack. Gerard, taking Oludara's cue, stood beside it, rapier pointed at the skull. The skull, faced with three opponents, turned and flew into the woods at incredible speed. The jaguar raced after it.

Gerard looked to his companion.

"We can't catch them," said Oludara. "But if I'm correct, we'll corner one of them soon enough."

Oludara waited in the shadows of an alley just off Olinda's Main Street. As he expected, Catarina passed by on her afternoon walk to the bakery, out to pick up the day's leftovers for the refuge. She walked quickly, head held down, looking neither left nor right.

"Catarina," he said, stepping out behind her.

She turned and he could see the burn marks upon her face. His hand had taken much worse, requiring half a jar of ointment and a roll of bandages to treat. Then again, he wasn't an enchanted jaguar with almost impervious skin.

Catarina's eyes darted from side to side and for a moment, he thought she might run. Then, Gerard stepped out from his hiding place on the other side of the street, and she dropped her shoulders in resignation.

"I tried to warn you," she said. "I told you to go away before you got hurt. No man can face a Comacang and live."

"Comacang?" asked Gerard.

"That's what my tribe used to call them. Evil men who can send their heads flying into the night."

"That thing is a man?" asked Oludara. "But who?"

"Who do you think? Sibaldo. The one with the most to gain. Twelve thousand cruzados a year isn't enough for him; his greed is without limits."

"Why don't you warn the captain of the guard?"

"Didn't you listen? He received his mill from the captain general, owner of the entire captaincy, by indication of the king himself. None here would dare raise a hand against him."

"What about the Jesuits?" asked Oludara. "No doubt they would burn him if they knew."

"How would I prove it to them? And if they burn him, what do you think they will do to *me*?"

"You're telling me that giant, flaming skull is his head? And his body stays behind?" asked Gerard.

"The enchantment is powerful, and he is not the first."

"And no one notices a headless body?"

"No doubt he locks himself away when he does it. And his manor is heavily guarded; no one goes near without permission."

"We could work together," said Oludara. "We have faced worse than Sibaldo."

She looked into their eyes and nodded reluctantly.

"But I must warn you," she said. "These killings are secondary—a diversion as he searches for his true objective. His greatest desire is to find the Lake."

"What lake?" asked Oludara.

"The Enchanted Lake. It appears only once in a lifetime, and tomorrow is the night. We can't let him find it."

"Why?"

"Because it grants whomever finds it a wish."

"And what does Sibaldo want?"

"Would you risk waiting to find out? Can you fathom what a man that ravenous might possibly request with a wish?"

"We will trap him tonight," said Oludara.

Catarina shook her head. "I doubt it," she said. "He doesn't go out on his hunts every night; he has to keep some semblance of a normal life. He'll almost certainly be at the *outeiro* tonight."

"And what is that?" asked Oludara.

"A poetry battle. He never misses the chance to show off."

Inocencia came jogging toward them. She stopped beside Gerard and put a hand on his shoulder as she caught her breath. Then she noticed she was touching him and pulled quickly away, her face red with embarrassment.

"Where have you been?" she asked. "The outeiro is about to start! You can't miss it." Then she spotted Catarina. "What happened to your face?" she asked.

"Just a bit of sunburn," replied Catarina.

The patio of the Jesuit College had been transformed for the spectacle to come. Above the crowd, colored flags dangled along strings. Circling the patio were huge flower wreaths, their fragrance carried through the crowd with every breeze that passed. To the front, a wooden stage had been erected under a canopy. Behind it hung a canvas with a painting of Mount Parnassus, as if the famous Greek orators would come that night to stand before it and recite their verses. Torches and colored lamps illuminated the patio from one end to the other. The color and gaiety of the festive scene surprised Gerard, who was accustomed to the more somber aspects of the Catholic Church.

He sat on a log near the back, Inocencia and Oludara on either side. People filled the rows before them, and others stood on all sides. Most were dressed in what appeared to be their finest, clothes Gerard expected to see in church, not at an outdoor festival.

A young girl in a blue dress approached the stage and Inocencia leaned over to whisper, "That girl will announce tonight's theme. All the poets must end their poems with it."

The girl said, "Tonight, the theme is 'Our Lady of the O'." The audience clapped and cheered, and the girl curtsied and sat down.

"'Our Lady of the O'?" asked Oludara.

"It is the pregnant Virgin Mary," said Inocencia, "waiting in expectation for the baby Jesus. She's quite popular around these parts."

From Gerard's other side, Oludara leaned in and whispered, "I begin to understand why you are a Protestant. Less confusing."

Gerard agreed with the assessment, but to not risk offending Inocencia, responded with an ambivalent shrug.

The first poet, a balding man around forty years of age, took the stage. After a short applause, he recited his poem:

"In a glorious dream
Gabriel came to Mary
And asked her to carry
A child supreme
Our sins to redeem
This task she assumed
And in her womb bloomed
For nine months she bore
The savior, our Lord
Our Lady of the O"

The poem received a general applause, and many more like it followed. Inocencia's smile grew as the night went on, and Gerard felt good to be by her side. On his other side, Oludara's head drooped and jerked as he nodded off time and again.

At one point, a giggling man in soiled working clothes staggered onto the stage. From the look of him, Gerard judged him a drunken farmer. The man cleared his throat, spit on the ground, and spoke:

"I have an ass
Who's not worth the poop
He drops in my soup
After eating my grass
And letting it pass
It tastes like the gutter
But I eat it like butter
Then I pray like a friar
My bowels won't catch fire
To Our Lady of the O."

The group of Jesuits who stood to one side looked none too pleased with the poem, but many in the crowd roared with laughter. Gerard looked at Inocencia and saw her blushing.

When she caught him staring at her, she said, as if in apology, "Some poets are better than others."

The other poets kept to the religious theme for the most part, although a few slipped in jokes that Gerard didn't understand, but imagined were aimed at others within the community.

After a long pause in which no one took the stage, the girl in the blue dress returned and asked, "Do we have any other poets tonight?"

At that, Sibaldo stood up in the front row. Gerard elbowed Oludara, who jerked awake and looked around, confused. Sibaldo held himself rigidly on stage. After a long applause from the crowd, he began his poem with a deep, echoing voice:

"How could one virgin womb possibly buttress such weight?
Easier for us sinners to hoist a thousand boulders
Than tote a single hair of Christ's head upon our shoulders
Only a heart of infinite compassion could conflate
With Christ's divine body, yet not desecrate
A flesh and blood so sanctified
It absolved our sins, when it died
To give all praise and devotion is little reward
To she who permitted the manifestation of our Lord
Our Blessed Lady of the O."

The poem received the heartiest applause of the night. Many stood in their enthusiasm as Sibaldo bowed.

Beside Gerard, Inocencia fumed. "He has no right," she said. "The man gives nothing to charity, yet acts so pious."

Sibaldo strode from the stage, and the girl appeared again.

"I hope you all enjoyed tonight..." she begun.

"Wait!" shouted Inocencia, standing.

As all eyes turned to her, she blanched. She looked down at Gerard and he smiled and nodded, offering his support. At this, she regained her composure.

She walked toward the stage, saying, "There will be one more poem tonight."

The whispers and gasps outweighed the applause as Inocencia took the stage. Once again, she searched out Gerard, looked straight at him, then returned her attention to the crowd and recited her poem:

"I see, from your reaction
Your surprise, that one so humble
Would dare, her verse to mumble
Yet, is not the satisfaction
Its greatest, when performing an action?
The feeding of those with needs
Is the calling the pious man heeds
Twelve thousand cruzados aren't worth dust
If the owner won't spare a crust
To feed Our Lady of the O."

The poem received great applause, although many looked around nervously as they did so. Sibaldo stood, furious, as if about to speak, but when he looked at the crowd around him, strode out of the patio instead, flanked by his ever-present guards.

Inocencia bowed her head and returned to her seat beside Gerard.

"I'm so embarrassed," she said. "I shouldn't have done that, should I? Sometimes I forget I'm a nun."

"Sometimes I forget too," said Gerard. Then, realizing what he'd said, he turned away to hide his embarrassment.

"I should go," stuttered Inocencia.

"Please," said Gerard. "Let us escort you back to the refuge."

Keeping her eyes to the ground, she responded with a nod.

Oludara sat on one of the beds in their rented room and watched Gerard, seated on the other, oiling his harquebus. Gerard caressed the gun a bit too sensually as he worked. The man's increasing infatuation with the nun had begun to worry Oludara. Gerard seemed to think of nothing else, and in a moment of danger, that could prove costly.

His thoughts were interrupted by a knock at the door. Their landlord, a tailor, opened it before they had time to respond.

"There's someone downstairs to see you," he said.

Oludara could only shrug at Gerard's quizzical glance. Without speaking, the two headed downstairs to discover Catarina waiting for them.

"Hello, Catarina," said Gerard, looking around. "Is Inocencia with you?"

"Of course not," she said. "I came here to talk about our plans for tonight."

"Good," said Oludara. "We have much to discuss."

They were interrupted when a man carrying a halberd stepped into their midst. Oludara recognized him as one of Sibaldo's guards.

The guard addressed Gerard. "The Dom Romani requests your presence for lunch at his residence."

Gerard looked at Oludara, but Catarina whispered from beside him, "Go there. See what he wants."

Gerard nodded and returned his attention to the man. "Tell Dom Romani we accept his kind offer."

The guard nodded curtly and strode off.

"Be careful," said Catarina.

"We will," said Gerard.

Oludara silently hoped that Gerard could keep his wits about him.

"Find me at the refuge after your lunch," said Catarina. At that, she headed off.

Oludara and Gerard retrieved their equipment and set out, only to come across Inocencia on the street minutes later.

"Where are you headed?" she asked.

"To Sibaldo's house," replied Gerard.

"Why?"

Gerard looked to Oludara, waiting for an excuse, but Oludara just sent the problem back to him with a discreet shake of his head.

"Um," said Gerard. "We're going to try and convince him to donate to the refuge."

"With your weapons?" she asked. "We prefer peaceful petitions, not threats."

"It's nothing like that. You know how one needs to be careful on the roads these days."

"I suppose so," she said, with a voice lacking conviction. "Please don't do anything foolish."

"Don't worry," promised Gerard. "We're just going to have a friendly chat."

Oludara's first glimpse of Sibaldo's plantation was the guard bastion, poised between road and river, with four guards on top and three pieces of heavy artillery poking over the edge. From there, the sights grew even more impressive, as he and Gerard passed a water-driven sawmill, irrigation channels, and a private church, more ornate than many within the town itself. Three galleys, two large enough to port guns on the prow, lay anchored in the river, and a two-masted caravel floated beside them. Beyond the mill and slave house, rows of sugar cane stretched out as far as Oludara could see. The fortune necessary to pay for an operation of that size was a sum he couldn't fathom.

To no surprise, Sibaldo's house was equally magnificent. A rock-solid construction painted an immaculate white, the two-story house stretched so far, it seemed more appropriate as a warehouse than a residence.

Guards ushered them in, and Sibaldo met them in an immense antechamber, one with exquisite paintings decorating its walls and works of gold arranged upon cabinets carved from dark, solid wood.

"Welcome, Gerard," said Sibaldo. "Your slave can wait here."

Oludara bristled, but had heard such comments so many times that he had almost gotten used to them.

"He's not my slave," said Gerard, "he is my equal in all that concerns my banner."

"He can wait here anyway," said Sibaldo.

"If he does not sup by my side, I'll have none."

Sibaldo gave him a furious look, but motioned them to follow and turned around. He led them down multiple corridors, each with its own rich decorations, until reaching the dining room.

Sibaldo sat at the head of the table and Gerard and Oludara sat along one side. Sibaldo shouted a command and three slaves—two women and a young boy—carried in their food. They were not from the Guinea region like Oludara; he imagined they must be from the Kingdom of Kongo, farther down the African coast. The three slaves stared wide-eyed when they saw Oludara at the table and the boy even gasped, but a hiss from Sibaldo caused them to lock their eyes upon the floor, not to be raised again.

Like everything else around Oludara, the meal was the most extravagant he had ever seen. Sibaldo's slaves first served a pigeon pie and leg of lamb. An intoxicating smell rose from both dishes.

"What are those spices?" asked Oludara, his mouth watering.

"Saffron and cinnamon," said Gerard. "The most expensive spices in the world."

"Ten-thousand réis to the pound," added Sibaldo.

The three ate in silence. Gerard, in particular, seemed to savor every bite. As Oludara ate, he spotted slaves peeking into the windows from time to time, staring at him with wide eyes and open mouths before ducking away. He recalled that the current price for slaves was twenty-thousand réis. That meant that white men gave a slave's life the same value as two pounds of the saffron he ate. After making that morbid calculation, Oludara lost his appetite.

The meal continued with leafy salad containing garlic and peppers and ended with a caramel custard. Gerard devoured all he was offered. When the meal finally ended, Gerard sat back with his hands upon his round belly, a satisfied look upon his face. Oludara wondered how he could enjoy a meal in the face of an enemy, but then again, Gerard had never been one to turn down good food.

"I thank you for the meal, Dom Romani," said Gerard. "It is, without a doubt, the finest feast I've enjoyed since I set foot in this colony, almost five years past."

"You are a man of good taste, Gerard," replied Sibaldo. "You should stop associating with those nuns at the refuge. Instead of dirtying their hands with the natives, they should be shackling them and sending them to work in the sugar mills."

The insult seemed to bring Gerard back to his senses.

"I don't think my choice of friends is any of your business, Sibaldo. And speaking of business, why don't we discuss ours? Why is it you called us here today?"

"I want you to leave Olinda, Gerard. Turn away from what is none of 'your business', as you so nicely say, and I will reward you handsomely."

"You ask me to take money and ignore everyone you've killed in your quest for power?"

Sibaldo looked back and forth between Gerard and Oludara, as if weighing his next words. "I ask you to take what I offer and not become the next victim. I ask you to be more reasonable than others who have sat at this table before you."

Gerard frowned, but asked, "And just what kind of reward are we talking about?"

"Two thousand, five hundred cruzados."

Oludara couldn't believe the sum; it totaled a million réis. Even Gerard choked upon hearing it. Sibaldo obviously took them seriously. Someone must have told him something which frightened him.

"If you don't want it for yourself, Gerard," continued Sibaldo, "give it to your impertinent nun. Think of what she could do for her refuge."

"I'll think about it," said Gerard.

Sibaldo studied Gerard in silence, then said, "No you won't. I can see that in your eyes."

Gerard made no reply.

"Beware, Gerard van Oost." Sibaldo growled the words.

"Thank you for your hospitality," said Gerard, standing. "But I believe it's time we headed out."

"I agree," said Sibaldo. He called for the slave boy. "See them out," he commanded.

The slave boy, never taking his eyes from the ground, led them away. At the door, he dared one glance into Oludara's eyes before ducking into the house and slamming the door.

As he and Gerard headed down the path, Oludara looked back to see thick, black smoke rising from one of the house chimneys.

"I don't think Sibaldo is concerned with warming his house in this heat," said Oludara. "We must leave this path as soon as possible, for that is the signal for an ambush."

"I have little doubt about that," agreed Gerard.

Gerard and Oludara found Catarina waiting for them in front of the refuge.

"What took you so long?" she asked. "And what is that stench?"

"Sibaldo set an ambush and we were forced to flee through the mangrove swamp," replied Gerard. "You wouldn't believe how many crabs I had to pull from my boots."

Gerard had rarely had the pleasure of visiting a more odorous place: a mire of shoreline saltwater packed with creatures both dead and alive.

"So he called you there for an ambush?"

"Actually, he made us a generous offer to leave him alone."

Catarina cocked her head and studied him.

"You needn't worry," he said. "If we'd accepted, do you think we'd have had to come back like this?"

"Night approaches," said Oludara. "We must make a plan."

"I know where the lake is," said Catarina. "Just follow me and we can set an ambush of our own."

"How do you know its location?" asked Oludara.

"My mother saw it in her youth. Years later, she showed me the place. We need only wait there and it will appear."

"Why did you not tell us before?" asked Gerard.

"I needed to make sure I could trust you. How do I know you won't try to wish for something worse than Sibaldo?"

"Do you trust us now?" asked Gerard.

She nodded.

"Then let us be off," said Oludara.

As the three turned to leave, a voice said from behind them, "Where are you going?"

They turned to find Inocencia there, a look of surprise on her face. As she came closer, she crinkled her nose, but said nothing of the smell.

"Catarina was just seeing us off," said Gerard. "Tonight, we hunt again for the beast."

"Why didn't you find me first? Gerard, will you speak with me alone for a moment?"

Gerard motioned for Oludara and Catarina to wait and followed her. She led him to the garden behind the refuge. In one of the trees, four bright blue birds with red spots on their heads chirped and danced in a most unusual fashion. They jumped around in one big circle, right in front of a green bird.

To break the awkward silence, Gerard asked, "Those are strange birds. What are they doing up there?"

"The green one is the female; the males dance for her. At the end of the dance, she will choose the one she likes best for mating."

At that, both she and Gerard turned red and looked away. Gerard took a deep breath and reminded himself that Inocencia was a nun.

"Don't go, Gerard," she said. "My heart fears for you."

He turned and stared at her. She stood so close to him, he could smell her perfume. It smelled of jasmine—a scent he adored. He failed to recall the last time he had smelled a woman's perfume. His heart pounded and he forced himself to speak.

"I must finish what I came here to do. With Oludara by my side, you need not worry."

"Are you sure?"

Gerard stared off. "We've had our failures, but we've always come out alive."

"Will you pray with me?"

"You know I'm not a Catholic."

"It doesn't matter."

Gerard considered giving in to her request, when Oludara appeared around the corner.

"We must leave," he said. "The gate closes mere minutes from now."

Gerard turned back to Inocencia. "I must go."

"Then I will pray alone," she said. "Every minute, until you return."

As much as it pained him, Gerard turned away from her and raced down the hill with Oludara.

They followed the Catarina-jaguar through the moonlight for three hours: first along roads, then through woods, until, without warning, she stopped and sat on her haunches. She took one glance back at them, then motioned forward with her snout.

Oludara followed her gaze to see an opening in the woods, its limits clearly defined by a ring of trees. Oludara couldn't help but notice they were brazilwood, the trees from which came a rich, scarlet-colored dye coveted by all of Europe. Trees which the Portuguese cut down and carried back home by the tens of thousands each year. Trees which gave the colony its name.

"Not much of a lake, Catarina," said Gerard.

Catarina, unable to speak in her jaguar form, responded to the jest with a low growl.

"What do we do now?" asked Gerard.

"Keep an eye out for Sibaldo," replied Oludara.

"Do you really think a giant, flaming skull can sneak up on us?" asked Gerard.

"He did last time. His flame appeared just before he struck. Let us split into a triangle, each one on a different edge of the clearing. Do you understand, Catarina?"

The jaguar nodded and the three of them took up positions at different edges of the clearing. With the great distance between them, several hundred feet, Oludara could barely make out the silhouettes of his companions from the dark woods behind them. As he squinted to make sure they were all right, he was surprised to see a light appear in the middle of the clearing, like a lamp being lit. The light grew in intensity, and as it did, Oludara could see water spreading out from it. The water rose until it touched the ring of brazilwood trees. The light glimmered a fierce yellow, making the clearing look like a giant pool of gold.

Then, another light caught his eye when a fiery ball lit up just behind Gerard. Oludara cursed when he saw it, but his curse was cut short by a woman's scream. The voice he recognized instantly.

"Olorun!" he cried.

In a split second of decision, he decided it would be quicker to skirt the lake than cross it, and he set off racing around the edge.

Gerard spun to face the flaming skull and readied a shot when Inocencia's scream froze him in place. The skull had knocked her down and set fire to a corner of her robe which she rubbed in the grass to put out.

"Look at what I found," said the Sibaldo-skull, its hideous jaw moving with the words.

"Inocencia," said Gerard, "what are you doing here?"

"I followed you," she said. "I had to know you were all right."

"And I followed her," said Sibaldo. "Very convenient. Now, I'll burn her alive if you don't toss down your weapons and step away."

Gerard threw down his harquebus and unbuckled his belt, allowing the rapier to fall. His mind raced for something to do.

"Now, stand up, you impertinent bitch."

Inocencia stood.

"Walk toward that light in the middle of the lake. Go slowly."

Inocencia stepped into the shallow water of the lake, and Sibaldo's macabre head floated through the air behind her. As they moved out over the lake, Gerard spotted a form sneaking through the woods. Moments later, the Catarina-jaguar charged from the bushes at a run. Sibaldo turned and she pounced at him, but he dodged and she splashed into the water.

"I'll kill her!" he screamed, and dashed, jaw open, toward Inocencia. His fire burned twice as bright.

Catarina threw herself in front of him and took the brunt of the attack. His mouth bit deep into her shoulder and she roared in pain. The pair crashed into Inocencia and sent her sprawling into the water.

Gerard ran to his harquebus and readied the shot. "Run, Inocencia!" he yelled.

Inocencia, however, sat in paralyzed fascination as Sibaldo and Catarina rolled through the water. Catarina suffered, an ugly rip opened along her side and bled profusely. None of her attacks seemed to faze Sibaldo, but with every moment, she weakened.

Gerard rushed forward into the water, searching for an angle for his shot.

"Sibaldo, behind you!" he shouted, and to his relief, the ruse worked. The skull paused its attack and turned around. Gerard took his shot, and the ball crashed into him just above the nasal hole, forming a tiny crack in the skull.

Sibaldo screamed in pain and Gerard charged forward as the skull shook from side to side. In a daze, it floated toward Inocencia and she screamed. Gerard lunged forward, ramming his harquebus into the creature's eye socket and shoving it out of the way at the last second.

Sibaldo jerked free and floated in front of Gerard, staring at him from the hollow sockets. Gerard stood firm, harquebus gripped across his chest. Inocencia looked back and forth between them in horror.

Then, as if searching for something, the skull spun around until focusing on a point behind it. Gerard spotted the object of Sibaldo's attention: Catarina dragged her dying feline body toward the light in the middle of the lake.

"Stop!" yelled Sibaldo, and he flew in her direction.

Gerard chased after, but it was obvious Sibaldo would reach Catarina with time to spare. From one side, however, he caught movement, and Oludara's ivory knife came flying. It walloped the skull and chipped a shard of bone from the crown.

The skull wavered as Gerard and Oludara converged on it. Gerard slammed it with his harquebus and Oludara searched the water for his knife. Sibaldo, in a fit of rage, bit at Gerard. Gerard held his gun up in defense, but just before the head reached him, a silver cage appeared around it and fell into the water, plunging the skull with it. Sibaldo screamed and trashed from side to side, but every touch of the silver bars sizzled as it burned him.

"What on Earth just happened?" exclaimed Gerard.

"I think she made her wish," said Oludara, pointing to the jaguar's unmoving body, collapsed just within the source of light.

Inocencia ran to Gerard and threw herself upon him, crying.

"Gerard," she said between sobs. "I've never been so scared."

"It will be all right," he said, patting her back awkwardly.

"What were those terrible monsters?" she asked.

Gerard looked at Oludara, his eyes pleading for him to be the one to tell the news. Thankfully, his friend obliged.

"That skull-thing is Sibaldo. Or at least his head."

"What?"

"And that," he said, pointing toward the jaguar, "is Catarina."

"No." Inocencia said it with an aversion that frightened Gerard.

"It is," said Gerard, turning Inocencia to face him. "And she gave her life to save us."

"But perhaps..." said Oludara, thinking.

He walked toward the light and placed his hand upon the jaguar. He mouthed some words Gerard couldn't hear and below him, the jaguar shriveled and changed, turning into Catarina's naked body. She opened her eyes and sat up.

"What is going on here?" asked Inocencia, eyes wide.

Gerard could feel her heart beating in panic.

"We'll explain everything," he said.

"Fools!" screamed Sibaldo. "You're wasting wishes. You could have money, power, fame, anything. And you use it on cages and half-breeds?"

"Enough!" said Oludara. His dagger, which he had recovered, waved menacingly in his hand.

Gerard gently pushed Inocencia away and removed his shirt, which he gave to Catarina. She thanked him with a nod and covered herself.

"Inocencia," she said. "Please don't look at me like that. My curse is gone now."

When she held out her hand, however, Inocencia shrunk back. Catarina lowered her head in resignation.

Oludara said to Gerard, "Do you desire to make a wish? This is your only chance."

"No," said Gerard. "I've had my fill of the heathen magic this day."

"And you?" Oludara asked Inocencia.

"Gerard is right," she said. "This place is unholy. I just want to leave."

"You two are right to refuse," said Catarina. "Every wish has its price. Mine cost me my life." She looked at Oludara. "No doubt saving my life will cost you even more."

Oludara shrugged. "Let it be, then. I would not take it back."

"Please," said Sibaldo. "Let me make my wish. It will only take a moment."

Gerard ignored the request and went to the bank to find a long branch, which he placed through the bars in the cage so that he and Oludara could carry it.

"No!" yelled Sibaldo. "You don't know what you're doing!" The skull banged the sides again, but jerked back when the silver burned it. "Wait," he said, pleading. "You must take me back to my body before sunrise. I'll die if you don't."

"That I can believe," said Gerard. "But I think we have time to stop by town first."

Oludara climbed Olinda's main street toward the top of the hill and his rendezvous with Gerard.

After returning to town the previous night, they had gathered a mob and taken Sibaldo's flaming head back to his house. Sibaldo, faced with death or humiliation, chose the latter, and allowed the mob into his house to watch the reunion of his his head with his body. The man now awaited trial, and Oludara had little doubt he would pay for his crimes with his life. The only doubt was who would get to him first: the church or the crown. No doubt both would be more than happy to confiscate his wealth. In either case, Oludara hoped the refuge would receive something. Gerard, now a local hero, had been glowing all day, and Oludara was glad to see his friend so.

"Psst!" Someone called to him from the darkness of an alley.

Oludara placed a hand on his dagger and paced alertly toward the voice. A child's head peeked out at him: the slave boy who had served his meal at Sibaldo's house.

"Thank you for what you did," said the boy.

Oludara nodded in reply.

"Your courage has set an example for us. With Sibaldo gone, some of us decided to flee. We head for the wilderness to form a *kilombo*." Oludara didn't understand the word, the boy had slipped back into his own language. "Sorry, he said, I mean to say, 'settlement'. We will form our own settlement."

"Good luck," said Oludara.

"Do you not wish to come? You are not Ambundu like us, but you have earned great respect. You could be a leader. Flee from your master and come with us."

"He is not my master," said Oludara, "he is my friend. I will soon return to Ketu; my place is not here."

"Do you really think so?" said the boy.

"What do you mean?"

"They will never let you return to Africa."

"Gerard will see me back."

"You call him 'friend', but I have learned never to trust a white man."

"This one I can trust."

"We will see. When the darkest moment comes, then you'll know if he is true. In any case, I wish you well." The boy turned to go. "My name is Landu. Find me, if you ever need my help."

"And I am Oludara."

"I know," said the boy, smiling. "That is a name we will not soon forget."

At Olinda's highest point, in the light of the setting sun, Gerard stood side-by-side with Inocencia, staring out over the town and the ocean beyond.

"Finally," said Gerard, "a night to relax."

"Yes," said Inocencia, smiling. "Did you hear? We gained two new recruits today at the refuge. You'll never guess who."

"Who?"

"Sibaldo's daughters."

Gerard couldn't help but laugh. "Then I suppose poetic justice is more than just a literary device."

Inocencia looked up at him. "How long will you stay?"

"Word spreads quickly," said Gerard. "Someone visiting from Porto Seguro has already petitioned us to go and face a creature which plagues that town. We'll leave on the morrow."

Inocencia couldn't hide her frown. She turned away.

"Inocencia, I know it will be hard, but please try to accept Catarina."

Inocencia shook her head. "After what I saw, I can't even look at her anymore. How could she harbor such an evil thing inside her? But this is your last night in the city, Gerard. Let's talk about something else."

Gerard, trying to think of something to say, looked out over Olinda. Churches and other buildings dotted the town, their red rooftops poking up through the lush, green vegetation. Beyond, the city grew along a chain of gorgeous hills. Beautiful, but not practical.

"The city shouldn't have been built on these hills," he commented. "It should have been built down there by the reefs, where the ships come in." He pointed down to the port, a strip of beach protected by enormous reefs. The beach held only a small fishing village and some warehouses.

"That's a terrible place for a city," said Inocencia. "It's surrounded by a swamp."

"Nothing a few dikes and canals won't fix."

"Leave it to a Dutchman to suggest building dikes!" For the first time that day, Inocencia laughed, and the sound made Gerard tingle. "Olinda is just fine where it is," she said, "thank you very much."

They watched the end of the sunrise and said nothing as the sky darkened. A screeching whistle caused them both to jump and they turned in unison to see a firework streaking through the air. Several more followed closely behind.

"Those are for you, you know," said Inocencia. "How I love to watch them."

They watched the show in silence.

When it was finished, Inocencia said, "It's time for me to go to bed." She looked down and bit her lip. "Thank you for everything, Gerard."

Gerard tipped his hat. "It was my pleasure."

As she walked away, just for a moment, Gerard imagined what she looked like beneath that shapeless dress, then quickly turned away, embarrassed.

Oludara watched as Inocencia said something about going to bed and headed off. He could see the looks of yearning between the two, and wondered how they could be so foolish as to ignore them.

He approached Gerard and said, "Hello, hero!"

Gerard's face flushed red and he said, "Hello. Took you a while to get here."

Oludara stared toward Inocencia. "It looks to me as if I came at the right time."

Gerard said nothing, only looked up at the stars.

"Why do you not go to her?" asked Oludara.

"What?"

"She desires you, Gerard. Why do you not take her in the way a man does a woman?"

Throughout the countless terrors the two of them had faced together, Oludara had never seen Gerard so pale. At that moment, however, he thought the man might faint.

"She's a woman of the cloth!" he said in reply.

"What does that mean? Do her robes make her less fertile?"

"It means she has sworn to never know a man in that fashion."

"She is obviously having second thoughts. I see the way you two look at each other."

"You'll never understand!" Gerard, face red, walked away stiffly.

Oludara could only shake his head. "Most likely, I never will."

The next morning, Oludara and Gerard went to the refuge to say their goodbyes. Catarina looked terrible, her eyes red and her hair frazzling out from her hood. Oludara embraced her and she accepted it gladly.

Gerard tipped his hat to her and said, "Thank you, Catarina. You saved Inocencia and most likely us as well. I know she's been avoiding you, but give her time, she'll come around eventually."

"I don't know," said Catarina. "She thinks I was possessed by the devil. But it doesn't matter. I stopped Sibaldo and my conscience is clear."

When Inocencia stepped into the refuge's reception, Catarina bowed her head and rushed away, as if on some errand.

Gerard had to clear his throat twice before speaking. "We came to say goodbye."

"Thank you both for coming," said Inocencia. "Your deeds are *digna cedro*."

"What does that mean?" asked Oludara.

"It is Latin for 'worthy of cedar'. Buried cedar doesn't go rotten, so the documents held within last for hundreds of years." She turned toward Gerard and looked him in the eye. "Some deeds are worth preserving forever, even if it's only within our hearts."

Gerard flushed red.

"It is an admirable saying," said Oludara. "These Romans had great wisdom, much like my own people."

Inocencia stood on tiptoe and kissed Gerard on his cheek. In response, he removed his hat and bowed low.

"We must be going," he said. "There are other places which require our help."

As the two of them walked away from Our Lady of the Immaculate

Conception, Gerard looked back only once. As foolish as Oludara found Gerard's insistence on not touching the nun, he had to give him credit for his iron will.

The jaguar paced through the woods, seeing if he could find any other females in heat.

The smell of the enormous female had faded away; the jaguar wondered if she had moved on to another territory. The unusual ball of flames he had seen from time to time had also disappeared. In any case, he was glad things had returned to normal. Once more, he was master of his domain, with nothing to fear.

He caught the faintest whiff of smoke. Perhaps the ball of flames had not gone away after all. Curious, the jaguar followed the scent until he arrived at a clearing. He peeked through the bushes and spotted two men—one dark and one pale—sleeping near a campfire.

The dark one slept peacefully, but the pale one tossed and turned in his sleep. The jaguar sniffed the air and thought he understood. Perhaps he wasn't the only one who had been anxious for a mate these last few days.

Chapter 11

The Catastrophic Ending of Gerard and Oludara's Brazilian Exploits

HE CICADAS FELT the tremors first. The males began clicking, one by one, until their clamorous song echoed through the Backlands. Shortly after, grasshoppers and hundreds of other insects joined in.

As the tremors grew, a red-footed tortoise ducked into a hollow log and hid within its shell. A group of white storks leapt away from their lakeside bath and flew gracefully south, searching for safer waters. Agoutis fled into their burrows, not daring to peer out. Even below the water, piranhas circled in a frenzy, trying to locate the intruder which disturbed their waters.

The random tremors, however, soon stabilized into ordered beats: ponderous footsteps reverberating through the earth.

Part I: The Rise of Woodsfather

Oludara and Gerard sat at the table of Heliodoro Gonçalves, chief magistrate of the town of Porto Seguro. Before them lay a magnificent meal of roasted goat, sweet potatoes, and spiced eggplant, topped off by an alcoholic beverage made from sugar which Heliodoro called *cachaça*. The town's elite had spent a week wining and dining the two, ever since they defeated a demon known as the Cavorting Goat, one Oludara would just as soon forget. The two had accepted the invitations, even though it wasn't like them to spend so much time in one place. Though neither mentioned it, the reason for their dallying hung between them like a cloud: their imminent separation.

Heliodoro's daughter, a brunette of fifteen years, brought in a coconut pudding with prunes. She smiled broadly and bent low before Gerard as she placed it upon the table. Gerard gave a curt nod and turned away, oblivious to her flirting.

"So," asked Heliodoro. "Where are you off to next?"

Oludara looked to Gerard and the two sat in silence, as if avoiding off the question. After some awkward moments, Oludara finally offered a response:

"I do not know what Gerard will do, but my time here in Brazil is done. I go to collect my family and return to Africa."

Oludara still hadn't resolved his problems with Arany. After countless attempts to convince her of the importance of returning to his ancestors' land, she still refused to go to Ketu with him. Just thinking about it made him nervous.

Heliodoro, however, who had no knowledge of their problems, accepted the statement with a nod.

"And you, Gerard?" he asked. "What will the legendary explorer do next? Do you also long to return home?"

It was a question neither of them had broached, and Oludara held his breath in expectation of what his companion might say.

"I'm not sure," said Gerard. "I fear my adventuring days are done, though. Without Oludara, there can be no Elephant and Macaw Banner. Perhaps I will take up commerce, like my father. I have contacts both here and in Europe, and there are many goods lacking in this colony which I could import."

Heliodoro raised an eyebrow. "Well, you can rest assured that Porto Seguro will welcome you with open arms if you choose to set up shop here. This town might not be as large as Salvador or Olinda, but we have much to offer."

"I appreciate it."

"I don't know, Mr. Gonçalves," said Oludara. "Adventure swarms to this man like flies to fruit. Gerard van Oost a trader? That I'd like to see."

Heliodoro grinned. "Perhaps you're right, Oludara. But don't worry; if he comes to stay with us, we'll make an honest man out of him."

Standing just behind her father, Heliodoro's daughter looked at Gerard and winked. Gerard coughed and returned his attention to his meal.

Minutes later, a knock sounded at the front door. Heliodoro stood and said, "Excuse me, I'll go see what that is." When he returned, he said, "You'd best come with me."

Outside, they found a man in a fancy helmet and doublet. He wore a fine rapier at his side.

"Gerard van Oost?" he asked. "Of the Elephant and Macaw Banner?"

"That is I."

"You and your bannermen are summoned with all haste to Salvador."

"The governor sent someone all the way to Porto Seguro to call on these men?" asked Heliodoro.

"Not just them. He sent ships to every port, calling in all his banners."

"What's going on? I'm chief magistrate here and I've heard nothing of this matter."

"Not even I know, and I'm one of the governor's personal guards. But one thing is sure, the matter is urgent." He turned his attention back to Gerard. "You must gather your banner with all haste and meet us at the port. Our ship, the Santa Teresa, will take you to Salvador."

Gerard looked at Oludara.

"Well then, it appears I'm headed to Salvador. You'll accompany me that far, won't you?"

"It will shorten my trip to Arany and Taynah," responded Oludara. "How could I refuse?"

Oludara stood beside Gerard in the governor's office. He had come to the meeting more for curiosity's sake than for any intention to embark on another adventure. That, and he still hadn't gathered the courage to say goodbye to Gerard.

They weren't the only ones in the room. Several other men waited impatiently. All of them were armed, and most wore clothes more suited to the wilderness than a governor's office. One of the men, to Oludara's distaste, was Belchior Grilo, who now led his own banner. Grilo only spared one sneering glance at Oludara, then ignored him.

They waited for half an hour for Governor Veiga to arrive. The governor entered wearing a blue doublet and gray cloak, with a fine, gray hat to complete the ensemble. He gave no greeting, ignoring everyone as he strode to his desk. Oludara saw Gerard's face crinkle at the sight of the man. Gerard had never been friends with the old governor, Governor Almeida, and even less so with his replacement.

But that reaction was nothing compared the the way Gerard tightened up when, just after the governor, another man stepped in: Antonio Dias Caldas. Antonio stiffened as well, squinting at the two of them, but said nothing. After that icy reception, he nodded to the others in the room, even Grilo, although with less enthusiasm.

"From this point on," said the governor, looking around the room, "I'm putting all banners under Antonio's command."

Gerard made a choking sound beside Oludara.

"Very well, Governor Veiga," said Antonio. Then he pointed toward Gerard. "But this one you can send away. I don't need him, and I certainly don't want him."

"Fine with me," said Gerard. "I wouldn't serve this scoundrel in any case."

"You're not fit for shoveling his dung," said Grilo.

"Enough!" shouted Governor Veiga. "Antonio, Gerard's experience will be invaluable; I demand you take him."

Antonio's face knotted with disgust, but he said nothing.

"And you, Gerard," said the governor, "need to learn your place. Antonio has served me well. You, however, have done your deeds in service to yourself."

"What service has Antonio done that I have not? Have I not fought dozens of perilous creatures to relieve the settlers of this fledgling colony? Or do you refer to Antonio's other business, the capturing of natives as slaves?"

"The slaves are a consequence of Antonio protecting our settlements from the Indians. Any Indian taken in just war can be used as a slave. Or do you argue against the king's edict?"

"I don't argue the king's edict, I argue against Antonio's interpretation of what qualifies as 'just war', when he enslaves children from peaceful Christian villages."

"Your fondness for the Indians blinds you to their savagery, Gerard. Antonio understands that, and that is why he leads."

"My wife is a Tupinambá," Oludara said, trying to control his fury.

"Half the men in Brazil have Indian concubines," replied the governor, waving away the comment. "We could fix that problem if the king would send but a thousand Christian women."

Oludara gritted his teeth and said nothing.

"Governor," said Antonio. "Gerard coming with me is out of the question. I am in first encounter with him. Only your presence here prevents me from consummating our duel."

"Then you have my order to put it aside until you have completed your task. I can't afford to lose either of you while Woodsfather is alive. Once it is slain, you have my permission to kill each other. Do you understand?"

Antonio nodded grudgingly.

The Governor stared around the room, daring anyone to speak, then continued, "And that is why I have called all of you to Salvador. A creature of enormous size has awoken in the Backlands. The Indians call it Woodsfather. It has destroyed numerous villages, and they have come to us for aid."

"And since when has a call of help from the natives meant anything to you?" challenged Gerard.

Governor Veiga shot Gerard an angry look, but answered his question. "His rampage brings him ever closer to the coast and to Salvador. You all have a single order: stop him before he gets here, or die in the attempt. This task will not be easy; the creature is said to be invincible."

"We've killed plenty of things that people said were invincible," said Gerard.

"Not like this one," said Antonio. "The creature is gigantic, over a hundred feet tall."

At that, incredulous murmurs broke out around the room. A creature of that size would outweigh every monster ever faced in Brazil put together.

"There is a rumor the beast can be slain through the navel," said the governor.

"Like the Kalobo," said Oludara.

"This giant would crush your puny Kalobo beneath its feet and pick its teeth with the bones," sneered Grilo.

"I'll believe that when I see it," said Gerard.

"You will," said Antonio, his expression earnest.

"Antonio leads, his orders are final. Antonio, you'll have all the bannermen, a hundred militia, and an army of Indians at your disposal. Warriors from many tribes have come to offer their aid."

Oludara turned to Gerard and asked under his breath, "All that for one creature? He must be serious about its size." When Gerard merely shrugged in response, he added, "You should not go along with this madness, Gerard. Refuse him."

He was surprised when the governor addressed him. "Everyone goes. Including you."

Oludara stood tall and faced him. "This is not my fight. I came here only to collect my family and return to Africa."

"You are part of Gerard's banner and have been called to serve, same as everyone else."

"My service to Gerard's banner is ended."

The governor looked him in the eye. "If you do not go, you will never receive passage from Brazil."

Oludara frowned. From the governor's eyes, he knew it was no bluff. With a reluctant lowering of his eyes, he gave his nonverbal assent.

The fleet set out the next day, sailing up the coast to meet with the Tupinambá contingent. The impressive fleet, which contained a dozen light ships and forty pieces of artillery, became even more impressive when it joined up with a hundred enormous canoes at the mouth of a river. All told, Oludara estimated their force at some three-hundred Europeans and three-thousand Tupinambá warriors.

The Tupinambá also brought with them an unusual pajé, who joined Antonio on the flagship. The pajé wore so many feathers pasted to his body, he looked more like a giant, green parrot than a man. Oludara never saw him speak to anyone, and no one on his ship could say why he had joined them, but all the Tupinambá treated him with deference. He disappeared for hours at a time into Antonio's ship, at which times, lines of white smoke drifted from one of the portholes.

Gerard had been sick through most of the short trip up the choppy waters of the coast, but improved once the fleet entered the calm water of the rivers. Oludara, on the other hand, felt every day more anxious. As best he could tell, they were headed straight toward Arany's village. After their first day on the river, he found Gerard to voice his concerns.

"Gerard, is this not the river that leads to Arany's village?"

Gerard seemed taken aback by the question. He studied the horizon carefully before responding.

"It very well could be. We've always come at it inland, haven't we, never from the coast? But it does seem we're headed in that direction."

After that, Oludara could not stop worrying about Arany and Taynah. He wished to confront Antonio and learn more of the man's plans, to know if his family faced danger, but he had no way of boarding the flagship; the fleet did not stop a single time after entering the river.

On their third day, they reached a fork. Oludara was sure he'd been here before, and when he looked toward Gerard, his companion's steeled face showed he recognized it as well. As the fleet's flagship neared the fork, Oludara watched helplessly and prayed a silent prayer to Olorun for the ship to take the left fork, away from his family and deep into the wilderness.

To his dread, they turned right.

The fleet stopped in a deep, wooded valley, just a few days from Arany's village, giving Oludara his first chance to confront Antonio. He found Antonio calling out directions to his men.

"Put two falcons over there, behind those bushes," said Antonio, referring to the cannons, which had different animal names, based on their size. "And a camel up there, higher."

Oludara interrupted him. "Why did you not heed my calls upon the river to stop?"

"Because we have no time to waste," said Antonio, without even looking.

"Why are we setting up here?"

Antonio ignored him and yelled out another order to his men. "I need a row of the carriage guns over there, on that ridge."

Oludara grabbed his shoulder and spun him around, "Why are we here?" he demanded.

Grilo and two of his bannermen saw the exchange and approached with interest. Antonio pushed away Oludara's hand and responded, "Because Woodsfather is nearby, and coming this way."

"How do you know?"

"Because we've been calling him this way, that's why. Now help with the setup or get out of the way!"

It took Oludara a few moments to consider the implication of his words.

"You baited him down this river?" asked Oludara.

"This valley is perfect for an ambush."

"You fool! He'll pass right through Arany's village."

"Who?" asked Antonio, irritated.

"I have a wife and child with the Tupinambá there."

Antonio only shrugged, but Grilo responded, "Who cares? I have half a dozen bastards with Indian women. You can go make some more when we're done."

Oludara stepped forward but Grilo pulled a hand from behind his back to reveal a knife at the ready. The hungry look in Grilo's eyes showed how much he wanted to use it. The other two soldiers leveled their harquebuses at Oludara.

Antonio studied the scene calmly. "I don't have time for this right now. Let's do the job the governor sent us here for, then we can settle all our arguments once and for all."

In despair, Oludara backed away. The voyage had given him time to reflect on what was most important to him, and now, when he knew he might lose both Arany and Taynah, the realization of how much they meant to him struck him like a blow. If they still lived, he resolved to do whatever necessary to keep his family together, even if that meant staying in Brazil and abandoning his ancestors—who would surely curse him forever.

Oludara ran looking for Gerard, whom he found setting up a row of small cannon with some natives. As Oludara caught his breath to speak, Gerard spotted him and commented, "I have to give Antonio credit. This really is the perfect spot for an ambush."

"Gerard! The creature approaches from upriver. Antonio's been calling the monster this whole time. We must reach Arany's village before the creature does."

"How did he call it?"

Oludara shook his head and looked around. Below them, in the middle of the river, he spotted the "parrot pajé" dancing upon a raft. A fire burned beside him, giving off a thin line of white smoke.

"Him," Oludara said, starting down. "We must stop him."

Gerard grabbed him. "Don't bother," he said.

"Why?"

"Because you're too late."

The brief moment it took for him to pause and consider Gerard's statement was enough to hear and feel what he had missed in his distress: tremors shaking the ground, a pounding approaching from the distance. Antonio yelled more commands, but all movement ceased when the giant rounded a set of hills in the distance.

Woodsfather had the look of a human turning into a tree, or vice-versa. The creature, immense beyond belief, towered over the forest canopy. Oludara judged it close to two-hundred feet tall. Patches of bark splotched the creature's brown skin, and its ears splayed out like two gnarled pieces of wood. The tip of its nose to the top of its wrinkled forehead formed one long, outward curve, and scraggly hair frizzed out from the back and sides of its head. Twelve-foot fingernails resembling crooked branches spread ominously from its fingers. The creature's navel, a hole like the knot in a tree, stood prominently in the middle of its protruding belly. Around the navel, the skin's color was lighter, contrasting with the skin around it and forming a perfect circle, like a target daring them to shoot. However, Oludara judged the hole to be no more than three feet wide, an impossible shot for cannon at that height, if the balls could even reach it.

Woodsfather trudged slowly under its ponderous weight, but each deliberate step carried it at least fifty feet. A look of madness pervaded its round eyes, and an evil smile spread across its lips when it spotted the army in the valley before it.

Many of the naked natives around him loosed their bowels at the sight, and Oludara had no doubt that most of the European trousers had been soiled as well.

Oludara broke the silence with a single word: "Olorun!"

Antonio was the first to move, calling out last-minute commands to his men, slapping the ones still too scared to move.

Oludara looked to Gerard and said, "We cannot stop that."

"We must try," responded Gerard. He went into action, rotating a cannon toward the creature, taking aim.

No we don't, thought Oludara, *we must live.* He had not wanted this fight, and had no stomach for it. His only thoughts were of getting back to his family, and for that, he would have to wait for this mad battle to end. He held no illusions that the group could stop that monster, with or without his help, so he had to wait for an opportunity to get past it.

"I'm sorry, Gerard," he whispered under his breath, "but not this time. Not this battle."

He walked deliberately to the crest of the hill and found a place to sit and watch the fight.

The group had not been ready for the attack. Only half the cannons had been loaded, and the men scrambled to load the others. They also hadn't had time to hide everything properly; most of their ambush lay in plain sight.

When Woodsfather came within a few hundred feet, bloodlust in its eyes, Antonio gave the command for the front cannons to fire. Only four or five of the front dozen cannons fired. Oludara spotted a couple of balls bounce off the beast's legs and splash into the water below. In response, the creature uprooted an entire tree with one hand and threw it toward a row of cannon.

From then on, the true chaos began. The artillerymen fired as possible, but the shots came few and far between. The harquebus fire was more constant, and the natives attacked bravely with bows, clubs, and axes, but like the cannon fire, all of it served for nothing.

Instead, combatants died by the score, as Woodsfather crushed them with hands, feet, rocks, trees, cannons and anything else within its grasp. Grilo and his band fled into the woods. The parrot pajé stood defiantly on his raft, chanting to the last, but Woodsfather disintegrated the man and his boat with one deadly splash of its foot. For an encore, it picked up a canoe and swung it down on a caravel, smashing the ship in half.

Despondency swept over Oludara as he imagined the damage the creature must have done, stepping through the clay longhouses of Arany's village like anthills.

"What has Antonio done?" he asked himself.

When Woodsfather finally had its fill of destruction, it trounced away southeast—toward Salvador. As it disappeared over the horizon, Oludara left his perch to aid the wounded.

Gerard he found unhurt, and Antonio had survived the battle with only minor wounds. The toll of lives, however, was staggering. Out of over three thousand men, only a few hundred remained standing, with another five-hundred or so too wounded to travel. The other thousands lay splayed around the valley, many of the remains no longer recognizable. Antonio rallied all those still capable of travel.

"I'm leaving five men to care for the wounded," he said. "Everyone else get ready, we set out immediately."

Oludara, however, could only think of Arany and Taynah. As the group readied to leave, Oludara sneaked down to the river and located a rowboat from one of the ships, still intact. He felt bad about leaving Gerard without a word, but didn't want his abandonment to cause him any trouble. With so many dead, they would never miss him.

Just as he was about to push off, a shot whistled by him and a sneering voice came from behind, sending a chill up his spine.

"And where do you think you're going?" asked Antonio.

The noise brought dozens running, including Gerard.

"I must see to my wife and child," said Oludara.

"You're staying with me," said Antonio, with a note of finality. "I need every man I can get."

"No more," said Oludara.

"We need to kill the beast, not worry about Indian whores."

Oludara, ready to stab Antonio in the eye, jumped from the canoe and unsheathed his knife. Gerard placed himself in his path.

"Don't do it," said Gerard. "It gains you nothing."

Oludara almost pushed him away, but looked into his earnest gaze and calmed himself.

"You are right. I must put my family before my pride." He turned and headed back toward the rowboat.

Antonio cleared his throat and Oludara looked back to see him motioning to some men, who aimed their guns at him.

"Very well," said Antonio. "You can leave, but not in my boat."

Oludara had to control himself once again, but finally nodded and started off on foot, wishing to waste no more time.

"Wait," said Gerard. "I'm going with you."

"Nonsense," said Antonio. "The governor gave you an order."

"I'll stay with my friend."

Antonio was about to say something, but paused and stroked his beard in consideration. Some thought caused him to grin.

"Fine by me, then," he said. "When this is over, the governor will have you in chains for desertion."

Oludara knew it was no bluff, but had no time to waste arguing with Gerard. With a curt nod, he showed his thanks to his friend, and the two set off.

Behind them, Antonio said to his men: "I always knew they were cowards."

Part II: The Search for Sacy

Gerard had somehow kept up with Oludara's charge through the wilderness, digging deep to keep pace with his companion's maddening sprint. They covered in a day-and-a-half what they would have taken three or four to traverse at a normal pace. As they neared the village, his first glimpse of it confirmed the worst of his fears; the palisade had been destroyed, the stout logs snapped and sprawled around like a child might break a pile of sticks. Beside Gerard, Oludara cried out in anguish.

Beyond the ruined palisade, the scene only worsened. Knocked down, crushed, and hurled away, all five of the massive longhouses had been destroyed. Tiny huts and lean-tos thrown together from sticks and palm leaves provided shelter for the handful of people who still remained. The remnants of the tribe's women did not run out to greet them in typical Tupinambá fashion; instead, they just turned to stare with vacant eyes, their children grasped tightly at their sides.

Then, Gerard spotted something which almost made his heart stop. Taynah's pet sloth, the one which slept with her every night and which the villagers had named "Lazy", lay crushed on the ground. Oludara noticed it also.

"What have I done?" he wailed.

At that, a faint cry of "Oludara?" sounded from one end of the village. Oludara gasped and ran toward the sound. Gerard, racing behind, spotted Arany laying beneath a lean-to. He looked for any sign of Taynah, but saw none. His heart tightened within his chest.

He arrived just as Arany opened her eyes to look up at her husband, who knelt beside her and cradled her head. She could barely focus her eyes, and beneath her bruises, Gerard could see she had a broken leg and a caved-in chest. The mere act of breathing must have been an agony, and Gerard doubted she would survive another hour.

Arany, with great effort, wheezed out her words. "I waited for you," she whispered. "I held on while many others died around me."

"I'm sorry," said Oludara, tears welling in his eyes. "You and Taynah. I'm sorry. I have failed as both husband and father. I'm sorry I wasn't here."

"Sorry you weren't here to die? Not being here was the best thing you ever did. Instead of dying with us, you can now save our daughter."

Oludara shot up. "She's alive?"

"Yes. During the massacre, Sacy appeared from nowhere and took her away."

"Olorun be praised!"

Gerard added a silent prayer of his own.

"Go find her," said Arany.

"I will not leave you like this!"

"Don't waste time crying for the dead. You want to be a good father? Find our daughter. You want to be a good husband? Do what I ask and go now."

Oludara made no attempt to hide the anguish on his face. His lip quivered for a moment, then he bent down and cried. Gerard's heart went out to him.

"Go now, please," said Arany.

Oludara looked into her eyes. "I'm sorry."

"Stop saying that, you fool."

"I love you." He placed his forehead upon hers.

Arany closed her eyes and allowed Oludara's tears to roll down her cheeks. Gerard looked away from their intimacy.

After a time, Arany pulled her head from Oludara's grasp.

"Goodbye," she said, with finality.

"Goodbye."

Oludara stood, resolute, and said, "Gerard, you heard her. Let us be off." He strode away, without looking back.

"Goodbye, Arany," said Gerard, tears flowing freely.

"Please take care of them, Gerard van Oost."

"Until the ends of the Earth, if that's what it takes."

She nodded, satisfied. As Gerard walked away, he heard Arany finally release the wheezing sobs she had courageously withheld in Oludara's presence.

Before Gerard could find Oludara, Cabwassu appeared from one of the makeshift huts, running towards him.

"Wait!" said Cabwassu. "Where are you going? You just got here."

"Arany asked us to find Taynah with all haste."

"Oh, right," said Cabwassu. "Let me go with you."

"Aren't you needed here?" asked Gerard.

"The tribe is finished. We have buried the dead. Those who are left must find their own way, join another tribe. My way is revenge. I will revenge myself upon Woodsfather."

"No man alive can revenge himself on Woodsfather."

"I will put an arrow into his eye, I swear, even if it is the last thing I do." Cabwassu stared off into the distance. "He crashed into our village, caring for nothing. He killed and killed, like he took joy in it."

"I don't understand any of it. What is this creature? Why this senseless destruction?"

"He is one of the Ebemongeera, the Earth-Shakers."

"One of them? You mean there are more of those things?"

"Two more. The three of them are enemies. The hero Soomeh put them to sleep long ago, so that men could live in peace. Something must have woken him."

"Dear God! I hope the other two don't wake up as well." Gerard pulled his goatee. "Then again, perhaps they would fight each other, instead of killing us."

Cabwassu shrugged. "I wouldn't know. Yandir might have known, but he's dead."

"Yandir too? And Jakoo?"

Cabwassu nodded sadly. "But that reminds me. Yandir left you something."

Cabwassu ran to Yandir's hut, the only structure still standing from the original village. He came back holding a corked gourd.

"He knew you were coming," said Cabwassu. "He said you would need this. We call this drink 'closed body'. Nothing can harm you after you drink it, at least for a time. It will give you the strength of a hundred men. It took him months to make it; it was the last thing he did."

Gerard took the gourd gingerly and stared at it.

"What?" asked Cabwassu. "Something you want to say about heathen magic?"

The thought had passed through Gerard's mind, but it was distant now, just a whisper.

"No," he said, storing the gourd in his pack. "I'm honored he spent so much time to make this for me. He was a great man."

"Well," said Cabwassu, "it seems that you've changed."

"Five years can change much in a man. Now we'd best get going."

"Just give me a minute to grab some food and a bow."

Cabwassu ran off and Gerard went looking for Oludara. He found him sitting on a stump just beyond the palisade. Oludara gazed into the distance and breathed heavily. Gerard waited nearby in silence, giving his companion time. After some five minutes, Oludara finally spoke.

"Gerard, I know not if I have the strength. What does one do, when you know you will never again see the one you love most in the world?"

Sad memories came back to Gerard, and he answered as best he could. "Consider it a blessing that you have the chance to say goodbye. Most of the time, we never get that chance. Then, go on living, as best you can."

In askance, Oludara looked at him.

Gerard, eyes tearing up, added, "It is what I did with my father."

Oludara nodded and the two remained in silence until Cabwassu appeared beside them, equipment in hand.

"Well," he asked, "are you two ready or what?"

The group wandered deep into the forest in their search for Sacy. Cabwassu told them that the imp had been spotted frequently in the woods to the south, and while Gerard tried to organize their search as much as possible, Oludara hindered them with his frantic impatience. Oludara seemed almost mad, and Gerard had never felt so nervous. Close to exhaustion, Gerard propped himself against a tree and Cabwassu threw himself down into the grass.

"What are you doing?" asked Oludara.

"We need to rest and get our bearings," said Gerard.

"We can't stop until we've found Taynah."

"Nonsense. First we ran to the village, now we're running through the forest. I'm on the verge of collapse. We've seen no sign of Sacy and need to calm down before we miss something."

Oludara rested his hands on his hips and gritted his teeth. He seemed on the edge of an explosion, but Cabwassu, sniffing around, interrupted him.

"What are you doing?" snapped Oludara.

"I smell something," said Cabwassu.

"Unless you smell a one-legged imp, I don't want to know."

"I smell smoke. Tobacco smoke."

Gerard and Oludara snapped to attention at the words.

"Follow me."

Cabwassu followed the scent like a hound. He led them to a rock wall with a small crevice on one side.

"This must be it," said Oludara.

He led the way in, Gerard and Cabwassu close behind. Inside, they found a cave lit by flickering torchlight. In one corner sat Sacy, cradling the sleeping Taynah in his young arms. His pipe sat to one side, giving off a fine line of smoke. The imp stared at the toddler, seemingly enchanted, so much so that he didn't notice them enter.

"Olorun be praised!" exclaimed Oludara. "She's safe."

Sacy jumped at the words and squeezed Taynah protectively. Oludara approached him, hands stretched forward.

"Thank you, Sacy, for saving her from Woodsfather. I owe you much."

Sacy twisted the child away from him. "Where were you when Woodsfather attacked? How do I know you'll keep her safe?"

Oludara froze and his body tensed.

"What do you mean, Sacy? Of course I'll keep her safe. I'm her father."

"Not a very good one. I'd make a better father than you."

Gerard saw Oludara's eyes narrow in fury.

"Hand me Taynah, Sacy. Now!"

Oludara lunged forward and Sacy disappeared without a sound, taking Taynah with him. His pipe remained where he had left it, the only sign he and Taynah had been there at all.

After a fruitless search through the woods for Sacy, Gerard suggested a visit to Yara, and, for lack of a better plan, the other two reluctantly agreed. They returned to the same lily-pad covered lake in which they had found her years before, and Oludara called out her name until her head and ruby-colored hair arose from the water. Wildflower's flower-covered head bobbed beside her.

"It has been years since your last visit," said Yara, "and I doubt you've grown the courage to share my lair for a night, so you must want something of me. What is it?"

"Yara," said Oludara, "we need your help to find Sacy. He has taken my daughter, Taynah."

Yara sneered at him. "Things far more important than Sacy require my attention at this moment."

"Nothing is more important than my daughter," said Oludara.

"Nonsense. An ancient being named Woodsfather is on the loose. He will kill us all if he is not stopped."

Oludara responded in an irritated voice. "We know who Woodsfather is. The beast killed my wife and caused the capture of my child. We fought it with thousands, but mere hundreds survived. Woodsfather left without a scratch."

Yara shook her head. "Attack it with a hundred thousand men if you wish, it will make no difference."

Gerard knew his companion would be loath to change the subject, but he didn't want to lose the opportunity to learn something of the creature.

"Can you stop it?" he asked.

"Take my power and Wildflower's and Curooper's and double them all and it would still amount to little more than a spit in the face to Woodsfather. Only a god can stop that creature. Soomeh did it." She sighed with desire as she spoke the hero's name.

"So Soomeh was a god?" Gerard glanced at Cabwassu as he said it, who shrugged.

"He was close enough," said Yara.

"What happened to him?"

"After he put Woodsfather to sleep, he went away. No one knows where, nor why."

"Can you call him back?" asked Cabwassu.

"Every village in a hundred leagues is trying," said Yara. "I doubt I'd have more luck than them. Only the most powerful of magic can stop Woodsfather, that is what we must seek."

Gerard snorted.

"What, Gerard? Will your god stop Woodsfather?" she said with a sneer.

"Perhaps," he responded, "though in ways we are not made to comprehend."

"Easy enough to say."

"Cabwassu mentioned some other things called Earth-Shakers?"

"Yes, the Ebemongeera," said Yara. "Besides Woodsfather, there is Gorjal the giant, and the Great Worm. Something awoke the Great Worm recently, and I believe it's wanderings below the earth are what caused Woodsfather to awake as well. It is only a matter of time before all three once again torment us." She shuddered.

"What if we could make them battle each other instead of us?"

"It is an intriguing idea, those three have fought each other enough. But three Ebemongeera would do much more damage than one alone. And though they fought for millennia, none ever killed the others."

"It might be worth a try," said Gerard.

"Or it might get you killed."

"Enough of Woodsfather," interrupted Oludara. "I care nothing for these monsters, I only want my daughter back. Is there anything we can do to make you help us find Sacy?"

"No. My powers are focused on my wards. I must protect myself from Woodsfather until I decide what to do. Come, Wildflower."

At that, Yara dove, her fish tail flashing over the water before disappearing underneath. Wildflower gave them a sad look before dipping down.

Oludara looked beyond consolation, and Gerard had no idea what to do next. They had spent two days to reach Yara and a dead end.

Then, without warning, Wildflower surfaced at the edge of the lake.

"Wait here until morning," she said. "I can help."

At that, she turned into a pink dolphin and dove back down.

After a long night, through which Gerard and Cabwassu patiently put up with Oludara's unending lamentations, the sun rose and Wildflower climbed out of the lake. The water trickled down from her as she stepped toward them, but within seconds, she stood completely dry, her golden hair billowing out in curls.

"Hello, Gerard," she said. "Hello Oludara." She looked at Cabwassu and said, "And I remember you from Arany's village, but I don't think I ever knew your name."

"Cabwassu," he replied with one of his demonic smiles.

"You can call me Wildflower." She returned her attention to Oludara. "Sorry for the not-so-warm welcome yesterday, but Yara doesn't allow me to speak to others."

"Yet you may speak to us today?" asked Oludara.

"As you know, I agreed to serve her every other moon. Lucky for you, my moon of service has just ended, and my moon of freedom begun." She held out a hand and showed them a yellow, translucent gem with a hole in the middle. Gerard could just make out a faint light in it, to one side. "I borrowed this from Yara," she said. "We can use it to find Sacy."

Wildflower turned the stone over in her hands, and the light remained in the same direction, like a compass. It pointed east.

"Amazing," said Cabwassu. "What is it?"

"A finding stone," she said. "The light is faint, which means Sacy is far away. Near Salvador, most likely."

Gerard caught the look of defeat on Oludara's face, just before the man fell to his knees. It was the same look Oludara had given after their meeting with Way-Krig, when his will had finally broken.

"Why must I continue to fail?" he wailed. "Sacy saved her from danger only to place her in Woodsfather's path once more. Why must I be tortured so?"

"We don't know that for sure," said Gerard. "Sacy can probably keep her away from Woodsfather."

"Time and again, I failed her and I failed Arany. The shame I bring to my ancestors is endless; it is better I die here and now."

"I can get you to Sacy before Woodsfather gets there," said Wildflower.

The glimmer of hope which appeared in Oludara's eye seemed almost as maniacal as the gloom which had resided there moments before.

"How?" he said, grabbing her arms.

"I thought you might require transport, so I called them last night."

"Them?" asked Cabwassu.

Wildflower whistled and a chorus of whinnies sounded in return. Gerard turned to spot three black horses, each with only three legs, hobbling toward them. At first, he thought their heads were bowed, then realized, just like the headless mule, they had no heads at all.

"Watch out!" he shouted, drawing his rapier in a flash.

Oludara leaped beside him and drew his dagger. Cabwassu fitted an arrow. The creatures pulled back.

Wildflower placed a hand on Gerard's sword arm. "Put your weapons away. Those are your mounts."

The others looked to him and Gerard, putting his trust in the girl who had saved them more than once, sheathed his rapier.

"I appreciate the thought, Wildflower, but how is riding crippled, headless horses going to help us get..."

At that moment, dark wings unfurled from the horses' backs.

Gerard's jaw dropped. *Could it be true?* he thought. His childhood dream had been to fly a Pegasus like his hero, Perseus. As the horses came closer, he saw the membranes on the wings. They looked like bat's wings, not the white, feathered wings of Pegasus he had pictured so many times.

Well, he thought, *close enough.*

The three men mounted the creatures, although Cabwassu took a bit of coaxing.

Once they were ready, Wildflower said, "I must lead them. They do not know the way."

"How will you lead them?" asked Gerard.

She placed the gem in her mouth and outstretched her arms. Black feathers sprouted from her body, and her arms became wings. She turned into a black bird with a collar of white feathers around its neck, then grew to impressive size, almost as tall as Gerard. The bird spread its massive wings and launched into the air, and the horse beneath him sprung up after her.

They flew for hours, and Gerard marveled at a view never before seen by any man. His spirit soared during the trip and his mind wandered again and again to Perseus and his legendary steed.

Near the end of their journey, however, a terrible sight brought him back to reality. Below them, Woodsfather, towering above the coastal trees, crashed through the forest. As they passed over the giant, it became ominously clear that it headed in the same direction, and wasn't more than a day out from Salvador.

The group circled and landed in a forest clearing, within an eagle's view of Salvador and All Saint's Bay. After the group dismounted, the horses flew off and Gerard watched them go with a sigh. Wildflower transformed back to her normal form.

"I didn't think you could turn into something so large," said Oludara.

Wildflower blushed. "My powers have grown during my time with Yara."

Gerard took a good look at her. Physically, she appeared the same, just a child, but her bearing had changed. She acted older, more mature. Of course, their last encounter had been years back.

She placed the gem into Oludara's hand. It glowed brightly, toward the south.

"Sacy is near," she said. "Now I must go find Curooper. Perhaps he will know what to do with Woodsfather."

At that, she turned into a falcon and sped away.

"Somehow," said Gerard, "I doubt it."

"Let us be off," said Oludara, impatiently. Gem held before him, he strode into the woods and Gerard and Cabwassu followed behind.

Minutes later, Oludara stopped them with a raised hand. Sacy sat upon a log on the path ahead. Taynah chased a white butterfly, doddering behind it with her toddler's walk.

"We must remove his hat," said Oludara, "as you did last time."

Gerard nodded and prepped his harquebus for the shot. Cabwassu also readied his bow.

"Don't bother," said Sacy. "I already know that trick."

The group froze.

"Lower your weapons and step forward."

Resigned, the three stepped into the open. Sacy picked up Taynah, still grasping for the butterfly, and turned to face them.

"You have been my friends," said Sacy, "and I am sad it must end this way, but Taynah is mine now. Say your goodbyes, for you will never find us again."

"Sacy," said Oludara, holding up his arms in a gesture of peace. "Let us talk."

At the sound of Oludara's voice, Taynah turned to him and yelled, "Daddy!"

She stretched her arms toward Oludara and Sacy pulled her away. She struggled against him.

Gerard froze, as did the others. He knew that any quick movement could scare Sacy into disappearing. He deliberately raised his harquebus, but Oludara motioned him down.

"That's enough, Taynah," said Sacy, struggling to keep his hold on the toddler. "Goodbye, Gerard. Goodbye Oludara."

At that, Gerard saw something disappear, yet Sacy, wild-eyed, remained in the same spot. Gerard turned, shocked, to see Taynah in Oludara's arms. Oludara stared at his daughter open-mouthed.

"Good Lord!" said Gerard.

"Chew my bones!" yelled Cabwassu.

"Olorun!" shouted Oludara. "What have you done to my daughter,

Sacy?"

"She's mine!" screeched Sacy. "That proves it. Come here, Taynah. Come back to daddy!" Begging, he held out his hands.

Taynah ignored the imp's pleading and hugged her father tightly, a happy smile playing across her face.

"She's mine! Mine! Mine!" said Sacy. Then he fell to his knees, sobbing. "Why can't she be mine? Why can't I have a child? Why does this accursed body never grow old?"

Oludara, a look of disgust on his face, turned and walked away. Cabwassu shrugged his shoulders and followed.

Gerard, however, looked with pity upon the sobbing Sacy. He took a step forward.

"Sacy..." he said.

Sacy only buried his face in his hands and cried harder.

Gerard had collected Sacy's pipe after their last encounter. He pulled it from his pack and laid it reverently beside the imp. Then he took out his own tobacco pouch, the one he had purchased before their first encounter, and placed it next to the pipe.

Without another word, he turned and followed Oludara.

Gerard and his companions walked in silence toward Salvador, until Oludara broached the subject of Taynah.

"What happened to my child?" he asked.

Gerard could only shake his head. Cabwassu, however, offered an answer: "It is what happens when someone lives with a creature like that; the magic invades the body."

"Does that mean she has become like Sacy?"

"I don't know," replied Cabwassu. "I don't think so. If she had stayed with him for a year, she might have grown a tail or something. She hasn't been with him for too long. I think it will wear off."

Oludara seemed nauseated by the mention of his daughter with a tail, and he broached the subject no more.

They soon reached Salvador's outlying buildings and farms. The city had changed much in the last years, and now extended well beyond the old wall. The wall itself, crumbling and abandoned, provided little protection. Only a few bastions remained. With the monsters of the interior no longer a threat, the defenses of Salvador had been refocused from land to sea, to prevent an invasion by the French or English. No one could have predicted the coming of Woodsfather. In the path of an unstoppable horror, the city stood practically defenseless.

Without warning, Oludara said, “It is here we must part.”

“What?” said Gerard, jumping in surprise.

“I will head down to the docks and hire a boat.”

Gerard and Oludara had split the many rewards they had earned over the years, and Oludara had collected far more than enough to sail back to Africa.

“We must warn Salvador of the danger!”

“And put my child at risk? Sorry, Gerard, I will leave that to you. From here on, she must be my only concern.”

Five years came rushing back to Gerard and his head dizzied with the memories. A powerful depression set upon him, but he nodded.

“Goodbye,” he said, holding out a hand.

“Goodbye, friend,” said Oludara, clasping it firmly.

“Ge-rad,” said Taynah, pointing at him.

Gerard couldn’t contain the tears as Cabwassu and Oludara said their goodbyes. This parting had come too quickly, too wrong after all their time together. But there was nothing he could do; Oludara had been out of his mind for days, his worry making his every action panicked. But in the end, he was right. He had to care for his daughter at all costs, and that meant leaving Salvador immediately.

As Oludara walked away, down toward the lower city and the docks, Cabwassu slapped Gerard on the back and asked, “Let’s go?”

Gerard nodded and turned toward the upper city. Palm trees stood high above the houses. Orange trees in full bloom peppered the landscape with orange spots. The city was a beautiful sight.

With Woodsfather close on their heels, however, Gerard doubted he would ever see that same view again.

Part III: The Ravaging of Salvador

Gregorio Bras, recently promoted to Provincial of the Company of Jesus, leader of all the Jesuits in Brazil, strode toward the governor's mansion. Something out of the ordinary was happening in Salvador, and no one had told him a thing about it.

To his surprise, he spotted Gerard van Oost heading in the same direction. A native whom Gregorio had never seen before walked by his side. In all the years he had lived among the Tupi, he had never seen a man with as many face piercings or as many scars as this one. He looked a veritable demon in the flesh.

"Gerard!" called out Gregorio. "What brings you to Salvador?"

"An emergency," Gerard replied, showing no sign of stopping.

Gregorio raced to catch up. "Then I suspect our motives are the same. May I accompany you?"

"Of course," said Gerard. He finally paused to shake Gregorio's hand. "It's good to see you, Gregorio. This is Cabwassu; a warrior chief of the Tupinambá and a good friend."

Cabwassu gave an exaggerated smile that made him appear even more frightening. Gregorio shook his hand.

"It's good to see you as well, Gerard. I was pleased to discover you heeded Inocencia's call to aid Olinda. I hear you made quite an impression."

It might have been his imagination, but Gregorio thought Gerard turned red at the words.

"It was nothing," said Gerard. "We'll speak of it later. My business with the governor is urgent."

"I'll wait here," said Cabwassu, "and leave the talking to you."

As Gregorio and Gerard approached the door to the governor's palace, the guards crossed halberds, blocking their entrance.

"None have permission to enter today."

"I am Gerard van Oost, of the Elephant and Macaw Banner. The matter is urgent."

The two seemed to consider the words, until Gregorio added, "I am

Provincial of the Company of Jesus. Will you bar my entrance?"

It was the first time Gregorio had invoked his title in such a fashion, and as he expected, the reaction was immediate. The guards pulled back their halberds and waved them both through, not even taking the time to announce their visit. Gerard raised an eyebrow at him, but Gregorio ignored it. Without a word, he strode in and headed for the governor's office.

From behind his desk, Governor Veiga jerked up in surprise when the two of them burst into his office. Two richly-dressed men in chairs turned to gape at them.

Without any formality, Gerard burst out, "The city must be evacuated, immediately!"

The governor's two guests gasped in shock, but that was nothing compared to the commotion which broke out behind them. Gregorio turned to see Gerard's companion Oludara struggling against two guards to gain entry to the office. Strangely enough, in his arms he carried a small girl of mixed descent, a toddler less than two years of age.

The governor nodded to the guards and waved them away.

As soon as the men freed him, Oludara said, "He already knows, Gerard." He cast an accusing eye at the governor. "Yet there is no evacuation. The docks are closed, as are the gates."

"What?" said Gerard.

Gregorio glanced at Governor Veiga, who didn't seem at all surprised. The governor turned to the sitting men and said, "Could you please excuse us?"

The men reluctantly obeyed, excusing themselves and tipping their hats to to all as they left.

"Can someone tell me what's going on?" asked Gregorio.

"Woodsfather is upon is," said Oludara. "It will tear this city apart."

Gregorio had heard news of this Woodsfather creature ravaging the Backlands, but had heard nothing of it approaching Salvador.

"Is this true?" he asked the governor. "Why wasn't I told?"

"And more important," said Gerard. "Why haven't you sent everyone away?"

"I just found out," said Governor Veiga. "And I didn't want to create a city-wide panic."

"Do you know what happened to Antonio's force?" asked Oludara.

"I know you failed, or Woodsfather wouldn't be here."

"It wasn't a failure," said Gerard, "it was a massacre. The beast is a giant, almost two-hundred feet high. Not even cannon can wound it. It is unstoppable."

The governor placed his elbows on the table and his head upon his hands. After some time, he said, "If the creature passed through Antonio's group without a scratch, it will decimate the militia here. Gerard, you have defeated creatures I can only imagine. I beg you, please, find some way to stop this abomination. Save Salvador."

"I will do all I can to help. Just allow Oludara to leave with his child."

"Nonsense. I've heard enough of your banner to know you are an inseparable pair. Your strength is in your partnership. Of that much I am certain."

"I will leave," said Oludara. "I swore to my wife to protect my child. To you, I owe nothing."

The Governor stood up behind his desk. "No! No one is leaving Salvador." He paused and calmed himself. "If you succeed, I will send you and your daughter safely back to Guinea with a hundred cruzados for good measure."

"And if I don't?"

"If you die in the fight, your daughter will receive a land grant so large that every suitor in Brazil will line up to marry her."

Gregorio could see the anguish on Oludara's face. Either way, Woodsfather would arrive and his life was at risk. By taking the governor's offer, at least, he could guarantee his daughter's future.

"Write up the contract," said Gregorio, "and I will guarantee it."

Oludara studied Gregorio's eyes, then nodded.

"Scribe!" called Governor Veiga.

He set the scribe to writing the contract and turned to Gerard. "And you, Gerard? Will you also make demands of me to save those I am sworn to protect?"

"No," said Gerard. "I will die here if I must, and consider my life well spent. Unlike Oludara, I have no family to look after when I die."

"Thank you, Gerard. I was wrong to say you serve only yourself, and I am sorry for it."

Gerard only nodded in response. Gregorio checked the contract and signed it as witness. Then the three said their goodbyes and left the governor's mansion to discuss strategy. Cabwassu joined them.

Before anyone else could speak, Oludara looked to Gregorio. "Please, Gregorio. Will you take Taynah and protect her? She is all I have left."

Gregorio reached out and took the toddler into his arms. She looked up at him with a friendly giggle and he instantly liked her.

"Just as Father Miguel gave his life to save you," he said, "I will give my life to protect her, if necessary. In that respect, at least, I believe I can equal my predecessor."

Oludara looked around, then pointed down to one of two artillery towers which protected the docks. "Take her to that fort, there, in the low city. It is strong—one of the best structures. It will be the safest place when Woodsfather comes. With any luck, he will remain here in the upper city and not venture down the cliffs."

"Very well. May God bless you all."

As Gregorio turned to carry Taynah down the gigantic flight of stairs to the docks, he heard Gerard say, "Now, what can we do to prepare?"

Those words lost all meaning just seconds later, when a rock the size of a house flew over the northern wall and crashed into the Customs House, spraying pieces of the building in all directions.

Bloodied and covered in dust, Gerard paused to consider his next move. He and Oludara had run from bastion to bastion, urging the artillery men on and doing their best to help aim for the beast's navel, but all for naught. They had watched shot after shot fail. They had stood helpless as Woodsfather crushed buildings on every side, and they had run for their lives time and again as the creature batted away every cannon which dared fire upon it. Hundreds had died. Cabwassu ran after the beast, shooting arrow after pointless arrow into its impenetrable hide, until Gerard lost sight of him.

Gerard looked desperately for any artillery still standing, but could see none. He watched as Woodsfather lifted a merchant's stall and threw it into a building, wrecking both in the process. The awesome power of the creature daunted him; Gerard had never felt so helpless.

Oludara crouched beside him, trembling in exhaustion. Gerard placed a calming hand on his shoulder, which only caused him to jump in surprise.

"Sorry," said Gerard. "Any idea what to do next?"

Oludara shook his head sadly. His shoulders dropped and he fell to one knee, resting.

Returning his attention to the creature, Gerard was terrified to see it sliding down the long cliff—a distance as great as the creature's own height—toward the low city.

"Oludara..." said Gerard.

"Curse my luck! We must do something before the creature reaches Gregorio and Taynah."

As Gerard and Oludara rushed toward the stairs, Woodsfather paused its destruction and turned to look out over the bay.

"What's it doing?" asked Gerard.

At that, a splashing echoed from below, followed by an atrocious smell not unlike rotten vegetables and vinegar. Gerard looked down to see Woodsfather pissing a massive indigo stream. The bizarre urine whipped aside dockside carts and booths on its way into the ocean. The creature, so assured in its dominance of the battle, had stopped to pee.

"God help us," said Gerard.

From the tower crenelations, Gregorio watched as the giant pissed a torrential, indigo stream toward the bay. A compulsion came over him. In a vision, he saw that he must do something, or Salvador would be doomed.

He looked around for ideas. Terrified soldiers peed their pants and trembled, making no movement toward the half-dozen cannons, primed and loaded, which stood upon the ramparts.

"Be not afraid," said Gregorio, making the sign of the cross over them, one by one. "Have faith in God and he will stand by your side."

He heard giggles and turned to see Taynah mimicking him, making the sign of the cross at everything on the tower: the soldiers, the flag, the cannon.

The cannon?

"Not a bad idea, child," he said.

Gregorio blessed one of the cannons and all its shot, then turned toward the soldiers.

"Fire this one," he said.

The soldiers looked at each other, none daring to anger the beast.

"Fire this one!" he commanded.

One of the soldiers nodded nervously and, with the help of the others, turned the cannon carriage toward Woodsfather. They lit the fuse and fired.

The shot sailed true, striking Woodsfather in the thigh. When it struck, Woodsfather howled with such force that all present covered their ears. On the creature's leg, Gregorio spotted a mark from which trickled a liquid like sap.

Its howl complete, Woodsfather turned in their direction and fixed its gaze upon the tower. The beast's terrible eyes upon him, Gregorio could utter no more than a whisper.

"Protect us, o Lord."

At Woodfather's howl of pain, a shout went up around Salvador. Oludara couldn't help but add his voice to the chorus.

"Olorun be praised, the beast has been wounded!" he cried out, raising a fist. "Someone has found a way."

"With a thousand more pricks like that," said Gerard in a dry tone, "we just might kill it."

Oludara spotted the trickle from the creature's leg, and had to agree.

Another shot fired, and this time Oludara located the source: the tower where he had sent Gregorio with Taynah. This second shot missed its massive target completely.

"Isn't that where Taynah is?" asked Gerard, echoing his thoughts.

"Is he mad?" asked Oludara. "He would risk my daughter in this way?"

"We don't know who's firing those shots."

"It doesn't matter."

Oludara ran for the stairs just as Cabwassu came rushing toward them from the city.

"Take the potion!" he called.

His message given, Cabwassu ran along the cliff, head level with the creature who paced through the low city below him. Arrows in hand, he released them one after another with incredible speed toward the creature's eye. One of them struck and Woodsfather paused to pluck it out. It looked toward Cabwassu in rage and slammed its fist into the cliff just below him. The rock collapsed below Cabwassu and he plunged down. Oludara, racing down the steps, saw Cabwassu's remains at the bottom: wrecked and lifeless.

Behind him, Gerard cried out in despair, "Cabwassu!"

Oludara realized his run to the tower would do nothing, the creature would reach it well before him. He turned to Gerard and ripped the pack from his back. Gerard didn't even seem to notice. Oludara pulled out the gourd and shoved it into his companion's chest.

"We have no time to grieve!" he yelled. "Remember Taynah. Remember Cabwassu and honor his last command."

Gerard shook his head sadly but took up the gourd. He chugged it down, a small stream escaping down his goatee in the process. Oludara watched for some change but could spot none; Gerard only lowered the gourd and stared at it curiously.

Then, without warning, his eyes widened and he straightened up. His body shuddered and he clenched his fists.

"Well," he said, "isn't that surprising?"

⤙◇⤚

For some reason, the creature had slowed down to strike at something on the cliff, giving Gregorio just enough time to escape the tower. He grabbed Taynah and raced down the circular stairs, not pausing until he came out the lower door.

As they rushed outside, Gregorio looked up to see the monster looming over them, preparing to strike the building with a fist. They had but one option.

As he ran for the water, he asked, “Child, can you swim?”

She grinned and lunged from his arms, diving into the waves and paddling out.

“Amazing child,” said Gregorio, tossing off his frock and exposing the white undergarments underneath. “Can barely walk and already knows how to swim.”

He jumped in after her, grabbing her with one arm as he passed and pulling them through the waves with all his strength. He looked back just in time to see Woodsfather smash apart the tower. Gregorio dove beneath the water with Taynah as the rubble came crashing around them.

Yandir had not lied; Gerard could feel strength in his body he had never known before. To test it, he grabbed a piece of rubble which weighed easily a hundred pounds and hurled it at Woodsfather. The rubble crashed into the back of Woodsfather’s head at unbelievable speed and disintegrated into a cloud of dust with the impact. The creature took no notice.

“Amazing,” he said.

“We need to help them!” screamed Oludara, as the creature smashed the tower to pieces below them.

Gerard tested his legs and wasn’t disappointed. He sprinted down the staircase like a gazelle, covering in thirty seconds a distance which would have normally taken him ten minutes. He rushed to the tower’s remains and tossed rocks one way and another, searching for Taynah and Gregorio. Something in the water caught his eye and he looked up to spot the two of them surface behind the waves and wave down a carrack. The ship turned toward them, lowering a rope ladder as it approached.

That concern resolved, Gerard returned his attention to Woodsfather. It had doubled back along the beach and busied itself with kicking down the warehouses along the dock, one by one. Gerard looked around for something with which to attack the beast and spotted a group of soldiers cowering at the cliff base. He vaulted at them with incredible speed, causing them to cringe into fetal balls.

"Were you the ones in the tower with Father Gregorio?" he asked.

One of them nodded.

"How did you wound the beast?" he asked.

"Father blessed the cannon balls."

"Which ones?" asked Gerard.

"Those." The soldier pointed toward a cannon and shot within the rubble.

The crew of the carrack *Sao Pedro* stared open-mouthed as the Provincial of the Company of Jesus stepped upon their deck, dripping wet in his undergarments and carrying a curly-haired toddler in his arms.

Gregorio wasted no time with explanations. "Who's the captain of this ship?" he called out.

A stout man in a black hat stepped forward. "That would be me. How can we help you, father?"

"You must fire upon the beast immediately. I'll bless your shot."

"We saw you wound the beast, but I'm afraid I can't help."

Gregorio once again called upon his most commanding tone. "You would go against a man of God?"

"It's not that. My cannon are fixed. They're for shooting at ships, not giants. From here, I couldn't shoot higher than the creature's toes, if that."

"Well then, what can shoot at giants?"

"You might try that one. I'm sure they have something that can shoot at it."

The captain pointed toward a Spanish galleon, fleeing at full speed. Even from the side, Gregorio could spot more than a hundred cannon poking out from the ship.

Oludara orchestrated Gerard's attacks against Woodsfather. He helped Gerard sort through the tower rubble in search of cannon balls and guided his throws.

Gerard performed marvelously. Some of the balls bounced off the creature, but others damaged it. Gerard had managed two solid wounds to the chest and one near its groin. They had also managed to avoid the creature's wrath, as it searched around furiously for a cannon, not a man.

"Now try for the head," said Oludara.

The shot would be difficult at such an angle, but Oludara decided it was worth a try. Gerard took careful aim, turned back, and hurled the ball high.

The ball lost a good deal of speed on the way up, but struck true: near the top of the head. The creature's head lolled around and it clutched at it with its hands. After a moment of wobbling, it fell to one knee and braced one hand upon a building, one of the few still standing in the low city.

"Climb up, Gerard!" urged Oludara. "Crawl into its ear, or strike the beast in its eye."

"Do you jest?" asked Gerard.

"This is your chance."

Gerard took a breath and rushed forward. He leapt upon the rubble of one building, jumped over to the two-story building on which Woodsfather rested, then sped up the creature's arm and toward its head.

Woodsfather noticed the movement and brushed at Gerard like a fly with its gnarled claws. Oludara gasped at the sight, but when the creature turned, he saw that Gerard had grasped some moss upon its back and was working his way up. Oludara could do nothing but watch and wish the best for his companion.

Gerard tried to enter the ear, but root-like hairs blocked his way. Instead, he braced his feet against the creature's head and yanked upon the earlobe. Oludara could see the ear rip away from the head, a thick spout of resin streaming from the wound.

The creature howled and clawed at Gerard, who was forced to stop halfway. Dropping to Woodsfather's shoulder, he dodged the claws and left the ear dangling. He then made a leap for the creature's nose and prepared to attack the eye.

Woodsfather, apparently guessing Gerard's intent, did something Oludara would never have expected: he leaned forward and rushed his head toward the ground. Oludara's heart stopped for a moment as the creature's forehead—right near the point where Gerard hung—slammed into the hard ground with a sound like thunder.

After a short chase and a verbal berating by Gregorio, the galleon *Santiago* stopped its flight and allowed the priest to board. Taynah, still in his arms, laughed in delight.

In Spanish, Gregorio addressed the captain. "I want you to turn back and unload all your cannon upon the beast."

The captain shook his head. "Sorry, father. It's hard enough to hit a wall from a ship, much less a moving target."

Gregorio pointed back toward Woodsfather, who for some inexplicable reason had slammed its face into the ground.

"He's not moving now," he said.

The captain frowned. "My concern is for my men. I need to get them out of here."

Gregorio stood at his full height and addressed not only the captain, but all on board. "Would you contradict the Provincial of the Company of Jesus, sent here by King Philip himself?"

The sailors muttered to each other and many made the sign of the cross. The captain still looked doubtful, but Gregorio stared him down. A look of resignation appeared, and Gregorio knew he had won one more tiny fight in the day's impossible battle.

Oludara ran to the crater made by Woodsfather's head. He cared no longer whether the creature noticed him or not, but to his luck, it had turned its attention elsewhere. Inside the crater, he found Gerard, his body pressed into the ground beneath. Oludara fell to his knees beside the unmoving body.

Oludara placed a hand on his companion's arm, which, to his amazement, felt intact. No bone had been shattered, nothing crushed. Impossible, but the body appeared whole and unharmed.

"Gerard! Gerard!" he shouted.

After a period of time which passed so slowly Oludara had no idea how long it took, Gerard opened one eye. His voice croaked out: "That hurt."

"Gerard, you're alive!"

Gerard raised one arm, then another, and Oludara pulled on his shoulders to sit him up.

"Alive and intact, it appears," said Gerard.

"Yandir's magic was great indeed."

Gerard gave a reluctant nod of agreement. "Where is Taynah?"

"I saw them flee on one boat, then move to another, larger one. They are far from here and safe."

"You don't mean that galleon, do you?"

Oludara looked to where Gerard pointed and saw the ship, much closer than when he's last seen it, turning to line its cannons at Woodsfather. After all he had suffered that day, he could not believe it.

"For Olurun's sake, why?" he called out.

The captain led Gregorio below deck to show him which cannon could possibly be expected to hit the beast, perhaps a dozen, and he blessed them all. Then they returned above deck where he blessed some mortars. Over a hundred artillerymen scurried to load them as the ship came in line with the creature.

The captain had given orders for the cannons to fire the moment they got a line on the creature, and there was nothing left to do but wait and watch.

As the prow guns came in line with the beast, two cannons fired. Both shots fell harmlessly, one crashing into the cliff behind Woodsfather and the other not even clearing the water. Nearby, the captain growled.

"Trust in God," whispered Gregorio while he gripped Taynah tightly.

Another few shots went off. The only effect Gregorio noticed was the collapse of a house wall nears Woodsfather's feet.

"Trust in God," Gregorio repeated, this time loud enough for those around him to hear.

The next round of shots wounded Woodsfather. It howled and looked toward them. When another shot flew its way and again struck true, it became furious. It stepped into the water and waded toward them.

All around Gregorio, men made the sign of the cross. The shots came seemingly at random and in the general panic, missed far more than they hit.

"Have faith!" shouted Gregorio, this time loud enough to be heard even below deck.

Woodsfather, water up to its waist, picked up a fishing boat and hurled it at the galleon. Everyone ducked as it careened toward them at amazing speed, knocking into the main mast and snapping it off. The impact jerked the galleon sideways and many fell overboard, careening from the deck, netting, and crow's nest. Gregorio barely held on to Taynah.

As the ship rocked back and forth, echoes of cannon fire came from the upper city. Gregorio was amazed to hear it, those cannon had been silent since early in the battle. To his even greater surprise, the creature howled as the shots wounded it. Gregorio squinted to see Jesuits on the cliffs, directing some loose cannon which had been hastily placed these. His brothers had come to the rescue, and pride surged within him. On the lower beach, he swore he saw a man throwing cannonballs, but shook his head at the sight, thinking it more likely an optical trick than a miracle of that size.

He returned his attention to Woodsfather, who continued toward the galleon. The water slowed the creature's already ponderous pace, yet it would still be upon them at almost any moment. At the same time, Gregorio noticed something different, a confusion in Woodsfather's eyes which hadn't been there before. It had obviously not expected such resistance from mere men. One of its ears dangled, ruined, and it bled sap from at least a dozen wounds.

"We must continue to fire," he said to the captain. "Another solid hit will break its will." The captain nodded and ran under deck.

The next volley of shots went off, but only one struck the creature. Gregorio knew there couldn't be more than a handful of cannon left to fire, and reloading was an impossibility at this point, the barrels hadn't had time to cool and they'd never get the ship back around, anyway. He dropped to his knees in prayer.

A final round went off and Woodsfather wailed miserably. Gregorio opened his eyes to see it clutching its face. Another shot came from the city and Woodsfather arched its back in pain.

With one last gaze of hatred at the galleon, Woodsfather turned away. It made its way northeast, up the coast and away from the city and the bay.

A cheer went up from the crew and Gregorio, smiling, bowed his head in a prayer of thanks.

Oludara did not join in the exuberant cheer which went up around Salvador. Instead, he waited impatiently at the docks for his daughter's return. As he waited, he gaped at the city in ruins around him. Rubble was strewn as far as the eye could see, and slicks of sticky resin lay splattered everywhere. The number of bodies was atrocious, perhaps a thousand. One in particular, that of Cabwassu, caused him pain to see.

Some thirty minutes after Woodsfather's retreat, Gregorio and Taynah, escorted in a rowboat crewed by Spanish sailors, finally reached the docks. Taynah shouted, "Daddy!" when she saw him and a strain of relief mixed with his fury. He wasted no time grabbing his child from Gregorio's arms.

"I ask you to protect my child," he yelled at Gregorio, "and instead you call danger toward her at every moment?"

Gregorio bowed before speaking. "I'm truly sorry, Oludara. My faith carried me away. I received a vision, one which told me I had to act, or that all would be lost."

Oludara knew within his heart the priest was right. If he had not acted, Salvador and everyone in it would have been destroyed. This fact, however, did little to make up for the anger and anxiety he had felt during the battle, which he took out on the priest.

"You are insane," he said.

"I put my trust in God, and he defended us."

Oludara shook his head and went in search of Gerard.

Gerard, Gregorio, and Oludara, the latter with Taynah cradled in his arms, buried Cabwassu outside the city. Each gave him a hero's farewell in his own particular way. Gregorio provided a short eulogy, praising his loyalty and bravery. Oludara placed Cabwassu's bow across his chest and thanked him for his sacrifice. Gerard had planned only to say a short prayer, but on the spur of the moment, he poured water into the gourd that had contained Yandir's potion and drank a toast to Cabwassu, Yandir, Jakoo, Arany, and all their fallen friends. He left the empty gourd upon the warrior's lifeless chest.

An unexpected duo surprised them on their way back to the city: Diogo and Moara. Gerard, overjoyed to see the two, couldn't help but embrace them both.

Once everyone had said their greetings, Gerard asked, "When did you arrive in Salvador?"

"We missed the original summons and arrived too late to join you," said Diogo. "We tried to catch up, and met with Antonio's group on their way back."

"Antonio has returned?"

Diogo and Moara both responded with a nod.

"We came looking for you," said Moara. "The governor has summoned all of us to the plaza."

Gerard had little desire to speak with the governor, but accepted the summons. On their way back to the city, Gerard could only stare in disbelief at the wreckage. Hardly a building stood undamaged. The toll in human life was phenomenal. Woodsfather's attack had set the city back years, perhaps decades.

From across the plaza, Governor Veiga called him over. A contingent of guards surrounded the governor, their uniforms in tatters, just like everything else in Salvador.

"Where have you been?" asked the governor, irritated, as they approached.

"Burying the dead," Gerard replied dryly.

"You've no time to waste on that. The beast is wounded; you must find a way to finish it off before it recovers."

"Wounded?" asked Oludara. "We've given it a few scratches, that is all. It is far from dead. My people have a saying, 'Do not attempt what you cannot bring to a good end'."

"There must be some way," said the governor. Looking at Gerard, he asked, "What happened to your show of strength? I've never seen the like."

"That magic is gone. Cabwassu is gone." Gerard choked on the words. "We have nothing left with which to fight the beast."

"It must be stopped! If it destroys the mills..."

"I care not for the mills," said Gerard.

"It heads north," said Gregoio, "toward Olinda."

When Gerard thought of Inocencia, his despair only deepened. Then, as if the scene couldn't get any worse, Antonio strutted across the plaza toward them, followed by a few dozen bannermen and natives. As he approached, Gerard could see the fury in his eyes.

"And what took you so long?" the governor asked Antonio.

The question did nothing to help Antonio's mood, and he rushed at Gerard, shoving him. Gerard stumbled back but stayed on his feet. Some of Antonio's men stepped forward but Moara and Diogo moved to Gerard's sides and everyone halted.

"How did you get here before us, you scoundrel?" said Antonio. "You deceive me and try to rob my glory? I'll have your head."

"Enough!" yelled Governor Veiga. "I have no time for arguments. I need all of you."

Antonio fought to control his anger and turned to the governor. "You know I'll follow your commands, but killing that beast is impossible."

"The Jesuits wounded it by blessing the cannons. You can take ships and fire at it from the water."

Antonio paused to consider the words. "Very well."

Diogo looked to Moara, who nodded. "We'll accompany you," said Diogo. "To make up for our failure to get here sooner."

"I'll go as well," said Gerard. "I cannot allow that creature to destroy another city without a fight."

"Good," said Governor Viega.

"Think on this, Gerard," said Oludara. "Your death will gain nothing."

"Perhaps," said Gerard. "But if I don't try, and that thing reaches Olinda, I'll never forgive myself."

Oludara, who had just lost his beloved, understood.

"In that case," said Oludara, "I'll go as well. You'll need someone to watch your back." Oludara stared at Antonio, making his double meaning obvious.

"I'll go with you as well," said Gregorio.

"No!" said Oludara. "This is a warrior's fight, and there are more than enough to die at Woodsfather's hands. Send some of your priests to bless the weapons. This time, protect my daughter, as I asked you before."

Gregorio closed his eyes and held his hands together in prayer, then nodded. "You are right," he said. "I have no place in the battle to come."

"I need your fastest ships," said Antonio, "loaded with cannon."

The governor looked down at the harbor and grimaced. Gerard followed his gaze. Much like the city, few ships remained intact.

"Take whatever is left," said the governor. "I'll write the order."

In the end, the group took three ships, which was all they had men for anyway. Only sixty bannermen and militia remained, and they rounded up a few hundred gunners and sailors to go with them. Antonio took the lead ship: the Spanish galleon *Santiago*. Diogo and Moara took control of a second galleon, and Oludara and Gerard took the final ship: the carrack *Sao Pedro*. Gregorio and a group of Jesuits went from ship to ship, blessing the cannon and the crew's weapons. He boarded Oludara and Gerard's vessel last.

Gerard feigned protest at a Catholic blessing his weapons, but quickly relented and allowed Gregorio to bless his rapier and harquebus. When Gregorio held a hand toward Oludara's knife, Oludara shook his head.

"My knife already has a blessing of its own," he said.

Gregorio seemed ready to argue, but held in whatever he was going to say. Instead, he held his arms out toward Taynah. Oludara, who had no delusions as to their chances against Woodsfather, squeezed his daughter and felt as if his heart would burst.

"Be good," he told her. "Remember your mother and father. Please."

Tears poured from his eyes as he handed her over to Gregorio.

"Teach her of my people," he said. "And her mother's. Find her a good marriage."

"Don't think of such things now," said Gregorio. "May God bring you back to her safe."

"Please," said Oludara.

Gregorio nodded sadly. "I will do all you ask. I swear it."

Oludara was shocked when Gerard knelt before the priest, but Gregorio blessed him without comment. When Gregorio and the other Jesuits set off in a rowboat, Oludara gave Gerard a quizzical look.

"What?" said Gerard. When Oludara said nothing, Gerard blushed and said, "I know, I know. We may have our differences, but we all serve the same God. And of one thing I'm certain: God is the only one who can save us now."

Part IV: The Final Battle

Strangely enough, the chase up the coast provided Oludara's first moments of quiet contemplation in a week. He knew nothing of cannon or sailing, so nothing was expected of him. Gerard, having some knowledge of artillery, spent time training with the gunners.

At one point, as Oludara stood on deck and watched the coast pass by, Gerard came and stood beside him.

"Gerard," said Oludara. "There is something I want to tell you."

"Go ahead."

"I want to apologize for when we parted, just before Salvador. I know I was abrupt, but my mind was not my own. First Arany, then Sacy. A mad rage to protect my daughter had gripped me, and I could think of little else."

Gerard said nothing, so Oludara continued.

"Now, here on this ship, one way or another, we face the end of our time together. Either we die or we separate; there is no other path."

"I know," said Gerard. "Those are ominous words, but I agree. This is an ending for us."

"So let me not be so abrupt this time. You have been a fine companion, Gerard, and I have no complaint of our time together. Even though I lost Arany..." At this, Oludara choked and had to compose himself. "What I want to say is, I had many doubts when we first set out. I considered abandoning you in the wilderness more than once."

Gerard showed no surprise, just nodded, and Oludara again continued.

"But I'm glad I did not. It was five years well spent. The best five years of my life, in fact. And I have something great to show for it all: a wonderful daughter to carry on my line."

At that, Gerard smiled. "I'm glad to hear you feel that way. She will grow to be a fine woman, no doubt. 'Great', as Kooka called her. She will make you proud."

At those words, Oludara finally released the panic which had gripped him ever since the ride up the river toward their first meeting with

Woodsfather. He relaxed, even while holding back from Gerard a terrible certainty which haunted him: the feeling he would die that day.

His relaxation lasted but a moment, before being broken by a shout of warning from the lead ship.

"What was that?" asked Oludara.

"I believe we've found the beast," replied Gerard, a finger pointing up the coast.

Well up the shore, an unmistakable form stood and towered over the trees. Woodsfather spotted the ships and loped in their direction, the powerful stamp of its feet louder with every moment. It bent down and when it straightened, held a palm tree in one hand. Oludara saw an arm move forward and, to his terror, launch the tree into the second ship, snapping two masts and dumping much of the crew into the ocean.

Gerard rushed below deck to the cannons, and Oludara could do little but watch. The captains of the three ships shouted orders to take them farther out, but it soon became clear they wouldn't have time; they had skirted too closely to the coast.

Woodsfather rained a relentless hail of trees and rocks upon the ships. The second ship, with Diogo and Moara, went down first. It suffered multiple strikes to the hull and sank without firing a single shot.

Antonio's ship managed to turn and fire at Woodsfather, striking it twice, which only enraged it more. It lumbered into the water towards them and, despite the captain's best efforts to evade it, reached them with the water up to its chest. The ship managed a final shot to Woodsfather's chin before the creature brought a fist down upon it, splitting it in half.

On Oludara's ship, the captain attempted to flee, turning toward the ocean. Woodsfather, far enough away it must have realized it couldn't catch them by wading out, dunked its head underwater.

Oludara watched in panic, waiting for the creature to reappear. When it came up, it lifted an enormous rock into the air. It hurled the stone at them, which passed through the ship's hull and splashed on the other side. Oludara, launched from the collapsing ship by the impact, prayed Gerard had not been in the stone's path.

Gerard lay upon the beach, too exhausted to move. His harquebus had weighed him down on the swim, but he had refused to let it go and still clutched it in his hand. His rapier also hung by his side. He didn't muster the strength to open his eyes until a slap across the face caused him to do so. Oludara knelt above him.

"We must flee!" he said.

Gerard used what force he had left to pull himself up. A terrible sight greeted him: the few survivors ran haphazardly around the beach as Woodsfather stamped them out of existence, one by one.

In a nervous gesture, Gerard reached up to adjust a hat which was no longer there, lost when the crashing water sucked him from the ship. Quickly assessing the situation, he saw the only possible cover from Woodsfather's towering gaze lay in the woods beyond a row of dunes.

Oludara must have seen it as well, because he set off in that direction. Gerard followed, his steps weighed down by the loose sand of the dunes. Woodsfather ignored them for the time being as it crushed other targets, and they reached the trees without incident. Moving cautiously, they found Antonio, Moara, and Diogo crouching in the woods as well. All three held harquebuses.

"Anyone else make it?" asked Gerard.

"None that I've seen," said Moara.

"We must find a way to flee," said Oludara. A pounding of sand from Woodsfather's footsteps alerted them that he searched the dunes nearby.

"We're here to fight it," said Antonio.

"With what?"

Without warning, a tree uprooted next to them, revealing Woodsfather's face staring down. The group split, everyone running in different directions.

As Gerard ran, he spotted a giant foot coming down nearby, right over Diogo.

"Diogo," he cried, "look out!"

His warning came too late, however. Diogo tried to swerve, but was crushed under the edge of the creature's foot. The impact hurled Gerard to one side. He had only a moment to lament the loss of his friend when, to his terror, he rolled over to see Woodsfather staring straight at him.

Woodsfather glared at the human below him with the same rage he had felt while killing the last thousand of them. The sparse woods provided little cover for these last few, and their useless attempts to hide amused him. The one at his feet, a bit rounder than most, made no move to run. Woodsfather would stamp him out quickly and move on to the next. He raised his foot for the blow.

At the last moment, however, something unusual made him stop. One hairy creature rode in on top of another and stopped just in front of the man. The creature on top, a tuft of red hair sticking up from its head, looked like a muscular young man. The creature beneath was a boar, much larger than most in the forest, but still not more than a bug to Woodsfather. Beside the two, a colorful parrot landed on the ground and transformed into a girl with flowers in her hair. The curious threesome was enough to make him pause.

"Woodsfather, stop!" shouted the hairy young man, using some magic to echo his voice far beyond his size. "Stop this senseless rampage."

The young man spoke in Woodsfather's language, one older than time, the only one he had ever known. The thing spoke terribly, but still the sound was music to Woodsfather's ears. He thought the language had been forgotten by all but him. For the first time since his awakening, the rage went to the back of his mind. Hearing his language reminded him of a time before people came to his land—before his enemy Soomeh had tricked him to sleep. Perhaps not all was lost after all.

This creature was but a toddler to him, couldn't be more than three millennia old, the time Woodsfather had slept. Three thousand years was but a piteous moment in the life of one who had lived for a million.

"What are you?" Woodsfather responded, his booming voice making the amplified shout of the other sound like nothing more than a bird's cheep.

"I am Curooper," responded the creature, "a protector of the forest."

Forest protector? Woodsfather liked the sound of that. This Curooper was nothing more than a child, but one with potential. With ten-thousand years, perhaps, Woodsfather could mold him into something of worth.

"If you wish to be a forest protector," he said, "help me kill these children of Soomeh."

"Why do you slay them?"

"I slay them so that Soomeh will return to save them. Then, it will be his turn to die."

"People are no great friends of mine, but I will not destroy them without reason. The All-Father Maire-Monan created them, just as he created us."

Foolish child, he thought. *I should never have listened to one who looks so much like the humans.*

"Created *us?*" he bellowed, rising to his full height. "No one created *me!*"

The red rage returned. He would slay all the fleshy man-creatures, and all who protected them. Even if it took a thousand millennia to smash them beneath his feet, he would kill every last one.

He kicked the three puny creatures, sending them flying. He then returned his attention to the man-creatures. They had fled into the woods again, but he would find them. That much he knew.

The remaining survivors—Gerard, Oludara, Moara, and Antonio—had taken advantage of Curooper's conversation with Woodsfather to hide. When Woodsfather spoke, his deafening voice booming in some unknown language, they had to cover their ears to keep them from bursting.

Hiding within some bushes, they watched as a kick sent Curooper, his boar, and Wildflower flying. Wildflower transformed into a bird mid-flight and spun dizzily through the air, but Curooper and the boar crashed through the trees, out of sight.

Gerard took inventory of the situation. Almost miraculously, he still held his harquebus, and his powder cartridges had remained closed and dry during the swim. He took the opportunity to load and offered the powder to Antonio and Moara as well, who accepted without a word. The loaded guns were next to useless against Woodsfather, but having his loaded at least made Gerard feel more comfortable. Beside him, Oludara breathed heavily.

"We must get away," said Moara.

"No," said Oludara. "Woodsfather will rip apart the entire forest looking for us. We must end this now."

"Are you mad?" asked Gerard.

"I've had enough."

With that, Oludara charged the creature.

"It appears your friend has gone mad," said Antonio.

Oludara grabbed Woodsfather's ankle and hauled himself up. He navigated through the bark and moss on the creature's leg.

"I think I understand his plan," said Gerard. "He will attempt to reach the creature's navel. We must provide him cover. Moara, hand me your harquebus. You keep loading while I fire..."

Gerard looked back to see why Moara had not placed the harquebus in his outstretched hand. Antonio, rapier drawn, stood over Moara's unconscious body. Gerard could only stare up in disbelief.

"What have you done?" he asked.

"What I should have done long ago. Draw your sword, van Oost. Live or die, today I have my revenge."

Hand over hand, Oludara made the arduous climb up Woodsfather. He reached the creature's thigh before it took notice of him, and even then, it didn't seem concerned. It continued to scan the ground while it absentmindedly scratched at him with its massive claws. Oludara ducked just in time to avoid the first pass.

Oludara had expected Gerard to recognize his plan immediately and find a way to distract the beast. If he didn't, Oludara wouldn't stand a chance.

"Curses, Gerard," he muttered under his breath. "What are you doing?"

"I'm not going to fight you, Antonio," said Gerard. "We have more important things to do."

"If you won't fight," said Antonio, "then die."

Antonio lunged at him, and Gerard rolled away just in time. Reluctantly, he unsheathed his rapier.

The two combatants circled as Gerard's eyes flicked back and forth between Antonio and Oludara. From the corner of his eye, he could see Woodsfather scratching at Oludara, and knew he had to do something. At a lunge from Antonio, however, he was forced to return his full attention to the fight.

Gerard parried the thrust, but Antonio's hand snaked back too quickly for a riposte. Gerard spotted a root near Antonio's feet and circled to one side, causing Antonio to counter his movement and line them up again. Gerard feigned a lunge, and Antonio took a step back onto the root, momentarily losing his balance.

Gerard, with no time to lose, disengaged and grabbed his harquebus. He made a desperate shot at Woodsfather and struck the creature's back, causing it to turn and take its attention from Oludara.

Antonio, recovered, charged in and Gerard used his gun to block a thrust at the last moment. Then he tossed down the gun and scrambled to recover his rapier.

At a shot from below, Woodsfather jerked his hand away from Oludara and turned around.

It took you long enough, van Oost, thought Oludara.

Oludara wasted no time in climbing higher. He made his way up to waist level and worked around toward his true objective: the navel.

Woodsfather, however, returned his attention to him. The creature seemed to finally grasp his plan, and instead of clawing at him, it scooped its massive hand upward along the skin. Oludara had no choice but to let go or be crushed.

He landed on the beast's palm and it raised him toward its face. He considered jumping off, but knew the fall would kill him. Instead, he unsheathed his ivory knife and waited. With luck, he might have a chance to plunge it into the creature's eye.

Woodsfather curled its fingers around him. To Oludara's relief, the long nails didn't allow the creature to close its fist all the way and squeeze him to death. It did, however, close enough to make him lose his breath and his grip on the knife, which plummeted to the ground. Helpless, he waited for death as Woodsfather studied him with its enormous eyes.

Gerard, using all his skill to keep Antonio at bay, risked a glance at Oludara, only to find him in the grip of the giant. Gerard saw a streak of white as Oludara's ivory knife fell from his hands. His glance cost him a nick to the shoulder, as he only partially blocked Antonio's next attack.

We are lost, he thought. Diogo had fallen. Oludara had lost his knife and was certain to die. It would take only moments for Woodsfather to turn his attention to the swordplay between Antonio and himself and crush them both with a single step. He considered dropping his guard entirely and letting Antonio kill him first. At least then, one of them might have a chance.

Just then, a feathered flash of color flew between the two combatants, causing them to both step back. The parrot crash landed beside them and transformed into Wildflower.

"What are you two doing?" she shrieked. "Oludara is in the hands of Woodsfather."

"I know!" said Gerard.

At that, Antonio lost no more time with the girl and lunged at Gerard, who turned away the blade at the last moment.

"Oludara dropped his knife," he panted out. "Get it to him, or he is lost."

"Where is it?"

"Over there!" He used his free hand to point in the creature's general direction.

Wildflower shook her head but asked no more questions. Instead, Gerard could see a curved orange beak sprout from her mouth just before he returned his full attention to Antonio.

After staring at Oludara for some time, Woodsfather finally lost interest and pulled Oludara back with a slow, sure movement. For certain, the creature prepared to hurl him to his death.

I have failed them all, he thought, *Arany, Taynah, Gerard*. He turned his thoughts to Ketu. *I failed my father and my ancestors, all those who came before me, those who made sacrifices so I could one day bring honor to our family. Instead, I will never again see our homeland.*

His vision blurred and in his mind's eye, a fuzzy form took shape. A voice came to him: his father's.

You have never failed us, my son. And we have never left you.

As the vision became clear, he saw his father smiling at him. Behind his father: his grandfather and grandmother, both long dead. Behind them, a hundred others, all reaching out to him, all giving him hope in his despair.

A shrill squawk shattered the image. He opened his eyes to see a toucan perched on Woodsfather's finger, his ivory knife in its massive beak. He could feel Woodsfather's arm begin its forward motion for the throw. Without hesitation, Oludara grasped the knife and slashed the creature's skin between the thumb and fingers.

The enchanted blade sliced cleanly through the bark-like skin and fibrous muscle beneath. Woodsfather howled and released him, and Oludara crashed into its shoulder. As he skidded off, he grasped at the mossy covering and grabbed a thread of it, hanging high in the air and not losing his grip on the knife.

He wasted no time in scrambling down the creature's chest. When Woodsfather tried to swat at him, he let go, putting his life into fate's hands and dropping the last twenty feet to the navel. With a miraculous grab, he caught onto the navel and hung on. His shoulder screamed in pain as it caught the weight of his body.

Although Gerard had far more training with the rapier, Antonio's incredible speed compensated, leaving them deadlocked. Also, Gerard's scruples of aiming any kind of killing blow limited his choices. Gerard's worry for Oludara, coupled by the stressful combat, wore on him.

When Antonio paused his attack to catch his breath, Gerard chanced another glance at Oludara and saw that, by some miracle, he had escaped the creature's grasp and hung onto some moss at its shoulder. More than ever, Oludara needed a distraction.

"Antonio," he said, "I have no more time for this."

Antonio laughed. "You can't beat me, Gerard."

"Once again, I think you may be right."

On purpose, he left an opening to one side and prepared himself. Antonio saw the opening and rushed in, plunging the rapier through the side of his gut. The pain was worse than Gerard had imagined, but, he somehow managed to retain consciousness.

Antonio stared at him wide-eyed as Gerard pulled himself forward along the blade and struck the side of his head with his rapier's pommel. The blow sent Antonio sprawling.

Gerard didn't even wait for Antonio to hit the ground. Instead, he searched desperately for an unfired harquebus. He spotted Antonio's gun and, as he raised it, prayed it had been loaded properly. He saw Oludara hanging from Woodsfather's navel and the creature getting ready to slap him with its palm. Gerard aimed for the beast's eye and shot.

The shot struck true, and Woodsfather screamed. On reflex, it lifted both hands to its eyes, giving Oludara the seconds he needed to pull himself up and into its navel.

Shortly after Oludara disappeared, the creature screamed and convulsed. It jerked from side to side and clawed desperately at its belly. Woodsfather spun around madly, knocking down trees and throwing up clouds of dirt as its feet slammed the ground. Eventually, it fell to one knee, still clawing at the stomach region. After what felt like the longest minute of Gerard's life, the creature finally fell, face first, the shock of the impact knocking Gerard to his knees.

Sword in his side and dizzy from loss of blood, Gerard staggered up and rushed to find his companion. He reached the beast's side and hacked with his rapier, slashing the skin but doing little else. He called for Oludara, but heard nothing. A squawk came from his side and a toucan landed beside him, changing into Wildflower.

His voice desperate, Gerard called out, "Wildflower, help! He's still in there. Is there anything you can do?"

To his amazement, Wildflower transformed into a massive, hazy creature. Its body moved without a definite form, as if a child had modeled an ogre from clay. With two huge arms, the ogre-like creature grabbed the gash Gerard had made and ripped Woodsfather open. With a stench of rank, rotting leaves, the creature's guts poured out. Inside them, Gerard spotted the tip of Oludara's ivory dagger. He pointed it out to Wildflower, who yanked out the creature's innards enough for Gerard to free his companion.

Gerard slapped at Oludara, then beat his chest, yet he didn't breathe. He tried again and again to revive him until, defeated, he fell to his knees and looked away. Beside him, Wildflower sobbed openly.

Footsteps alerted him and he turned to see Curooper and his boar approaching. The boar hobbled on three legs; the other one dangled beside it, broken. Curooper, bruised and battered, held his ribs as he moved.

He placed a hand on Wildflower's shoulder. "What's wrong?"

She pointed to Oludara and again covered her sobbing face in her hands.

Curooper stared at the lifeless body for a time before responding. "Don't worry, Little Flower, it's not yet his time." He looked around.

"They won't let him go just yet."

"They?" asked Gerard, looking around but seeing nothing. "They who?"

Curooper knelt and placed a hand over Oludara's heart. "Can't you see them? Your friend walks with many, Gerard. It is you who walk alone."

Gerard, about to ask a question, swallowed it down when Oludara lurched up and gasped for breath. Oludara opened his eyes and scanned around, as if searching for something. When his gaze fell upon Gerard, the two of them traded smiles.

Wildflower squeezed Curooper and he yelped in pain, again clutching his ribs. She released her grip and kissed him tenderly.

Gerard laid a hand on his friend's shoulder.

"You did it," he said. "I don't know how, but you did it."

"And to think," said Oludara. "I had a premonition that I would die this day."

"You did," said Curooper, matter-of-factly.

Oludara gave him a puzzled look but asked nothing. Instead, he stared off and said, "In the end, I received aid I had not expected."

"Well of course you did," said Wildflower, beaming. "You two can't do anything without me! How many times does that make now that I've saved you?"

Oludara smiled and braced himself to stand.

"Curooper," said Gerard. "You spoke with Woodsfather, didn't you? What did it say? Why did it do this?"

"Revenge," replied Curooper. "Madness, and revenge. Nothing more."

The boar squealed and Curooper said to it, "Sorry, friend. Here you go."

He took the boar's injured leg in his hands and gently pushed it back into place. After speaking a few words, he released the leg and the boar walked on it again as if nothing had happened.

Curooper mounted the boar and said, "Come, Little Flower. It is time to go."

Wildflower placed herself behind him and the two started off.

"Wait!" said Oludara. He pulled something from a pouch at his belt and handed it to her. "Don't forget Iara's gem."

Before riding off, Curooper turned back one last time and said, "Shame you had to kill him. Two Ebemongeera remain. If they awaken and discover Woodsfather is dead, they will become bold."

"I hope I never meet them," said Oludara.

"Yes," agreed Curooper, "hope that you don't."

At that, he turned the boar and rode off.

Oludara looked quizzically Gerard and said, "Gerard, do you realize you have a sword stuck in your side?"

Gerard's concern for his friend had made him forget that fact. He looked down to see the blade still firmly implanted, the blood seeping out freely.

"Why yes," he replied, just before he fainted.

Part V: The Journey Back

Gerard opened his eyes to the sight of green. Someone had placed him in a makeshift lean-to built from branches and palm leaves. The smell of roasting fish permeated the air. He tried to sit and felt an almost unbearable pain in his side. Taking deep breaths, he managed to pull himself up on the third attempt.

Looking around, he first spotted the source of the fishy smell. Moara sat by a fire, roasting a fish over some sticks. Far to the left, he spotted crosses marking a row of fresh graves. To the right, Antonio sat tied to a tree.

Oludara appeared at one end of the campsite, carrying an armful of sticks. He spotted Gerard and hailed him.

"Gerard, you've awoken!"

Oludara dropped the sticks near Moara and knelt by Gerard's side.

"How do you feel?" he asked. "You've been asleep for days."

"The pain is intense. I've had better health, to be sure." Gerard looked to the graves and asked, "Are we four the only survivors?"

Oludara nodded sadly.

"What's he been like?" asked Gerard, motioning toward Antonio, who stared at the two of them from under his tree.

Oludara frowned. "I want to speak to you about that...when you're better."

"Nothing you can't say now."

"His hatred for you remains. He will stop at nothing until you are dead. I see no reason to take him back to Salvador and leave you in peril. After his treachery, we have every right to kill him."

"You know I would never kill a man."

"I know. I will kill him for you."

Gerard shook his head. "Don't even think of it. Justice will be served in Salvador."

It took two more days for Gerard to mend enough to walk, and the group started the long trip back to Salvador. As proof of their conquest, they chopped off Woodsfather's smallest toe, but even that turned out to be a heavy load, and Oludara and Moara had to pull it in a makeshift cart they had pieced together from the debris of a cannon carriage. The two of them took turns pulling the load and leading Antonio along by a rope.

In contrast to their triumphant victory over Woodsfather, a gloom hung over the group. Almost no one spoke, each keeping to his own thoughts.

At the end of their first day of travel, it was Antonio who finally spoke. He called to Moara as the latter prepared the nightly fire. Oludara and Gerard had left camp to gather wood.

"What's everyone so damn depressed for?" asked Antonio. "I'm the one who's tied up!"

"Don't be a fool, Antonio. Oludara lost his bride. Gerard grieves because his friend returns to Africa, leaving him here alone in Brazil."

"And you?"

"I lost my friend, Diogo, in case you didn't notice. Once again, I am alone."

"Let me go," said Antonio. "The two of us can travel together, like the old days."

Moara could not hide her disgust at the suggestion. She spat on the ground in reply.

After that, Antonio returned to his silence.

Oludara awoke to the sound of a "psst!" He looked around camp, but saw nothing out of the normal. Gerard and Moara lay asleep. He looked at Antonio, to check his bonds, and found the man wide-awake and staring at him. It could only have been Antonio who woke him.

"Slave..." said Antonio.

After all this time, Oludara couldn't believe the man still referred to him as "slave".

"I want to tell you something," said Antonio.

"What is it?"

"You're nothing but a worthless mule. That's all you'll ever amount to."

Antonio had ignored him for so long, Oludara had no idea why he would say this now. Antonio sneered at him, a look of disdain in his eyes. It seemed out of character, even for Antonio.

"Worse," continued Antonio, "you're a coward. You should have killed me when you had the chance. As soon as I'm out of these bonds, I'll cut your friends up and save you for last."

It was as Oludara had feared. Without a sound, he pulled his ivory knife from his belt.

"You think you'll use that?" said Antonio. "You don't have the guts. Give it to me so I can put it to good use, slitting all three of your miserable throats."

Gerard would curse Oludara for this action, but it didn't matter. How could he return to his homeland and leave a scorpion in his friend's bed? He stood and strode toward Antonio. As he approached, Antonio's eyes lit with...what...madness? Expectation?

"That's it, you worthless wretch. Let's see if you amount to half a man, after all."

Oludara pulled back and aimed a strike for Antonio's neck, but as he stabbed forward, a hand grasped his arm. Oludara turned to see Gerard.

"What are you doing?" he demanded.

"What I must do."

"Why do you insist so?"

"Just look at him! Look at the hate in his eyes."

Oludara pointed at Antonio, but was embarrassed to discover that the derision and sparkle had disappeared from the man's eyes, leaving only resignation.

"And so you thwart another of my plans, van Oost," said Antonio. "Forever, you are the thorn in my side."

"You wanted Oludara to kill you?" asked Gerard.

"Better killed than humiliated."

"That's nonsense."

Antonio stared off and made no reply.

Gerard sighed as they came within sight of a sugar mill. Their journey to Salvador had almost ended.

Unexpectedly, Moara said, "This is where I depart."

"What?" asked Gerard.

"I will never return to Salvador. My place is in the wilderness."

"Moara..."

"My mind is decided. I lost my tribe, I lost my people, I lost Diogo. I was put on this Earth to walk alone."

"Nonsense," said Gerard. "You could come with me."

"No. You are the wanderer, van Oost. There are no roots which bind you; your home is where you make it. I must return to the land of my ancestors, where I should have stayed all along."

Oludara acknowledged the sentiment with a knowing nod of his head.

"Very well," said Gerard. "I wish you the best."

"And I to you."

The three traded embraces and goodbyes. Antonio remained silent through it all. Gerard stared in silent melancholy as Moara walked back up the trail and disappeared into the woods.

He turned back to see Antonio sitting cross-legged in the middle of the path. The man had said nothing since his taunting of Oludara two nights previous. In fact, little had been spoken by anyone during that time. Oludara gave a tug on Antonio's rope and said, "Get up!"

Antonio shook his head in response.

Oludara threatened him with a fist. "No tricks. I would not delay our return any longer."

"I want to speak to Gerard."

Gerard, curious, asked, "What do you want?"

Antonio focused on nothing as he spoke. "Gerard, I beg of you. Please don't lead me into Salvador like a dog. Let your slave kill me, or let me go."

"No," said Gerard, "you'll come with us and stand judgment."

"There is no justice for me."

"What does that mean?"

"My whole life has been an injustice."

"Enough of this," said Oludara, impatient. "Let us drag him the rest of the way."

Antonio ignored him. "Would you hear my story, Gerard?"

Gerard sat down and took a drink of water from his canteen, then poured a sip into Antonio's mouth, who accepted it gratefully.

"I suppose it can't hurt," said Gerard.

"Gerard..." said Oludara.

"I would hear his words."

Oludara tossed down the rope angrily and strode off a few paces, turning his back to the two.

"My family never had much," said Antonio, "but things got worse when my father killed a man in an argument. He was sent to Limoeiro. Have you heard of the place?"

Gerard nodded at the name of the infamous Lisbon prison. Antonio continued: "Two years later, he received a choice: stay in prison for life, or take his family and settle in Brazil. He chose the second, obviously. He probably should have chosen the first. Shortly after we arrived, he caught my mother cheating and killed her and her lover. He was hung soon after."

At that, Antonio paused and took a deep breath before continuing. "My sister and I were orphaned. She was eight and I, six. We were separated into boys' and girls' homes, and I saw her from time to time. At least until someone kidnapped her. Then I never saw her again. At nine, I fled from the refuge. Since then, I've made my own way in this world.

"Tell me, Gerard, how many could have raised themselves up from that place, all the way to the counsel of the governor himself?"

Gerard nodded, genuinely impressed. He had never heard this tale, and doubted many had.

"Please, Gerard," said Antonio. "I have no family, no friends, only my dignity. If I return this way to Salvador, I will have that no longer. I would rather die and be remembered for my past than live on like this."

Oludara, furious, rushed toward him.

"What do you know of dignity?" he shouted. "You who trade in slaves! I was taken from my home, my people, tossed into the hold of a ship crowded with men as one might coop chickens for market. In the darkness, we lived on the edge of starvation. Disease, rats, and our own filth were our closest companions. Those who died, rotted for days or weeks until the slavers took the time to throw them overboard.

"Eaten away by lice and hunger, we arrived on a deserted beach, where the slavers could cull away the dead and dying in peace, and bring back to a minimum of health those still worth selling. *That* was how I arrived Brazil."

At that, Oludara, barely able to control himself any more, strode off. Antonio waited until he had walked away and looked back to Gerard.

"That one understands," he said. "Let him kill me. It's the most merciful thing you can do."

"I need time to think," said Gerard.

He walked away to sit by himself. Killing Antonio was unthinkable. Reason told him he should bring Antonio to justice, but the man's story had moved him, as had Oludara's, who in five years had never spoken in such detail of his macabre trip to Brazil. To release Antonio would be to pretend nothing had happened. Quite the opposite, Antonio would be considered a hero, stealing glory from the deeds of others.

Glory, thought Gerard. That had meant everything to him once. It had been his entire reason for coming to Brazil. In the colony, he had become more famous than he could ever have imagined. Now, however...

In the end, one thought overcame all: *better to die unknown with a clean conscience, than famous and full of regrets.*

The scales had been weighed in his mind. He stood slowly, walked to Antonio, and pulled out a knife.

Oludara rushed toward him. "You're not really thinking of this, are you, Gerard?"

"Antonio may hate me, but he's a brave man. People follow him."

"He is a snake. He has no respect for human life."

Gerard paused at those words. "Antonio," he said, "I will release you on one condition: that you never again capture the natives or deal with slaves of any kind."

Antonio raised his eyebrows. "You would rob me of my livelihood?"

"A livelihood at the cost of others' lives? Did you not listen to Oludara's story?"

Antonio looked at the ground. "I heard him well enough. It was a devil of a tale."

"There are other means of living."

"If that's what it takes to maintain my dignity, so be it."

"You still think of yourself? Do you not understand, now, tied up and approaching Salvador, the way those others feel?"

"I suppose you're right, Gerard. Perhaps I do. I swear I shall never again enslave or sell another man. I swear it on...on my mother's soul."

Gerard nodded and moved forward, but Oludara grabbed his arm.

"Stop this! He will take credit for defeating Woodsfather, then turn against you."

Gerard almost yanked away from the painful grasp, but paused to consider the words of his friend. He knew Oludara was probably right, that he was making his greatest mistake, but he had to act on his beliefs. To show his sincerity, he gently peeled away his friend's hand.

"The fame doesn't matter any more, Oludara. In the end, all that matters is the soul. No matter what Antonio chooses to do, my conscience will be clear."

"My people have a saying, Gerard, 'He who claps his hands for a fool to dance is no better than the fool.'"

"My people also have a saying. 'If someone strikes you on the right cheek, offer him the left one as well.' "

With that, Gerard bent down and cut the rope.

As the three approached Salvador, the giant toe trailing behind them, word spread quickly. As they passed through the outer dwellings, people paused in the rebuilding of their houses to gawk and mutter among themselves. By the time the group had reached the main plaza, a huge crowd had formed, cheering and calling on them to tell their tale.

Oludara looked to Gerard, who beamed at the cheers.

"I thought the fame no longer mattered," he said.

Gerard blushed. "Well, it's not all that bad, either."

Antonio stepped up onto a block of rubble and the crowd quieted.

"Woodsfather is slain!" he shouted.

The crowd cheered and chanted Antonio's name, at which he held up a hand to silence them.

"Do not cheer my name," he said. "Gerard van Oost is the true hero this day."

Cheers of 'Gerard van Oost' burst from the crowd and Antonio once again raised a hand to silence them.

"Not just Gerard," he said. "But the many who followed us. Many gave their lives. Diogo, our old friend, died bravely." With that, he took off his hat and recited a long list of the dead. He bowed for a minute of silence before continuing. "I'm forgetting someone..." he muttered.

Oludara straightened up.

"Oh yes," said Antonio. "Moara also. She was a great help."

Oludara said, “What?” but the cry of the crowd washed him out. They rushed forward to congratulate Gerard and Antonio.

Oludara pushed his way toward Gerard and shouted, “Do you believe it? Still he says nothing of me!”

“Well,” said Gerard, “at least he didn’t take all the credit. It’s a start.”

Oludara fumed. “You sound like the full-bellied child who tells the hungry child to ‘keep good heart’!”

“We have another saying, Oludara. It goes, ‘You can’t change the world in a day.’ ”

With that, the surging crowd pushed them apart and Oludara stamped off angrily.

Furious, Oludara scoured the streets of Salvador for any sign of Gregorio and Taynah.

“That fame monger, Gerard van Oost,” he muttered under his breath. “I’ll change *his* world in a day! Fool that I was to ever trust a white man.”

Oludara wished only to find Taynah and leave Salvador as quickly as possible; he could stand no more.

“Oludara!”

The call of his name interrupted his thoughts.

Still angry, he turned and yelled, “What?”

A child, ten or eleven years old, had called him. The child had dark brown skin and curly black hair, but was not a native African. More likely, he was of mixed birth.

At Oludara’s angry response, the child cringed back. Then he turned and ran in the other direction.

“Wait!” shouted Oludara.

The child froze at the command.

“What do you want?” asked Oludara, this time in a gentler voice.

“Your friend was looking for you. He told the crowd it was you who killed Woodsfather, and that all praise should be yours alone.”

Oludara felt relief and embarrassment in equal measure. After five years together, he should not have doubted his friend so quickly.

Nevertheless, he spoke his mind.

"No one wants to hear that," he said.

"You're right," agreed the child. "The crowd ignored him and continued chanting his name and Antonio's."

Oludara's anger returned and he scowled. Once again, the child shrank back and Oludara composed himself. He knelt down to make the child more comfortable.

"It doesn't matter," he said. "Let van Oost have his fame; I want none of it. I might as well still be a slave, for others to receive the benefits of my labor."

"No!"

The child's emphatic shout surprised Oludara and caused the child to cover his mouth in embarrassment.

"What was that?" asked Oludara.

"I mean..." the child stammered. "My mother is a slave. My father..."

"Her owner," completed Oludara, removing some of the burden from the boy's telling.

The child nodded and continued. "I never thought I could hope for anything in this life. But then, one day, I heard of you... Not everyone ignores your name in the stories, there are many who repeat it with pride. You give me hope, to do great things. May your gods protect you!"

At that, the child shoved a tiny circle of wood into Oludara's palm and ran off.

"Wait!" said Oludara.

This time, the child did not stop. He disappeared down one of the city streets.

Oludara turned over the piece of wood in his hands to discover a rough painting of his face. Underneath it were written the words 'OLUDARA HERO', with both of the 'R's reversed.

His knees weak, Oludara sat heavily on the ground. He stared at the tiny painting for a long time, the tears flowing freely from his eyes.

At twilight, the crowd dispersed, and Gerard was called upon to visit the governor. He found the governor's mansion under repairs, but the office intact. Upon entering, he was surprised to find Oludara already waiting with Governor Veiga. He had been searching for Oludara for hours in vain. In one arm, Oludara held Taynah, in the other hand, he gripped some kind of wooden circle. Gerard reached up to tip a hat which was no longer there.

"Good to see you, Oludara," he said. "Good to see you, Your Excellency."

"No need for formalities, Gerard," said Governor Veiga. "I owe you both a great debt."

"I expect my reward," said Oludara.

"You will receive your one hundred cruzados and safe passage to Africa. I will send you with trusted men, to prevent any treachery along the way."

Oludara nodded and Governor Veiga turned his attention to Gerard.

"In your case, Gerard, I'm afraid my reward will not be fitting of your service."

"I understand, Governor," said Gerard. "You have a city to rebuild."

Governor Veiga frowned and stared out the window. "I wish it were so simple. News has reached us that Philip of Spain has taken control of Portugal and united the two realms. As such, he in now sovereign of Brazil."

Gerard frowned in understanding. "And Spain is still at war with Brabant and the Low Countries."

"William of Orange has been declared an outlaw. Did you not fight alongside his brothers in Mookerheyde?"

Gerard nodded. "They lost their lives in that battle."

"Philip has not yet turned his attention to Brazil, but any day now, a ship will arrive and demand the allegiance of all who live here. You are an enemy of Spain, Gerard, and on that day, you will become our enemy as well. I won't arrest you, but I also can't offer you harbor. You should leave as soon possible. I'll pay for your passage to Europe and give you the same hundred cruzados as your friend."

Gerard knew it wasn't the governor's fault, but he couldn't help but be irritated. "After all I've done, I'm to be rewarded with exile? If that is how courage is rewarded, then I take my leave gladly."

He bowed stiffly and as he turned to leave, spotted Oludara out of the corner of his eye. A thought crossed his mind and he turned back to the governor.

"Book my passage to Africa, not Europe. That is, if my friend here will have me."

From the way Oludara's face lit up, Gerard knew he would.

"Perhaps there are still some adventures to be had there?" asked Gerard.

"Indeed, much like Brazil, there are many monsters there in need of taming."

"Very well," said Governor Veiga. "I wish you both the best."

"Does the ship leave soon?" asked Gerard.

"On the morrow."

"Good. A friend once told me, 'The dawn does not come twice to wake a man.'"

Oludara's smile broadened.

A crowd had gathered at the docks to send off the famous Gerard van Oost. When the rowboat came out to take Gerard and Oludara to their ship, Gerard waved a gorgeous new banner—blue with a richly embroidered elephant and macaw—a parting gift from the governor. The crowd cheered his name, and more than a few shouts of 'Oludara' could be heard as well. From the high city, the governor called out a command and a row of cannon fired in their honor.

From out of the crowd, someone yelled, "We will not forget you, Gerard van Oost!"

"I will miss Brazil," Gerard sighed. "I have never felt so alive. But I have also met the greatest friend a man could have, and am glad to depart with him."

"Just when I thought I would put the adventuring life behind me, it follows me home!" said Oludara. "But it is well. It would not suit me to grow old and fat." He tickled Taynah, who giggled. "There is magic within my girl, and I must keep my wits."

Gregorio came forward from the crowd.

"Gerard, Oludara," he said, nodding to them, "you are truly warriors of God. I see why Miguel sacrificed himself for your cause."

"Thank you," said Gerard, bowing.

"May I bless Taynah?"

Oludara hesitated, but nodded. Gregorio made the sign of the cross on her forehead.

"Safe voyage to you, and God bless you all, wherever you may go."

At that, he departed. Oludara turned and stepped onto the rowboat with Taynah. Gerard, about to follow, was held back by a hand on his shoulder. He turned to find Antonio, who quickly pulled his hand back, as if embarrassed.

"Gerard..." he said.

"Yes, Antonio?"

For the first time since Gerard had met him, Antonio seemed to struggle with what to say. He looked at the ground for a time, then looked up at Gerard's hair and raised his eyebrows, as if seeing something for the first time.

"You lost your hat," he said.

"Yes, during the shipwreck."

"I hear it gets hot in Africa."

"So I've heard," said Gerard.

"They say there are deserts there the size of Europe."

"So they say."

"Then I suppose you'll need a new hat."

With that, Antonio pulled off his hat. "Take mine," he said.

Gerard hesitated for a moment, knowing how much Antonio prized it, until the man insisted, "It's a good hat, van Oost. Governor Veiga gave it to me when I lost my last one."

"It's a marvelous hat," said Gerard, taking it in his hands and admiring it. "Thank you, Antonio. It won't be the same without you around."

At that, Antonio gave him a half smile. "Most likely not."

With those words, Antonio walked away.

From atop the ruins of the Church of the Immaculate Conception, in contrast to the subdued tones of the rubble, a scarlet macaw perched upon a fallen cross—leaning to one side yet still standing—and stared out over the aquamarine vastness of the Bay of All Saints.

The macaw spotted two men, one white and one black, sailing away upon the deck of a galleon. As a child danced playfully around them, the two men stared at Salvador. Half an hour later, the ship left the bay and the two men turned their gaze east, toward a perilous journey across the wide sea.

Epilogue

An Ending, of Sorts

T IS SAID that Gerard and Oludara traveled together for many more years, and that their adventures took them to the very ends of Africa...and beyond.

But those tales must wait for another day.

END

Acknowledgements

Before this novel, when these tales were being launched as standalone stories, I had the chance to acknowledge hundreds of people who helped me along the way. In this space, I'll focus on the people who have most contributed to this series.

First off, let me thank my editor David Stokes, who made this project happen. I'd also like to mention the long list of amazing editors who have published one or more of the stories, starting with Douglas Cohen, Shawna McCarthy and Warren Lapine, who published the first story back in *Realms of Fantasy* in 2010. After them, many others honored me by publishing these stories around the world: Roberto de Sousa Causo, Douglas Quinta Reis, Leandro Luigi del Manto, Martin Šust, Cristian Tamas, Rudy Martinez, Margret Helgadottir, Tony C. Smith, Pei Liu and Cor van Mechelen.

Many partners and friends have made significant contributions to the series's diffusion, including Fabiano Pandolfi, José Maia, Jeremy Tolbert, Ursula Dorada, Carolina Mylius, Paulo Ítalo, Ernanda Souza, Tânia Rösing, Moisés Baptista, Leo Carrion, Victor Marques Batista and Vitor Severo Leães. I must also thank the De Lage Landen Group for their sponsorship and the Brazilian Cultural Ministry for their incentives, without which, the series would not be nearly what it is today.

Many professionals have been fundamental in my development as a writer, including Aliette de Bodard, Tony Pi, Russel Bittner, T. L. Morganfield, Al Bogdan, Enéias Tavares, Duda Falcão, A. Z. Cordenonsi, Cesar Alcázar, Marcelo Cortez, and Felipe Castilho. Others have been great inspirations along the way, such as Catherine Schaff-Stump, Jeannette Kathleen Cheney, Cory Doctorow, Steven Silver, Terri-Lynne DeFino, M.G. Ellington, Dan Goldman, Lawrence M. Schoen, Jeff Wheeler, Jim C. Hines, Dru Miller, Lawrence Santoro, Mike Brotherton, Beth Dawkins, Christian Lykawka, Gerson Klein, Nuno Venâncio, Tabajara

Ruas, Társis Salvatore, Adriana Amaral, Tiago Castro, Clinton Davisson, Patrícia Langlois, Eduardo Müller, Samir Machado de Machado, Christian David, César Silva, Artur Vecchi, Max Mallmann, Simone Saueressig, among others. Also on that list are the beta readers for this novel: Ana Cristina Rodrigues, Victor Vargas, Douglas Cohen, and Terra LeMay. I should also thank many groups which have influenced my development, including Critters, Viable Paradise, Speculations, Codex, SFWA, AGES, Zoetrope, and CLFC.

I must thank my family, especially my parents, Antoinette and Charlie, and my siblings: Stephen, Anne, Lisa, and Michael. Also my in-laws, Ana Maria Gusmão de Lima and Luiz Fernando Corrêa de Lima, and my eternal inspirations: Fernanda e Lynx. After all these decades, my family's support has been unwavering.

As I always say: it takes one person to write a book, but thousands to create the writer.

Thank you all so much.

About the Author

CHRISTOPHER KASTENSMIDT was born in Texas and now lives in Porto Alegre, Brazil. Christopher was a Nebula Award finalist and winner of the *Realms of Fantasy* Readers' Choice Award for his novelette "The Fortuitous Meeting of Gerard van Oost and Oludara".

Christopher ran Brazilian video game developer Southlogic Studios for a decade before its sale to Ubisoft Brazil, where he served as Creative Director. He participated in the production of thirty internationally-published video games, totalling millions of units sold.

Christopher has a Bachelor's degree in Electrical and Computer Engineering from Rice University and a Master's degree in Social Communication from the Pontificia Universidade Catolica do Rio Grande do Sul. Besides writing, he lectures at UniRitter university on scriptwriting, game design and video game production.

To learn more about The Elephant and Macaw Banner series, please visit www.eamb.org, where Christopher posts news, artwork, and in-depth explanations of historical and cultural references used in the stories.

CPSIA information can be obtained
at www.ICGtesting.com
Printed in the USA
LVHW050453030322
712449LV00004B/144

9 781911 486312